A TIME TO LOVE

Dr Sheila
with affection
& admiration

Bnd

A NOTE ON THE AUTHOR

Bríd Mahon was born and lives in Dublin. She has worked as a folklorist, journalist and author of children's books. She is the author of *Land of Milk and Honey: The Story of Traditional Irish Food*, also published by Poolbeg.

BRÍD MAHON

A TIME
TO
LOVE

POOLBEG

A paperback original
First published 1992 by
Poolbeg Press Ltd
Knocksedan House,
Swords, Co Dublin, Ireland

© Bríd Mahon 1992

The moral right of the author has been asserted.

A catalogue record for this book is available from the British Library.

ISBN 1 85371 221 3
10 9 8 7 6 5 4 3 2 1

Cover design by Pomphrey Associates
Set by Mac Book Limited in Stone 9.5/13
Printed by Cox & Wyman Ltd, Reading, Berks.

To my family, my friends, and to Dublin, my city

Acknowledgements

I am deeply grateful to my friend Caitriona Downey for reading the manuscript and for her invaluable advice and encouragement. I thank Sean McMahon for his editorial skills and Jo O'Donoghue of Poolbeg Press, for her interest and enthusiasm. And last but by no means least I thank my friend Marion Cronin for keeping me at my desk with cups of coffee and words of cheer.

*To everything there is a season, and a time
for every purpose under the heaven:
A time to be born and a time to die;
A time to plant and a time to pluck up that
which is planted...
A time to weep and a time to laugh
A time to mourn and a time to dance...
A time to love*

(Ecclesiastes 3)

Dramatis Personae

Peg Woffington—Actress
Charles Coffey—Man of letters
Lord Darnley—Scottish aristocrat, Jacobite rebel
David Garrick—Actor-Manager

Supporting roles
Máire Rua—the Lady of Lemineagh
Mrs Slany Woffington—Peg's mother
Polly Woffington—Peg's sister
Conor Woffington—Peg's brother
Kitty Clive (*née* Raftor)—Actress
Madame Violante—Impresario
Captain O'Kelly—Smuggler
The Foundling—Pickpocket
Sarah Pepys—Landlady
Mr Quinn—Actor
Jennie Tatler—London urchin
Belle Tudor—Courtesan
Jimmy Maclean—Highwayman
Alice Morgan—Widow
Patrick Taafe—Squire
Margaret Leeson—Whore
Mr Elrington—Manager, Aungier Street Playhouse
Samuel Johnson—Man of letters
Mr Rich—Manager, Covent Garden Playhouse
Sarah, Duchess of Buckingham
Mrs Bellamy—Actress
Mr Fleetwood—Manager, Drury Lane Playhouse
Owen M'Swiney—Actor
Charles Macklin—Actor
Zara—Peg's maid and confidante
Mohamet—Peg's blackamoor
Prince Charles—Young Pretender
Captain Maurice O'Connor—Mercenary
George Ann Bellamy—Actress
Colonel Caesar—Landowner
James Wilding—Drummer boy
Susanna Cibber—Actress
François de Voltaire—Writer
Marie Dumesnil—Actress
Madame Denise—Niece of Voltaire
Armand de Richelieu—Aristocrat
Duchesse di Condi—Aristocrat
Duc di Condi—Aristocrat
Signor Angelo—Swordsman

Lionel, Duke of Dorset, Lord Lieutenant of Ireland
Simon Winchester—Valet to the Duke
Thomas Sheridan—Manager, Smock Alley Play-house

Also
Kathleen McEnroe
Mrs McEnroe
Mr Carey
Dottie Carey
Gaoler
Trinity student
Apprentice weaver
Dean Swift
Buck Whaley
Henry Loftus, Earl of Ely
Sir Francis Dashwood
London housewives
The thin woman
The fat woman
The barrow woman
Rumplestiltskin, Mr Rich's dwarf
Priscilla Stevens, Mr Rich's wife
Lord Burlington
Violetta Burlington
Madame Flaubert
Lord Sandford
Samantha Gunning
Mrs Gunning
Maria Gunning
Elizabeth Gunning
Messenger boy
Dublin buck

Crowd Scenes
Cast of *The Beggar's Opera*
Members of the Dublin Corporation and City Guilds
 at the Riding of the Franchise
Medmenham monks
Crowds at the hanging of Jimmy Maclean
The Mohocks
Street vendors
Smock Alley audience
Drury Lane audience
Covent Garden audience

AUTHOR'S NOTE

Peg Woffington was a child of the Liberties who became the greatest actress of her day. Born in 1718, red-haired, green-eyed, wilful, reckless, beautiful, generous, she became the toast of Dublin, London and Paris. Hers was a rags to riches story. The Dublin and London she grew up in were exciting, expanding, with fine buildings, shops, parks, arcades and theatres. They were also the haunt of highwaymen, whores, rogues and cut-purses brought vividly to life in *The Beggar's Opera* in which she was to make her stage debut. A role that would lead her on to heartbreak, happiness, fame and disaster.

She bewitched many men and four were to shape her destiny. Charles Coffey, the writer with whom she had her first love affair and who set her feet on the first rung of success.

Patrick Taafe, hard-riding, hard-drinking squire who gambled away vast estates and introduced her to the infamous Hellfire Club in the Dublin mountains where she so nearly lost her life.

Lord Darnley, handsome, aristocratic, who plotted the return of the Young Pretender, Bonny Prince Charlie.

David Garrick, the actor who changed the face of the English stage, the most gifted actor who ever trod the boards.

Peg's friends and acquaintances included the famous, the scandalous, the gifted and the good. Jonathan Swift, dean of St Patrick's Cathedral, with the whiff of brimstone and generosity of a saint, Margaret Leeson, keeper of Dublin's most notorious brothel, Samuel Johnson, wit and man of letters, the beautiful, tragic, penniless Gunning sisters from Co. Mayo who became the "beauties of

London", Jimmy Maclean, England's best-known highwayman, Buck Whaley, whose uneasy spirit still haunts the parks and squares of Georgian Dublin.

Running through Peg's life were the threads of her great-grandmother's story, the incomparable beauty who sold her favours to the grim Cromwellian General Ireton to save her estates and paid the price with a curse so terrible that it was never mentioned aloud.

In choosing a historical figure for the heroine of my novel I have tried to be faithful to her story after my fashion. Where there was tension between historical fact and fiction I remembered that first and foremost this was a novel and I had a story to tell. History and fiction are so interrelated that, as Brian Friel once said, "historical fact is a kind of literary artifact." This is the story of a tempestuous woman who lived in a tempestuous age, and of what happened to her and of the might have been.

PROLOGUE: IRELAND
1651

The coach and six rattled furiously down the twisting road, bumping over stones, scattering ducks, hens, geese and ragged children in its path. Women in scarlet petticoats, shawls thrown hastily across their shoulders, stood at their half-doors and wondered at the haste of the mad driver lashing the steaming horses on to greater effort.

Brawny men laid down scythes, glad of a respite in their never-ending task of hacking gnarled roots like skeleton claws, clearing the arid land of stones, and strained to catch a glimpse of the legendary Máire Rua drive by. Men and women alike crossed themselves and muttered a prayer in Irish for the repose of the soul of her husband, Conor O'Brien, who had fallen to Ireton's soldiers. It was well known that the Cromwellian general feared O'Brien more than any other man in Clare and had planned his death, sending five of his best marksmen, disguised as huntsmen, in the path of the Irish rebel. They had succeeded in mortally wounding the handsome nobleman, but in turn, had been caught and hanged in Cratloe woods by O'Brien's followers. Ireton had sworn vengeance and now all north Clare waited in fear for the burnings and reprisals, aye and hangings, that were bound to follow.

Inside the coach Máire Rua extracted a mirror from her reticule and examined her face. She was still handsome despite her thirty-six years and the rigours of bearing eleven children to two husbands; well-arched, dark eyebrows, aquiline nose, small firm well-shaped mouth and cleft chin. She had painted her face skilfully but her wide-set emerald eyes with their sweeping lashes were shadowed with strain. She frowned and unpinned the dark

i

red hair so that it fell in rippling curls around her shapely shoulders. It was her pride and glory. Conor used flatter her, tell her that when she wore her hair loose she looked virginal, young. She would need looks, all her wiles, all her wits for the task facing her: a desperate errand to Ireton's headquarters in Limerick, an errand that would end either in a pardon for all, or destitution for herself and her children, eviction and transportation for the servants and retainers and the lash, or even death for the foolish men who had followed Conor on his mad enterprise. When the natives rebelled, the Cromwellian showed no mercy.

Despite her recent loss, her anguish, her fear, she had taken time to dress in her most becoming gown, blue silk cut fashionably low, the bodice criss-crossed with silver lace, jewelled pendant nestling between the curves of her round breasts. She pondered on what she would say when she met Ireton face to face. Could she charm him as she had in her day enchanted so many other men? Born into the Irish aristocracy, the daughter of Torlach Rua MacMahon, hereditary Gaelic lord of Clonderlaw, and Mary O'Brien, youngest daughter of the third Earl of Ormond, she had been a noted beauty even as a young girl, with a sunny disposition masking a will of iron. Hers had been an idyllic childhood, brought up in a big house, filled with the children of Torlach Rua's three marriages, with aunts, cousins, and Uncle Donough, the most powerful man in Clare, lord of castles at Bunratty, Clonroad and Clarecastle. To affirm his loyalty he had introduced English and Dutch settlers to his estates, some of whom became wealthy merchants and artisans. They settled in Ennis town and were soon on visiting terms in the great MacMahon household.

Days were spent riding, hunting, fishing with her

siblings and cousins, attended by grooms, servants, and tutors. In high summer she liked to take picnics to the Burren, the most famous beauty spot in north Clare. Here she and Conor had pledged their love, sealed their union during a thunderstorm and arisen from their stone bed soaked to the skin, hair streaming, vital, happy, hungry for life—for each other. She loved that wild pagan place with its ancient stone forts, hundreds of miles of craggy landscape, twisting valleys and great shelved highlands. Loved the fissures and crevices that chequered the rock-strewn fields which were ablaze with wild flowers and plants the most exquisitely unique to be found in Europe. She smiled wryly at the thought of what the Cromwellian general had said of the Burren: "Here there is not water enough to drown a man, not trees enough to hang him, not soil enough to bury him."

These indeed were troubled times. The rebellion of 1641 had meant that in the decade that followed Ireland had been torn asunder by a savage and destructive war and the end was not yet in sight. The Lord Protector of England, Oliver Cromwell, had come and gone and now the land of Ireland was being divided amongst the Cromwellian soldiers and adventurers, the old Irish banished beyond the Shannon, driven to the Atlantic's edge, "to hell or Connacht," Cromwell was reputed to have ordered.

Whatever the truth the soldiers had left behind them a trail of scorched earth, ruined monasteries, desolate homesteads. Embittered, dispossessed men and women driven westwards wandered the roads of Galway, Mayo, Clare, agitating, planning, plotting revenge. Having nothing left to risk they had nothing to lose. Many would welcome a holocaust.

Yes indeed this year of Our Lord, 1651, was Máire's

worst yet. First there was the death of the much-loved twins, the pretty eight-year-old daughters, carried off by the smallpox, buried in Coad church which looked down on the blue waters of Lake Inchiquin. Above their graves stood a limestone cross inscribed:

"Here lyes the bodies of Mary and Slany ny Brien, Daughters to Conor O'Brien and Mary Brien alias Mahon of Lemineagh. Anno Domini, 1651."

She had thought this her greatest tragedy; needed all of Conor's love to help her survive her ordeal, to hold her close at night, to wipe away her tears, to blot out the memories of her dead darlings. Only in the passion of their love-making could she find relief from her anguish. But the Parliamentary army was closing in on the west and there was plague and devastation on the land. Conor and his royalist friends were fighting back; there seemed a glimmer of hope on the horizon. Talk of aid from the continent, the Stuart was in Scotland. There were rumours he was poised to invade England with a Scottish army, rumours that the English themselves were divided, weary of the austerity of their Puritan rulers and the drabness of their lives. A victory for Charles could alter the odds of war, change the mood of England, lift the scourge from Ireland's back. But Conor and his ilk could not bide their time. They would drive Ireton and his soldiers home to England in the wake of Master Cromwell.

David Roche, self-styled colonel of the poorly equipped Irish army, foster-brother and confidant of Conor, besieged a parliamentarian garrison at Carrigaholt, while Conor held the Pass of Inchecroghan. It was there on 24 July he was attacked and slain by the English soldiers. The date was burnt into her brain. He was thirty-four years of age, in the prime of his manhood; her lover, her sweetheart, her life. He had filled her days with laughter, had so pleasured her nights that she had prayed that the world would cease to spin on its axis, and that time would stand still. Oh, she had known what it was to be married to a dry stick of a man, young though he was—or were rumours correct that he had loved others of his sex best? There had been no love between Daniel Neylon and herself, only wealth and land and the binding together of two powerful families. She had been married at eighteen years in a magnificent gown of French silk, by Bishop Neylon, uncle of the groom, in Ennis Cathedral. Her bridal night had been a disaster, like so many that followed. She had gritted her teeth and told no one of her frustrations and humiliations, had dutifully borne her husband three sons. Five years later she watched dry-eyed as his coffin was carried to the graveyard on their estate at Dysert O Dea; his death had been the result of a drunken brawl. She was a widow of twenty-three, her passions unslaked, beautiful, wealthy, owner of 400 Irish acres and a magnificent castle. This time there would be no interference from family or friends. She was her own mistress. She had married Conor O'Brien for passion, lust, love, perhaps all three and what did it matter! She had borne him eight children in eleven years, and never regretted her choice, knowing full well she was more wife than mother, more mistress and lover than wife. And now she must pit her wits against that most wily of soldiers, Ireton. Must hold her property; the castle and lands of Dysert, the broad acres of Castle Smithson which she had inherited from Conor's grandmother. Above all she must save the sweet mansion of Lemineagh, her beloved home, with its mullioned windows, wooden staircase, spacious rooms. Carved in stone above the lintel of the great door was the legend: "Built in the year of Our

Lord, 1648, by Conor O'Brien and Mary Mahon wife of the said Conor."

These she must secure for Conor's sons and daughters. Not for nothing had the MacMahons and O'Briens and, indeed, the family of Daniel Neylon her first husband struggled and contrived to hold their lands against plantation, wars, and the greedy eyes of Norman and Elizabethan adventurers. They had played England's game, changed sides, sworn allegiance to Plantagenets, Tudors, Stuarts—whoever happened to be on the throne. She knew full well what happened to rebels, their wives and families: the Viscountess Fermoy who had been hanged on the charge of having killed an Englishman; the rebel Colonel Fitzpatrick's mother sentenced to be burnt at the stake as a witch; the Countess of Antrim charged with complicity in a massacre, stripped of her estates and banished.

They were passing through the city gates, and townsfolk were turning to watch the rocking coach, the foaming horses, the crazed driver with his high crowned hat and ragged coat, a hand-me-down from his beloved master, and with which he refused to part. Máire Rua rapped sharply on the window; "*Tóg bog é*— take it easy you fool. I wish to arrive with some semblance of dignity." Her servant cursed in Irish the Cromwellian soldiers who had filled his master with shot and the fools and knaves of Irish who had let it happen. At first he had defied her, refused to take her to the Limerick garrison until she had laid a whip to his back, and in a fury for the length of the journey had taken his misery out on the unfortunate horses goading them on to greater speed until she was sure the coach would overturn before journey's end.

A guard on duty attempted to intercept them at the entrance to Ireton's headquarters but one look at the wild driver, the half-dead horses and the painted lady within was enough. He waved them through. With a mighty oath the driver drew up at the great oaken door, let down the steps and Máire Rua dismounted with as much composure as she could muster.

From a window in the castle the commander-in-chief of the Cromwellian army in Ireland watched the lady mount the steps. He knew who she was, having already been given tidings of her headlong flight to see him. Spies, Irish renegades, kept him informed. Though he despised the lot they were necessary to keep the peace of this benighted land and control her ignorant, ragged, subversive inhabitants with their gibberish language and their pagan superstitions that passed for religion. He barked an order to his servant: "Bring Madam O'Brien to my private apartment, and see that those unfortunate horses are watered and fed."

"And the servant, sir?"

"Throw him into a dungeon if he makes trouble. Better still fill him with ale, the stronger the better. Make sure that an Irish renegade is present to act as interpreter. I want a report of what he says, of any rebel plans for revenge."

Ireton was standing, looking down on the courtyard when Máire Rua was ushered ceremoniously in. "And your business, Madam?" he said curtly without turning around.

Máire Rua swallowed her ire. Her temper matched her hair but she was determined to control her tongue. The stakes were too high for self-indulgence. She would play the part of the perfect lady, match rudeness with meekness. "I have come to beg clemency for me and mine," she said softly, "And to swear my allegiance to England and Lord Cromwell."

"Indeed Madam. Your husband was a traitor and has

paid the price. His estates are forfeit."

"And you will throw a defenceless woman and children on to the roadside." She allowed a sob to escape, threw out her hands. "Will you not at least grant me the courtesy you would your wife, daughters, and allow me to sit in your presence. I am distraught, weary with the journey and humbly crave your indulgence."

Moodily Ireton swung around and was just in time to catch her as she swayed. He carried her to a couch and shouted for a servant to bring wine. He growled at his minion, "Hold up her head. Make her drink. Here give it to me, you dolt. You are ruining her gown."

At this Máire Rua's eyelids fluttered and opened and he found himself gazing into the most beautiful eyes of any woman he had ever known: milky white irises, dark green pupils, shaded with thick black lashes. Her red hair, smelling of fragrance, covered her shoulders, like a cloak. As she caught the goblet she brushed his hand and that dark controlled Puritan quivered, knew the first stirring of his sex.

He helped her to her feet and barked another order to the servant who scurried away. He removed himself to sit behind his desk struggling for self-control. He was a lusty man, had not known a woman since coming to Ireland. In another time, another place he would have bedded her. He cleared his throat and said gruffly, "I cannot help you. Your husband was a rebel. All wantons must pay the price." He was talking wildly, the words had slipped out. Had she bewitched him?

Colour flooded her cheeks and she stood up, her air of helplessness gone. "By the gods above," she swore, "an my husband were alive and you called me wanton you would have been dead at my feet. Know you that my stock is as

viii

good as any king or commoner who ever ruled your kingdom. Know you that my father, Torlach Rua Mac Mahon, was high sheriff of Clare and loyal to the English government. Know you that my uncle, the Earl of Thomond, swore his allegiance to King James. My husband Conor was a fool, led into a mad escapade through his love for his foster-brother David Roche. I begged him to desist. I implored him on my knees." Tears were streaming down her face. Impatiently she brushed them aside.

Ireton had an overpowering impulse to take her in his arms. "What can I do?" he said helplessly. "Your husband knew the penalty before he took up arms. He has been a thorn in our side for long. Our enemy. A quick death was too good for a rebel. I would his head had been spiked over Limerick city as an example to all."

She drew in a shuddering breath, then leaned across the desk and slapped his face, her nails drawing blood. Her cloak had fallen back and he could see the tips of her rounded breasts. He felt his sex uncurl, harden. Dear God in another moment he would have her on the floor. "Leave me woman," he said hoarsely, "ere I have you thrown in gaol."

She was beside him, mopping the blood with a silk ribbon she had taken from her curls, kissing the ragged red claw marks that ran from eye to chin. "I need a protector, a husband," she sobbed. "I am sorry. If you will forgive me, help me."

How it happened he never knew, her arms were around him and he was kissing her hungrily, unlacing her bodice, carrying her to the couch. With trembling fingers she undid the buttons of his breeches, then he was riding her, while she panted and moaned and their limbs and tongues entwined; and then he took her again.

ix

A week later he ordered one of his officers, Cornet John Cooper, a dour Yorkshire man, who held the lowest commissioned rank in the cavalry regiment, to marry the lady. The ceremony was performed by a hastily summoned Calvinist preacher. On her wedding night Máire Rua lay with Ireton, as she had done for seven nights, and when she left the garrison with her new husband on the following morning she carried a pardon for all on the estate and the deeds of the ownership of her houses and lands to be held in perpetuity for her sons.

The journey back to Lemineagh was sombre, even the driver seemed subdued. Much against his will the Cromwellian soldiers had cropped his hair, and thrown him into the river to wash away the lice. His ragged tail-coat had been burnt. He now wore a grey jacket and breeches, a cast-off of the commander general, a fact which filled the garrison officers with unholy glee. He sat stiffly upright while the horses, fresh and mettlesome, pranced along. Máire Rua fingered the ring which Ireton had given her before they parted, a token of his protection, and glanced speculatively at her new husband. She had scarcely noticed him at the wedding service. She would have been prepared to marry a doddering beggarman to secure her lands. He was not ill-visaged but wore a sullen expression. She guessed his age to be about twenty-six.

"Before we reach my estate, it might be advisable to make a few things clear." It was the first words she had spoken to him since the wedding.

"I have nothing to say," he growled. "You'll speak when you're spoken to. I'm master."

She leaned back in her seat. She was enjoying this interchange. Much worse had he been smitten by her, grovelling at her feet. His hostility and ignorance were easier to manage.

"Listen you fool and mark well my words, for I shall not repeat what I have to say. We are wife and husband, but only in name, and so it shall remain."

"I'll have my rights." He glared at her from under beetling brows.

"You have no rights," she reminded him coolly. "It was a marriage of convenience for us both. Your gambling debts were paid and you were saved the humiliation of being drummed out of the army or worse. I am an Irish aristocrat while you are an English yeoman but I forgive you this. My servants and retainers will slit your throat if I but give them the word. You are entering enemy territory my friend."

"If Ireton hears of this," he threatened.

"The commander general will spike your head on the battlements of Limerick Castle. He has promised me this if you give me cause."

He swore under his breath. He had been a fool to marry her but he had little choice. His mates had told him how lucky he was. To bed Ireton's woman, to become master of her castles and lands.

"I am not an unreasonable woman," she was saying. "So long as you give me no cause I shall not throw you to the wolves. You will have your own apartments in the castle, a good hunter to ride, money enough in your pocket for modest pleasures. In Limerick and indeed in Ennis town you will find drabs for your appetites. If you gamble heavily and lose, Ireton shall be told—or indeed," she seemed amused, "there may be no need. My people can read the straw in the wind. It would be better if this matter was settled amicably before we reach Lemineagh."

He knew she held the upper hand, but could not

forbear one last taunt. "At least you bear the name of a loyal soldier of the Commonwealth, and not that of a renegade Irishman. Do you still lust after him, or will Ireton continue to satisfy your needs?"

She stared him full in the face, eyes cold, deadly. He put up a hand, began to bluster. "You should listen to what I say." Her voice was quiet but he knew she meant every word. "If ever again you mention the name of my dead husband, Conor O'Brien, I swear I shall kill you with my own two hands."

She was weary and heartsick when the coach drew up outside the great door of Lemineagh. Tired and lost and lonely for Conor. She had triumphed and won, but at what a price. Children and dogs came tumbling out to embrace her and be kissed; the servants stood silently to attention in the hall. They had heard the news long before she had arrived. They were relieved but anxious and looked to her for reassurance. She gathered herself together and smiled. "I am back. All is well." She signalled to her butler. "Seamus, you will show John Cooper my husband to his apartments in the north wing. He will dine alone." Her maid came forward and bobbed. "Yes, Alice," she said in answer to the unspoken question. "You will take my travelling bags to my apartment. I shall sup at six o'clock with the children."

Hastily she swept up the winding staircase to a room at the top of the keep. Her nurse sat by the fire, her face in her hands. Máire Rua went on her knees beside the old woman. "Don't Nanna. There was nothing else I could do. Don't upbraid me. I could not bear it."

"You betrayed us." The old woman got heavily to her feet. "I nursed your mother. When you were born she put you into my arms. You supped the milk of my breasts. God forgive me, I think I loved you more than my own." Slowly she went over to the table and lifted a pitcher. Then looking Máire Rua in the face slowly spilled the milk on the floor. Appalled, Máire Rua looked on. She knew what the action meant. The curse was as old as time.

"I have spilled the milk, I have cut the loom," the old woman said implacably. "You know the result. Your sons will have no issue. The line you have dishonoured will die out."

"I had no choice," Máire Rua shouted. "I have nine children to provide for. It was death and destitution for us all."

The old nurse shook out her grey locks. She had the second sight. Máire Rua dreaded what she would hear.

"Last night the banshee cried for me," the old woman keened. "My time is near, I go to join my sons who fell at Limerick: my grandsons who died at the pass of Inchecroghan."

"Oh for God's sake. You are like the raven of doom. I want no more talk of death, no more of your superstitions, your ancient curses. Know you I have a Cromwellian under my roof. He is my protection. He will tolerate none of this."

The old woman laughed and Máire Rua thought, "She has lost her wits," then shivered and crossed herself at the prophesy: "No good will come of your actions. It is written that on the day your Cromwellian husband lusts after you and curses the name of Conor O'Brien he will die by your hands."

Weeping, retching, Máire Rua stumbled from the room. Outside her frightened maid waited, helping her mistress to the great bedchamber. For a long time Máire Rua lay across the four-poster bed, sobbing her heart out, then composing herself she sat up and ordered the maid to fetch her a brandy. Quickly she tossed back the amber liquid in one long gulp, felt the blood course through her veins, felt her courage return. "I have acted well," she told herself, "I have done only what was necessary to salvage my pride, to secure my children's inheritance."

Slowly she got to her feet and shaking out her hair went to the window and for a long time gazed fixedly down on the countryside below. She regarded the broad acres that stretched far as eye could see, the nearer gardens fragrant with blossoms, the orchards heavy with fruit, and away in the distance the dim blue hills and the everlasting restless sea. Let old women keen and lament. She, Máire Rua, came of no peasant stock, but of right royal lineage. She and hers would survive. Come what may.

ACT I

DUBLIN, LONDON
1728–1730

In Dublin's fair city
Where the girls are so pretty

T he autumn of 1728 was drawing to a close in a day of soft winds and slow drifting clouds that constantly changed shape as if an artist was drawing a wet brush across the heavens. Sun warmed the cobblestones of the streets of Dublin and mellowed the red brick of houses. Outside the Fountain tavern in Church Lane a gaudily dressed young sprig, propped against a wall, could be heard singing the latest doggerel in a drunken voice: "In Lucas Club he spends the day," he warbled, "and for a month won't miss a play." At that moment his bleary eyes focused on a couple of men in ragged clothes, who had set down their poles nearby, and he raised a languid hand. Grinning at each other the chairmen helped him into the sedan and then went trotting briskly away in the direction of Fishamble Street and the Smock Alley Theatre.

By now more than eighty years had passed since the arrival of Oliver Cromwell, Lord Protector of England, at the little fishing village of Ringsend outside the city walls, but he was still remembered in the Liberties of Dublin as having ordered his soldiers to quarter their horses in the Protestant Archbishop's Palace, of putting a Papist to death in the cabbage gardens and of closing down the Playhouse before riding off at the head of his army to bring fire and pestilence to the rebellious Irish outside the Pale.

Dublin had kept her head down for a decade or more until word was brought that Cromwell was dead. With the restoration of the monarchy bonfires were lit in the Liberties and toasts were drunk in the town houses of the gentry. Before long, the king with the long dark curls, seductive voice and the way with women had set the fashion for wanton living in the two kingdoms. Masked balls, the equal of anything seen in the Palace of Whitehall in London, were held in Dublin Castle. Fashionable ladies painted their faces, took lovers, gentlemen diced and drank themselves under the table, the lower orders indulged in cock fights and nude wrestling. Gin-parlours proliferated and the theatre became more popular than ever. Hitherto female parts had always been played by pretty boys; now, for the first time in history, actresses trod the boards. At first they were considered to be audacious: adventuresses, women of no account. All changed when King Charles invited a young actress from Maypole Alley to his bed. Soon every young woman with her way to make in the world determined to go on the stage. Kings mightn't be very plentiful but the playhouses were filled with randy old roués, young bucks who rode horses and women with equal vigour and could pay for both, country yokels new to the city, ripe for fleecing, reckless highwaymen who lived as if each day were their last. If a girl kept her head she could make a fortune, might even marry a man of substance, better still become mistress of a noble lord. If Nell Gwynn could do it, why not another? Even when Restoration days were no more than a golden memory the lure of the stage beckoned them on.

❧

Two young girls could be seen making their way down Fishamble Street in the deepening twilight. Kathleen McEnroe, blue eyes sparkling, paused, the better to make her dramatic announcement.

"I'm leaving Dublin on the evening tide."

Peg Woffington, red-haired with freckles, screwed up her face in disbelief.

"You're what?"

She stood considering the news and was almost knocked off her feet by the chairmen from Fountain Street on their way to the Playhouse.

"Who are you going with, if I may make so bold?" she demanded, when she recovered her breath.

Kathleen tittered.

"Mr English, the actor from Smock Alley."

She weighed her basket of oranges in one hand and with the other smoothed a kiss curl on her forehead.

"He fancies a fumble with me."

Peg made a shocked face.

"He has a wife and family. You told me so yourself."

"Who cares? That old Máire Rua you're always boasting about had three husbands. I'll be famous like her."

"What will I tell your mother?" Peg demanded distractedly. Mrs McEnroe was her mother's best friend.

"Least said, soonest mended," Kathleen said airily. "I don't want to be stopped."

"Promise you'll come back when you're a great actress. I'll go backstage to see you." Peg had been Kathleen's slave ever since her family had moved from a fine house in the High Street to a run-down cottage in George's Lane.

Kathleen tossed her head so that her curls danced.

"A right fool I'd look with you hanging around. Only gentlemen will be allowed call."

She thrust the basket at Peg. "Here, I'm finished with hawking. Sell the oranges and pay your debts, else you'll be locked up in the Marshalsea and eaten by rats."

"Out of my way, wenches," a passing horseman called out good-humouredly.

Peg stood her ground.

"This street is gone mad with the traffic. First I'm near knocked down by an old sedan, now you're trying to run us down like dogs."

The young man chuckled, amused by the flash of temper and the pitch of voice, low and seductive for one so young.

"My apologies, sweetheart."

With a sweeping bow he doffed his feathered hat and then jumped to the ground to tie the reins to an iron post.

A tall, angular girl with large feet and hands and an expression of deep discontent who had at that moment joined them stiffened like a wary cat.

"That's Captain O'Kelly," she whispered. "He's a smuggler with a price on his head."

"Mind your own business, Kitty Raftor," Peg said sharply. "Putting in your nose where you're not wanted."

"Making up to every dog and devil you meet," Kitty shouted. "Playing the lady and your family owing money all round."

"Faith, then, your huckstering grandmother will see that she gets her pound of flesh," Kathleen McEnroe taunted the newcomer. "Peg comes of good stock. Máire Rua was one of the gentry."

"Cromwell's whore," Kitty jeered. "She lived in old God's time. There's a curse on the family."

Peg made a drive at her tormentor, lost her balance and went stumbling under the wheels of a crested coach on its way to Smock Alley. Horses reared, the driver cursed, oranges scattered around and she felt a sickening blow. After that she remembered no more.

When she came to her senses she found herself on a sofa in a room bright with candlelight and the soft glow of a fire. A man with reckless blue eyes was looking down at her. There was something familiar about him. Then she remembered.

"You tried to run me down. Galloping along like a madman."

He grinned.

"You're like the cat with nine lives."

He held out a glass.

"Here, get this down."

Obediently she swallowed and the strong, sweet liquid stung her throat. She sat up in alarm.

"What did you give me?"

Time and again her mother had warned her of the dangers of strong drink and the danger of abduction.

"A punch of French brandy, hot water and honey, sweetheart, favourite tipple of His Honour Lord Wicklow. I'll warrant he's entertaining his boon companions in the Playhouse with an account of the slut who threw herself under the wheels of his coach for love."

"I was pushed," she argued but the savoury smell of the cooking-pot distracted her mind. A pale woman in a low-cut red velvet gown was ladling food into bowls. Peg recognised her at once as the Frenchwoman who had lately arrived in Dublin.

She swung her feet to the ground and stood up.

"I know your name. You're Madame Violante and

you're going to open a booth."

"You talk too much," the Frenchwoman snapped. "It ees time you go home."

"Feed her first," the captain said easily.

Hastily Peg sat up to the table for fear he would change his mind.

She had to admit that the soup was good, thick with lentils, flavoursome with chunks of smoky bacon, as she hungrily mopped up shreds of meat and leeks with crusty bread. When she had eaten her fill she propped her elbows on the table and studied the room, which was comfortable with oak furniture and a well-stoked fire.

"Is this a love-nest?" she asked politely. Kathleen McEnroe had often spoken of such places and she wished to appear worldly wise in the company in which she now found herself.

The captain choked on his wine.

"Did you hear that, Violante? Our secret is out. I think your quest for Polly Peachum is at an end."

Idly he began to whistle a tune from *The Beggar's Opera*, which had taken London by storm. Everyone knew the words and music—whistled by apprentice boys, sung by the Trinity students, performed on fiddle and pipes by musicians at every street corner. Next moment she and the captain were singing in harmony:

I would love you all the day;
Every night would kiss and play,
If with me you'd fondly stray
Over the hills and far away.

By the time they had finished even Madame Violante was tapping her feet in time to the music.

Captain O'Kelly raised his glass in a toast to Peg. "To your success, m'dear."

"She is 'alf starved and the bones stick out," Violante protested; yet Peg knew she was pleased.

"Nothing a few meals won't cure," the captain said lazily. "I never fancied unripe fruit myself but the town will go mad for her." He stretched, got to his feet, took his cloak from a nail and went out the door, beckoning Peg to follow.

She linked him out of Copper Alley and into Cork Hill cutting across into Dame Street, wishing her friends could see her now but they appeared to have vanished. Not that she cared. She told herself she had better fish to fry, dancing along, feet keeping time to her thoughts.

"Tell me about yourself, then," he ordered.

She knew he was trustworthy, that she could confide in him.

"There's me and the twins, Conor and Polly. They're four years old. I'm eleven. Father died of a fever and we had to move to George's Lane."

"And now you have taken to the streets selling oranges and no doubt other desirable commodities."

"I was only obliging a friend," she said grandly. "My mother was well born. I take after my great-grandmother Máire Rua who owned castles and things." She stole a glance at his face to see if he was suitably impressed. "Máire Rua married three husbands. Now she's a ghost."

"One husband is enough for any woman," he said absently, his mind on the sailors he was engaged to meet in the Dead Man's Head and the contraband he planned on running in.

They had arrived at the top of George's Lane. Through the open door of the tavern she could hear voices, some singing, more arguing. A sailor spied the captain and raised his tankard of beer, shouting a greeting.

"You said I'd be good as Polly Peachum," she whispered, holding on to his arm.

He paused and looked down at her. "Madame will be trying-out tomorrow morning. Can you read?"

"I was sent to the Quakers' School in the Coombe," she said proudly.

"You'll be all right so. Handle Madame carefully. The French are notoriously temperamental."

"I will," she promised fervently.

She was shabby and skinny with tangled red curls, and eyes like emeralds.

"Egad, when she fills out she'll turn many a head," he thought and on an impulse tossed her a sovereign. "To make up for the loss of your oranges."

She gazed at the gold piece in her hand. "I'm not allowed to take money. My mother will kill me."

"Tell her it's a hansel for luck," he said impatiently and had disappeared into the inn.

❦

Slany Woffington was a fragile-looking woman with something of Peg's colouring, only more faded, and was considered highly strung, as befitted a woman of breeding. It was her proud boast that she had been christened Slany for Máire Rua's favourite, the child-aunt buried in Coad graveyard in Co. Clare. For the past couple of hours she had been distracted with worry; now, at the sight of her daughter's flushed face and shining eyes, her temper flared.

"And where were you, Miss, until this hour of the

night?" she demanded. "Kitty Raftor brought me word that Kathleen McEnroe had run off with an actor from Smock Alley and that you had gone with them on the boat." Peg side-stepped her mother. "I was safe and well, taking supper with Madame Violante and Captain O'Kelly. Look what I got." She held out her hand.

"Do they think we're beggars or what?" With an angry movement Mrs Woffington thrust Peg aside and the sovereign went rolling across the floor to disappear down a hole.

Peg dodged around the room. "I'll ready up the fire," she said quickly, hoping to distract her mother. "It's almost out." She began to turn the fan bellows with more vigour than skill so that sparks flew up the chimney. In the flames she could make out a shining castle.

"Tell me about Lemineagh," she coaxed.

Her mother's face softened. "Ah, Lemineagh. So many rooms I could never count. We had a banqueting hall and a *grianán*, where I used to play."

"Tell me about my father." Peg had heard the story many times but never tired of listening.

Her mother seated herself down on the creepie stool. Her eyes had a dreamy look. "Your father was the best stonemason in Dublin. When Lemineagh was sold to pay the debts, he was brought down from Dublin by the new owners to repair the property…"

"Then you got married."

"What else was there for me and I alone in the world? My father lost everything at the gaming tables."

"And then what happened?"

"Lemineagh was the last to go. My father rode out on his favourite mare on a day of rain and high wind. His body was found in Lake Inchiquin. It killed my mother." She gave a great sigh and got to her feet. "I blame all our misfortune on the curse the old nurse laid on my grandmother. But there, I've wasted enough time talking. I've your father's supper to prepare and the room to make tidy. It's time you were in your bed where the twins are this last hour or more."

"Is that for him?" Peg whispered, nervously watching her mother fill a mug with buttermilk.

"Who else? Isn't this All Souls' Night, when the dead return home? The poor man will need sustenance after his long journey back."

Peg shivered. Thinking about her dead father worried her. "Tell me about Máire Rua."

Slany Woffington stood with a knife in one hand and a loaf of bread in the other, her mind far away. "My grandmother killed the Cromwellian she was forced to marry, when he insulted the memory of Conor, the husband she loved best. Afterwards they tried her for murder in Ennis town. Ireton's ring saved her life. She was riding home when her hair caught in a tree in Toonagh Woods and strangled her. She still haunts the place where it happened. Her pendant is all I have left of our fortune. One of these days I'll redeem it from the pawnshop."

Peg hugged her mother. "When I'm an actress and make my fortune I'll buy Lemineagh back for you."

"Foolish child." Slany Woffington kissed her daughter and for a moment dreamt of that house in Clare, the orchards, the gardens, the sweeping lawns running down to the sea. Then she pulled herself together and, taking the Spanish combs out of her hair, examined herself in the cracked mirror over the mantelpiece. She had skin so fine as to be almost translucent and even in hard times washed her face in buttermilk.

"Do you remember your father's friend, Mr Coffey?" she said. "I heard he married the Lady Jane Sandford. Ah well, some go up in the world, others down."

"I'll go up in the world," Peg boasted. "Madame Violante has engaged me to play Polly Peachum in *The Beggar's Opera*. It's likely the Lord Lieutenant will come to see us."

"Do you tell me so? Let you not forget that your ancestors were Earls of Thomond before his like ever set foot in this country. More fitting it would be to be praying for your dead father's soul than chattering on about upstarts. That Kathleen McEnroe has your mind astray with her talk of the Playhouse."

Mrs Woffington was a woman of quickly changing moods. Now she assumed an expression of deep humility and, falling to her knees, began to intone the prayers for the dead: "Rest in peace, O Christian soul, in the name of God the Father who created thee."

"Amen," Peg muttered, a lump in her throat at the image of her dead father wandering about the graveyard in his shift.

Later, when her mother had fallen asleep, Peg crept back into the kitchen and in the darkness scrabbled around the floor, her fingers finally closing on a withered herb she had hidden under the floorboards, and the lost sovereign, which she carefully placed on the mantelpiece. Tomorrow she would redeem Máire Rua's locket from the pawnshop and pay Mrs Raftor something on account. She pictured Kathleen McEnroe on the London stage, bowing and smiling, everyone clapping and cheering, and hoped Violante would give her the part. She was sure the captain would help.

Back in bed she put the yarrow under her pillow, muttering an incantation which Kathleen McEnroe had taught her and which could only be used on this one night of the year:

Good night, good yarrow, good night to thee.
Tell me who my true love is to be.

She was sure she would dream of the captain but instead found herself walking in Toonagh Woods with Máire Rua. "You'll be famous some day," her great-grandmother told her. When she looked up, Máire Rua had vanished and her place had been taken by Mr Coffey, who was once her father's best friend and was now husband to the Lady Jane Sandford and a person of importance. He took her hand in his and she was filled with such happiness that she wished the dream would never end.

2

I n years to come, taking a final curtain-call in Drury
Lane or Covent Garden, Peg would sometimes be
transported back to her early days, memories resurrected
by the voice of an Irish footman in the gallery, the whiff
of a musky perfume that Violante had once worn, a
glimpse of a dark-haired orange girl so like her childhood
companion, Kathleen McEnroe. In an instant the theatre
would blur, the face of the prince in the royal box, beaming
fatuously down, become indistinct, the sound of applause
die away and the fashionable London theatre change into
the booth in the Liberties of her native city, where she had
made her name as Polly Peachum. Out of the shadows
would steal the ghosts of her companions of yesteryear;
diminutive highwaymen, pickpockets, cut-purses, gaolers,
doxies, the cast of the long-forgotten *Beggar's Opera*.

With an effort she would banish the past, smile, curtsey
to royalty, throw kisses to the gallery and retreat to the
wings, while the house continued to ring with applause.
She would remind herself fiercely that she had achieved
her ambitions, was rich, famous, sought after, the toast of
the town. Yet all the while a still, small voice in her head

would repeat: "Once you were young, happy; the world was before you. What happened? Why did things turn out as they did?"

There was never any doubt, from the first performance on that cold New Year's Night of 1729, *The Beggar's Opera* was destined to catch the imagination of the town. Somehow Violante, herself failed acrobat, failed actress, had wrought a small miracle. Somehow she had brought together a group of unruly youngsters and, within a few short weeks, by some magic had moulded them into a company of actors, disciplined, sparklingly bright, with angel voices, playing the parts of sleazy denizens of the London underworld.

Everyone loved the catchy music, the libretto. Dublin possessed no Alsatia, sanctuary for all sorts of rogues, no highwaymen the likes of Captain MacHeath, hero of the story, no Mother Redcap, born into the aristocracy, who kept an infamous brothel and acted as fence in Blackfriars, the most notorious quarter of Alsatia...But to know such places and people existed, to see them brought to life on the stage, brought a frisson of fear and delight to the most law-abiding citizen. That the opera was based on fact, that a well-known justice of the peace had played a double role for years, outwardly respectable but in fact the king of the underworld, until fate caught up with him and he ended his life on the gallows, only added spice to the story.

Off-stage Peg was the quietest, most biddable of the players but costumed, painted as Polly, the gaoler's daughter, she lived in another's skin, headstrong, bold, bewitching, determined to seduce the doomed highwayman to do as she wished. No one could wriggle her hips like Peg, and when she winked at Peachum and called out in a saucy voice: "A woman knows how to be mercenary, papa. We have it in our nature. If I allow Captain MacHeath some trifling liberties, why I have this gold watch and other visible marks of favour to show for it," the booth resounded to the shrieks and catcalls from the fishwives, apprentices, redcoats and their whores.

It wasn't until Mr Charles Coffey, who wrote about the theatre for *Faulkner's Journal*, attended the opera, in the company of Captain O'Kelly, that the town sat up and took notice. He wrote a glowing account of the production, praising the youthful acting, tuneful songs and imaginative sets, and gave special mention to young Peg Woffington, who played the part Polly Peachum with such *joie de vivre*.

After that came the rich merchants and their well-endowed wives, the Trinity students, goldsmiths, tanners, clock-makers, carpenters. Even the Huguenot community, sober-faced weavers who seldom visited any place of amusement, could be seen to attend, tapping their feet in time to the music, humming the songs under their breaths. Before long the players were lionised by rich and poor alike, given money and fruit by the dealers and street vendors, invited to entertain the guests in the fine houses of the town. Lady Westmoreland, in her day a famous beauty who had spent time at the court of Versailles and taken part in amateur theatricals there, had had a little theatre specially built in the attic of her mansion in St Stephen's Green and invited the Lord Lieutenant to a special performance of the opera, for which she paid Violante a purse of gold. Peg had never been so happy in all her life, the pet of fashionable society, destined for greatness, a success. Her mother was content and the twins enjoyed the baubles thrown her on stage, the gingerbread, oranges, apples showered on her by the inhabitants of the Coombe, who considered her one of themselves.

"I wonder where my Kathleen has got herself to?"

Mrs McEnroe, plump, good-humoured, was busy sharing left-overs with her friend and neighbour, Mrs Woffington. Food was cheap and her mistress, careless, extravagant, turned a blind eye to the goings-on of her cook.

Peg considered the possible whereabouts of her erstwhile friend.

"She's probably travelling the roads of England with a company of strolling players. Either that or she's acting in the Covent Garden Playhouse." She swallowed a portion of pork pie and concluded: "One of these days I intend to make my name on the London stage."

"My parents visited the court of Charles II after his happy restoration," Mrs Woffington said nostalgically, remembering lost glories. "My grandmother Máire Rua could have been a great actress, if she hadn't been born into the aristocracy. She swept General Ireton off his feet, though she had little time for the Cromwellians."

Mrs McEnroe, who was a law-abiding soul, reminded herself that her friend was a widow in straitened circumstances and should be forgiven her boasting. All the same, but for her own good nature, the Woffingtons might often have starved. She poured out two glasses of wine which she had filched at some cost and said darkly: "Last night I dreamt of a riderless coach."

Mrs Woffington poked the fire and a shower of soot fell down. "It is a well-known fact," she announced, "that the banshee follows old Irish families. Everyone heard her wailing the night before my father was drowned."

In the orange glow Peg saw a faery woman in a black coat combing her long grey locks. Outside the wind was blowing a gale though the month was July.

"Mark my words, we'll hear of a death," Mrs McEnroe prophesied. "I always dream sharp."

❦

Next morning chaos reigned in the City Hall as the various guilds assembled for the "Riding of the Franchise," an event which took place every four years on the anniversary of the Battle of the Boyne.

In her apartment in Copper Alley, Violante stuck a patch on her face and added a spot of rouge to her chin while Peg helped her into her gown, a marvellous creation of French silk with a low-cut neckline and three-quarter sleeves, the navy skirt caught up at one side, revealing a pink petticoat. Richard Baldwin, Provost of Trinity College, had issued her with an invitation to view the procession from his rooms. They frequently drank a dish of tea together and conversed in French. He was a well-meaning old man who did his best to keep order and discipline the students, though there was a constant conflict between Town and Gown. Duelling had become so popular that when a gentleman sued for a lady's hand, the only two questions ever asked were: "What family is he?" and "Did he ever blaze?"

"Will the captain be joining you, Madame?" Peg enquired as they went out into Fishamble Street. She hadn't laid eyes on him for more than a month but hugged to herself the thought of their last meeting, when he had squeezed her waist. She had gone home in a daze of delight.

"*Mon capitaine* is away on the travels, you comprehend," Madame said vaguely, bowing to every passing acquaintance, as she seemed to float along. She was as close as an oyster about his movements, though the world and his wife knew him for a smuggler who sold fine wine and brandy to the innkeepers of the town. Matt Carey of the

Dead Man's Head was his best customer.

After a night of rain and high wind the day had dawned gloriously sunny. Signs swinging from shops and taverns were freshly painted, arches of greenery spanned entrances to alleys and courtyards. Away in the distance Peg could make out a group of students decking the statue of King William in the centre of the Green with an orange sash and a flaming cloak. When the parade was over they would parade the streets arm in arm with their companions, forcing honest citizens into the gutter, would drink to excess, fling bricks through shop windows, tie gunpowder squibs to street lamps to plunge the place into darkness. But as yet they were mostly sober, content to bandy insults with the crowd around.

A green oak-bough had been nailed over the entrance to Trinity College and here Violante took her leave of Peg, mincing along the college cobbles while Peg squeezed herself in to the front of the crowd.

"Egad, but your green bonnet becomes you. Where's Madame? Not eloped, I trust."

She wheeled around in delight, unable to believe her ears. And there he was, handsome in plumed coat, cloak, sword at the ready, Captain O'Kelly, the dashing cavalier of her dreams.

"Madame was invited by the provost to a window seat. I think the place is full," she added anxiously, afraid he would leave her.

"Then I'm an outcast like yourself," he said, slipping an arm around her waist. She was sure she would faint with the joy of it all.

A cheer went up as the Lord Mayor's coach came into view, followed by the city fathers on horseback. Trumpets sounded, kettledrums rolled, bagpipes shrilled to the passing guilds, preceded by open carriages decorated with ribbons. Peg waved to the Sparks twins, Lucy and Larry, dressed as devils with painted faces and wearing horns, black breeches and shirts. Two of the most talented of the actors in the booth, they ran the streets at will, since their parents were locked up in the debtors' gaol in the Marshalsea, with little hope of release. Kitty Raftor, her rival on stage and her avowed enemy in everyday life, rode by in the shoemakers' carriage, got up as Cinderella on her way to the ball. Goldsmiths and silversmiths, all splendidly attired, swung by. After them marched the Liberty weavers, small dark Huguenots, wearing high coloured wigs and silk sashes. There was bad blood between them and the Ormond butcher boys, Catholic to a man.

A simpering student with a painted face made a grab at an old man's hat.

"Honour King William of pious glorious and immortal memory who saved us from popery, slavery, brass money and wooden shoes," he bullied.

He had drunk a pint of port at one go for a wager and could scarcely stand upright. "Remember the glorious Boyne," he hiccoughed.

"Remember Limerick," the old man shouted, his voice surprisingly strong for one of his years.

At his words a hush fell on the Green so compelling that the sound of passing footsteps was an army on the march. In an instant the mood of the crowd had changed, grown sullen, stories recalled of the defeat of the Irish at Limerick by the Williamite forces more than thirty years before. Patrick Sarsfield, Earl of Lucan, had led his "Wild Geese" into exile and they had taken service in the armies of Europe, soldiers of fortune whose rallying cry, "Remember Limerick," had turned many a tide of battle.

A stone struck the statue of King William and with that the riot erupted. Weavers and butchers broke ranks to attack each other with bottles and knives, redcoats rode up, steel flashing, and even the women took sides. Quickly the captain unsheathed his sword and waded into the fray, as the drunken student, the cause of it all, went down under the hooves of a maddened horse. Sobbing with fright, Peg took to her heels. In her headlong flight she lost her green bonnet and remembered her mother's dire warning: "Wear green for grief."

In the early morning Violante accompanied by Peg made her way to the Sheriff's prison down by the quays. Matt Carey of the Dead Man's Head had been first with the news that the captain had been taken after a night of violence. A bitter east wind had blown up and the festive arches of greenery and gay streamers of the day before fluttered ragged and torn. Somewhere around, a bell tolled. Peg crossed herself, remembering Mrs McEnroe's dream and her mother's talk of the banshee.

When they reached the Marshalsea, Violante bribed the turnkey, a shambling giant wearing a tattered velvet coat, and he led them through the gloom of the debtors' quarters where links and yellow candles threw eerie shadows on green mouldering walls. Then they were descending into the lower depths, where drabs stripped to the waist were fighting for the favours of their gaolers, and on past to an alcove where three prisoners were chained to a wall.

"I'm due for a rise in the world," joked the captain, battered and bruised. Beside him the simpering student giggled inanely.

"There I was making my way through College, a humble sizar, emptying slops, waiting on tables, pleasuring my betters when I could have been holding up coaches like my gallant friend." He leered at the captain. "Or were you a smuggler, dearie? What matter, we're all friends here."

A yellow-haired boy, little older than Peg, wept as he tried to explain his case. "I'm innocent. A butcher attacked me and I pushed him away. Somehow the knife twisted and someone got killed. It wasn't my fault."

Violante gave them brandy which she had brought along and bribed the warder with gold. He promised to have them moved to better quarters until their fate was decided.

❧

A week later they were sentenced to the gallows, for when the process of law worked at all, it did so with devastating swiftness, and for a penniless student, an apprentice weaver without connections and a smuggler with a price on his head, no mercy was shown.

On the night before the hanging, they took a last farewell of the condemned. Moonlight filtered through the prison bars and countless stars, an immeasurable distance away, filled a radiant sky. Peg thought wistfully of that enchanted country where her mother once lived and longed to be safe in the fairytale mansion of Lemineagh. She felt hollow inside, unable to accept the fact that on the morrow the three prisoners would be no more than scarecrows dancing in the wind.

"Don't cry for me, Polly Peachum," the captain teased. "Take care of Madame for me," he said, and she promised, would have promised her life away, though she felt burdened enough with a feckless mother and the helpless twins.

"There was a lake in Wicklow I used fish," the young weaver remembered.

"'By the waters of Babylon we sat and wept when we remembered thee, O Sion,'" the student jeered. "Jesus, I hate a melancholy wake. Give us a kiss, Captain, or sing us a song."

The captain whistled the opening bars of the harlots' chorus from *The Beggar's Opera* and they all joined in.

> *In the days of my youth I could bill like a dove;*
> *Like a sparrow at all times was ready for love.*
> *The lips of all mortals in kissing should pass*
> *Lip to lip while we're young, and then lip to*
> *the glass.*

Afterwards when Peg tried to recapture that night all she could remember was moonlight and the three of them singing and drinking. Early next morning they were hanged from the same arm of a three-cornered gallows in Thomas Street, in the Earl of Meath's Liberty.

❦

Violante sold the booth to the notorious Buck Whaley, and invited Peg to accompany her to London. It had been the captain's last wish and Mrs Woffington agreed that it must be obeyed, else his spirit would know no rest. In addition to which, Madame had been lavish with money and promises of a great future for Peg. Matt Carey hired a coach to take them to the North Wall, where the ship waited to sail with the tide. In a fit of goodwill he produced a hamper of food for the journey, which could take anything up to three weeks, depending on wind and weather.

"A few trifles to keep you in good heart," he said, wiping eyes which continually leaked and planting wet kisses all round. "A couple of fowl, done to a turn, a bottle of brandy, another of wine, cheesecake to which Peg is partial. Funeral meats for the captain, a gallant gentleman."

"Be sure to remind the king if you meet him that my parents were once invited to the court," Mrs Woffington said bravely. "When I was young I wanted to travel the world."

"Travel broadens the mind," Mrs McEnroe conceded. She had come for the ride and to remind Peg to seek out her errant daughter Kathleen in London.

Peg hugged and kissed her mother and the twins. She could feel Conor's heart thumping and was sure her own would break with the loneliness of it all. Whistles were blowing, a sailor was holding the rope-ladder steady. It was time to depart. She bit her lips as she began the climb, lonely at leaving her family, the town, scared of the dark waters below.

They were safely on board, slowly inching out into the bay, sails swelling, billowing, figures on the quayside growing smaller and smaller. She thought she could make out the spires of Christ Church and the turrets of Dublin Castle. Daly's Inn, where the rakes of the town gathered each night to drink and carouse, before riding out to the Dublin hills to the Hellfire Club, was nearby. Buck Whaley was said to practise black magic. He had the Sparks twins in his keeping but Peg had no fear for them. Nothing could touch them. They believed in nothing, were afraid of no one. Treated everything as a joke. If they could survive, so too could she. Defiantly she tossed back her red hair, the salt spray slapping her face, giving her courage.

"Please God, don't let me be homesick," she prayed. "Let me be brave like Máire Rua."

YOUTH'S A STUFF WILL NOT ENDURE

In delay there lies no plenty;
Then come kiss me, sweet and twenty,
Youth's a stuff will not endure.

(*Twelfth Night*, II, iii)

3

Peg never forgot the foundling. That dark, enigmatic Scottish noble, Lord Darnley, had called him her dark angel at their first meeting and she had been too upset to protest to the man who would one day become her lover.

She thought of the foundling as something different. Ragged and dirty he might be, hair black as the soot on his face, but he gave an impression of light, brightness. He had an air of irrepressible gaiety and a smile that would melt a stone. It was odd that she had never discovered his name. He must have been called something, she reasoned long after, given a name in the Foundling Hospital where he was left abandoned, or by the grim Puritans who ran the Charity School, or even by his old master, the sweep. Surely the boys he had grown up with would have nicknamed him. Yet if that was so, he had never divulged it. From their first meeting she had felt there was a bond between them, though she had no way of knowing that one day he would save her life. After that terrible night he vanished forever, back into Alsatia, grim underworld, haunt of thieves and cut-throats.

She was leaning over the rails as the ship ploughed its way across the Irish Sea on that first morning out, when he appeared out of nowhere. The moment he opened his mouth she knew he was from the Liberties.

He said: "What's your name?"

She didn't answer and he repeated the question.

"I'm Peg Woffington, if you must know," she said impatiently.

He looked around furtively. "Can you keep a secret?"

"That all depends."

"I stowed away last night."

She examined him critically: a small, thin boy, scarcely up to her shoulder, clothes so ragged that they might have been held together by a prayer and a pin; face grimed with soot, hair that stood up in spikes, great grey eyes that looked at her trustingly.

She didn't want to be bothered and said crossly: "If you're caught you'll likely be put in the hold or worse."

He twisted one leg around the other. "Did you ever see anyone strung up?"

Down below, a shoal of fish leaped and twisted to disappear in the patchwork waters. Seabirds were rising out of the foam, their mournful cries a dirge for the captain and his dead companions. Now all that remained of them was a handful of bones in a limestone bed inside the prison walls.

"Go away and leave me alone." She was near to tears.

He wiped his nose with a sleeve. "I've nowhere to go. I'm a foundling."

She felt a sudden gush of pity for his plight. Unwanted infants were left in a basket outside St James's Hospital under cover of darkness and taken in at daybreak by a grim-faced porter. Most of them died. The few that survived were sent to a Charity School. It was the worst fate that could befall any child.

She looked at him sadly. "Did they beat and starve you?"

He eyed her through long, dark lashes. "No one dared touch me. We were fed mouldy bread, lumpy stirabout, fat a dog wouldn't eat, but I was lucky: I could steal the eye out of your head." He grinned. "I used to climb over the wall of the orphanage and make my way into Patrick Street, stealing bread, oranges, anything I could lay hands on. I brought a share back. It kept us alive. Someone ratted and I was flogged half to death. An old fellow who came in to sweep the chimneys took pity on me and engaged me as his helper. He'd tie the brushes around me and I'd climb up the chimneys quick as a flash. He had a fierce temper but I made him laugh."

She didn't believe the half of what he was telling her but he had a hungry look and impulsively she made an offer.

"I can get you some food. The lady I'm travelling with is seasick. She won't miss what I take. Chicken, a lump of cheese, bread. I think there's wine."

He danced with delight and she looked around fearfully. "Be quiet or you'll be caught."

He grinned impishly. "My old master always said it's better to be born lucky nor rich."

His luck held. When next she laid eyes on him his face was clean, his hair combed, and he was wearing a trousers too long and a coat too big. He confided that he had been adopted by the crew; the captain had spared him because he was said to resemble the wooden boy carved on the ship's prow, a talisman against pirates and shipwrecks. Sailors were superstitious by nature and a sweep was considered to bring good luck. Still Peg felt anxious about his future.

"What will you do when the ship reaches land?"

"Make my way to London and apprentice myself to a master-thief I heard tell of. He keeps a school for pickpockets in a place called Blackfriars. I'll be the best thief in London. I have the talent."

Blackfriars in Alsatia had been the setting for *The Beggar's Opera* but none the less real for that, a known haunt of ruffians and thieves. She tried to dissuade him but he scoffed at her fears and boasted of all he would do.

She didn't see him again until the ship reached Holyhead. Passengers were fighting their way ashore, intent on securing a place for themselves in one of the stage-coaches lining the harbour. Violante was using her as a buffer. She heard a voice in her ear whisper: "For luck, Peg," and found he had slipped her an embroidered purse containing a few coins. She turned to thank him but he had vanished into the crowd. She treasured that purse for years, which by some magic seemed never to be empty. She kept it until it was destroyed in a fire that was to change her life utterly. But all that was away in the future and London was beckoning her on.

❦

Belle Tudor, the most famous courtesan in London, was held to be responsible for the death of the Duke of Marlborough's son. He had squandered a fortune in jewels and gowns on her and when she dismissed him for Jimmy Maclean, the famous highwayman, he had lost no time in gambling away what remained of his inheritance at cards and had then made his way to Buttons Inn in Great

Russell Street, where he challenged his rival to a duel.

Jimmy Maclean had no equal with pistols or sword. In vain he had reasoned with the distracted young man but in the end had been forced to accept the challenge. The duel was fought at dawn in Hyde Park and the young nobleman had been fatally wounded. With his dying breath he had whispered that it had all been worth while for a night in Belle's arms. Marlborough was so enraged at the death of his heir that he offered a reward of five hundred guineas for Jimmy's capture, thus sealing the fate of England's most popular "gentleman of the road."

Now London town was agog for the next chapter in the story. Billy the pot-boy in Buttons Inn was a simpleton. His mother, a drunken fishwife, had dropped him on his head down a basement as an infant, and since he had learnt to talk he seldom uttered a word of sense. But he was kind, with a shock of fair hair and innocent eyes, and people liked him; besides which he had one great gift: he could sing like an angel. One night in Buttons he had sung "Greensleeves" for Belle and so impressed had she been that she had taken him to her bed.

"He follows her around like a dog after a bitch on heat," Peg's new-found friend, Jennie Tatler, grumbled. Jennie's sister was an actress in a booth in Southwark Fair and her grandmother kept a stall in Covent Garden. Between them they knew all the gossip of the town.

"She promised she would pleasure him once more if he brought her twenty guineas," Jennie continued. "She might as well have asked for the moon. It was all a ploy to get rid of the poor fool."

"He might save a lifetime and never succeed," Peg said sadly.

She was fond of Billy, who filched food for her from

Buttons and kept watch as she wolfed down stale pies and seed cake. But for him she might have gone hungry. Violante spent most of her time drinking gin in the company of Sarah Pepys, their landlady, a good-natured slut of a woman who kept a lodging house in Bull Alley behind the Garden. Mr Quinn, a broken-down actor, also lodged in the house. He had taken a fancy to Peg and lent her his dog-eared copy of Shakespeare's works. She loved to watch him as he described parts he had played: long thin body and hands, a face so expressive that by the lifting of an eyebrow, the curl of his lips, he could convey the anguish of Hamlet, prince of Denmark, the craftiness of the hunchback Richard III, the savagery of Caliban the deformed slave in *The Tempest*, or the mischievousness of Oberon, King of the Fairies, in *A Midsummer Night's Dream*.

He wore his wig at a rakish angle, favoured flamboyant clothes which had seen better days, and painted his face. In years to come she would remember that mellifluous voice and would compare it with David Garrick's and marvel at the twists of fate, by which one man could become the greatest actor of his day and another, seemingly equally talented, end his days in a run-down house in a dingy alley.

The first lines of Shakespeare he taught her were from *Julius Caesar*. He was sitting on a broken-down stool in the kitchen reciting, while she mouthed the words after him:

Forever, and forever, farewell, Cassius!
If we do meet again, why, we shall smile!
If not, why then, this parting was well made.

Violante, who was preparing to go on the town, pushed her way forward intent on fixing a beauty spot at her mouth.

"An invitation to kiss," she simpered, throwing the old actor a flirtatious glance. She was forever making up to him.

Jennie Tatler had told Peg that Mr Quinn's tastes lay in another direction. "Boys," she had whispered, "he buggers them."

Jennie was common. Peg admired Mr Quinn and was of the opinion that Violante was making a spectacle of herself, prinking and posing instead of doing what she had promised. She determined to have it out with her once and for all. "You brought me here under false pretences," she said, angry at the interruption. "I thought to go on the stage and make my way and all you do is drink gin and make eyes at every man you meet."

Mr Quinn beat a hasty retreat, which he always did when trouble was brewing, and Violante gave Peg a resounding slap on the face. Sarah Pepys thought it time to intervene. She was a good-natured woman who liked a laugh and hated scenes.

"Compose yourself, Madame," she begged. "Quinn always had a taste for boys, though nowadays he finds them hard to come by. The young are mercenary and Quinn, poor wigh, grows old."

Violante adjusted her wig. "Bah, with you it is both *jalousie*. Soon I stage *The Way of the World*, an elegant comedy the town will adore. It ees a question of a licence from the Lord Chamberlain."

Nothing had turned out as Peg had expected but she was enjoying herself too much to care. She ran out of the ramshackle house in search of Jennie Tatler, who had promised to take her to Pudding Lane to see the Roman column two hundred feet tall, that marked a spot near where the Great Fire of London had started. They went through Covent Garden and into Russell Street. Billy was sitting in the Cock Fighting Pit in Birdcage Walk, gambling all his money in the vain hope of a win.

"That fool will end up in Bedlam the way he's behaving," Jennie said, squinting at the blood and feathers flying around.

"Don't mention that place," Peg begged. She had visited Bedlam, where lunatics were locked up in cages, tormented by visitors who poked sticks through the iron bars.

❧

A mellow autumn was followed by the hardest winter in living memory. Heavy snow fell. Then came a great frost. Violante took Peg skating on the Serpentine in Hyde Park, where they met up with the cook from Buttons Inn. The three of them crossed arms and went gliding over the icy lake so fast it was like flying. In the evening the moon came out, the sky glittered with stars, lanterns flickered as though they were fireflies and people sang songs. That was the best time of all. When the Thames froze over the lord mayor of London held a Frost Fair. Bonfires were lit on the ice; oxen were roasted; musicians played drums and pipes and old men sang ballads; acrobats turned cartwheels, and booths on London Bridge selling pies and sausages and hot mulled wine did a roaring trade.

Belle Tudor, a vision in diamonds and white furs, had been invited by the lord mayor to present the cup to the winner of the best sporting exploit of the fair. It had been won by a reckless buck who had risked his own neck and that of his coachman, driving a coach and four across the river of ice. Billy the pot-boy stood as near to Belle as possible. There was something different about him, Peg thought, something about the way he stood, no longer hunched up. But it was the sound of his voice that stopped her in her tracks. He was quoting Shakespeare in a voice Mr Quinn might have envied:

> Is there no pity sitting in the clouds.
> That sees the bottom of my grief.
> Past hope, past cure, past help.

She made the sign of the cross. "Mother of God, he thinks he's Romeo and that Belle is Juliet?"

She caught his arm, peering into his face: "Billy! What ails you? What are you saying?"

He blinked, bent over, face crumbling, foolish, bewildered eyes staring at her in fright. Muttering some nonsense about a highwayman on a monkey, he shuffled away.

When she returned to Bull Alley that night it was to find that Violante had bolted, leaving no message. Sarah Pepys and Mr Quinn were drinking gin, well into their cups.

"Where has she gone?" Peg demanded distractedly.

"It is my belief that she has eloped to Paris with the cook from Buttons." Mr Quinn tapped his nose. "I have heard rumours."

Sarah Pepys tittered. "He admired her skating. Tumbled her under London Bridge."

Peg could have shaken them both. "Did she leave any money for me?"

Sarah Pepys wagged a finger. "It was not within her competence to do so. He is now her husband in all but name."

"Legal capacity," Mr Quinn brought out carefully. "Right to cognizance."

"Winner take all." Sarah Pepys laughed so much she tumbled off the stool and lay on the floor in a drunken stupor.

"What's to become of me?" Peg shouted hysterically.

Mr Quinn carefully raised his glass, splashing his velvet weskit.

"Join a band of strolling players," he enunciated carefully. "Travel the roads of England like the great bard himself."

Carefully he rose to his feet, bowed in Peg's direction and collapsed on the floor beside Sarah Pepys, his drunken snores keeping time with hers.

Worn out with day's happenings, Peg climbed the stairs to her attic bed and fell asleep almost at once. In her dreams she was with a company of strolling players, travelling the roads. Billy, wearing a monkey's mask, sat in a tree, pelting them with acorns. She awoke with a start. Someone was throwing stones up at her window. She stood on the bed to look out. In the courtyard below she could just make out a figure dancing around like a dervish. She put out her head and heard Jennie Tatler's reedy voice soar up: "Jimmy Maclean was taken and now Billy has gone to Belle's with the reward."

4

They ran through Covent Garden in the direction of St Paul's Cathedral. Peg's heart was thumping, breath coming in uneven gasps.

"I don't believe Billy betrayed the highwayman," she panted. "Why would he do a thing like that?"

"For the reward, of course," Jennie said scornfully. "He would have sold his own mother for a night in Belle's bed."

"How did he know Jimmy's hiding place?"

"Didn't he take him food every day? The landlord at Buttons trusted Billy."

"Where was he hiding?"

Jennie sighed. "You might as well know, since the harm is done. He was hiding in Leicester Fields."

❦

Belle Tudor lay motionless in the four-poster, reputed to be the biggest bed in London. Beside her a dark, handsome man stirred in his sleep. In his dream Edward, Earl of Darnley, was walking the Coolins, dark, remote;

he gazed on rushing mountain torrents, listened to the clash of antlers as two stags locked in mortal combat, filling that wild space with sound and fury.

He awoke with a start and sat up, listening. The heavy curtains of the bed excluded all light; the darkness was almost tangible, yet something had roused him. He was one of those people who awake fully alert, who are in full possession of all their senses, the moment they open their eyes. Quietly he got out of bed and lit a candle. Belle hadn't moved. In the flickering light her face was smooth, unlined. Golden hair spread fan-like on the pillow, breasts rising and falling gently. In her sleep she might have been a young, innocent girl, though she was thirty years or more.

Belle was a drug. He came to her worn out by his obsession: planning the downfall of the Hanoverians and the restoration of the Stuarts, and she would listen in silence until his emotions were spent. Only then would she pour him the wine from the vineyards of Normandy first bottled for the Duc de Richelieu, that strange, ugly, noble man with lineage centuries old. She said he could entice any woman into his bed with that wine and that low, caressing voice.

Darnley's tongue clove to the roof of his mouth. He longed for a draught of the crystal-clear waters, ice-cold, sharp, to be found only in the mountain streams of his beloved Scotland. Last night he had drunk himself nearly crazy, drunk until his loins were on fire. Belle had been well schooled in the art of sexual pleasing: she had been the mistress of d'Orléans, the greatest libertine in France. He would never understand her. She was an enigma: greedy, generous, sensuous, indolent, at times gripped with a religious fervour, only to become again worldly, practised, sophisticated. She had once taken part in a black mass with some members of the court at Versailles. Afterwards she had been shriven by the Bishop of Paris and had immured herself in a convent in repentance. Growing bored with the foolish storms that at times rocked the community, the gossip, back-biting and the petty penances the nuns practised on themselves, she had left and returned to London where she had been born. She would sell her body for a king's ransom or give herself for nothing to a struggling artist, a highwayman with a price on his head, a fool with the voice of an angel. Some day she would return to the nunnery at Poitiers, she said, do penance, make her peace with God.

He yawned tiredly, the smell of stale perfume, candlegrease, spilt wine, semen in his head, threw back the shutters and gulped in the night air. He sensed rather than saw that the square was thick with shadows. Watching from their vantage point behind a tree Jennie clutched at Peg's arm.

"Lord Darnley seems to be Belle's latest conquest."

❦

"What is it?"

Belle had joined him. At that moment the moon broke free of its cloudy anchorage to sail across the rooftops, lighting up the fashionable London square, revealing a girl in a white silken robe at the window, a man in shadows at her shoulder and a figure kneeling in supplication below.

"Who's there?" Belle called down.

That husky voice it was his heaven to hear! He

struggled to tell her that he had brought her the gold, to remind her of her promise, but the words were twisted in his mouth. He would sing her song and she would understand. In the stillness of the night the clear voice rang out, like the death song of the thorn bird that impales itself and sings the more exquisitely as it expires.

Greensleeves was all my joy...
And who but my lady, Greensleeves?

"Mother of God, it's Billy the pot-boy," she whispered. "I must go to him."

"Don't be a fool, Belle. I'll give him money to pacify him." Lord Darnley disappeared into the room and returned almost at once, leaning out to toss a shower of silver that fell with a clatter on the cobbles. Immediately the shutters closed with a finality that quenched all hope for the desperate figure below.

Billy plucked at the strings of his purse, flinging handfuls of gold in the air, leaping like a crazed juggler. As if on cue, the innkeeper of Buttons, cudgel in hand, emerged from the shadows. A harridan voice screamed. "Judas. The reward was five hundred guineas. You sold our Jimmy for twenty pieces of gold."

Men were advancing with stones, broken bottles, knives; closing in.

Peg made to dart forward to Billy's help but Mr Quinn, now sober, face white under the moonlight, held her back.

"Past hope, past cure, past help," he said.

She began to scream. Billy had used the self-same words, watching Belle at the Frost Fair. Had he foreseen his terrible end?

It was finished: the square silent in the moonlight; rats slinking out from their holes; beady eyes examining the crumpled mess that had once been an angel's voice; greedy tongues licking the cobbles stained red. There was no one to see Lord Darnley emerge from the house, lift up the broken body and carry it in to where Belle waited in tears.

❦

Arm in arm Jennie and Peg made their way back to Bull Alley.

"I hate Belle Tudor," Jennie said viciously. "Failed actress turned great whore."

"Belle would have taken Billy to her bed," Peg said in a choked voice. "It was all Lord Darnley's fault."

Next day Mr Quinn invited Peg to accompany him to the Covent Garden Playhouse to distract her mind. It was her first visit to a London theatre and she was almost sick with excitement.

"*A Midsummer Night's Dream* is my favourite Shakespearean play," Mr Quinn said solemnly, rouging his lips. "I once played Oberon, King of the Fairies."

Sarah Pepys tittered behind her hands. "A part he's been playing off-stage ever since."

From a vantage point under the gallery Peg looked down into the pit, the benches covered in bright green matting stretching to the apron stage where orange girls shouted their wares. The house was filling up with citizens dressed in their best. In the boxes painted ladies flashed fans, gossiped, called greetings to friends; gentlemen rolled dice, played cards, drank from silver flasks and threatened to run each other through if they

suspected cheating. In the "gods" there was bedlam
with apprentices, soldiers, fishwives, whores, shouting,
laughing, engaging in fisticuffs to settle arguments.
Wearily Mr Quinn mopped his brow with a square of
scented silk. "'Lord what fools these mortals be,' to
quote Puck, my dear Peg. I fear the theatre is finished."

Yet at the commencement of the play the house
settled down to enjoy the enchanted romp of fairy
mischief and teasing love in the palace and woods of
Athens. Peg longed with all her soul to be on stage,
playing Titania, Queen of the Fairies, and for days
afterwards went around reciting Oberon's lines:

> Through the house give glimmering light
> By the dead and drowsy fire;
> Every elf and fairy sprite
> Hop as light as bird from briar,
> And this ditty after me
> Sing, and dance it trippingly.

"I am determined to become a famous actress," she
told Jennie Tatler as they wended their way in the
direction of Belle Tudor's mansion. "I shall serve my
apprenticeship with the strolling players of England.
Your sister Rose must put in a good word for me."

Jennie tittered uneasily. "Are you scared of what
we'll see?"

Peg tossed her head of red curls. "Dublin is a great
place for wakes. We like to give the corpse a good send-
off."

"All the same, it was a queer thing for Belle to do,"
Jennie said darkly. London had been astounded when
Belle sent around notices of Billy's wake on black-edged

cards, embellished with a skull and crossbones, an hour-glass and an old man clutching a scythe. In the centre was the fell phrase:

Nymph, in thy orisons
Be all my sins remember'd.

Belle's house was shuttered, the knocker wrapped in flannel to deaden the sound. On the steps a deaf-mute, face plastered with white chalk, rolled his eyes and pulled his hair in an agony of despair.

"That poor soul must have loved Billy," Peg said, eyeing him curiously.

Jennie sniggered. "You're easily fooled. He's an actor from the Playhouse. Belle pays him sixpence an hour."

"All the same, it's good money," Peg argued. She was feeling the pinch since Violante had left and longed more than ever to go on the stage. She had not the slightest doubt that she would be a success.

A servant wearing black gloves ushered them into a long hall, where the mirrors were covered with black and pictures were turned to the wall. All the clocks in the house had been stopped at the hour of Billy's demise.

A slim figure in a medieval gown of green velvet with a heart-shaped neck and wide, flowing sleeves sat in the great drawing room, keeping watch at the bier. A lace wimple covered her golden hair.

"Greensleeves." The word was out before Peg could stop herself. In her confusion she forgot to kneel and pray for the dead. She stood on her toes, craning into the coffin to look at the corpse. Whatever fearful damage had been done to Billy's body, his face had been spared.

All signs of idiocy had been wiped away by death and his once slack mouth was firmly closed. He was like the effigy of a Norman knight she had once seen in the vaults of Christ Church Cathedral in Dublin and she wondered which was the real Billy, the fool everyone mocked or the boy who had sung so beautifully and spoken words of love at the Frost Fair.

Reverently she bent and kissed his marble forehead.

"Good-night, sweet prince, and flights of angels sing thee to thy rest!" she said solemnly.

Jennie Tatler pinched her arm: "Show-off. Do you think you're Mr Quinn, or what?"

Belle covered her face with her hands and made strangled sounds. Was she laughing or crying? In an agony of embarrassment Peg fled from the house, deaf to Jennie's hungry cries, to the clatter of plates and glasses in the dining parlour where the funeral meats were laid out and the mourners were eating and laughing.

❦

Sarah Pepys had let Violante's room to an Irish girl named Margaret Leeson who had come to London with a recruiting officer and was soon deserted.

"I come from a poor holding in County Wicklow, little more than a cabbage-patch," she explained to Peg, who was watching her settle a golden wig on a head of wiry black hair. "When I was ten years of age I sucked Alick's cock. He was the landlord's son. After that he stole anything that I asked him to."

Jennie Tatler had tried to explain what Belle's "French tricks" meant. Was this what Margaret Leeson was talking about? The thought made her sick. She had seen

Belle in a different light since the evening of the wake, had admired Belle's green velvet gown, been impressed by the deaf-mute on the doorstep, the clocks all stopped, the pictures turned to the wall. It was like something you would see in the Playhouse. Besides, everyone knew that Belle had been reared at the court of France and was descended on the wrong side of the blanket from King Charles, the Merry Monarch with the beautiful mistresses and the packs of yapping spaniel dogs. Only a common whore the likes of Margaret Leeson would boast of such conduct.

"I don't wish to hear any more of your murky past," Peg said loftily and minced out of the house into the gloom that was Bull Alley. Covent Garden was bathed in sunlight. She caught the scent of flowers, the smell of the good earth, the vegetables, fruits, odours she would for ever associate with the markets in the Liberties. At that moment she longed with all her heart to be back in Dublin with her mother and the twins.

Jennie Tatler was seated on the steps of Buttons Inn, her small shrewd face greedy as she pushed hot pancakes into her mouth. Her wispy hair blew in the wind, getting in the way. Companionably she moved to make room for Peg. "Take that hungry look off your face and have something to eat," she ordered. "I swear you're starved by Sarah Pepys. I hear she's got a new lodger— a whore, no less. Is she keeping a brothel or what?"

"She needs the money," Peg said peaceably. She had no wish to quarrel with Jennie and sought in her mind for some distraction. "Get her to read your hand," she coaxed. "She's good at the fortunes. She might promise you a handsome husband or maybe that you'll go on a long journey."

"I am."

"You are what?"

"I'm leaving tomorrow morning with the acting company from Southwark Fair. Rose arranged it."

"I'll go with you, Jennie," Peg said eagerly. "Remember how we planned it. Mr Quinn is always urging me to become a strolling player. He says it's the only way to gain experience. Besides, there's nothing to keep me in London now that Violante has vanished."

Jennie scowled. "It's no use. I did my best for you. Rose wouldn't hear of it. We'll be playing in castles and places. You'd be a laughing-stock with your Irish brogue."

Peg couldn't believe her ears. "You're not...you can't go without me."

"Oh, shut up," Jennie said, driven beyond endurance. "You'll never make an actress."

"One day I'll be famous, Jennie Tatler," Peg shouted. She was so upset her voice cracked. "Your Rose is no better than Margaret Leeson. I'll show you all. One of these days you'll be sorry."

"It's not my fault," Jennie whined miserably. "At least you can say goodbye." She held out a grubby hand but Peg had turned away and was running blindly across the piazza, by the cathedral, across the busy thoroughfare of the Strand, down a flight of stone steps that led to the river. In her misery she had no eyes for the slender wherries carrying passengers out to the waiting ships, was deaf to the laughter and good-natured banter of river folk in their gaily painted houseboats. Jennie was false. She would never again trust a living soul. She was a failure. She might as well be dead. Wave after wave of the most searing loneliness swept over her.

"Please, God, let me go home," she sobbed. "I swear

I'll be good, I want my mother and Polly and Conor."

❧

Sarah Pepys was reading the crystal ball for Margaret Leeson.

"There are men all around you and a long journey before you. A lecherous fellow with the initial *A* will come back into your life."

Margaret Leeson rattled her bangles. "Aye, that will be Alick. He never got over me. Where is the journey taking me?"

Sarah Pepys said testily, "I wish you wouldn't keep interrupting. One of these days I'll call up the spirits. I feel the power stirring in my blood. Did I tell you I saw the gallows in Jimmy Maclean's hand?"

Mr Quinn helped himself to snuff. "Belle Tudor visited Newgate yesterday. Jimmy was playing cards in the taproom, on a winning streak and too busy to lay her."

Peg sat on a stool, face in her hands, wishing she were miles away. "What use is money and poor Jimmy facing the gallows?" she said in a cranky voice.

Margaret Leeson smirked. "Money is always useful."

"For what, pray?"

"So that he can bribe the hangman to do the job properly and pay a few strong men to pull on his feet to make sure he goes quickly."

Mr Quinn brushed snuff from his velvet weskit. "The hanging is fixed for April Fool's Day. We'll have a public holiday. We must all go along to pay our respects."

"I wouldn't miss it for a fortune," Margaret Leeson sniggered. "Good for business."

"Aye, a hanging is as good as a carnival," Sarah Pepys said cheerfully and opened a bottle of gin to celebrate the coming event.

5

F rom where she stood on the platform at Tyburn Tree she could see the countryside for miles around, stretching out mistily green in the morning haze. Crowds were still arriving, Londoners in their Sunday best, sober country men in their homespuns, women in colourful cloaks and hoods, barefooted rosy children, young boys and girls dressed in bibs and petticoats. Some had come on horseback, others had travelled in carts and waggons, while still more had made long journeys on foot and, footsore and weary, they settled down to witness the hanging. Down below the platform they were drinking from flasks and bottles, toasting the highwayman, toasting each other, emptying their purses, throwing their money, rings, jewels, all they possessed up to the golden-haired giant as he lived the last hour of his life.

A grandstand known as Mother Proctor's pews was filled with the gentry in brocades and silks, high-crowned wigs, feathered hats. A stir was created as Belle Tudor arrived to take her place beside Lord Darnley, dressed in black velvet. Peg was incensed. How dared they show their faces here on this of all days? Had they no shame? But for Billy's obsession with Belle, but for her careless greed in demanding a purse of gold, the poor fool would still be clattering pots in Buttons Inn and Jimmy still free to roam the roads at his reckless will.

She hadn't wanted to come to the hanging, never thought to stand where she now found herself, had had her fill of death the night poor Billy was stoned. But Sarah Pepys had insisted and in the excitement of the journey, following the cart bedecked with flowers on the highwayman's last journey, she had forgotten the end. Four strong men—Mr Quinn had explained they were Jimmy's brothers—had carried the coffin. Behind them trotted the jiggers, all bulging muscles and stupid red faces. They would pull on Jimmy's feet to hasten his end. By the time Peg reached Tyburn she was parched with the thirst for the road had been long and dusty; she longed for a juicy orange to ease her throat, but the hawkers gathered around the platform were too taken up listening to Jimmy's last speech to bother calling out their wares. Oranges, meat pies, gingerbread, toffee apples, all went unsold. Jimmy was telling them that on his last night in gaol an Irish prisoner had entertained the company with song. He would like to hear the ballad again. He whistled a few bars. Did anyone know the words?

Of course Peg knew them, all Dublin did. On an impulse she called up, though she hadn't wanted to draw attention to herself, didn't feel like singing, only wished that the hanging was over and done with.

Beside her a man shouted: "Ring! Ring!" as they did when a fight or wrestling match was about to take place in the streets, and good-naturedly the crowds fell back, allowing her to make her way forward. A jigger hoisted her onto his shoulder, the hangman bent down and helped her up onto the platform, and she found herself standing beside the most famous highwayman in all England. He was over six feet tall, wearing a suit of brocade, golden hair tied back with a scarlet ribbon. She averted her eyes from the rope of hemp which he wore as carelessly as a silken scarf round his neck.

Gallantly he kissed her on the cheek and she found herself blushing.

"Your name, sweetheart?"

"Peg Woffington, sir. From Dublin."

"And what brings you so far afield, sweetheart?"

She took a deep breath. "I came to London to be an actress. I have had no success."

He slapped his thigh in delight. "Dress up as a gentleman and they'll swing out of the rafters to see you."

Around the platform a great roar of laughter went up at his sally, to die away when he held up his hand for silence. "Peg from Dublin will sing me out."

She waited, heart thumping, while the musicians tuned up, then her voice rang out sweet and clear as a bird's. The crowd was clapping in time to the music, the hangman, his long lugubrious face creased in a smile, bowed to the highwayman and together they trod a measure.

"All together now," Jimmy shouted and across the heath the singing swelled in the final chorus, while the musicians played as never before.

O fal, diddie, fal diddie fal
Fal, diddie, fal diddie rare O
Fal diddie, fal diddie fal
Fax fal diddie, fall diddie rare O

The crowd went wild with excitement, shouting, hugging each other, the hangman was swinging the rope over the tree, pulling the noose, and Peg was being lifted down from the platform. She turned away, didn't see Jimmy strung up or the rumblers dance their mad jig. A great sigh went up and the crowd pressed forward to pay their last respects to their hero before he was nailed in his coffin.

❦

Peg had put a distance between herself and the crowd grown sullen, the twisted tree where that handsome body had swung, the hangman drinking himself insensible. In a small grove of trees she threw herself down and covered her eyes, trying her best to blot out her last picture of Jimmy, gold ear-rings jingling, scarlet open-necked shirt and the chain of hemp around his neck. How had he felt when the hangman had tightened the noose, when he was swung off his feet, when the jiggers had pulled on his feet? How long did it take to be strangled?

Someone had hands around her neck, someone was trying to strangle her. She struggled wordlessly, the hands were creeping up, covering her eyes while a merry voice called out: "Guess who?"

She hauled herself up and saw the foundling grinning broadly.

"You frightened the wits out of me," she said crossly.

His face fell. "It was only a joke."

She dusted down her skirt and examined him. Spiky black hair, tattered suit. "Still as ragged as ever," she said spitefully.

"Working dud," he said cheerfully. "You should see me when I go courting."

She couldn't help laughing. "Did the master-pickpocket take you on?"

"I'm his most promising pupil." He executed a jig. "I heard you sing for Jimmy. You were the best turn of all."

"Don't remind me of it."

He rattled a handful of coins.

"The pickings were easy today. There's a tavern over the heath where the ale is good and we can eat our fill."

"That's the first sensible thing you've said since we met. I'm nigh dead with the thirst—and now that I think of it I'm just as hungry."

A bush festooned with ribbons and rags marked the old-fashioned tavern, long and low, built of wattles and clay. Inside pandemonium reigned as customers shouted orders and maidservants bustled around with platters of goose, mutton with oysters, ham, puddings flavoured with ginger and nutmeg, well-laced with sack. There was even a large pink blancmange on offer.

When she was finished Peg wiped her mouth with her sleeve and sighed with satisfaction.

"That meal was the best I've eaten since coming to London."

The foundling helped himself to a wedge of Cheshire cheese and drained a tankard of beer to the dregs. "We've a cook in our lodgings who took a hatchet to his wife when she criticised his mutton pies. He once worked for a duke. He's the best there is. Come to Blackfriars with me, there'd be a welcome for you, we could team up together, you singing, me stealing."

He gave her a grin so infectious that she wanted to do as he asked but though she was tempted, she sensed that times were changing, Alsatia no longer the sanctuary it had once been. "I'm not nifty with my hands like you. I'd never live it."

It was growing dark in the inn; maids were bustling around with rushlight candles, customers growing rowdy, singing more raucously, shouting orders more vociferously. A row broke out: a couple of sailors pulled knives. The innkeeper tried to eject them without success. Peg realised it was time she was making tracks for Bull Alley. Reluctantly the foundling followed her out the door. "I can't go with you yet," he complained. "There's good pickings still here."

"I know." She was disappointed but knew he must satisfy the master-pickpocket in Blackfriars, by bringing back a full purse. Yet she was scared to leave him: the road ahead would be lonely and she wasn't sure of the way.

"Want to be lighted home, mistress?" A figure holding a torch of flaring pitch and tow had come silently out of the shadows. There was something furtive about his movements, something false about the voice, the cap pulled well down hiding his face. Stranger still was the fact that he hadn't attempted to strike a bargain or even ask for payment.

"I don't trust him," the foundling whispered, clutching her arm.

"He's only a link boy," she said impatiently. The

torch flickered, moved away, and she hurried after the guide, afraid she would lose him.

"I'll be safe," she called back. "Let you take care."

"I was born lucky," the small voice said in the darkness. On an impulse she ran back and planted a kiss on his cheek. He looked so small, so defenceless. She thought of Alsatia, that den of thieves and cut-throats, and prayed that his guardian angel would take care of him.

"Don't do anything reckless." She knew it was foolish advice but she had a premonition of danger.

"Ah, go off and don't bother me," he muttered and turned back to the inn.

Tyburn was now far behind; it seemed they had been walking for hours, the link boy in front, his torch like a will o' the wisp beckoning her on. Twigs cracked under her feet, broken branches tripped her, strange night sounds made her jump with fright. Then the pattering began. Was it an animal on the run? Was that the sound of a coach, a voice? Was the place haunted like Toonagh Woods? Jimmy a ghost, like Máire Rua? Why hadn't she stayed with Sarah Pepys and Mr Quinn, instead of making a spectacle of herself getting up on the platform singing. She didn't want to think about Jimmy Maclean. All she wanted was to be safe in Bull Alley though her bed be lumpy and the mice keep scuttering around the floor.

They had reached the outskirts of the city and her heart began to lift. She even managed to hum a little air. There were people about, the occasional horseman, soon there would be lights, streets, shops. She didn't care that the link boy hadn't uttered a word for the length of the journey; he had been as good as his word, brought her back to London. Even if he vanished this minute she could find her own way home. Unsuspecting, she followed him round a corner into an alley, dark, smelling of urine, shit. A rat scuttled between her legs and she screamed. As if this was a signal, the torch was suddenly extinguished and the link boy whistled three times. Too late she remembered the doggerel all London knew:

> *Though thou be tempted by the link man's call,*
> *Be wary; trust him not at all;*
> *Before you're home, he'll quench the brand*
> *And share the booty with the murdering band.*

Menacing figures were creeping out of the shadows, brandishing hatchets and knives. Everyone knew of the Mohocks, the London gang who dressed as Indian braves and stalked the streets at night, terrorising respectable people, torturing nightwatchmen, forcing whores to stand on their heads in barrels of tar so they could prick their private parts. Like the other night-time gangs, the Nickers and Bold Bucks, they were seldom if ever brought to justice.

They were circling around, whooping, chanting obscenities. Their war-dance would be followed by rape.

In the shadows something moved. A voice in her ear whispered: "I'll get help." But she knew it was useless. No one could help her now.

❦

The coach and four travelling along the London road needed no guiding hand, which was as well for the driver was half asleep, his thoughts on home and the tasty supper the cook would be keeping for him. She was a fine sonsy woman from the same part of Ireland as himself and usually game for a tumble. With a bit of luck he would coax her into his bed in the coachhouse behind the Grosvenor Square mansion where his aristocratic master lived. He was rudely brought to his senses by a figure which had taken a flying leap and was pulling itself up by the horses' manes. With an oath he pulled on the reins and the coach rocked to a halt.

"You young spalpeen," he howled in a fury. "I'll have the skin off your back."

The boy winced where the whip caught him across the arms. "It's the Mohocks," he panted. "They've a girl."

"I'll go to the help of no bloody London whore," the coachman screamed.

"She's as Irish as you," the urchin yelled back. "She sang at Tyburn today."

Below, the coach door swung open and a tall man, handsome in velvet and lace, jumped out. "Bartley, why have you stopped?"

The voice was cold and the coachman cursed under his breath; before the night was finished he would pay for this delay.

"Begging your honour's pardon, it's the fault of this fellow stopping the horses, says the Mohocks have a girl."

Even before he had finished a scream had shattered the night. Pulling his pistol the gentleman was gone, running swiftly in the direction of the alley. Panting and puffing, the coachman dismounted and followed his master. The foundling had gone to ground.

Peg had been dumped unceremoniously into the coach, the driver had mounted his perch, applied his whip with such vigour that the startled horses bolted. "Whoa there," he shouted, pulling fiercely. Feeling the bit, they steadied down to an easy trot.

She was sick, smelt blood, cautiously opened her eyes. Beside her a man in velvet and lace sat nursing a still smoking pistol. Timidly she touched his hand and drew back in alarm.

"You're bleeding..."

"I winged a couple of ruffians." He sounded tired.

"You saved my life, sir."

"Not I, but a ragged young urchin who almost overturned the coach in his efforts to get help. Who is your dark angel?"

"A foundling I met on the ship. He must have followed me. I thought he was a ghost. He's a pickpocket and lives in Blackfriars."

"In Alsatia, the rogues' sanctuary? Well, well. You should pick your companions with more care or you'll come to grief as you so nearly did tonight."

There was something about the gentleman that puzzled her, she was sure she had seen him before. "Were you at the hanging?"

He didn't answer and she persisted. "You were with Belle Tudor. You are Lord Darnley."

His head ached. He disliked prying wenches, who caused nothing but trouble.

"Hold your tongue," he ordered sharply. "You've done enough damage for one night."

Tears threatened to choke her. It was all too much. The hanging, then the fact that she had been almost killed by the Mohocks, now this haughty voice blaming her. But for Belle Tudor none of this would have happened.

"It wasn't my fault," she cried.

"If you utter another word," he threatened, "I shall throw you out on the road where you belong."

She felt the blood rush to her head, felt the urge to strike out, leaned across and slapped his face.

He fingered his cheek. When he spoke again his voice was oddly detached. "Why on earth did you strike me?"

"It was all your fault," she wailed. "You and Belle Tudor."

"What has Mistress Tudor to do with this?"

"I was there the night Billy was murdered," she hiccoughed. "I saw what happened."

He sighed. "Belle is a fool, I told her so. There is no one more dangerous to trifle with than a witless boy."

"And what of Jimmy, cold in his grave?"

"Your bold highwayman carved out his own destiny."

"It was a fearful way to go, strung up on a tree," she said sullenly.

"He died as he lived, surrounded by an admiring throng, with a pretty girl to sing his last dirge."

"It was the least I could do."

"And you gave the pot-boy his epitaph at the famous wake. Belle was impressed. 'Good-night, sweet prince.'"

"You're mocking the dead. Billy can't answer you back."

"Ah yes, how did the Bard put it? 'The undiscover'd country from whose bourn no traveller returns.'"

She squeezed herself into a corner and sat weeping noisily.

"Dry your eyes and be quiet," he ordered wearily and

threw her a handkerchief.

She blew her nose on the square of linen. A coronet was embroidered in one corner over the letter D. She stuffed it into her pocket and brooded on how unfairly she had been treated and all she had suffered through no fault of her own: Violante running off, Jennie Tatler betraying her. She tried not to think about Billy or Jimmy Maclean. A niggling voice reminded her that Lord Darnley had saved her life and she had behaved like a fishwife, slapping his face. She wanted to explain she was truly sorry but the right word wouldn't come and he sat there turned away like a statue, not throwing a word to a dog.

With a clatter the coach drew up before a handsome redbricked mansion in a fashionable square. The coachman dismounted smartly from his perch and rolled down the steps. Peg made to follow Lord Darnley but he waved her back.

"Stay where you are. My coachman will see you home. Where do you live?"

He sounded so curt that she became confused, blurted out, "George's Lane in Dublin."

His shoulder hurt where the hatchet had caught him. He longed for bed.

"Where in London?" he asked patiently.

"Bull Alley behind Covent Garden." She was chattering nervously, unable to stop. "I suppose I'm lucky to have a roof over my head. When Violante ran off, Sarah Pepys said I could stay. She's not the worst and I like Mr Quinn. He was once a famous Shakespearean actor."

He hadn't really noticed her before. His coachman had picked her up, carried her back. After that she had been a whining voice, an irritant in the darkness of the coach. Grosvenor Square was bathed in moonlight so bright that it was almost day. A lantern hung over the door of his house and a street lamp had been lit. She was hanging out the window and, as he glanced up, he saw her clearly for the first time and was shocked by the likeness to someone he had once known.

"What is your name?" he said gruffly.

"Peg Woffington, sir."

"You should go back where you belong."

She drew in a deep breath. "It is my dearest wish, except maybe that one day I hope to become a great actress."

She was so young, little more than a child. "I can grant you one wish at least. To go back to your hovel in Dublin like the fisherman's wife in the fairy tale."

She wasn't a fishwife, didn't live in a hovel, tried to explain.

"I come of good stock. My mother was of the gentry. Only for the cursed Cromwellians we would have castles and—and money and things. They backed the Stuarts."

Had she said the wrong thing? She looked at him anxiously. He smiled and then he did something so wonderful that she fell in love with him on the instant. He reached up and kissed her hand just as if she were a great lady.

"Good-night, my fellow Jacobite," he said gravely.

Elated, beside herself with delight, she recited in as good an imitation of Mr Quinn's voice as she could muster:

Forever, and forever, farewell!
If we do meet again, why, we shall smile!
If not, why then, this parting was well made.

Impatiently the horses pawed the ground. With a nod from his master the coachman shook the reins and the coach clattered away in the direction of Covent Garden.

For a long moment he stood on the steps of the mansion, his thoughts on that lonely grave in the highland glen where one with the same dark red hair and green eyes slept the eternal sleep of the dead. Then like a man in a dream he shook himself awake, forced himself back to reality.

She is the most exasperating wench it has been my misfortune to meet, he told himself wryly. Were she a little older and I not bound for France—why, who knows? She has a nice taste too for a Shakespearean line. What was it Feste sang in *Twelfth Night*? In sudden exuberance at being alive, he threw back his head and sang out:

In delay there lies no plenty;
Then come kiss me, sweet and twenty,
Youth's a stuff will not endure.

But only an owl and a cat on the prowl heard the clown's foolish words.

❧

A footman bearing a crested letter had called to the house in Bull Alley, with such news that Sarah Pepys collapsed in a chair, Mr Quinn wreathed his face in an infrequent smile and Peg danced an Irish jig on the flags. Arrangements had been made for Mistress Woffington's return to Ireland and money had been lodged to her account in La Touche's bank in Dublin. Sarah Pepys had not been forgotten. A golden sovereign was solemnly handed over by Lord Darnley's servant "in appreciation of her kindness to a girl with red hair."

Margaret Leeson declared that she was fed up with London, where the gentlemen were white-livered misers and a girl went in dread of her life from ruffians that roamed the streets. She had made up her mind she would accompany Peg back to Dublin as paid companion.

❦

At the stagecoach inn on the Strand Peg took her farewell of Sarah Pepys and Mr Quinn.

"I shall think of you every day," Sarah Pepys wept. "Now I have no one to fetch ale from Buttons, light the fires or eat the fine meals I cook."

Peg repressed a giggle. In all the time she had been in Bull Alley a pan had never been greased or a cooking-pot put to use.

Mr Quinn pressed his dog-eared Shakespeare into her hands. "I shall miss you, my Portia. I have taught you all I know. It was no little task. Someday you will grace the London stage. Till then let this book be your Bible."

"One day you will come back to London and make your fortune. I saw it written plainly in the lines of your hands," Sarah Pepys added for good measure. "Maybe

you will repay me for all I have done for you," she
finished hopefully.

The stage had arrived. The moment of parting had
come.

"Good-bye," Peg wept, her heart breaking with
loneliness. "God care for you both."

As the coach clattered away, the last she saw was the
small, dumpy woman, wearing a gown cut too low and
a wig of bright hair, arm in arm with the broken-down
actor enter the Coaching Inn, and knew they would
remain there until the golden sovereign was spent.

Margaret Leeson complacently arranged her gown of
crimson silk to the best advantage and announced her
plans to the coach at large while the men leaned
forward, avid for every word.

"It is my intention to set up a bawdy house in
Dublin," she boasted loudly. "I intend to furnish the
rooms with well-sprung beds. All the ceilings will have
mirrors and the walls will be hung with venery prints.
I intend to become a greater courtesan than Belle Tudor."

Peg sat gazing out the window, her mind drifting
down the year that had passed, remembering the good
things that had happened. Skating on the Serpentine
in Hyde Park with Violante, exploring the town with
Jennie Tatler, meeting the foundling again, singing her
heart out at Tyburn with Jimmy Maclean—best of all
the day Mr Quinn had taken her to the Covent Garden
Playhouse to see *A Midsummer Night's Dream*. She would
read all Shakespeare's plays, learn the sonnets by heart,
remember all he had taught her.

They had moved out on the London road, leaving
the city behind, the coach-wheels gathering speed,
saying it all for her:

"Good-bye to London, Good-bye to Sarah Pepys, Good-bye to Mr Quinn, Good-bye to Lord Darnley..." She took the square of linen she had carefully washed and ironed, and pressed the embroidered coronet to her lips. She would never forget him. He would be her secret.

Margaret Leeson was prodding her in the ribs. "Listen to what I'm telling you. You can become one of my harlots. Take the highwayman's advice and dress up as a man. Set a new fashion in seduction."

Peg tossed her head. "I shall have nothing to do with you once I return to Dublin."

Margaret Leeson laughed raucously and leaned forward to address a redcoat, who was lecherously eyeing the breasts that threatened to spill out of her bodice.

"Let me tell you, officer, that drab is fit for nothing but the back-street hovel where she was reared."

ACT II

DUBLIN, 1735–1739

Fair daffodils, we weep to see
You haste away so soon:
As yet the early-rising sun
Has not attain'd his noon.

("To Daffodils" Robert Herrick)

6

The horse's hooves raised a cloud of dust on the winding road that ran west of the city. In the morning light, midges and flies danced over the river and a hungry fish made a silver arc in the air before disappearing to the fast-flowing waters below. Horse and rider were well matched. A glossy rowan-red mare ridden by a handsome, straight-backed, dark-haired man, reins held loosely in square capable hands. Charles Coffey had given the mare her head ever since he had left the large stone house some five miles beyond Chapelizod, the site of the legendary Isolde's tower. He patted the silken flanks as he guided her in through the great iron gates of the Phoenix Park, the finest in the two kingdoms. This was the part of the ride he loved best, cantering down an avenue of smooth-barked birch and needle-sharp pine that led to a sunlit opening. In the distance a herd of deer browsed peacefully. A peacock flaunted disdainful feathers, a red fox on the prowl disappeared into a nut grove. On this autumn day the air was clear, clear as the spring water, *fionn uisge*, which had been corrupted by the townsfolk to Phoenix and from which the park took its name. There were, to be sure, follies like the recently erected Magazine Fort, castigated in verse by Jonathan Swift, Dean of St Patrick's Cathedral:

> *Behold a proof of Irish sense!*
> *Here Irish wit is seen.*
> *When nothing's left that's worth defence*
> *They build a magazine.*

Coffey smiled wryly as he recalled the verse. "A country for rogues and fools," he thought bitterly, then resolutely put away the thought. Useless to dwell on the vanity and stupidity of men in such a place and on such a morning. His own story was nothing of which to boast.

Deliberately he switched his mind away from the time he had spent in the Sandford Mansion. The week ahead would be good. Tonight the new Theatre Royal in Aungier Street would open its doors, with a production of *The Twin Rivals*. On his review would depend the success or otherwise of the theatre. He would invite his landlady to accompany him. For a moment he dwelt uxoriously on Alice Morgan's charms. When he worked late into the night, she encouraged him, bringing pots of fresh coffee laced with whiskey, leaning over his shoulder, reading what he had written, her hair loose, the smell of her soft moist flesh exciting his senses. He had held off for too long. He should have married a woman such as Alice or at least bedded her long since.

His thoughts strayed to his mockery of a marriage. He had been flattered the evening in Daly's Club some ten years before, when the Earl of Sandford had made the surprising suggestion that he, a penniless Papist, should marry his sister, the Lady Jane.

"She is smitten with your charms," Sandford had

drawled. "She pines for your company. I am disposed to let her have her heart's desire."

And he, fool that he was, had believed the story, convinced himself that Sandford wanted the marriage for more wholesome reasons than was the case, to introduce strong peasant blood into a line that had become tainted. All the Sandford males were born crippled. He had allowed himself be duped, though from the beginning he sensed there was something amiss. Only two people had witnessed the nuptials in the ivy-clad chapel on the estate, Sandford and his valet, a dark, surly man who spoke little. Afterwards he had watched uneasily while his bride, the silver-haired beauty with the strange orange-brown eyes, had passionately embraced her brother, had known shame, betrayal when she had refused him that night in the four-poster bed. A month later, frustrated, drunk, he had taken her by force, consummated their union. He had expected tears, recriminations, anything but her smile of contempt. That had been their first and only coupling. Five months later she gave birth to a crippled but otherwise healthy boy, christened Jeremy after her brother.

Long before that he had learned of the incestuous relationship that had existed between the Lady Jane and her brother since childhood. She had taunted him with the truth and he had sworn to let the world know but Sandford had stayed his hand. Who would believe the word of an Irish peasant who had dared marry above his station? He would be laughed out of town. It was then they made their devil's pact. He would hold his tongue, the Lady Jane would play the part of the loving wife, the devoted mother, Sandford would be his patron. It had all worked out, he had been introduced to the best clubs, to the most fashionable houses, to men of power and prestige:

Faulkner, owner of Dublin's most influential newspaper, Sam Leadbetter the goldsmith, patron of the arts, who had fingers in every pie.

Even granting his undoubted talents, his rise had been meteoric. Before long he was acknowledged the most important theatre critic in Dublin, his plays were produced in the Smock Alley Theatre and in London's Drury Lane and Covent Garden. His romance, set in the south-west corner of Ireland, a place of rocky indentations where desperate men lured unwary ships to their doom and lived on the spoils, had been an overnight success. Few knew that he had been born and brought up in the townland he so vividly brought to life.

A year after his marriage the earl and his sister went on an extended tour of Europe, leaving the boy in the care of a nurse. In their absence Coffey frequently visited the Sandford Mansion to keep up appearances. It was no great hardship. He enjoyed the fresh air, the tranquillity of spacious gardens, tree-lined walks, enjoyed fishing the Liffey that meandered its way through the estate, relished the convenience of working in the well-equipped library, a blazing fire at his back, a silver decanter of mellow whiskey at his elbow. But the magnet that drew him again and again was the lonely crippled boy they had left behind.

Eventually they returned, gave a great ball and the charade was resumed. But Sandford was restless; he had decided to marry and produce the heir he needed, since the estate was entailed. He took himself off to London, inspecting the ladies of rank on offer, and when he had made his choice went hunting in the south of Ireland. Consumed with rage and spleen the Lady Jane took stable-boys, workmen on the estate, even her brother's valet to her bed. Before long there was talk in Daly's, scandalous details related behind fluttering fans in ladies' boudoirs, embellished as port circulated after dinner in the great houses of the town. In the end Coffey could take no more and arranged his passage to the colonies in the New World. It was then fate intervened. A week before his nuptials, the fifth earl was killed on the hunting field. Pity for the wretched woman, affection for the lame, neglected little boy, were the factors in his decision to remain. He would visit Chapelizod a couple of times a month, oversee the estate, guide and direct the young boy in his studies. Duty done, he would live as he pleased. His writings assured him a comfortable income; he had friends he respected, whose company he enjoyed.

A fastidious streak made him avoid the town's brothels but occasionally he visited Paris, where he enjoyed the favours of a countess who kept a salon and entertained men of letters. In London he had an affair with an actress who professed to adore him. But lately such amorous adventures had begun to lose their flavour. Increasingly he was aware of the passage of years, the wings of grey in his hair, the lines deeply etched on his face. The Lady Jane had turned violent, was drinking heavily, ill-treating her servant, creating hysterical scenes when he appeared, threatening to kill herself if he stayed away. Her physician bled her frequently to quell the choleric outbursts but it seemed that nothing helped.

He shook the reins and delightedly the mare broke into a gallop. When his thoughts were clearer he would come to a decision. Meanwhile there was the play tonight. Let what happen might, it was in the lap of the gods.

❦

Margaret Leeson opened an eye, aware that the Honourable
Patrick Taafe had left her bed some time in the early hours.
She stretched lazily and felt her bruises, her lips curling in
a satisfied smile. He was a good horseman and a mettlesome
lad and had kept her awake half the night. A long lie-in
would be good for her health but for the madam of a house
life was not easy. She pulled the bell-rope and waited
impatiently for Lizzie, who came in puffing and panting,
set down her mistress's breakfast-tray on a small table
beside the bed, then drew back the hangings, allowing the
mid-morning sun to flood the room, sparking off the
mirrors that lined walls and ceilings. Margaret Leeson
propped a pillow behind her shapely shoulders and spread
a slice of toast liberally with orange preserve. Silently Lizzie
poured coffee, added sugar, cream, listened to the orders
for the day.

"As soon as you have helped me dress and tidied my
room, you will iron my petticoats and launder my lace.
After that you will reserve two seats in the lattice of the
Playhouse in Aungier Street. Is Mrs Sally Hayes still abed?"

"Yes, ma'am. She ate no breakfast, sickening for
something I'd say."

Margaret Leeson pulled a face. "Not the pox I trust. I
expect her to accompany me to the Playhouse tonight; the
town will be there."

She scrutinised her face in a hand mirror. "My physician
says the new French powder is bad for the complexion,
contains white lead or some such. My face is my fortune,
that and my pussy, or so I'm told." She laughed
immoderately and Lizzie tittered sycophantically, then
winced as pain knotted her gut.

Her mistress frowned. "You're breeding again. Get cook
to make you up a powder of pennyroyal and aloes before

you're too far gone. Connie left it too late, remember."

Lizzie remembered only too well. A young slip of a girl, not more than thirteen years. Nothing had helped. Not the gin bath, not the bitter draught, not the ride in a hackney around the rutted country roads. In the end Lizzie had taken her to Mother Macklin. Connie huddled in a chair, covered with brown stains, feet raised on a stool, skirts pushed around her thighs, legs apart, shivering, despite the roaring fire, the cup of rum the old woman had forced down her throat.

"Holy Mary, Mother of God, pray for us sinners," Lizzie had prayed, as old Macklin squinted, pushed in the pointed knitting-needle. Connie had screamed while the blood ran down her legs. Two days later she died, calling for her mother, long dead, for a priest who refused to visit a house of ill-fame. She had been scared of hell fire, damnation, had begged that she would not be buried in a pauper's grave. The madam had kept faith, fair dues to her. Connie had been given a respectable burial, a coffin, flowers, all the girls dressed in decent mourning.

Margaret Leeson's strident voice brought her back to earth.

"Don't stand all day gawking, there's work to be done. Remember, I'll have no bastards around the house."

Nervously Lizzie twisted her hands. "Yis, ma'am! I mean no, ma'am."

Good-naturedly, Margaret Leeson flung a shoe at her maid's head and lay back on her pillows, contemplating her lush body with some pride.

Lizzie scurried from the room, nursing her forehead, where a lump was rising.

Say what you would, Margaret Leeson wasn't the worst: the pickings were good, the girls generous with money and cast-offs. She muttered a prayer that her flux would come soon.

❦

Peg was wedged in the crowd of onlookers outside the Playhouse in Aungier Street, where entertainment had been laid on for the citizens: a display of fireworks which lit up the gathering dusk with marvellous colours and shapes, a band playing martial airs and popular tunes. A guard of honour in full regalia stretched from the cobblestones to the colonnades of the new building, and a space had been set aside for the use of coaches and chairs.

Mr Elrington, dapper manager of the theatre, standing stiffly at the entrance and holding a branch of lighted candles, awaited the arrival of the Duke and Duchess of Leinster.

"Why kiss my garters, if it isn't young Woffington herself." Though almost four years had elapsed since she had last laid eyes on Margaret Leeson, Peg recognised the Dublin madam at once—loud as ever, rouged, patched, stylishly got up in a honey wig and spectacular gown of red velvet, draped with panniers.

"Gad, the stench around here will give me a fever. Come along inside and share your news. Mrs Sally Hayes was to accompany me but I left her entangled with the law, an eminent barrister, no less, and here I am on my lee-lane."

She gave a throaty laugh and men turned to stare. Reluctantly Peg trailed behind her into the vestibule and up the wide staircase to where Lizzie awaited her mistress in the lattice. With much rustling of petticoats Margaret Leeson sat herself down, arranging her skirts in folds, and accepted the box of sweetmeats her maid held out.

"Off with you now, Lizzie, and see that the house is kept in disorder in my absence." She hooted with laughter at her wit and turned her attentions to Peg.

"Well, and what's your news? Are you married or in some man's keeping or what?"

Peg was tempted to fabricate, to pretend something impressive had happened to her, but one look at her unpainted face, drab gown, down-at-heel shoes, would give the lie to this fantasy.

She said unwillingly: "I did a little acting with the Sparks twins when I came back to Dublin. The Earl of Meath opened a theatre for them in the High Street but it didn't last."

"Fancy that. What did they call themselves?"

"The Undertakers."

"Bloody gruesome, if you ask me. Did they finish up in the boneyard? Jesus, I must remember that *bon mot*. And so you were left high and dry. Ah well, the only way for a girl of spirit to better herself is to pleasure a man of money. Lucy Sparks is Meath's doxy and he blind as a bat and rising eighty. Larry, her twin, is Buck Whaley's new fancy."

"'Burnchapel' Whaley earns his name," Peg said angrily. "Riding around on a Sunday morning, tossing lighted pitch on to the thatch of Catholic chapels. Only last week a child in George's Lane was burnt to death. Whaley should hang. He gets off with murder."

"The devil looks after his own." Margaret Leeson bit on a sugared almond, made a face and tossed the box over to Peg. "Take the lot, fatten you up, rot your teeth." She leaned across the ledge surveying the house, shouting greetings, bandying jokes with students in the stalls below.

"I see Sam Leadbetter in Sligo's box with Charles Coffey, the critic. Coffey is lodging with Alice Morgan, widow of our late lamented lord mayor. She's hot for him, I'm told. He'll succumb any day now, if I know the signs. I think I'll join them."

She swept off as the sound of a trumpet heralded the appearance of the duke and duchess, accompanied by the lord mayor of Dublin and his mayoress, patriotically gowned in green silk. In adjoining boxes the duke's entourage settled themselves comfortably, the men in gold-frogged brocades and curled wigs, the ladies enamelled figurines in silks gleaming, cascades of fine lace at bosom and waist, jewels throwing off sparks in the candlelight.

Peg drew back into the shadows. Meeting Margaret Leeson had unsettled her, brought back the past all too vividly: her time in London with Violante; the house in Bull Alley where they all lodged; Mr Quinn who had promised great things of her, called her Portia, given her his cherished copy of Shakespeare's works; the day Jimmy Maclean had been hanged, the excitement of singing up on the platform with the golden giant, people cheering, loving her, wanting more. The advice he had given her. "Dress up as a gentleman and they'll swing out of the rafters to see you." One New Year's Eve she had taken his advice, well almost...Times had been bad, her mother ailing, the landlord threatening them with eviction. Unknown to anyone she had dressed up as a man in a pair of breeches her father had once worn and her mother's black coat, borrowed a wig from a neighbour, and made her way to the High Street. A blind fiddler had joined her. She had sung "Greensleeves," songs from *The Beggar's Opera* and popular ballads and had been showered with money. Afterwards as she shared the takings with the old tinker, he had said they should join forces. "You singing, me fiddling." He reminded her of the foundling in far-off Alsatia. Was he still alive, she wondered.

She had been tempted to repeat the performance but fear of her mother had stopped her. If only they could manage better. Money seemed to melt through her mother's fingers. All the money Lord Darnley had lodged to her account in La Touche's bank in Dame Street had long since been spent on fripperies. Polly, like her mother, acted the lady. Only Conor had sense. She wished he were older but he was still a boy, not yet twelve. She had lied to Margaret Leeson about the Earl of Meath's theatre. The place had been no more than a romping ground for the bucks of the town, who expected to roger anyone taking their fancy. No one was interested in the drama. One night a young fop had tried to rape her on the stage. She had picked up a knife, one of the props, and threatened him. Lucy Sparks had put a story about town that she had gone berserk, slashing out, seriously injuring a young man. After that she was finished, never got past the stage-door of Smock Alley, couldn't even get an audition for the Aungier Street company, who were opening tonight.

A handsome young actor came downstage to speak the prologue, the curtains swept back and the house settled down to enjoy Farquhar's popular Restoration play, *The Twin Rivals*.

Though the play was comical and had a happy ending Peg shivered at the character of the rapacious madam. The wicked prospered and the good died young, she thought. Not only the good: the captain and his foolish companions, now dust in a limestone bed; Billy the pot-boy with his angelic voice; Jimmy Maclean, golden-haired, vital, laughing. There was no mercy, no hope for the poor. A maidservant had been hanged in St Stephen's Green for stealing a petticoat yet the likes of Buck Whaley could get off with murder because they had influence, power. She remembered the Mohocks in London, creating mayhem, murder, roaming the street without hindrance because they were wealthy. People made the excuse they were only "sowing their wild oats." She would like to be rich but more than anything she wanted to become an actress. If only someone would give her a chance.

Margaret Leeson was back in full flood, chattering loudly, while the house erupted into noise and the audience pushed their way out into the night.

"Gad, what an evening. I played hazard at the back of Sligo's box and won ten guineas." She fanned herself vigorously. "Sam Leadbetter invited us to join him in Daly's. They have a French cook and the best claret in town. Mr Coffey was keen to meet you. I'll introduce you to Elrington. He'll be there too. Come on, don't be all night!"

Like one in a dream, Peg got up out of her seat, pulling her shabby cloak around her shoulders, and followed Margaret Leeson down the stairs and out into the street. Maybe this was the answer to her prayers.

Daly's was crowded, full of noisy young bucks, elderly fops, wealthy merchants, a few women in low-cut gowns, high wigs, bold, avaricious faces. Sam Leadbetter, floridly handsome, bedecked with gold chains and diamond rings, was ensconced in an alcove, deep in conversation with Charles Coffey. Without waiting for an invitation, even a sign of recognition, Margaret Leeson flopped into a chair beside them, kicking off her shoes, declaring she was famished with hunger. Awkwardly Peg sat down by her side.

Leadbetter snapped his fingers and a succession of waiters brought platters of roast duck, beef baked in a crust, artichokes, oysters. Margaret Leeson ate ravenously, Peg picked nervously at her plate and the men ate soberly and well. Glasses were filled with Rhenish wine and red Burgundy, replenished, filled again. Then the port circled the table. Appetite sated, Margaret Leeson sat back and began to give an account of a quarrel that was tearing two of the town's leading families apart.

"Pinky and Buck Townsend are at each other's throats over who fathered her ladyship's bastard. This time the succession is at stake. It will be pistols at dawn in the Phoenix Park. Elrington gave me the whid at the Playhouse, before he went off to kip down with his latest fancy."

"You promised you'd introduce me to Mr Elrington," Peg burst out. "You said he'd be here."

Sam Leadbetter chuckled. "He's not keen on your sex, sweetheart. You'll have to make do with a different friend tonight."

Margaret Leeson turned to Charles Coffey, who had said little all night.

"Peg's randy all right," she confided, nestling up to him. "You should hear the stories Lucy Sparks tells of her doings in the Earl of Meath's Playhouse, copulating on the stage no less with one of the bucks; then pulling a knife."

Peg jumped up, knocking over a chair, and fled from the room, fighting back tears of embarrassment, rage. She should never have come, should have known only too well what Margaret Leeson was like; she would never again be able to hold up her head in the town.

Outside, the cold night air stung her wet cheeks. Footsteps were catching up and she quickened her pace.

Charles Coffey took her elbow and slowed her down.

"Allow me to escort you home. I am to blame. I apologise." She could feel the warmth of his hand on her arm. "I enquired for your family earlier at the play. Mrs Leeson mistook my interest."

She couldn't answer: tears threatened to overwhelm her. Had her father lived, none of this would have happened.

"I saw you in *The Beggar's Opera*. It was a great success." He was being kind, making things worse.

"It was a novelty," she said in a choked voice. "We were young."

"And now you are old." She knew he was mocking her and angrily pulled away but he held her fast, his arm encircling her shoulder.

"If you are serious about acting, perhaps I can help," he said in a warm, kind voice. "I could speak to Elrington."

Somewhere around, church bells were chiming the midnight hour, filling the night with radiant sound. A star fell through the heavens. She made a silent wish.

He pulled her close. "You should read poetry; it would develop your voice."

She remembered a poem she had memorised at the Quaker School as a child. It had been her father's favourite. She found herself reciting softly:

Fair daffodils, we weep to see
You haste away so soon:
As yet the early-rising sun
Has not attain'd his noon.

His deep-timbred voice took up the next verse:

We have short time to stay, as you
We have as short a Spring;
As quick a growth to meet decay,
As you or any thing.

She felt intoxicated. Was it the wine? The night air? His nearness? They had reached George's Lane and she stood outside the cottage, trying desperately to think of something that would prolong the parting, some excuse to meet him again.

"Will you really help me?" she whispered.

He bent down, took her face in his hands and kissed her on the lips. It was so light a kiss but it filled her with a foolish delight, a happiness she had never imagined.

"I'll remember this night forever," she said breathlessly. "Just the two of us here and a night full of stars."

He drew back, his voice fathomless. "What a good parting line."

"Shall I see you again?" He couldn't leave her now, go, just like that.

He turned away blindly, knowing he would burn until he met her again. He was like a green boy.

Who'er she be,
That not impossible she
That shall command my heart and me.

Until this moment he had not known what the words had really meant. Had Alice accompanied him to the theatre, he would be in her bed by now, at ease, content, not torn with this pain, this longing for a girl young enough to be his daughter. But at the last moment Alice had been stricken with a megrim and the gods laughed.

More than ever he regretted his mockery of a marriage, the wasted years.

In the darkness of the kitchen, lit only by the flickering embers of the dying fire, Peg undressed, letting her clothes drop to the floor, touching her pale skin, hugging the thought of him to herself. Square chin with a cleft, deep-set eyes, strong hands on her shoulders, his mouth on hers. And when at last she fell asleep, he was in her dreams, and the loneliness she had felt since her father's death was gone.

7

A lice Morgan let herself into the house in Smock Alley to which she had come as a bride. It was a spacious house of seventeen rooms, which took all her time to run, even with the help of a couple of maids, strong country girls not afraid of work, who polished and cleaned, lit fires, washed and ironed without complaint. She had lately engaged Mrs McEnroe as cook and housekeeper, so giving herself leisure for tasks she enjoyed. She took off her cloak of fine broadcloth, the frilled hood lined with silk, and arranged the flowers she had bought at the Castle markets, fingers busy with gold and bronze blossoms and lacy fern. She was good at flowers. Yet her mind was elsewhere, harking back to that fateful evening when Charles Coffey had arrived back from his weekend in Chapelizod, exuberant, smiling, inviting her to accompany him to the opening of the new theatre in Aungier Street. She had been as excited as a young girl with her first beau, ruffling through her wardrobe, tossing aside gowns of brocade, wools, in red, black, grey. Why were all her clothes so drab? Her husband had liked her to dress as befitted a matron. In desperation she had gone to her hope chest, unearthed her wedding gown, wrapped in tissue for so many years, held up the soft silk to her face, the colour emphasising the cornflower blue of her eyes. She stepped into it, had her maid lace her up. Her figure was still good, her waist slender as a girl's. Sensuously she smoothed the silk over her hips, touched the heart-shaped neckline. She would wear milky pearls. Her dressmaker had been French, an artist, and the wedding-dress had been her masterpiece. She had never worn it again. She slipped on high-heeled pumps and surveyed herself in the mirror. She had never looked so good. Later she washed her hair with rain water and perfumed soap and called the maid to help her brush the long golden tresses until they shone. Giggling together they had arranged tendrils of curls around her face.

"Heartbreakers" they were called. What a fool she had been. Like a girl in love for the first time. Yet it was the first time. Perhaps the fault lay with her upbringing. Her parents had been Puritans, godly folk, and she, their only child, had been protected from the world. Wary of fortune-hunters, too old to remember the dreams of youth, they had married her off to a dried-up man twice her age, one-time lord mayor of the city. He had been generous but insanely jealous, allowing her no friends of her own. Little more than a year before, he had died of an apoplectic fit, despite the surgeon's leeches, and left her the house and a tidy fortune. She also owned an estate in the New World which she had inherited from an uncle long dead, and which she never intended to visit.

In the beginning her widowhood had been like the lifting of a burden. For the first time in her life she was free to do as she pleased. Then loneliness set in. She found herself missing her husband, his moods, the demands he made, the few friends who used call and no longer came.

A child would have filled the void, the ache for love, but theirs had been a barren marriage. On an impulse she rented rooms to English actors engaged by the Smock Alley Playhouse next door, for a season of Shakespeare. One evening Charles Coffey had called to pay them a visit and she had fallen in love with him at first sight. There was something about him, the broad shoulders, the voice, the candour of his grey eyes. After that he called every evening and she made him welcome, preparing suppers for his actor friends, bringing up wine from her late husband's cellar.

When the season ended and the company departed for London, she was desolate. She would never see him again. Yet to her surprise he called next night to ask if she would rent him rooms. He moved in at once, flattering her that she made him so comfortable he would never leave. Every day they discovered common interests: books, music, civilised talk. She had a pretty soprano voice, could accompany herself on the violin; and when in the mood he would sing songs of his native place, in Irish, a language of which she knew nothing, only that it sounded melodious and was his first tongue. He said of the native Irish that all their war songs were merry and all their love songs sad, and she had been tempted to put her arms around him to comfort him but did not dare.

With a touching belief in the old saw that the surest way to a man's heart was through his stomach, she bought salmon in season, fresh oysters, had the gingerbread man call twice a week and the bakeshop deliver hot apple pies. Man of letters, wit, darling of polite society he might be, yet at heart he was a simple countryman and liked the old ways and customs best. She pandered to his every whim, celebrating traditional Irish feasts, serving roast goose at

Michaelmas and Christmas, bilberry pie on Garland Sunday,
a colcannon of potatoes, kale, onions at Hallowe'en,
slipping a ring and a charm into the barmbrack. Saturday
nights were sacrosanct when they took supper together in
her parlour. They usually had a coddle of smoked bacon,
onions, pork sausages, washed down with ale. She was able
to reassure him that the dish was a favourite with Dean
Swift. The German composer Mr Handel would shortly
visit Dublin for the performance of his new work *Messiah*,
and would lodge in her house. She planned on giving a
very grand dinner party, with the help of her new cook,
Mrs McEnroe.

Her thoughts raced on, remembering confidences,
anecdotes they had shared. They had stared together at
pictures in the firelight, flames shaping a wild promontory,
beacons lit by ghostly figures, as if to lure unsuspecting
ships to their doom on the merciless rocks below. He had
been born in such a place, had left it when he reached
manhood to become a hedge schoolmaster, teaching Latin
and Greek to the sons of landless men, paid for his labours
in sods of turf, eggs, fish. Tired of the life of hardship, he
had eventually made his way to Dublin, determined to
become a writer, to make his name. Once in his cups he
had been bitter about the Sandfords, his farce of a marriage.
He had never again referred to that part of his life and she
never questioned him, even when he returned from his
weekends in Chapelizod, taciturn, drained.

Over the months they grew more intimate. He took to
bringing her home specially chosen gifts: a fan he had
picked up in a shop by the river, a beaded purse, a singing
bird in a gilt cage, a phial of French perfume, a bottle of
good claret which they would share. She convinced herself
it was only a matter of time before he succumbed and made

love to her and her heart had lifted on that autumn day. He would come to her bed that night, she knew by the soft look in his eyes, the way he held her hand. Maybe the anticipation, the promise of fulfilment after the arid years of her marriage, had been too much but by evening she was prostrate with a megrim. It must have been midnight when he arrived home. Light-headed with the tisane Mrs McEnroe had concocted, she got out of bed, threw a lace robe over her flimsy nightgown, opened the door, holding up the lighted candle, willing him to look at her, touch her, but he passed unseeing, a man bewitched.

Mrs McEnroe had given her the first hint: a girl young enough to be his daughter, stage-struck, ambitious. "Her mother is a neighbour of mine, well born but fallen on hard times, an unpredictable woman, kind but airy, if you get my meaning, ma'am."

"If she's using him I'll kill her," she had sworn and Mrs McEnroe had looked at her mistress in pity, surprise. Afterwards she was furiously angry with him, determined to show him the door, but when the time came her courage failed her and she said nothing. At least while he was still under her roof there was some hope. Surely he would come to his senses. "Oh please God, let it be soon," she wept.

❧

That summer of her eighteenth year Peg was in love for the first time and while it lasted her mother, the twins, their good neighbour, Mrs McEnroe, were no more to her than black strangers walking the roads.

Coffey had kept his promise, spoken to Elrington and she was employed as general dogsbody in the theatre, at everyone's beck and call, running errands, cleaning up, acting as prompter, helping the wardrobe mistress. She was once a famous actress, but now she was pock-marked, had a puckered mouth and scrawny hair, but retained her old shrewdness.

"Old Meg sees everything that happens," she would cackle. "All the naughty boys and girls and what they get up to. Old Meg knew the two days." She would stab her needle at Peg. "Don't let them take advantage of you. Seize your opportunity when it comes. Always remember you'll need money when you grow old. I was a foolish girl in my time, now look at me." And Peg would look and pity Old Meg. But would her chance ever come?

Most of the actors treated her as maid-of-all-work, throwing her the occasional copper, for which she was grateful, though she had been brought up to loath charity. Elrington was a miser, seldom paying her the few shillings that were her due. Of the company Kitty Raftor was hardest to bear; she was so full of her own importance, with a prosperous grandmother and expectations. She boasted that one day soon she would shake the dust of Dublin from her feet and make her mark on the London stage. Even Elrington, thin-faced, precious in his mincing way, with his coterie of young men, was afraid of Kitty. She intimidated everyone. Peg's only real friend was a young Scottish actor, Dónal Bán MacLeod, named such though his hair was bright ginger. He had served his time in an apothecary's shop in Edinburgh, before throwing up his position to become a strolling player, finally making his way to Dublin. She was in Dónal's confidence, he in hers; she told him of her love of Charles Coffey, he told her of his passion for the stage carpenter, a giant of a man who loved only strong drink. Dónal had cures for every ailment, doled out potions and ointments for the gout, rheumatism, surfeit of drink. He was popular with the women of the company, often relieving an actress of an unwanted pregnancy with some concoction his grandmother had taught him to mix. But for him, Peg might have given up and stormed out of the Playhouse. But he counselled patience, said fiery temper went with red hair and must be subdued. And in the end she would laugh and have to agree.

She met Charles Coffey almost every night. He made it seem accidental. He had taken to attending every performance and would walk home with her when she had finished clearing up after the rest. Occasionally, if her mother and the twins were asleep, he would come into the kitchen and they would kiss and fondle, wordlessly. It left her limp with desire and she would cry herself to sleep in her pillows after he had gone.

Now and again he paid her mother a visit, bringing small gifts: a book, sweetmeats, toys for the twins. Mrs Woffington was delighted to renew his acquaintance: she played the coquette, relating endless stories of her early life in Lemineagh, pressing him to meals he was too polite to refuse, decrying her hospitality as a poor thing—she whose people had once entertained the nobility. Peg was coldly polite. Yet when she gave him a glass of wine, the touch of his hand was a quickening of nerve and pulse, a wild longing, a searing pain. Once he invited her into the small back room in Faulkner's printing works, where he penned his articles and essays, and kissed her lingeringly, running his hands over her body.

"Small bones," he said tenderly, "small-breasted, like a winsome boy."

That night she stood naked examining herself in the fly-blown mirror, longing to be voluptuous, desirable, with a body to set a man mad with love.

As the weeks passed there grew an urgency about his love-making, a hunger that seemed to match her own, yet he kept control and when she wept with desire he said there could be no future for them. He was married, with commitments; she was too young, her mind still unformed. He would help her, tutor her, asking nothing in return: she would stay free as a bird. She protested she would never leave him and during their conversations would question him about his life before they met, like lovers since time began. He told her stories of his youth. His people had been pirates, vultures, driven to desperate shifts because the land was barren, the landlord hard. Yet the place still held him and when he described the blue-grey hills, the quiet valleys, the enchanted seashore where the heron fed, cliffs where golden eagles nested, she longed to be there with him, knew she would throw away every ambition, follow him to the world's end and beyond, did he but lift a finger. In all that time Alice Morgan's name was never mentioned and she had no way of knowing that it was she and not the Lady Jane he dreaded to betray.

❦

It was St Brigid's Day, spring's first awakening, and people raised their heads thankfully to the pale sun, to the blue hills looking down on the town, optimistic that the winter days were at an end. Only Peg, making her way down Winetavern Street, had no eyes for the halcyon day, the brave show made by the stall-keepers, the flowers, the fruit, the gaiety of barrow-boys. She and Coffey had parted almost a fortnight before, when he left Dublin to spend a weekend in the stone grey house in Chapelizod. When a week elapsed she grew anxious, tormenting herself that he was tired of her, had been seduced again by the grandeur of the Sandfords and become re-enamoured of his wife, the Lady Jane. Then she tormented herself with thoughts of illness—a chill, the smallpox, a fever which had killed her father. She knew he lodged in Smock Alley; she had often passed the house but she hadn't dared mention even his name to Mrs McEnroe.

Desperation drove her in the direction of Faulkner's printing press and into the path of a messenger boy emerging from the office. He stood eyeing her cheekily. "I've seen you around before. Looking for old Coffey, eh?"

She swallowed her ire. "Do you know is he back in Dublin? I have a message for him."

"You're not the only one. Coffey hasn't come near us for days. Got a fever or the clap or something in that chapel place he visits."

"Chapelizod," she said without thinking.

He whistled. "You know all about him. The boss gave me a letter to take to his lodgings." He waved the missive in the air. "I hope he gets sacked."

She managed a smile. "I'll deliver it for you if you like, save you trouble. I'm on my way to Smock Alley."

He leered. "Think I'm a fool? Old Faulkner was most particular."

"Please let me have it," she heard herself begging.

"What will you give me? Exchange is no robbery."

"I've nothing to give."

"Oh yes you have." Roughly he caught her by the shoulders, squeezing her breasts, running a hand up her skirts.

She slapped his face. "You little beast..."

He kicked out and she fell to the ground. In a temper she jumped to her feet, boxed his ears and grabbed the letter out of his hand.

"You're a right vixen," he grinned. "Meet me tonight and I'll show you a thing or two."

She walked away, head in the air, and he shouted after her.

"I hope Coffey rapes you." Shrugging his thin shoulders, he went off in the opposite direction, whistling loudly.

Peg paused outside the fine four-storey house in Smock Alley to gather her courage before raising the knocker, a lion, mouth wide in a soundless roar. She muttered a prayer that Mrs McEnroe was not within earshot.

Alice Morgan, who had been gazing idly out of the window, ran down the stairs to open the door before the maid could arrive up from the basement. She had pictured a slut with rosy cheeks, a common air, but this girl was different. She had an air of breeding and her eyes were troubled.

"Please, I have a message for Mr Coffey." Her voice was husky.

"If it is a letter I shall see he gets it." Alice Morgan was cool, betraying nothing of the jealousy that was tearing her apart.

Upstairs a door opened and they both turned to watch as Coffey came down the stairs, wearing a brown robe and a week's growth of beard.

He said mildly, "I thought I heard voices."

Mutely Peg held out the letter.

He put a hand on Alice Morgan's arm. "This is Peg Woffington, daughter of an old friend of mine, long dead. I was expecting to hear from Mr Faulkner." He smiled at Peg. "Come up to my rooms and I'll let you have an answer."

He led the way up the stairs. Alice Morgan was last. As she reached his door he closed it gently in her face. Pressing her hands to her temples, she made the climb to her drawing room on the second floor, feeling utterly defeated. It couldn't be happening. The girl was too young, too vulnerable, as if something above and beyond infatuation was driving her. Could it be that she was *enciente*, but even that didn't make sense. A pregnancy was nothing new to a girl of her class, especially if the father was Charles Coffey. Angrily she brushed away her tears, pitying him, herself, the whole doomed business. The girl would bring him nothing but trouble. Of that she was sure.

In the study, long windows looked out to the place where the city had its beginnings. Peg caught his hand.

"Were you ill?"

"It was nothing, a fever. Oh Peg, I'm like a starving man away from you."

"I love you," she said softly. "I have loved you since that night when we met."

"You are too young."

"No."

"You have so much to learn."

"Teach me. Please..."

He held her face in both hands, then his arms were around her. He covered her face, her neck with soft kisses. Her eyes filled with tears and he paused.

"You are not ready?"

"Yes," she whispered. "I long for you. Kiss me. Touch me."

"Here," he said softly, "and here. Do you like that?"

Her eyes blazed like stars.

He lifted her up, carried her into his bedroom, undressed her and she lay waiting while he undid his robe.

He lay down beside her, covering her body with kisses, while she writhed in an ecstasy of desire. She nerved herself for the first thrust, the pain that followed, nails digging into his buttocks as he slid his hand around, under her, lifting her closer so that he was flesh of her flesh, bone of her bone. When he took her again, she experienced something over and above pleasure, a fulfilment that had come at last.

Somewhere there was a thud and they pulled apart.

"It's only a door banging," he said breathlessly but the spell was broken. He got up to dress. She tugged her shift over her head, ashamed of its grey poverty, of the rent in her skirt, her bodice too small, stained under the armpits.

"I should have come to him in silk and lace," she thought fiercely feeling her poverty a disease, as bad as the pox which could disfigure and kill, quench desire.

They went back into his study and she stood by the window while he rooted at his desk, picking up manuscripts, his voice matter-of-fact.

"If you will take this article to Mr Faulkner I should be obliged."

As if this were the reason for her visit, as if what had happened was nothing at all! To hide her tears she pressed her nose to the window. A bitter east wind had blown up and on the bridge spanning the Liffey, traders cowered for protection, their shrill cries lost in the scream of angry gulls swooping greedily, snatching up heads of fish, guts, bloody entrails on the cobblestones. The sight of the women's poverty, their unending struggle to earn a crust, fuelled her sense of misery and she snivelled.

"What ails you?" His voice was impatient.

She wheeled round. "I'm sick of the Playhouse, that's what ails me. Sick of being poor. Elrington hates me, the actors despise me. Last week I earned sixpence, thanks to your influence. But for Mrs McEnroe we might starve. She steals the leftovers from your landlady's table."

He winced. "Don't, Peg. I promise things will improve."

"Promises mean nothing, pay no bills. Yesterday my mother pawned her wedding ring; last week she pawned Máire Rua's locket to pay the rent. Today the twins are ten years old. I have nothing to give them, no gift to celebrate their birthday."

"I offered help before; you refused."

Impatiently she shook back her red hair, which had loosened in their love-making, her eyes hostile, angry. "I won't be a kept woman. I'm not Margaret Leeson." She laughed hysterically. "My mother says one is judged by the company one keeps. My people were aristocrats when yours were wrecking ships."

"I'm putting the finishing touches to a play," he explained patiently, as though addressing a child. "In a couple of months' time the company will set out on a summer tour, ending in the new theatre in Cork with a first production of this—" He held up the sheaf of manuscripts.

She made to say something but he interrupted. "I'll speak to Elrington. Force him to give you the lead, pay you a proper wage." He took a sovereign from his purse. "Take this, buy your twins whatever trifles they fancy: painted soldiers, a string of glass beads."

"I'll not take charity from you or anyone."

"It's not charity. Your father befriended me when I came to this city, seeking to make my way. I owe your family some recompense. You can pay me back some day, if it will ease your stiff-necked pride."

"Kiss me," she said, suddenly melting.

He opened the door. "For God's sake, leave me in peace." His voice was weary. "I'm too old for such scenes."

❧

Alice Morgan was packing her trunks, leaving Dublin for a visit to her sister who lived in Bath. "I need a change of air," she told Mrs McEnroe. "You will take care of the house, of Mr Coffey, when I am gone." Yet she knew she was fooling no one, least of all herself. She had been sickened, dismayed when she saw the sheets he had tried to hide away, the blood. "The girl was a virgin. He took her under my roof. How dared he do such a thing?"

Charles Coffey was standing in her room, summoned there like a servant. She warned herself she must be stern, not break down before him. "I do not know when I shall return," she said evenly. "I may even arrange to settle permanently in England."

He drummed fingers on the table. "Surely there is no need for such drastic action? A simple solution is for me to find other lodgings."

She busied herself folding gowns. "I should be obliged if you would remain until I return. A man in the house is a security. That is, unless you mean to set up an establishment elsewhere." Try as she might, she could not hide the bitterness.

"As yet I have made no plans," he growled. "Until such time I shall abide by your wishes."

Without another word he went out the door and she stood for a long moment, not feeling anything at all. "Thank God I am over the worst," she thought.

His footsteps descending the stairs sounded loud, firm. She heard the front door close with a bang and looked out the window. He was striding away, head erect, and she was swamped with desolation, misery washing over her, threatening to destroy her. She had to bite her hand to prevent herself from following after him, throwing herself on her knees before him for all to see, begging for his love. "I have no pride left," she whispered, "nothing."

She knelt by the sofa, burying her head in the cushions to muffle her sobs, for what had so nearly been hers and was now lost to her forever.

❧

At the beginning of June a heat-wave hit the city, the Aungier Street Playhouse closed down for the season and the company set out on tour, which would end in the newly built theatre in the Munster capital. Their final offering would be Charles Coffey's long-awaited play. He had battled with the management and in the end had his way. Peg was cast in the leading role. For weeks he had coached her and she had not spared herself. Yet at times she despaired of her acting abilities, felt she was a puppet dancing to his strings. On the night before her departure she went to the house in Smock Alley, to his bed. He had been insatiable and she had not protested, though weary with the weeks of rehearsals, the strain of trying to please Elrington, of reassuring a mother who alternated between bouts of gaiety at her daughter's change of fortune and irrational fears.

"Some of these Irish peasants are savage. They live in mud cabins. Animals and humans sleep in the one room— a clay floor, a turf fire, and great ropy curds to eat. You forget I was reared in the country."

Peg sighed. "It's high summer. The cattle will be out to pasture. We are strolling players. A bale of straw in a barn will serve as our bed, if we are lucky."

Her mother's face lit up. "In the old days strolling players came to Bunratty Castle, my uncle's place, and were well received. They stayed until 'Little Christmas' and put on a different play for each of the twelve nights. Shakespearean actors they were. Better than any in London."

Resolutely Peg put all thought of her mother's misgivings and stories out of her mind to concentrate on her lover, her arms holding him close...

"I shall miss you." She would die of loneliness.

Tenderly he stroked her face, kissed her lips. "Don't forget me, darling, pulse of my heart. Remember, I love you best of all."

It was the first time he had said this and exultantly she hugged his words to herself, told her foolish heart that one day they would be together for always, that everything would come all right in the end.

8

The fair-haired young man riding the dusty road had spent the night at the card-table in Shanbally Castle with Lord Cashel and a couple of hard-riding country gentlemen. Gambling was in the Honourable Patrick Taafe's blood. His father had married one of the richest heiresses in Ireland and had managed to lose his wife's fortune as well as his patrimony, before taking a toss on the hunting field which had resulted in his death. His son Patrick, brought up in the Ormond Butler household, had roamed the countryside at will from boyhood. By the time his maternal grandmother died, leaving him one of the finest estates in the south, he knew every field and stream of his inheritance, the thickets where game was plentiful, the lakes and rivers where fish rose to the fly, above all, the coverts, banks, stretches of land that made south Tipperary the best hunting country in Munster.

His last meet with the Tipperary Scarlets had been his finest hour: the fox sighted, hounds in full cry, horns sounding "Gone away," turf under his heels and fifty horses behind. Faintly beyond the stone wall he caught the music of the pack, had taken the gate in one glorious leap, followed by a thicket of fences. Across the silver waters the pack were running breast-high to the scent, Roisín Dubh his prize mare, her blood up, galloped like the wind. In front of them the river sparkled, disappearing between bank and bank, reappearing again, and they were over. Cashel, thudding behind, turf-clods spattering, and he, Patrick Taafe, going hell for leather, saw the hounds streaming to the cap in full cry, the doomed fox turn, teeth bared for the last-ditch stand. That day, leading the field, he had almost broken his neck, and on this fine summer morning, despair in his heart, he wished he had. Last night on the throw of a dice he had gambled and lost to Cashel the last of his stables, the best hunter in Ireland, his treasure, Dark Rosaleen.

Moodily he dug in his heels and the hack broke into a gallop. It was ill-advised to gamble when in one's cups. Cashel could drink them all under the table and sober up the instant the cards or dice were produced. Tomorrow he would set out for Dublin and Margaret Leeson's brothel. If he couldn't ride Ireland's most spirited horse, he could ride her gamiest whore. Yet he knew he was only postponing the hour of reckoning. He needed an alliance with wealth, an heiress to save him from ruin. Like father, like son. The thought afforded him little joy. A vision of the Lady Arabella FitzSimons swam before his eyes, though vision scarcely described the angular, sharp-featured lady, some ten years his senior and suitably rich. She had pursued him relentlessly since their meeting more than a year before at a ball in Dublin Castle, professing herself hopelessly infatuated by his charms. It seemed as if she was about to get her heart's desire.

His tongue was like wood pulp. No one had a better hand with the buttermilk than Deborah Dunning, a comely woman, beddable too, except he had no wish to cross his bailiff. As he dismounted at the farmhouse door he noticed the strangers chatting to Deborah; a young man with a painted face clad in second-hand finery, a wench in tawdry silk. Gypsies, he guessed, scavenging the countryside around, begging, poaching, filching anything not locked away. Odd that he hadn't seen sign of their encampment: their half-starved donkeys and ragged children were usually all over the place.

He reined in his horse at the door of the farmhouse and Deborah, cheeks flushed and eyes inviting, gave him a curtsey.

"No doubt you are thirsty after your journey, Squire," she said sweetly.

"Aye, that I am," he growled.

She clapped her hands and a dairymaid came out with a pitcher of buttermilk which he downed at one go. It was only then that he gave his attention to the strangers, the ginger-haired fellow, staring at him with open admiration, the wench, suspicion in her green eyes.

"Who are these people, Deborah?"

She smiled. "Actors, Squire. They had a mishap in the glen beyond, near the weaver's cottage. The old horse is half dead and the cart upturned."

He turned on his heels. "Tell them to get on their way. We have beggars and to spare roaming the countryside."

Peg stiffened. Not for the first time since leaving Dublin did she curse Elrington for giving them the broken-down cart and the old nag that should long since have been put down. With all the traps and costumes they had to carry there was scarcely room for one, let alone three—herself, Dónal Bán and Old Meg, now sitting in the thatched cottage, being comforted by the weaver's wife and inspected by his brood. It was, she supposed, only to be expected. Elrington resented her, hadn't wanted to give her the lead in Charles Coffey's new play. The rest had taken their cue from the manager. Only for Dónal Bán's friendship she would have been in despair. His unfailing high spirits had kept herself and the old wardrobe mistress in good humour for the length of the creaking journey, with its many mishaps, through Leinster into Munster.

He was explaining their predicament to the squire, sprinkling his conversation with "your honour" and "your lordship," waving his hands, giving his winning smile. But his attempts at flattery were not well received by Taafe who prided himself on his masculinity. Dónal was castigated by him as a vagabond, a catamite. At this Peg lost her temper and with eyes flashing told the squire what she thought of him.

Afterwards she thought he had taken it well, considering he owned the very ground under their feet and was used to the honey-tongued servility of his tenants and menials. She was not to know that it was the story of the worn-out horse collapsing in a ditch that moved him to make his offer, that and the fact that he was always ready for a fumble with a pretty wench. He was intrigued by the red hair and the green eyes, and passionate defence of her foppish companion. If she would get up on the horse with him, guide him to where the accident had occurred, he would see what could be done.

She wondered was she wise mounting the horse at his command, but their situation was desperate, stranded as they were here in the heart of the Golden Vale. Most of the men around were away at the fair of Cashel and they might beg their way back to Dublin, abandoning Old Meg to her fate, leaving the props behind, the company in the lurch and thus ruining her chance of a stage debut. Her career might be finished before it had rightly begun.

From the moment she had seen the horseman canter down the dusty road, she had felt a scratchy sensation in her fingers and found herself repeating the witches' refrain at the approach of King Macbeth, lately Thane of Glamis:

> By the pricking of my thumbs,
> Something wicked this way comes.

Yet on close inspection this Tipperary thane seemed harmless enough, typically upper class. Hard-riding, hard-drinking squireens such as he were to be found the length and breadth of the land. There and then she decided she would use her wiles, coax him into giving them a new cart, a fresh horse. Otherwise they would never see Cork.

They hardly exchanged more than a couple of words on the journey. She began by explaining where the horse had collapsed, that Old Meg had sought refuge in a nearby cottage. He grunted something about knowing the place, the weaver his tenant. After which he had relapsed into brooding silence broken only when she enquired about a few landmarks, a circle of stones where druids had once held rites, the ruins of a Norman keep. Only once did he volunteer information, pointing out a place where at the last meet a fox had gone down in a welter of black and white and tan bodies, to the baying of those hounds and the horsemen moving in for the kill. She guessed by the tone of his voice that it had been a milestone in his life and wondered why.

Some five miles south of the river the horse confidently turned in through a pair of iron gates guarding a walled demesne and went trotting down an avenue banked by blood-red rhododendrons.

"Blood-red was the sky when the high king of Ireland followed three red horsemen to his doom in Bohernabreena, Road of the Hostels," the old legend went. The king had broken his *geasa*, spells laid on him by the people of Faery, and he found the hostel in flames and all dead.

She shivered. A day of high summer was no time for remembering legends of accursed kings long dead. Firmly she put the story out of her mind, little dreaming that a time would come when she would find herself in Bohernabreena journeying to hell itself, and all because of the man with whom she now rode.

They seemed to be travelling for miles, the path twisting and turning, past hedgerows heavy with pink and white blossoms, shrubs with globular clusters forming a blue and white wall. Then, as sometimes happens when least expected, they reached journey's end. They had descended into a valley and before them a sweep of terrace framed a house of symmetry, grace. A house such as she had imagined Lemineagh to be. Grey stone glinting in the sunlight, mullioned windows reflecting green lawns and terraces, wooden staircases.

Her feelings for the owner of this jewel in the hollow of a hand were undergoing a change. For the first time she understood Máire Rua's wild journey to beg mercy of the dread Cromwellian, General Ireton, knew that she, Peg, would kill for such a house, make any bargain to keep it safe from greedy hands. She drew in a deep breath. "It is the most enchanting place I have ever seen."

Taafe shrugged. "My grandmother, the old countess, had the house built on the ruins of an earlier castle. It was designed by a famous English architect. Her ancestors buttled for a king and earned the family name. The Butlers were a great Norman family."

"And now this is all yours?"

He laughed mirthlessly. "And every stone mortgaged. My father's people, the Taafes, began their rise as grooms. From them I inherit my weakness." He looked so assured, so much in command, a legacy of hundreds of years of power, privilege.

"Your weakness?" she echoed.

"Gambling. On anything from a racehorse to the throw of a dice. Until today I was on a losing streak. Maybe you'll change my luck."

She gave him a brilliant smile and he felt himself quicken. What a strange creature she was, with those sparkling eyes, that vibrant hair. From what midden had she sprung? He would take her to the bedroom where the old countess had slept with her grooms when all the men of her generation had died in the wars. That was the other weakness he had inherited from the Butlers. Not only the men but the women also were great lovers, sensual even in old age.

His factor was waiting to see him in the hall, had urgent business that would not keep. With a muttered oath he left her to the care of an old man in knee-breeches and long silver hair who beckoned her to follow him through a baize door and down stone steps to the servants' quarters. She was given milk to drink in the stone-flagged kitchen and eagerly questioned by the red-faced cook, while barefooted scullions crowded around her, touching her gown, giggling, whispering.

Was she the squire's new "tally woman?" Did she know it was the custom in these parts for the landlord to bed any girl who might take his fancy? It was his right.

She had heard of the practice of *droit de seigneur*, but

laughed at the idea that their master had any rights over her. She was free, her own mistress. They assured her that he was good-natured and if she pleased him he might marry her off when he grew tired of her. He had done as much for Deborah who had been his "tally woman" for the best part of a year. She was the bailiff's second wife. She had done well for herself. Somehow the story shocked her, Deborah had such a pretty air of independence; yet she should have guessed there was something between them, a familiarity uncommon between landlord and tenant. For the first time since meeting him she felt apprehension. Would she be able to handle this man, used to taking what he wanted? She would make her excuses, leave on foot if necessary, but as if on cue the old servant was there, waiting to take her back to the hall where his master was waiting. For all that he was a menial, he had an air of authority that she found impossible to refuse.

To her surprise Taafe took her on a tour of the house and she played the game with herself that she was the *châtelaine*, this her domain: the oak-panelled dining room was where she took her meals; the morning room, fragile, graceful, a woman's room, where she ordered her household, then, duty done, called the dogs to heel and strolled out on to the terrace and down the broad steps to the garden below.

It was only when they reached the countess's bedchamber that her powers of invention ran out. She could never imagine owning this room, sleeping in that great four-poster bed, carved, tapestried. Everything about the room spoke of exquisite taste: walls lined with silk, slender chairs, a writing-desk, a dressing-table in fine French wood. And everywhere bowls and vases of crystal and porcelain, filled with fresh flowers, their perfumes filling the air. Light poured in through long windows which looked down on pleasant gardens and a lake where swans nestled. Far away, the Knockmealdown Mountains rose mistily blue into the sky...

He had come up behind her as she stood looking out, lifting her chin, kissing her gently at first, then more demandingly and she found herself responding, until he put his hand down her bodice and she panicked and broke free. He caught her before she could reach the door, threw her down on the bed, pinning her with his body.

"Let me go," she protested, struggling, but he held her too firmly.

He licked her ear. "I have arranged for a cart to take you and your baggage to Thurles. But first you must pay me."

"No," she said breathlessly, biting his hand.

He let out an oath; then gave a great belly laugh. "I love a good tussle, a gamy woman. Like Margaret Leeson."

Outrage gave her strength to break free. She rolled out of the bed, fell on to the floor, picked herself up.

"How dare you say such a thing to me?" she panted. "I am no whore."

At that moment the door opened and the old man in livery said quietly:

"It is time the lady was on her way. The cart is ready below, her companions waiting."

Taafe had worked himself up into a frenzy of lust. Had it been any other of his servants, he would have thrown him bodily out of the window, but the old man had been his surrogate father, tutor, valet, confidant, the only person in the world he trusted, listened to. Helplessly he let go of Peg. At the threshold she paused and looked back. There was pity in her eyes and a little regret. "I am truly grateful for your kindness, sir."

He said thickly, "I love you. I must see you again." He sounded foolish, fatuous. He had never been more serious in all of his twenty-five years. She smiled, a dimple playing in her cheek. "We open in the new playhouse in Cork a week from today. Perhaps the journey would be too far."

"I would journey to Hades and back to be with you." With a bound he had crossed the room, taken her in his arms, and was covering her with kisses that left her bruised and exhilarated.

As the horse and cart trundled down the drive, she turned to take a last look at the house. Standing on the wide step was a young man with a shock of fair hair and a look of longing. In an exuberance of spirits she threw him a kiss. It had only been an interlude, an hour's flirtation on a day of high summer, yet somehow his foolish declaration of love had touched some secret chord. He would be a dangerous man to trifle with, she told herself, yet perversely hoped they would meet again.

🐦

From an early hour country people had been arriving in Cork to celebrate "Lady's Day," the annual harvest festival which fell on 15 August. Citizens were out on the streets in great numbers watching the mayor and aldermen making their stately way to St Fin Barre's Cathedral for a service of thanksgiving. Hard on the heels of the civic dignitaries came the actors, a motley crowd. They too had entered the town by way of the Mardyke, a charming river-walk between two branches of the Lee, their carts and waggons festooned with bunting, the horses prancing along wearing ribbons and favours. Small boys ran around distributing handbills announcing that the Aungier Street

Players would, that very evening, present a tragedy never before seen on any stage. The young and beautiful Mistress Peg Woffington would play the lead.

It was seldom that a theatrical company made the long journey from Dublin to Munster's capital and few doubted that the new playhouse would be packed to capacity. It would be something to tell their children and grandchildren.

As the hours passed, excitement mounted; rumours circulated the town that army officers from the military post in Cove were making the thirteen-mile journey on horseback and, more exciting still, that no less a personage than Lord Cashel, accompanied by the Honourable Patrick Taafe, known to be the finest rider to hounds in Munster, was already on his way.

Peg, costumed in the scarlet flannel petticoat and velvet bodice of a peasant girl, had only one wish. That the ground would open and swallow her. In a few minutes the curtain would rise and her mind had gone blank.

"I can't remember my opening lines," she said, clutching frantically at Dónal Bán, who would not appear until the second act but had come up to lend his support.

"It's just first-night nerves," he whispered. "Once on stage you'll be fine."

"At the last moment Elrington orders me to adopt a brogue, so that the natives will understand what I say."

Kitty Raftor, resplendent in high wig and brocade, swept up. She was cast as Peg's aristocratic rival in the play.

"That should give you no trouble," she smiled maliciously. "You're used to consorting with peasants, whores and such low life."

"Shakespeare put it in a nutshell, Mistress Raftor." The pleasant Scottish voice held a sting:

The venom clamours of a jealous woman
Poisons more deadly than a mad dog's tooth.

"A pox on you, Dónal Bán MacLeod," Kitty hissed and swept off.

Behind the curtains Peg could hear the noise of the house filling up; orange girls shouting their wares, wealthy butter merchants seating themselves down in the stalls with many grunts and sighs, laughter and banter as Cork beauties invited the hard-riding officers to share their boxes, and the excitement as Cashel and his companions made a last-minute appearance and were welcomed by the lord mayor.

Peg was on stage, the scene the kitchen of a Big House somewhere in Munster. How she got there she couldn't remember. Behind the curtain a voice was whispering her cue and she mumbled: "Oh, how I long to see his darlin' face again..."

"Speak up," a man shouted from the pit.

"I dhreamt of him last night, and shure 'twas no wonder and I wid the shticks of yarrow beneath my pillow," she wailed.

From the stalls came a titter, from the pit a guffaw, and in her misery she tripped and fell flat on her face. Pandemonium broke out, the house rocked with laughter, cat-calls, booing.

Taafe's imperious voice from a box called down: "Give the girl a chance." From a wit in the gallery came the ready riposte: "Ease in acting comes from art not chance."

Scarlet-faced Peg got to her feet, eyes seeking out the tall young man who leant over the box, willing her to go on. His being there gave her courage. She would be damned if she would let them defeat her, would play the part in her own way, as Charles Coffey had coached her. Silently she counted to six, then moved centre-stage, speaking with a bell-like clarity that could be heard in every part of the house.

"I would put spells on him as Grainne did Diarmuid. He fled with her across Ireland and they made their bed in bracken and heather and in the quiet places of the woods where badgers and squirrels sleep."

As the momentum of the drama gathered pace, the laughter, booing, hissing died out, and for the next two hours she acted out the role of the simple country girl possessed by love and destroyed by jealousy. It was not a great play, the lines stilted, the plot commonplace, but the house listened rapt. Drained, exhausted, she bowed as the curtain came across and then made her way to the wings, to tumultuous applause.

❧

She lay on her bed in the inn, weeping into her pillow, for the triumph that had turned to ashes, the careless gaiety of the night that had ended in bloodshed. She had returned to a standing ovation and had been finally released to make her way to the greenroom, surrounded by admirers. Even Elrington had been moved to praise her. Soon after, the place had filled up with the mayor and his party, wealthy merchants, the officers from Cove and the gentry. Patrick Taafe had come determined to claim her, whispering loudly: "Come back with me, Peg, to Cluain Meala, the honey vale." Like most of the men he was well in his cups.

She had laughed, remembering that enchanted house and, flushed with success and happiness, had kissed him back, promised that she would come some day soon.

It was then that she saw him, held her breath, so sure was she that he was an apparition, a ghost from another world. She had left him behind in Dublin, with his explanation that he could not possibly come to Cork for the opening: pressure of business, his affairs in Chapelizod. He was standing apart from the people surrounding her. She pushed them apart and went to him. "How did you get here?"

"By stage from Dublin." His voice was strange. "Too late to see you perform on stage."

"I am not giving a performance now," she snapped.

Taafe came over to join her and after that the nightmare had taken over. Kitty Raftor, crazed with jealousy, explaining to Taafe that Charles Coffey was her paramour, had betrayed the Lady Jane Sandford, his wife; Taafe thickly challenging the man he saw as his rival to a duel. Distraught, she had appealed to Cashel to intervene, begged him to take his friend away. There had been uproar, officers and actors taking sides in the dispute. Someone drew a sword, someone else was hurt, blood was flowing, Elrington knocked to the ground, his favourite, a dark-haired boy with a fragile air, injured. Taafe had let off his pistol, blown a sconce of candle off the wall.

It was then that Dónal Bán had got her away to her room in the inn, assuring her it was nothing but a drunken brawl, advising her to have a good night's rest. She would never know rest again.

"Peg."

He was in the room, had come in noiselessly, was standing at the foot of the bed, his face in shadows.

"Leave me alone," she whispered. "Why did you come, spoil everything?"

He covered his face with his hands, she knew he was weeping.

"Don't," she begged. "Not tonight. It was nothing. We were all carried away with excitement."

"Oh, Peg. I missed you. *A mhuirnín, a chuisle mo chroí*, darling pulse of my heart." He was pouring out his love in torrents of Irish, as he did when deeply moved and as so often before she was melting in his arms, returning his wild kisses. He was stripping her to the skin, touching her, his body covering her, then like an arrow unleashed was piercing her, bearing down, until the whole world was breaking into a million pieces and she was washed in his love, satiated, spent.

Afterwards they made love again and she kissed his neck, the hollows of his shoulders. "We'll stay together for ever," she whispered. "Promise that it will be soon."

She longed for his reassurance but he had fallen asleep. For a long time she lay back in the darkness, trying to see into the future, knowing she would barter her career, her family, her very soul to feel he was hers forever, to still the storm in her heart. Little knowing that two years would elapse, and disaster and famine stalk the land, before their story was finally told.

9

I t was spring; spring in Dublin. In the gardens, parks and orchards of the town, apple trees blossomed, chestnuts, limes, oaks were heavy with leaves. Flower-sellers, their baskets ablaze with the colours of daffodils, lilies, peonies, forget-me-nots, paraded the streets calling their wares. Winter was gone and the Liffey sparkled with light; small boats bobbed and great white ships' sails softly billowed. Children played in the river Poddle that ran through the Liberties, screaming with laughter. Small dark weavers with high-crowned wigs left their looms idle while they gossiped with friends; nursemaids took the air with their charges in Grafton Street; the Beaux Walk on St Stephen's Green was crowded with fops in fancy waistcoats and powdered wigs; well-appointed matrons shopped in the markets of the High Street for brandied apricots, chocolate, marzipan for special supper parties. In Patrick Street their poorer sisters haggled with dealers at makeshift stalls, smelling fish for freshness, pressing stumpy fingers into fruit and vegetables, testing for soundness. Beside the cathedral a ballad singer sang in a cracked voice:

Come buy my fine wares,
Plums, apples and pears,
A hundred a penny,
In conscience too many,
Come, will you have any;
My children are seven,
I wish them in heaven,
My husband's a sot,
With his pipe and his pot,
Not a farthing will gain 'em,
And I must maintain 'em.

A sardonic-looking clergyman emerged from the cathedral close. He it was who had written the verse. He was in the habit of composing such doggerel when he worked on his sermons and pamphlets, in much the same way as the early monks had scribbled in monastic scriptoriums, filling in the margins of their manuscripts with strange and wonderful animals.

Peg, making her way along Patrick Street, had a sudden urge to accost the dean, to pour out her troubles to him, to tell him of the storm which she feared would shortly break about her head. Surely he of all men would understand. For as long as she could remember he had been the subject of scandal. His book *Gulliver's Travels* had been mocked as childish, satirised as an attack on humanity, labelled obscene, fit only to be burnt in the market-place. Yet it was as widely read as popular romances like *Moll Flanders* or *Robinson Crusoe*.

More scandalous still, at least in the eyes of the authorities, were the *Drapier's Letters*, published anonymously in 1724, denouncing Hanoverian George and his government in London for their attempts to foist a worthless currency on a downtrodden people. Dublin Castle had offered a reward of £500 for information about the author. But though £500 was more than a man might earn in a lifetime and the very dogs on the street knew who the Drapier was, none could be got to betray the dean.

Love had served him no better. Gossip had it that on his wedding night he had discovered his bride Stella was his half-sister. After that they never slept together again, though he made her an allowance and spent an hour with her each afternoon in the cathedral house, chaperoned by his housekeeper, Mrs Dingley, who sat tight-lipped, clutching her Bible, wearing hinged glasses.

He was in the habit of visiting St Paul's Cathedral in London from time to time. It was there he had met Vanessa, spoilt daughter of wealthy parents. She had fallen in love with the handsome clergyman with the literary reputation and the whiff of brimstone and followed him to Dublin. In a fit of pique at the coolness of his reception, she had left Dublin and rented a house in Celbridge in Kildare, where she set about writing a letter to Stella, demanding to know the truth of her relationship with the dean.

When Swift discovered what had happened he saddled his horse, not drawing rein until he reached Vanessa's house at Celbridge. He had thrown the letter in her face, vowing they would never meet again. And they never did. Three months later she was dead, people said of a broken heart.

Strange to think how this old man, plagued now by fits of vertigo and deafness, noted for appearing with wig askew and in shabby black clothes, had known two such tempestuous affairs. Surely he of all men would understand her obsession with Charles Coffey, her longing for independence. She took a few tentative steps in his direction but he had been swallowed up in the crowd. Greedy hands clutched his cloak, generous hands offered him fruit and fish, cajoling, coaxing, whining voices demanded his attention, his charity, his time. It was always thus when he went abroad. Defeated, she turned away. She had already made her decision: the die was cast.

That morning at rehearsal Elrington's face had been thunderous. Trouble was in the air. For weeks the company had been playing to half-empty houses, the coffers were bare, salaries in arrears. Shareholders like Leadbetter the goldsmith were forecasting ruin—closure of the Playhouse, even. Kitty Raftor, heiress to a rich grandmother who owned huckster shops and tenement houses, had no need to worry; Lucy Sparks could rely on the protection of her twin brother Luke, current favourite of Buck Whaley. Dónal Bán would make his way back to Edinburgh and no doubt do well on the stage there. Others like Old Meg could well end up in the gutter. And what of her own future? Charles Coffey, engrossed in his own troubles, would be of no help.

At that moment she was visited by an idea so bizarre that at first she smothered the thought. Yet on reflection was it so outrageous after all? Since that day at Tyburn, Jimmy Maclean's words had never been far from her mind. "Dress up as a gentleman and they'll swing out of the rafters to see you."

Without giving herself time to have second thoughts, she had blurted out:

"Why not revive *The Constant Couple* and let me play the part of Sir Harry Wildair?"

She could see they were shocked into silence. An actor named John Wilkes had made the part his own. Now

Wilkes was dead these three years or more but there wasn't an actor alive with the temerity to step into his shoes.

Elrington was the first to discover his voice: "A woman to play a man's part?" he croaked. "Have you taken leave of your senses, Mistress Woffington?"

"It was suggested to me by a gentleman of my acquaintance," she said coolly. Elrington was not to know that the gentleman in question was a long time dead, now no more than a handful of dust. She could see him wavering. So daring a venture would be sure to result in wide publicity; there would be talk; the town would be scandalised; seats would be taken. Kitty Raftor's sharp nose tested the air. "I shall play Wildair. The role will suit me."

Peg held her peace. "It matters little to me," she said lightly. "Just that my friend may be upset."

Elrington was of two minds. Kitty Raftor would be the ideal choice for the part, with her deep voice and commanding presence. Yet it would be foolhardy to antagonise the rakes of the town, risk making an enemy of the Honourable Patrick Taafe, who was capable of wrecking the Playhouse if his wishes were set to naught.

"If I do not play the part I shall go to London," Kitty threatened.

"Go and be damned to you," Elrington grunted and stumped away.

Peg closed her eyes in relief. She had got her wish: the gamble had paid off. She couldn't help wondering what the reckoning would be.

❧

Mrs McEnroe delicately raised her skirts as she roasted her shins and glanced sternly at her neighbour and friend:

"I hear tell that Peg is to appear in a breeches part, no less. Wagers are being laid by the bucks of the town, regarding the shape of her legs. It's my belief there will be a riot on the opening night."

Mrs Woffington dabbed her eyes in distress. "I did my best to dissuade her but she will have her way. When I think of our aristocratic ancestors I could weep for shame."

Mrs McEnroe sniffed. "Faith then, from all I heard tell, your grandmother Máire Rua was a lady who would stop at nothing to gain her ends."

"Peg is twenty years of age. I can hardly put a lock on her."

"Too true. Only today Mrs Carey remarked how lucky she is with no children to burden her."

"Mattie fathered brats and to spare in his time with the kitchen slatterns," Mrs Woffington said tartly. "And come to it, you had your own troubles with Kathleen. Do you ever hear trace or tidings of her?"

"Never a word. One of these days she'll turn up like a lady."

"Maybe so. As I always say, breeding will out."

Mrs McEnroe considered the discussion had gone far enough and produced a poke of paper from her apron pocket. "Mrs Morgan won't miss the few grains I took and a cup of tea will do us both good."

Soon the kettle was boiling and the place laid with the accoutrements of the tea-table. Slany Woffington stood back to admire her handiwork and sighed. One could always tell a lady by the fine china she used. If only she possessed a silver teapot and some silver spoons.

❧

It seemed as if every man in Dublin had made it his business to be present at the opening of *The Constant Couple* to see Peg play the part of Sir Harry Wildair. Boxes were filled to overflowing with the bucks of the town, galleries crowded with sweating apprentices, butcher boys, penniless students, redcoated soldiers; sturdy guildsmen filled the pits, while rich merchants and students in robes of crimson and gold, which denoted their rank and privilege, claimed seats in the stalls. The only females to be seen in the packed house were two titled ladies who went where and when they pleased, Margaret Leeson and her girls, Lucy Sparks, who was in the Earl of Meath's box, and a couple of independent whores. Indeed, the only notable absentee was the Honourable Patrick Taafe, forced to flee Dublin by irate creditors. "Poor Patrick," thought Peg. Unlucky in love *and* cards. Since their meeting more than two years before he had pursued her hopelessly. In another place, another time she might have succumbed, become his tally woman, might even have induced him to marry her. But they had met too late. She would be forever enslaved to the dark handsome man with the steady grey eyes. Something in that deep voice had ensnared her on the starry night outside Daly's:

> *Fair daffodils, we weep to see*
> *You haste away so soon.*

Her dresser settled the powdered wig on the titian curls and smoothed down the cuff of the blue brocade suit. "There now, my pet, you look a treat."

"Wish me luck," Peg said as she made her way to the stage.

If the play failed, if a riot should break out, if she were laughed off stage, there would be no second chance.

During the weeks of rehearsal, when she had to withstand the town's prurient interest, her mother's sulks, Kitty Raftor's jealousy, only the ghost of the golden-haired giant had given her courage. But then he had been reckless beyond belief and had paid the price, dancing his final jig at the end of a rope. Strange how she, with her soaring ambition, her need of security, so much admired gamblers, smugglers, highwaymen—men who never bothered to count the cost.

Charles Coffey was not attending the opening night, pleading family business in Chapelizod. He had deputed a raw young critic to take his place. Oh, the young neophyte would be fulsome in his praise, careful not to antagonise his mentor's whore. It was the first time she had faced the word and it stuck in her throat.

On stage the prologue had ended. She touched a unicorn's foot for luck with hands clammy with fear, forced herself to breathe deeply, willed herself into the part and strolled nonchalantly on stage, elegant in padded blue velvet breeches, with lace at cuffs and throat, powdered wig, sword at the ready—the epitome of every gallant who had ever gambled at cards, ridden to hounds, tumbled a wench. She made a sally and the house roared its approval. Bawdy remarks were shouted up, the fine figure she made, at the girth of her thighs, the curves of her legs. She dimpled, smiled, postured, played the part with verve, assurance, while they shrieked with delight at her quips, her asides, applauding her courage in filling a role that everyone said was doomed to fail. And when the play drew to an end and they finally allowed her to leave the stage, heaped with flowers and tributes, she knew she had achieved her ambition. Dublin loved her. She was a success at last.

❦

It was a cold autumn night and the deserted Playhouse held the lingering odours of the night's audience: sweat, candlegrease, scent, orange peels, pomanders and the stench of dead flowers. For half a year she had filled the theatre nightly and now the final curtain had fallen. Alone at her dressing-table, creaming her face of paint, she willed him to come. It was weeks since they had met. She shivered, felt gooseflesh on her bare arms and wrapped a dressing-gown around her bare shoulders. It was time she was dressed and gone home, yet she was reluctant to move. All the rest had left early, prepared to celebrate the night that was in it. Farewell autumn! Welcome winter! In the Castle the Lord Lieutenant was holding a ball. In the Liberties, people were building the Hallowe'en bonfires. Dubliners were making merry, dancing, drinking, risking life and limb as the bolder ones among them jumped over the flames for luck. It was magic to throw a lighted brand in the air and watch the sparks mark its flight. This was the night when the dead walked abroad, when faery folk rode out and when spells were cast.

"Good-night, good yarrow, thrice good-night to thee. Tell me who my true love is to be." Once long ago she had chanted the incantation and had dreamt of Charles Coffey.

Her heart lurched as she saw his reflection in the cracked mirror. He had appeared so noiselessly that for a heartbeat she thought him an illusion. He walked lightly on the balls of his feet, crossing the room in a couple of strides.

"Is your admirer, the Honourable Taafe, not with you tonight?" His voice was harsh, uneven.

"If you spent more time in Dublin you might realise that the run ended tonight." Wearily she pushed back her hair. She looked young, vulnerable. What he had come to tell her stuck in his throat.

"Some of the players were invited to entertain the guests at the Castle," she said. "The rest have gone to the bonfire. Old Meg is drinking herself stupid in the Dead Man's Head. I gave her a florin."

Why was she making it clear to him that they were alone in the place?

"Indeed." His eyes mocked her yet he seemed ill at ease. "And what of that elegant Peg, who showed such a leg, when lately she dressed in men's clothes."

She thumped the table in rage. "So you've heard the latest doggerel. Pray allow me finish it for you: 'A creature uncommon, who's both woman and man. /And the chief of the belles and the beaux.'" She laughed wildly. "Why don't you go back to Chapelizod where you belong? No doubt the Lady Jane has need of you."

"She's dead," he said tonelessly. "So is her son."

"Dead," she whispered.

He rubbed his eyes. "I buried them last week."

This was unreal. "What happened?"

"I found them in bed together. Coupling. Jeremy wasn't right in the head, you know. What they call in my native patch 'one of God's innocents.' I threatened to take him away. We had a scene. She attacked me and I struck her."

Peg looked at him, appalled. "You killed her?"

"Talk sense, for God's sake. A black eye, a bruise. It was the first time I ever raised hands to a woman."

"Then what?"

"In the night she took a boat on the river. In the

morning her maid raised the alarm. We found the two bodies, the boat upturned." He sighed, "I was fond of the boy."

"It must have been an accident."

His face twitched. "She left a letter. The marks on her body would bear witness to my cruelty. A sweet revenge. Buck Whaley, her kinsman, is out for my blood."

"Oh God, no." Peg put her arms round his and held him close. "Don't worry, darling. We'll go away until all this is past. To London, Paris, wherever you wish. No one will blame you."

He could feel the heat of her body under the flimsy gown and suddenly inflamed with desire, he kissed her savagely, forced her down on the floor, lay on her, while she stared at him with those eyes that had bewitched him. He was taking her, not the man she loved but a stranger, riding her brutally, as if he hated her, hated this coupling. She pushed him away and got to her feet, watching helplessly as he buttoned his breeches, his movements jerky, erratic.

"I must get back to Alice." He refused to meet her eyes. "I promised her it wouldn't take long."

"Just long enough to have your pleasure with me. Why did you bother?"

"Forgive me, Peg. I didn't mean to."

Something red exploded before her eyes. She wanted to kill him. Blindly she scrabbled on the dressing-table, fingers closing on a hard lacquered shell with brown and grey markings, his gift, his talisman. He was backing away at the look on her face.

"Please, Peg. Control yourself."

She flung it with all her force, catching him on the cheek. He wiped away blood and went out without another word. She picked up the shell, chipped, stained, and burst into a storm of wild weeping.

In the weeks that followed she was sustained first by anger, then by pride, and when these crutches failed was possessed by a longing, a hunger that gave her no rest. She abased herself, wrote humbly, pitifully, asking him to forgive her. She needed his love. He answered briefly; there was much to be done in connection with the Sandford Estate, of which he was executor and which would pass with the title to a cousin, an elderly don cloistered in Oxford. She comforted herself with the thought that he would return. He always did. He had sworn they were bound together by invisible bonds. To distract her mind, she made plans. They would rent a house outside the city, between sea and mountain. It was magic to walk there of a morning when the tide was far out, over that vast expanse of golden sand. Given time he would quite forget the Lady Jane...Alice Morgan...all that had gone before.

❦

Mrs McEnroe was on a mission for which she had no stomach. In the Woffingtons' kitchen she lowered her bulk into an armchair and demanded to know where was Peg.

Peg emerged from the bedroom at the sound of Mrs McEnroe's voice. Perhaps there was news, a letter?

"I've something for you." Mrs McEnroe's usual cheerful voice was grim. "Mr Coffey and Mrs Morgan were married this morning." She held out a letter. "It's all there."

Peg gripped the back of the chair. Around her the room seemed to swim.

"I don't believe it." She found difficulty getting the words out.

Mrs McEnroe pushed her into a chair and waved at Mrs Woffington to be silent. "Read what it says, Peg."

With trembling fingers Peg broke the seal. She could make nothing of the writing.

"Read," Mrs McEnroe insisted in a firm voice.

She blinked and the words cleared. It's the script of a play, she thought and began to read in a loud, clear voice:

> *Dear Peg,*
>
> *Forgive me for breaking the news to you in this way but everything happened so suddenly that there was no time to explain. Alice and I were married this morning in a quiet ceremony in St Patrick's Cathedral by Dr Delaney, a friend of Dean Swift. We sail by the evening packet to England and plan on spending some time in Bath with my wife's sister and family.*
>
> *Believe me when I tell you that this is not a marriage of passion, nor yet one of convenience. Alice and I are dear and trusted friends, binding ourselves together for companionship, affection. Please try to understand and remember, my dear, that you will always hold a special place in my heart.*
>
> *You bewitched me that night long ago in Daly's Inn, and for a little while I fooled myself we could be happy together. You were such a child, with such impossible dreams. I determined to help. Given time, you will one day become a fine actress. You have the passion, the imagination, above all the drive to succeed. I say this not to comfort you but so that you will see*

*more clearly what is best. I am too old for you,
Peg. A union between two people with such a
difference in age and temperament is doomed to
failure, once passion is spent. You are eager,
greedy for life, for success, as the young mostly
are. Someday you will meet a man who shares
your dreams, your aspirations, and you will make
him happy.*

*There have been ugly rumours in the town
since the Sandford deaths. Whaley has threatened
to kill me. Alice has convinced me of the danger
of delay. But I shall not burden you with my
troubles.*

*And now, my dear, good-bye and God
bless and keep you safe. Remember me most
kindly to your mother and the twins. I shall think
of you always with affection.*

Charles Coffey.

Peg crumpled the letter in her hand. "He's frightened
of what Whaley might do, running scared to England." She
was shaking and her mother was holding her, Mrs McEnroe
forcing whiskey down her throat, asking her was she all
right, was she in trouble. Did Peg know what she meant?

I'm still playacting, Peg told herself and smiled brightly.
"My health is fine, thank you for enquiring."

The veined hand patted hers. "Thank God for that. A
broken heart is easily mended. No man is worth a tear. I
should know. I buried three husbands."

She stumbled away into the bedroom, closing the door
behind her, throwing herself down on the bed. Her heart
was like stone.

❦

By the New Year snow was falling steadily, soundlessly all over Ireland, covering spires and turrets, castles and houses, towns and hamlets, so that it seemed for a little while as if the world were new born and children went mad with delight. Then came the great frost which turned rivers to iron and chilled the marrow. At first Dublin's two theatres, Smock Alley and Aungier Street, made brave attempts to entice an audience, lighting braziers in the pit, lining walls with wool. But as conditions worsened and illness swept Dublin, the actors found themselves playing to empty houses. On the last night of January the curtains came down, candles were quenched, the playhouses were shuttered and actors joined hundreds of citizens with no work, no money, no hope.

Peg took her farewell of Dónal Bán MacLeod at the North Wall where the ship waited to sail with the tide. He had taken passage to Holyhead and would make his way to Edinburgh. A week before, his lover, the burly carpenter, had hanged himself in despair from a beam in the Aungier Street Playhouse, surrounded by the sets he had made. Now there was nothing to keep the young Scotsman with the ginger hair and the sad eyes in a starving city.

"I'll miss you." Peg smiled through her tears. "I never thought to cry for anyone after Charles Coffey but you saved my life. I was tempted to end it."

He hugged her, comforting her as he had done in the past. "It was a pity things turned out as they did. I always admired Mr Coffey."

She remembered the nightmarish days that had followed his letter, when her flux had failed to come, time when she had lain awake knowing she was caught in a trap.

Strange how nothing had come of their hours of ardent passion but that swift savage coupling had resulted in this. Nothing was any good. Not the hell-ride in the broken-down hackney around the Dublin hills, not the gin bath nor the purgatives Mrs McEnroe made her drink. When more than two months had passed she asked Dónal Bán to help. He had given her a draught, a compound of special herbs, never known to fail. Hyssop, fleur-de-luc and an ingredient whose name she forgot.

That night she fell asleep the moment her head touched the pillow, had slept soundly for the first time in weeks, awoken in the early morning gripped in a vice of pain. Mrs McEnroe was there to minister, knew what to expect. She remembered her mother sitting by the fire, praying, Polly peeping around the door, bright-eyed with curiosity, Mrs McEnroe chasing her away, Conor with pity in his great green eyes.

Now months later she was beset by doubts. "Did I do right? At least if I had borne his child I would have had something left, a proof of our love." Dónal Bán's voice was comforting. "What else could you have done and starvation all around you? How could you feed another mouth? Best put it all behind you."

Whistles were blowing, sailors lowering the rope ladder. He kissed her lightly on the lips and was gone without a backward look.

Sails billowed in the sharp west wind, driving the ship slowly downriver, bound for the open sea. She watched and waved until the figure standing on deck was no more than a dot, and then turned back to a city gripped by fear.

1 0

Peg had been out since early morning searching for food. The winter had been the worst in living memory, a bitter spring had been followed by a miserable summer of wind and storm battering the crops into the ground. Now it was autumn, the harvest bad, food scarce and dear, the threat of famine, hunger on the faces of people walking the streets. For almost a year she had struggled to make ends meet, eking out her savings until they were gone. She had nothing left to pawn, no one from whom to borrow. But for the charity of Mrs McEnroe, employed by the Careys at the Dead Man's Head, they might have starved. Her mother had long since given up the ghost; most of the time she sat hugging the fire, talking drearily of time long gone. Sometimes Peg thought she hated the word Lemineagh, was sick of the past, longed only to shake the dust of Dublin from her feet, make her way to London where so many of her fellow actors had gone.

In the High Street the markets were empty but in Goodman's Alley she coaxed a butcher into selling her a marrowbone and a pound of beef. Daylight robbery, she thought bitterly, handing over the reckoning. A milkmaid in Thomas Street stopped to enquire the way to St Stephen's Green. She was on her way back to Buck Whaley's house with supplies; she had come from Chapelizod.

Chapelizod! The name brought back memories she would sooner forget. Isolde's Chapel. Once he had ridden back with such eagerness from the stone-grey mansion to be with her. He had explained that Chapelizod was the corruption of the Irish 'Isolde's Chapel', had told her the story of the star-crossed lovers, Tristan and Isolde. The princess had fallen in love with Tristan because of his voice. He had said that in time we forget names, faces, but the memory of a voice lives for ever.

She pulled herself together; useless to dwell on the past. "I'm one of the quality myself," she lied in her grandest manner, knowing the milkmaid favoured the gentry. "Lady Taafe be name. Me cook and maids are took ill and I'm forced to succour them."

Impressed with such condescension the girl sold her a couple of eggs and filled a can with milk, dropping a square of butter on top, offering to accompany "Her Ladyship home." Peg excused herself and gave a few coppers to two gaunt chairmen to carry her back to George's Lane.

Her mother was dozing in front of the fire when she reached the cottage. Polly had been complaining of vague aches and pains but she seemed somewhat better this morning, though listless. Conor was in bed, running a fever. She wrung out a sponge in cold water and bathed him, then went back into the kitchen to prepare food for the invalids, splitting the marrowbone with a heavy cleaver, adding pot herbs and onions and a few tired carrots. While the soup simmered, she whipped up a posset of milk curdled with wine, egg yolks, cinnamon, pouring the foaming liquid into a glass. Conor swallowed a mouthful, retched, then closed his eyes. In the days that followed he grew worse: a rash covered his body, swelling into raised pimples, then blisters of evil pus. Mrs McEnroe brewed tansy tea and made a two-milk whey; her mother prayed. Nothing was any good. Finally in desperation she sent a neighbouring child for the surgeon. It was midnight before he arrived, a small exhausted man carrying the doctor's silver-topped cane, shabby black bag, tools of his trade. He examined Conor all over and she knew the verdict by the look on his face.

Smallpox! That merciless disease. Those who survived might have no scars or only a few. Others lived blind, deaf, so marked that they might hide their faces, wear a mask to cover the ravages of the disease.

"Your sister and your mother are weak, at risk," he was saying. "They must leave the city. Have you friends, relations who would take them?"

Alas for Máire Rua, for the great house of Lemineagh, the graciousness, the hospitality of her ancestors. All gone, blown away by the winds of fortune, the Mahons, O'Briens and the rest. An old nurse's curse bearing fruit? Or was the cause the plantations that had sent prince and peasant alike scavenging the roads of what was once their land? She thought of her father's people, godly Quaker folk. All dead.

She shook her head. "There is no one."

The doctor made ready to go. "I can give you the name of a farmer's wife who lives just outside the city in Rathfarnham. She will take no one infected. Her charges are high."

"I'll manage." She would borrow from Sam Leadbetter.

The goldsmith charged astronomical rates of interest but she was weary parrying Matt Carey's lecherous overtures. Since she had played the breeches part it sometimes seemed that every man in Dublin considered her fair game.

I'll worry about my debts tomorrow, she thought, when Conor is better, when the weather improves, when the Playhouse re-opens. Dear God, let it be soon, before we are all consigned to the debtors' prison. She would carry the memory of the Marshalsea to her grave. Drabs fighting for the favours of the surly gaolers, rats scampering around the floor, walls dripping with fungus, shit on the floor.

Her mother was dozing in the kitchen. She lowered her voice. "What about Conor? Will he get better?"

"Bathe him to keep the fever at bay." He produced a spill of powder. "Try to get him to swallow this. It will help him rest. He won't last long."

"But he can't die," she said desperately.

"Pray the good God takes him," the doctor said crisply. "If he lives he may curse you for saving his life."

Next morning she saw her mother and Polly off on the coach for Rathfarnham, Polly in tears, her mother protesting "I want to nurse my son."

"Will you do as the doctor ordered? Do you want Polly to die?"

She knew her words sounded brutal but there was no other way. "I'll take good care of Conor. It's best this way. Mrs McEnroe will help. I'll send for you as soon as the sickness has passed." She kissed her mother. Polly turned her face away. The last she saw, they had their arms around each other and were climbing into the coach.

Mrs McEnroe, who had been keeping vigil at Conor's bed in her absence, produced a bottle from her capacious apron pocket. "A drop of whiskey I filched from the Careys."

Peg wiped her face of sweat and dust, and poured out a cupful, swallowing it in one gulp. "I needed that. I heard the banshee cry last night. She follows my mother's family."

"God between us and all harm." Mrs McEnroe made a sign to ward away evil. "Charon the ferryman is waiting to take your brother across the river Styx."

❦

She counted the cathedral chimes. "One, two, three."

Outside the cottage the night-watchman went by, voice calling: "Three o'clock, past three o'clock, and all well."

All was not well. Conor was dying. For twelve hours she had sat by his bedside, moving only to moisten his lips, wipe his forehead bathed in sweat. "I am on fire," he had cried over and over again.

For a little while now he had been quiet, his shallow breathing catching her heart-strings. He was sinking into the shadows, the person she loved best in the world, the gangling thirteen-year-old with his red curls and her own green eyes. She loved his enquiring mind, the quirky restless nature, which she understood. His ambition had always been to travel the world. As soon as he was old enough he had haunted Ringsend, the little fishing village outside the walls of the city, making friends there with sailors, old men who had sailed out on the ship *Ouzel*, more than forty years before. She had been reported missing, all hands lost. Then five years later she had sailed back into the port of Dublin, the crew safe and well, the hold bulging with gold. The story the sailors had to tell caught the imagination of the town. Taken prisoners by pirates on the high seas, they had been forced to man their own ship. After many adventures they had seized their opportunity, mutinied, dealt with their captors and sailed for Irish waters.

Conor's lips were moving. She bent to hear what he was saying:

"Read *Crusoe*, Peg." His voice was no more than a thread.

She got up stiffly from her chair and took down the well-thumbed book from the bedside table. It had been a gift one Christmas from Charles Coffey. Conor knew the story by heart.

"'If ever the story of any man's private adventures in the world were worth making public and were acceptable when published, the Editor of this account thinks this will be so…'" she began.

Conor smiled faintly and she continued: "'The wonders of Robinson Crusoe's life will scarce be believed…'"

❦

It was morning. She was still reading, her throat dry. "'And now to an account of how invaders came, ruining their plantation, and how they fought bravely and were defeated and three of them killed. But thanks to their prayers a storm blew up, destroying the enemy canoes.'"

His face was changing, had grown waxen, his breathing more laboured. His time was running out. Tears blurred the print. She improvised: "Soon after, Crusoe and his Man Friday recovered possession of the plantation, and lived in peace…"

He coughed, and there was a sound of rushing wind from lungs and nostrils, the death rattle; his head lolled to one side. Gently she closed his sightless eyes, kissed him for the last time.

She buried him in the Quaker cemetery near St Stephen's Green, in the grave with his dead father. Would her mother object, say Conor should be buried in consecrated ground in a Catholic plot? She was too tired to think about it. Only let Conor be happy, she prayed. In her mind's eye she saw the ghostly outlines of the *Ouzel*, Conor waving from the deck, and knew he was now sailing uncharted seas bound for the everlasting shores.

In the days that followed she experienced loneliness such as she had never known even when Charles Coffey had gone. She missed her mother, missed Polly, but Conor had been the core of her heart. She longed to lose herself in work but Elrington had fled Dublin like so many others and the Aungier Street Playhouse was dusty, deserted, except for Old Meg, who had made it her home, keeping a family of mice alive with the scraps of food Peg gave her.

She fed the last of the firewood to the dying embers, coals crackling, soot catching fire. A dram of brandy might help ward off a chill. Matt Carey might allow her credit if he was feeling lecherous, except that she was no man's fancy, thin as a rail, eyes circled with strain, lifeless hair. With an effort she got to her feet, pulled her shabby cloak around her shoulders and went out into the lane. In the cottage the chimney roared, belching smoke and flame.

Carey polishing glasses had his ears cocked for the conversation of a couple of pot-bellied customers who were leaning their weight on the counter and discussing a marathon gambling session that was taking place in

Daly's. Peg took her seat in an alcove, allowing the hum of conversation to wash over her. Strange how in times of disaster some still flourished like the green bay leaf. Oh, she would give Carey credit for his rise in the world. He had started life as a pot-boy, bullied, brow-beaten, half starved, until rising forty he had come into his own. His master died of an apoplectic fit and within a month Mattie had married the orphaned Dottie, thin-faced, shrewish and barren. It was a deep disappointment to him that he had no heir to inherit, to make up for the years of deprivation he had endured. Frustrated with Dottie's performance in the marriage-bed he turned to the kitchen slatterns. They bore him no ill-will, leaving when their time was due with a swollen belly and a heavy purse. Dottie made it her business to see that he had no further commerce with them once they had left.

He came over to the alcove where she was huddled beside the oak-beamed fire.

"Give us a kiss," he said.

She steeled herself for his greedy sucking lips, then pushed him away.

"I think I'm sickening for something."

Startled, he shied away. "Is it the pox? You should be home in your bed."

"Get me a punch," she ordered pettishly. An icy wave washed over her, followed by a rush of blood that left her feverish. "Please God, it isn't the pox," she prayed, and waited impatiently until he returned with a steaming beaker and a letter which he threw in her lap.

"Left be the post boy. I hope it means you can pay your debts." Grumbling to himself he shuffled away.

She took a gulp of the punch and examined the letter, recognising the well-formed hand so unlike her illiterate scrawl. Pictures assembled themselves in her mind's eye: the night he had come to Cork, the journey back, making love in the fields, bracken rough to their skin, a goad to their passion. They had travelled through Glendalough. Glen of two lakes. Scent of pine trees, a blackbird hopping across the grass, stabbing the earth with yellow beak. A cave high in the cliff; St Kevin's bed it was called. He had told her the legend. How the beautiful Kathleen had followed the hermit to his bed and, fearing for his chastity, he had thrown her into the lake. No skylarks winging, no young girl singing, only a lone monk brooding on what he had done. He had not thought the world and what followed well lost for love! Inextricably mixed in her mind was another picture. Their cottage, her mother and the twins asleep in bed, her hand in his as they read *Hamlet* by the flickering flames: "There's rosemary, that's for remembrance; pray, love, remember...I would give you some violets, but they withered all when my father died. They say he made a good end..."

She finished the punch, broke open the seal and read.

> *Dear Peg,*
> *This is the last time I shall write to you. It is so long since we met, a year, a lifetime. So much has happened, so many changes. By the time you read this I shall have taken ship for the New World, bound for Philadelphia, where Alice owns a plantation, left her by an uncle. Perhaps we are too old for such a venture but some good Quaker friends are making the journey with us and we are of stout heart.*
>
> *I met Mr Elrington recently in London and he tells me he hopes to re-open the Aungier Street*

Playhouse as soon as conditions improve and expects to revive The Constant Couple *with you in the part of Sir Harry Wildair. If ever you find yourself in London, Mr Rich, Manager of the Covent Garden theatre, is related by marriage to my wife. You have her permission to use her name.*

Remember me most kindly to your mother and Conor and Polly. A letter care of the Governor of the Colony will reach me if ever you need my help. Alice joins with me in sending you loving wishes for your happiness and prosperity, now and for always.

Charles Coffey

Something splintered in her heart. This then was the end. All along she had fooled herself, cherished the hope that some day he would grow tired of Alice Morgan and return to her. Tears filled her eyes and she touched their saltiness with her tongue, sorrowing for the girl she once was, for the dream she had known, for the love she had felt for this man who was weak and well-meaning and had never understood. She remembered sitting on his knee by the fire in his study, that well-loved voice reciting softly into her hair:

If to be absent were to be
Away from thee;
Or that when I am gone
You and I were alone;
Then, my Lucasta, might I crave
Pity from blustering wind, or swallowing wave.

He had put her away abruptly, got up, gone to the window and with his back turned said carelessly: "Richard Lovelace. I admire his poetry."

She shivered. One thing was certain, he was gone as surely as if he lay under the cedar tree in the quiet graveyard alongside her father and Conor. Carefully, methodically, she tore the letter into shreds, letting the pieces drop into the fire, watching the words curl, grow brighter before disintegrating for ever...loving...for always... Philadelphia...Alice.

She straightened her shoulders, rose to her feet and went out into the night. There was no moon, the sky was not dark at all, but shot with crimson like a river of blood. Even before she smelt the acrid ashes on the wind, she knew the cottage was on fire.

ACT II SCENE ii

STANDS A LADY ON THE MOUNTAINS

Stands a lady on the mountains,
Who she is I do not know;
All she wants is gold and silver
And a nice young man to love her.

(Old Dublin children's street game)

11

"**P**eg." A voice called through layers of sleep, pulling her up from a deep safe womb she had no wish to leave. She ignored the hand on her shoulder and snuggled deeper into the pillows.

"Peg," the voice insisted. A smell of fresh coffee, of toasted bread, of bacon filled her nostrils.

"Here's your breakfast," the voice said, sending her thoughts scuttling: flames leaping into the sky, their cottage in ruins. She shivered and pulled herself up in the bed. Mrs McEnroe was opening the shutters, admitting light, showing in strips across the patchwork quilt.

She examined the room. It was small and dusty, with a rickety table on which Mrs McEnroe had deposited the tray, what passed for a dressing-table, a commode and washbasin beside which were a jug of hot water and a towel.

"At least the sun is shining this morning," Mrs McEnroe said, turning around. "Eat up like a good girl. There's a dish of honey. Very nourishing."

Peg took a mouthful of coffee. "Mmm. That tastes good and strong."

"Aye, it will give you strength after what happened."

Peg buttered a slice of toast. "The Careys didn't dare cross you, when you suggested I stay?"

Mrs McEnroe's face creased in a smile. "How could they? Dottie can't boil an egg; Mattie likes pork and onions, and drinks too much, and him with a bad stomach. I cure him with whey, gruel and purgatives. One of these days his gluttony will kill him but until that happens I'm needed here."

Peg sighed. "What in God's name am I going to do?"

"You'll think of something, daughter. As the Good Book says, 'Take no thought for the morrow, for the morrow shall take thought for the things of itself. Sufficient unto the day is the evil thereof.'"

Mrs McEnroe tied the strings of her apron firmly around her ample waist and waddled away.

The bacon was crisp, the egg firm, just as she liked them. "I'll think of what happened when I've eaten something," she told herself. "It's only right to enjoy what Mrs McEnroe has cooked." But the smell of scorched wool and linen still permeated the room and her skin and nails were still black from scrabbling through the ruins of the cottage. Long after the fire had died down she had searched for the embroidered purse the foundling had given her on that day long ago. It had contained her few treasures: a locket holding a few strands of Conor's hair, a luck-penny, the embroidered handkerchief that Lord Darnley had given her that night in the coach. Funny she could scarcely remember his face. And the shell she had thrown at Charles Coffey. She used hold it to her ear, hearing the faint murmur of the sea. He had recited a poem in Irish in which a young man had promised his sweetheart marvellous gifts: gloves made of the skin of a fish, a silver house built on shifting sands, a ship with golden sails. Her heart had gone out to the nameless young poet with his impossible dreams.

She couldn't lie there brooding. There was work to be done, plans to be made. In a fever of anxiety she jumped out of bed, stripped off, washed face, body, hair, thankful for the hot water, the towels, the soap scrubbing away grit, cinders.

She sat by the open window drying her hair. "Rapunzel, Rapunzel, let down your gold hair."

In the lane Matt Carey's customers of the evening before were deep in conversation, their words drifting up, still discussing the marathon gambling session in Daly's. They had little to worry them, she thought sourly. Patrick Taafe's name was mentioned... gambling with Dashwood who had come over from London. Naturally he would have to be in the thick of it! Then, like a bolt from the blue, came the solution. She would seek Taafe out, become his tally woman, his whore, whatever he liked to call it. What did it matter now? Beggars couldn't be choosers.

She examined herself in a fly-streaked mirror, pinching her cheeks, biting her lips, longed for a pot of rouge, a fine gown, velvet shoes. Máire Rua had dressed in a blue silk gown, silver pendant nestling seductively between breasts, lace at neck and sleeve, when she set out to seduce the Cromwellian general. Every detail of that journey had been preserved in the folklore of her mother's family.

She borrowed half a guinea from Mrs McEnroe, promising repayment before the day was done, and set out for a second-hand clothes shop in Francis Street where the quality sold their cast-offs.

Enthusiastically the shopkeeper laced her up in a most appropriate green velvet gown with matching shoes. Who would see the ragged shift she wore underneath? She wasn't going to lie with Taafe in Daly's Inn. He could take her to the Honey Vale. Being mistress of that lovely house would make up in some way for giving herself to a man for whom she had no love, no tenderness. Anyhow, she was finished with love. She would insist on her mother and Polly joining them. She would employ Mrs McEnroe as housekeeper.

The shopkeeper produced rouge, kohl, powder and helped her paint her face, arrange her hair in fashionable curls, boasting the while of her own successes.

"I was lucky my gentleman set me up in this business. Times are hard, even the gentry are forced to sell their best gowns and fripperies. Later, when things improve, I'll make a killing." She affixed a beauty patch at the corner of Peg's mouth. "An invitation to kiss. I hope your assignation goes well."

For two days and two nights a gambling session had been in progress in Daly's. Buck Whaley was there, as were Henry Loftus, Earl of Ely, known as Lucky Loftus, Sir Francis Dashwood, a member of the Medmenham Monks, a satanic sect who held their black rites in the ruins of Medmenham Abbey in Buckinghamshire, and Patrick Taafe. When the liveried servant announced that a lady awaited the Honourable Mr Taafe's pleasure, he got up at once, glad of a respite.

Peg, warming her hands before the fire in an anteroom, was shocked by the sight of his pallid face, the coat stained with wine, his stock awry. She dimpled. "Are you glad to see me?"

"God's truth, you are the last person I expected," he said. "I was sure it was the Lady Arabella Fitzsimons back from London, good for a loan."

He held her out, feasting his eyes on her face and figure. "You are a sight for sore eyes, darling, in this benighted town where every second person is in rags."

"Dublin is so dull since they closed the theatre," she pouted. "I declare I am bored."

"You missed me, sweetheart?"

She smiled provocatively. "I have a fancy to sleep in your grandmother's room. I've never forgotten how lovely it is."

He ran his tongue around his lips. "I'd sell my soul to be there with you this minute but I can't leave town."

"Why ever not?" She wasn't really listening to the story of his hard luck; she had heard it all before. "I want you to do me a little favour," she interrupted. "I'm temporarily short of money. Leadbetter has my stock and valuables but he's left Dublin on business and I'm in something of a tizzy. Lady Ely—you know what a jade she is—demands that I settle my debts at cards." She dimpled. "All I need is fifty guineas—no, better make it a hundred."

He groaned. "I told you, I'm cleared out. I owe thirty thousand at the tables and the estate is mortgaged."

"Even twenty guineas," she heard herself pleading.

"I couldn't lend you fifty pence, m'dear."

She burst into tears. It wasn't all acting. "Our cottage was burnt to the ground last night; everything I ever owned is gone. Conor died of the smallpox and I was forced to send my mother and Polly away. I owe money to Matt Carey and Sam Leadbetter, I even borrowed from Mrs McEnroe to buy this second-hand finery." Savagely she rent her gown.

"If you came to me in rags, sweetheart, it would make no difference." He caught her up in his arms. "Don't worry, pet. I'll send word to Lady Fitzsimons. She's as ugly as sin but rich as Croesus. Once let her get wind of the word that I'm willing and she'll be over hotfoot."

She could feel his prick hard against her and pulled away.

"You are a fool and a failure, Patrick Taafe," she said in a passion. "God's truth, if I were a man I swear I'd go into that gaming room and sweep the boards."

He started to laugh and she lashed out at him in her rage.

"Listen to me, Peg." He caught her fists, held them in an iron grip. "You've given me an idea. Whaley has arranged a gambling session tonight in Squire Connolly's lodge."

"The Hellfire Club," she shuddered. "Where you expect to recoup your losses. I don't want to hear any more."

"For Christ's sake, listen. I'll wager Whaley that a lady will suddenly materialise in our midst. It's an unwritten rule that no female crosses the threshold of the lodge. Old Nick swears he can smell women a mile off. Like his master, Whaley, he hates your sex."

"I'll not hear any more of your crazy schemes." She was shouting and he was ordering her to keep her voice down. "All you have to do is wear the breeches. Dress up as Sir Harry Wildair. I'll introduce you as my nephew, Peter, lately arrived from London. Whaley likes them young and fresh. Then we'll reveal all, collect the winnings and I'll take you home."

"The whole of town saw me play Wildair." He was driving her mad with his talk.

"Whaley has never been known to put a foot inside the

Playhouse. He has no interest in actresses. He wouldn't know you from his washerwoman."

"And what of the rest?"

"Ely is a sportsman. He'll be glad to see Whaley bested."

"And what about Dashwood? He's a known satanist. It's common gossip he poisoned five wives."

Taafe smiled grimly. "Dashwood may have his quirks and fancies but he believes in neither God nor the devil."

She knew she was insane to listen to him but things were desperate and the gamble just might pay off. "What if they rape me?"

"Whaley's too depraved for such simple pleasures, my pet." His blue eyes had the look of a gambler willing to stake his soul in the hope of a win. "I might borrow more. Raise the stakes. Two hundred guineas at ten to one. It would net us two thousand. God's guts, Whaley will be the laughing-stock of the town when word gets around."

Her lips trembled. "Will you promise to take me away the moment the wager is paid?"

"Will you promise to lie with me at least once before the bell tolls for me?"

She softened. "Don't talk like that. When all this is over we'll plan something. Maybe we'll go to America."

"I'd go to hell and back with you," he said, hugging her so fiercely that she was sure every bone in her body would break.

She borrowed the Wildair costume from Old Meg in the Playhouse, fabricating a story of how she had been bidden attend Ely House to entertain the company for supper. Later when Mrs McEnroe appeared with a tray in the attic room she was told of the wager.

"Don't do anything foolhardy, daughter," the old woman pleaded. "Eat up the soup and the breast of chicken. I smuggled you up a glass of Mattie's port. It will give you strength for what's before you."

"Everything will be all right," Peg promised, her heart beating fast. "After tonight I'll have plenty of money for all of us. I'll slip out later, when it's dark. Try and keep the Careys occupied around ten o'clock. They must never know."

Mrs McEnroe's usually cheerful face was grim. "As the Good Book sayeth: 'Be sober, be vigilant; because your adversary the devil walketh about, seeking whom he may devour.'"

Peg crossed herself superstitiously. "It's the hunger that has changed us all," she thought. "That and poor Conor's death."

She was dressed and ready, with breeches, shirt, embroidered waistcoat, great coat, wig and sword, when the cathedral clock struck ten, the hour appointed. Making sure the coast was clear, she ran down the stairs. From the dining-room came voices, the clatter of dishes, Mrs McEnroe singing tunelessly.

A coach was waiting at the top of the lane, the ancient driver wrapped in a frieze coat, caubeen pulled well down over his eyes. Grumbling under his breath, he dismounted, turned down the folding steps and waited impatiently while she got in. Then without another word he resumed his perch, whipped the horses and they were away. Past Dublin Castle, turning into Bride Street, past the fashionable church that gave the street its name. A drunken student stood at a corner of Patrick's Close, swinging the great iron key of his room, looking for a fight. The cathedral was in darkness. From out the lanes and alleyways figures shuffled their way to the deanery, carrying pitchers and basins for their nightly ration of broth, their flittery rags whipped by the night wind. As a child her father had taken her to the harvest festival and she had listened to Dean Swift, beak-nosed, stern as the eagle carved on the pulpit, charging that the town was full of idlers who pretended to be more wretched than they were. "I have seen them pour their pitchers of good broth in the gutter," he shouted. "They sell their clothes, for their rags are part of the tools with which they work. What they crave is strong drink." Times were different now. People were really starving and the dean half mad with deafness and fits of vertigo.

Wearily she closed her eyes and when she looked again they were passing through the pleasant village of Harold's Cross. Before them was the road to Rathfarnham, after that the hard pull to Bohernabreena, Road of the Hostels, where a pagan king had ridden to his doom. "Great the slaughter, ravens sating themselves with the blood of the murdered king."

Why did the legend haunt her? The journey was no more than a jape. It would soon be over, and she and Pat Taafe would enjoy the reward. Far below lay the city, noisy, uneasy, familiar. Children playing a street game "Stands a lady on the mountains, who she is I do not know." Looms thudding, clocks chiming, bird and chicken squawking, watchmen armed with bills and lanterns crying out, "Ten o'clock, past ten o'clock and a fine night." Comforting everyday sounds she was used to. Here amid the dark hills all was different. Rattle of coach-wheels on stony roads, menacing command of a highwayman, "Stand and deliver."

All the stories she had ever heard of the Hellfire Club flooded her mind. In a panic she tugged at the door of the coach, shouting hysterically to the driver to turn back. A gust of wind screamed down the mountains, the door slammed in her face and she fell to the floor. By the time she picked herself up the coach had stopped and before it could start up again she was out, jumping, wrenching her ankle. She thought she heard the driver call out, "Journey's end" but his voice was carried away by the wind, a branch of mountain ash flew by, striking the horses into a frenzy, and the last she saw was the coach swaying crazily from side to side down the mountain path.

"God damn that fool of a driver and all his kind," she swore roundly, "that he may feel the bite of Pat Taafe's whip across his back."

Feeling the better for her outburst, she took stock of her surroundings. Some little distance off a grey building squatted on top of a hill.

Montpelier Lodge! Resolutely she put the other name it bore out of her mind and began the climb. As she toiled upwards, the wind dropped as suddenly as it had risen and the moon broke free of its moorings to sail overhead, lighting up the countryside for miles around. To the east were the peaks of Kilmashogue and behind them the Three Rock and the Two Rock mountains. Beyond that again was Tibradden and the dense wood of Glendoo. Northwards a ribbon of water snaked its way over Kippure and down the dips and valleys to join the river Dodder at Rathfarnham which ran its course through small villages to enter the sea at the little fishing village of Ringsend.

She touched her sword like a talisman, straightened her wig, squared her shoulders. The sooner this business was finished the better.

If Máire Rua could face General Ireton, that dread Cromwellian, with equanimity, she would not be overawed by a coterie of gamblers, bullies, painted fops who had allowed horror stories to circulate about their doings to frighten the natives. What were they after all but a crowd of hell-raisers?

She beat a sharp rat-tat on the door, which was opened at once by an old man holding a candle aloft. His eyes had the vacant stare of an idiot child and a dribble of spit ran down his chin. Without a word he beckoned her to enter and she found herself in a dark passage. Gritting her teeth, she followed him up a flight of uncarpeted steps. Floorboards creaked, a bat flew in her face, the wavering light of the candle threw grotesque shadows on the wall.

At the end of a stone passage the old man knocked and then opened the door, and she found herself in a room so brightly lit that it dazzled her eyes. A great fire of pine and apple wood blazed in an open hearth. Portraits of Tudor ladies in court dress, gentlemen in hose and ruffed jackets, lined the walls. Sconces of candles were set on a table where a robed figure sat with bowed head. Gathering her courage, she stepped forward and bowed formally.

"I am here at the invitation of the Honourable Patrick Taafe. Lord Peter Butler, at your service." In spite of herself, her voice quavered and she thought, Hell and damnation, where is the fool?

"We were expecting you, Mistress Woffington." The voice was so mild that it took her a moment to realise that he knew of her identity.

"Then the charade is over." She made her voice purposely bright. "If you would be so good as to declare yourself."

He raised his head and she found herself gazing into little eyes lost in a mound of fat.

"Sir Francis Dashwood at your service," he said quietly. Despite the heat of the room, her blood froze. This was the head of the Medmenham Monks, satanist, poisoner, murderer. With an effort she brought out, "I was expecting Mr Taafe."

"You will meet him presently." His little mouth creased

in a smile. He took her hand in his cold slimy fingers, slugs crawling over her skin.

"Don't upset yourself, m'dear. The wager will be honoured in good time but first you must make some recompense for your little prank."

He tittered, and Peg knew a moment of blind panic when she wanted to turn tail, to run from the horror before her to the safety of the dark night, to hide herself behind a boulder, in some wretched cabin, anything to escape the evil that permeated the lodge. But she was rooted to the spot.

Was it her imagination or were the eyes growing larger, protruding? He rose and, going to a cupboard, filled a beaker with some wine. "You will drink a toast."

She wanted to refuse but the words stuck in her throat. Her hand trembled as she raised the goblet to her lips, wine staining her lace cravat and coat: "...ravens sating themselves with the blood of the murdered king."

She was on fire, hammers beating in her head, the room spinning crazily around, breaking up. She closed her eyes as the ground rose up to meet her.

❦

She was out of her body, suspended in air, looking down on a small, fat figure bent over a naked woman spread on a cruciform table which was covered with a black cloth. Black candles flickered and the idiot acolyte waved a censer. Monkish figures were prostrate before the altar, before the terrible rite of the black mass. The satanic priest raised a chalice and drank, then kissed the breasts, the genitals of the naked woman, cold serpent's tongue, drawing her back into her body. In the candlelight something glinted. His penis was swollen, ringed with spikes. He was mounting her and she braced herself for the thrust, and was filled with such pain, revulsion, that she screamed, went on screaming, though she made no sound.

A hooded figure watched through a drugged mist. Insanely the old servant giggled, swung the censer in a circle, loosing coals that perfumed the air, burned the vestments, the altar cloth. Above her the satanic priest moved, took a candle, set fire to the acolyte's hair, turning flesh and bones into a burning torch. A scream of agony ended in a sobbing wail and the room was filled with the horrifying stench of burning flesh. Patrick Taafe, shocked sober, jumped up, knocking over chairs and kneeling figures in his frenzied dash to where Peg lay. She saw his wild eyes and glistening forehead as he gathered her up in his arms. After that she remembered no more.

Aeons later she swam back to life. Time and space seemed to whirl away until they were no more than pinpoints of light on the ceiling. She was lying on a narrow cot in a room with whitewashed walls. Watching over her was an old peasant woman and a soberly dressed man.

She tried to concentrate, couldn't hold the thread of her thoughts. On the bedside table a candle dripped grease, reminding her of something that had happened but she was too muzzy to remember.

"Go to sleep," a voice ordered, and obediently she closed her eyes, slipping back into the darkness, falling, down, into a bottomless pit.

She was wandering along the streets, bone weary, crying desolately, looking for something she couldn't find. She longed to lie down but some force drove her on. She was on a mountain. Demon birds were attacking her, driving their bills like knives into her private parts. The old peasant woman swam in and out of her nightmare, giving her drinks, changing her shift, sodden with sweat. She was happy once more, walking the roads hand in hand with Charles Coffey. He felt her pulse and said, "She's coming around. The worst is over."

She opened her eyes. Outside the window the sun was shining and she felt better but infinitely weary. The watchers were still at her bedside.

"Who are you?" she whispered.

"I am a doctor," a voice reassured her.

"How long have I been ill?"

"Two weeks."

"Where am I?"

"In a cottage in the Dublin hills."

The nightmare was returning; dark hair on his fat hands, evil eyes that hypnotised her, the shameful things that had been done to her body. "I want my mother," she wept. "I want to go home." She remembered the cottage had been burned to the ground and desolation engulfed her.

The doctor wiped her face with a towel. "Everything will be all right. Your mother is safe in the farmhouse in Rathfarnham with your sister. Money has been sent for their keep. Soon you will be reunited. Try not to worry. Go to sleep."

In the days that followed, the doctor paid frequent visits to the cottage, examining her, muttering words of encouragement. But it was the old peasant woman who nursed her, making the bed, emptying slops, bringing broth and egg-flips laced with wine, herbal drinks brewed in a little black pot on a turf fire. She was dumb and understood only Irish, but by signs Peg learned that she was a widow, her family scattered, her only wish to own a cow. Her skin was dry as yellow parchment and she smiled showing toothless gums but her hands were soft and gentle, and slowly Peg recovered her strength.

❧

She was dressed in a dark worsted gown and bodice, given her by the old woman, waiting for the doctor who was arriving on horseback to see her for the last time.

"I have arranged for a farmer to take you in his cart to Rathfarnham to join your mother," he said in his precise tones. She nodded assent and he produced a purse of sovereigns. "I understand there was a wager. These are your winnings."

She pushed the bag away. "I don't want their money."

He said soberly: "You cannot afford to refuse what was hardly earned. You must get away and soon."

"First tell me what happened to Pat Taafe?" she said faintly. The question had haunted her for days.

"He was found dead on the mountainside."

"What happened? I demand to know."

The doctor rubbed his chin. "Maybe it is better that you should. There was a duel, I understand. Sir Francis Dashwood and others were implicated. Mr Taafe was dead when I saw him."

Tears of weakness filled her eyes. "Poor Patrick. He thought he could somehow outwit them."

"Try not to dwell on the past."

She took up the purse, let the gold pieces fall through her fingers. "I must recompense you for your care."

"You owe me nothing. I was well paid."

She summoned a smile. "You were very kind; but for you I might have died."

He looked out the half-door of the cottage at the gentle hills. "Strange how nature can change."

Her mouth was dry. "What are you trying to tell me?"

"Your womb was lacerated. I asked no questions. It would have served no purpose. The damage was done before my services were sought. You will never bear a child."

His words slid away, meant nothing. She wondered how much he guessed, what she had revealed in her delirium.

As if he could read her thoughts he said, "My daughter lives in London. She writes and tells me that the Covent Garden theatre is putting on a season of Shakespeare. I'm sure you will do well on the London stage." He picked up his black bag and bowed. "Good-bye, my dear, and good fortune. A word of advice. Keep the details of your ordeal to yourself. Don't give the old woman gold. She has been paid with a cow, which is what she most needs."

He was gone and Peg was filled with an immense gratitude for the man who for a time had been her only link with the outside world and of whom she knew nothing, not even his name.

On her return to Dublin she paid a visit to Faulkner's printing house and combed back numbers of the journal until she had found the item she sought, headed: Mysterious Fire in Montpelier Lodge in the Dublin Mountains.

The story went on to describe how Squire Connolly's hunting-lodge in the Dublin Mountains, known locally as the Hellfire Club, had been gutted by a mysterious fire. No one knew the cause, though local people described seeing the devil on the rooftop as flames enveloped the building. Not that anyone gave credence to the folklore of ignorant peasants, the writer concluded. On the back page of the paper, a brief notice informed the reading public that the body of the Honourable Patrick Taafe, the well-known sportsman, had been found in a field in Rathfarnham. Foul play was not suspected. There was no mention at all of Sir Francis Dashwood.

For a long time she sat lost in thought. In her mind's eye she saw a fair-haired young horseman cantering down a dusty road in the Honey Vale, remembered how for an instant a shadow had blotted out the sunshine of that summer day and the words of Macbeth's witches had drummed in her ears:

By the pricking of my thumbs,
Something wicked this way comes.

He had been foolish, reckless. There had been no wickedness in him but coming events had cast their long shadow, though she was not to know then.

Had her heart been free when they first met would the story have ended differently? Somehow she didn't think it would. Gambling had been his passion, was in his blood, was stronger than the love he might feel for any woman. Had he died needlessly or was there somewhere a lesson to be learned? They were questions to which she might find an answer some day.

"Rest in peace, my dear," she prayed, and that night in bed she wept healing tears and no nightmares came to haunt her dreams.

❧

Within a week she had made her plans, settled the score with Sam Leadbetter and Matt Carey, rented an apartment for her mother and Polly in Aungier Street, invested a substantial amount in Le Fanu's Bank in College Green, sufficient to give them an income, and set a sum aside for Mrs McEnroe's needs.

"I'm grateful, child, but you are too extravagant," Mrs McEnroe chided her at their parting.

"I'm lucky." Peg lifted her chin as if to defy fate. "Shakespeare said it better for me: 'There was a star danced, and under that I was born.'"

Was it true, she wondered. So much disappoint-ment, so many tribulations. The price had been high, yet she had endured. She knew that courage, determination would see her through. Let the morrow come. She and hers would survive, come what may.

ACT III

LONDON, DUBLIN
1740–1743

If we do meet again, why, we shall smile!
If not, why then, this parting was well made.

(Julius Caesar, V, i)

1 2

He sat on the steps of the painted caravan, a lithe, brown-eyed, brown-haired young man, half listening to the gypsy's low voice, as she read Sam Johnson's hand, distracted by the sounds and sights all around him: intermittent colloquy of dogs, screams of children, clatters of spoons as an old crone with long grey streels of hair dished out tin plates of stew from a great iron pot, ribald laughter of men as scarlet-skirted girls whirled and turned cartwheels to the music of a fiddler, whose head was bound with a yellow handkerchief.

They had sighted the camp across a field and, tantalised by the smell of rabbit and bacon stew, had decided on the spur of the moment to trade their mare for supper, a bed for the night and a shilling to take them the rest of their journey. It had been a wise decision, he thought. They had taken it in turns to ride the mare for most of their journey but she was a bad-tempered beast which threw them whenever the road rose or a stone caught in her hoof or she sighted another of her kind. As they assured each other, it was a relief to be rid of her.

"You come from a city of spires," the gypsy was telling

the heavily built man, his face creased in a tolerant smile.

"Aye, you could call Lichfield that," Johnson agreed.

"You have a good heart which rules your head," she said peering intently at his hand. "You will live by the pen and become one of the best-known men in London; yet you will never know riches. Your wife whom you have for the time left behind is a much older woman." Johnson was impressed in spite of himself and David Garrick removed his gaze from a dark-eyed nubile girl who was ogling him from under her shawl, to examine this other bird of plumage, with her bright shawls and beads, as she made her divinations. His friend looked like a confirmed bachelor who never gave a woman as much as a second glance but he was very susceptible. As if she could read Garrick's thoughts the gypsy prodded him in the ribs. "Sit up, young man, and let me read what's in store for you. It's not often I meet your kind."

Amused by the sharpness of her tone, Garrick held out his hand. With a crooked nail she traced the line of fate. "You were born under a lucky star, young master. You will know power and fame and mix with the greatest in the land and when you die you will be buried with kings."

Garrick grinned. "Tell me more and you shall have my lucky sixpence."

"You are a man of some passion and will fall in love with a red-haired girl, but in the end you will marry for power, though the union will be a happy one."

"And how shall I make my fortune, old mother?"

"In the way you least expect. You will change your way three times and the final road will bring you riches and acclaim. You are a man of many moods and in your life you will play many parts."

"Tell me about the girl I am fated to love."

She threw away his hand in disgust. "Bah, what is love to one such as you! A red-haired wench with green eyes and a secret past she will never share. It will cast a shadow between you."

"'Love is not love which alters when it alteration finds,'" Garrick said glibly. He prided himself on his memory and was wont to air his knowledge of Shakespeare. It was a habit Sam Johnson deplored.

"'Men have died from time to time, and worms have eaten them, but not for love,'" the gypsy cackled, startling him with her knowledge. "My people travelled the roads with the strolling player who penned these lines in the days when Drake the pirate ruled the seas and saved England for Elizabeth the virgin." She got to her feet and Garrick saw to his surprise that she was immensely tall. With her black hair coiled in snakes around an ageless face, she might have been Medusa or in another light Prospero's daughter, Miranda, in *The Tempest*. "I have told you enough. It is time you began to tread the road that destiny has marked out for you." It was uncanny, he thought, even her voice had changed: it was that of a young girl.

It had taken the two men most of the month of August to cover the distance from Lichfield to where they were now, one hundred and twenty miles as the crow flies. They had been in no hurry, content to explore the countryside through which they were passing, to gossip with people who seldom journeyed more than a few miles from their homes.

Though they had started out with no more than a couple of shillings between them, they had not gone hungry. David Garrick was a born raconteur, with a captivating manner which he used with such effect on maidservants and housewives, that they were seldom without a meal or a place to lay their heads. Sam Johnson, heavily pock-marked and with the gait and bearing of a man older than his thirty years, was of a more serious turn of mind. Scholars and country squires they met on their journey relished his company and were only too willing to be hospitable to a man with whom they could intelligently discuss literature and the politics of the day. Garrick was equally at home with itinerant tradesmen and farm labourers, trading bawdy jokes, scandals and ghost stories. All in all it had been a summer they would not easily forget.

Dawn had scarcely broken when they left the encampment and crossed the fields to meet the London road running by the Thames. This was the most exciting stretch of the journey, thronged as it was with people from all arts and parts, sailing by in barges and boats, cantering along on horses, travelling on Shanks's mare. Leathery men, tanned by wind and rain, carried butter and corn from Suffolk; fresh-faced milkmaids from Cheshire, with proud straight carriages, balanced cheeses on their heads; boys with keen blue eyes and the look of the sea carted barrels of herrings from the fishing fleets at Yarmouth. On the outskirts of the city they came upon a red-cheeked woman respectable in bonnet and homespun skirt, as she sat on a flat stone lacing up her boots. She had driven her flock of turkeys, barefooted, all the way from Norfolk. A young girl rounded up wandering geese; bright-eyed children marshalled chickens and hens; hard-faced drovers from places as far away as the Scottish highlands prodded herds of weary cattle. All the dairy produce, the livestock, the mounds of fresh fruit and vegetables, would find their way to one of the four great London markets: Leadenhall, Newgate, St James's, Covent Garden. Everyone knew that

London was growing, sprawling out, that her demand for food and drink and everything else was well nigh insatiable. It was a place where a man with his wits about him might make a good living; a rogue engaged in sharp practice might net a quick fortune and lose it just as easily on cards and dice; and a young lad, new to the city, could all too easily find himself penniless and mother-naked because of the wiles of some painted whore. London was no place for the meek, the mild or the credulous.

Garrick who, eager for his first glimpse of the city and avid for a sight of the guildhalls, the shopping arcades, the royal palace of St James at Westminster where the king held court, had been striding along became suddenly aware that for some time now he had been talking to himself. Sam Johnson plodding along behind was in another world, walking the lime avenues of the cathedral town where he had been born and bred. Lichfield with its timbered and brick houses and well-stocked gardens was a town that had been taken and retaken many times during the years of the civil wars. Old Mr Johnson had kept a bookshop in the Market Square and when he died, his only son, with no head for business, had sold the shop and opened a school. David Garrick had been Sam Johnson's first pupil. Mr Walmesley, the town clerk, had been a friend both of the Johnson family and of the Garricks. He was a portly good-hearted widower with a bulbous nose, a tidy fortune and an interest in the law. When Mr Garrick, a recruiting officer on half pay, had died after a lengthy illness, Mr Walmesley had settled the sum of £100 on young David on condition that he go to London and enrol at the Inns of Kings. A solicitor in Threadneedle Street would see to his needs. David had been only too happy to oblige, and had set off without a backward glance. At times like this, he wondered had he been selfish in persuading Sam to close down the school and accompany him on his travels. He sat on a tuft of grass waiting for his companion to catch up. "Homesick for the schoolmastering?" he asked affectionately punching Sam's arm.

Johnson smiled thinly. "There mark what ills the scholar's life assail; toil, envy, want, the patron and the jail." He always seemed to speak in quotations even when the words were his own. He continued, "No, I was tired of beating knowledge into wooden heads. I would fain leave my mark upon literature." Exuberantly Garrick jumped over a puddle of water. "And I should like to become Lord Chief Justice of England. What was it the gypsy promised us? Riches and fortune for me, a girl with red hair and green eyes, the pen for you," he chuckled. "Strange how she knew about Tetty."

Johnson scratched his wig. "Did it surprise you, Davy, when I made up my mind to wed with Mistress Elizabeth?"

Garrick stopped dead in his tracks and was almost run down by an irate coachman. "I thought you had taken leave of your senses, Sam. She must be a score of years older than you."

"Aye that she is but a comfortable body, handsome too."

"But what possible reason can you have for taking such a step?"

"Think of it like this," Johnson said drily. "Marriage has many pains, but celibacy has no pleasures."

Garrick hooted. "Does she realise that you have ambitions to be a writer and have a mind above money."

"Don't be a fool, Davy. No man but a blockhead ever wrote except for money."

❦

More than six years had elapsed since Peg had seen London and the city was greatly changed: new buildings were going up everywhere; there were redcoats at every corner drumming up recruits. Moonfaced yokels new to the city, mere youngsters gathered around the recruiting officers like flies around a honey pot, dazzled by the offer of the king's shilling and the promise of adventure. By now half of Europe was caught up in the War of the Austrian Succession and England needed every man she could muster to the colours. A strumpet in a low-cut gown swayed past, clutching the arm of an elderly gallant and talking volubly in a Dublin accent. She might have been Margaret Leeson who had, no doubt, survived the Irish famine with no hardship to herself, and was probably this very minute entertaining clients from the Dublin garrison in her bawdy house. Her sort always made out.

At the stage-coach "set down" she engaged a hackney to carry her to Bull Alley which was even gloomier than she remembered. Sarah Pepys had changed greatly, grown scrawny and wrinkled with the years, her cheap flamboyance of earlier days replaced by a high-necked gown and a dusty wig. She peered short-sightedly at her visitor. "And who is this fine lady come to lodge with me? Do I know you, ma'am?"

Peg's heart sank. "Of course you do. I'm Peg Woffington. I stayed with you as a child."

Sarah Pepys simpered. "Why I do declare. How could I forget. Many's the time I've cried myself sick with loneliness for you. Let me give you a hug I'm that overjoyed to see you and you so prosperous I'm sure with a trunk full of fine things."

Tactfully Peg disengaged herself as best she could. She knew Sarah Pepys of old, doubted if the old woman had given her a second thought in the intervening years. Mr Quinn was different. She had retained a soft spot for the old actor who had taught her so much in the early years. When she mentioned his name, Sarah Pepys wept into her petticoats. "Poor Mr Quinn is no longer with me. It was the spirits that got him."

"Was it whiskey or gin?" Peg asked, surprised. "I had thought him a wine imbiber. I often heard him say he had the palate but not the purse for a good claret."

Sarah Pepys said huffily. "Lud, how you run on! Looking for guidance he was. There was a part, you understand, in the Playhouse. Mr Quinn as you will recall had a voice like velvet. There were rivalries, jealousies, feuds..." her voice quavered.

"And then what happened?"

"I held a sitting and called up a guide I know but a young fellow hanged for sheep-stealing came through instead. The wretch advised Mr Quinn to challenge his rival to a duel. Instead of accepting the glove as a gentleman should, the pesky actor pushed Mr Quinn into the river. The altercation took place in a tavern at London Bridge."

Peg was torn between laughter and tears. "Poor Mr Quinn. I liked him well. All the same, Sarah Pepys, you must take a share of the blame. You should know it's dangerous dealing with the occult."

"It was all the fault of that young demon," Sarah Pepys said mulishly. "They say the spirits like nothing better than the death of a human being."

Peg shrugged in disbelief.

"You'd be afraid of a ghost if you saw one," Sarah Pepys said, pushing her into the dingy kitchen.

"Ghosts if they do exist are harmless," Peg said vehemently. "It's the living we should fear." She spoke with such depth of feeling that Sarah Pepys's curiosity was aroused. "Tell me, did you have a sighting or what?"

"Never mind." She opened a bottle of whiskey. "I brought this from Dublin. It was to have been a present for Mr Quinn. We'll drink to his shade."

"Amen to that," Sarah Pepys said happily, holding out her glass and raising her skirts to warm her shins which were already mottled and scorched with heat. "Lud, sweetheart, you look that handsome in your fine cloak and gown," she said expansively, holding out her glass for a refill. "Did you come in for a fortune or what?"

Peg didn't bother to answer. Mr Quinn was the only reason she had come to Bull Alley. Looking around the dirty kitchen, with its decaying food, flies, unwashed dishes, cockroaches scuttling around the floor, she knew it had been a mistake. She could have engaged a decent room in Buttons Inn for what Sarah Pepys would demand. The journey from Dublin had left her exhausted, a week of heavy seas followed by six days on the road, often forced to sleep six to a bed in coaching inns, to fight off groping hands, bloodthirsty bugs. "If you will show me to my room," she said faintly, "I should like to wash and unpack."

Sarah Pepys led the way to the apartment formerly occupied by Mr Quinn. Once the best in the house it was now sadly in need of repair. It presented a picture of damp walls, broken furniture, chipped basins, a chamberpot that slopped over. A whey-faced child came scurrying up the stairs at the sound of her mistress's voice. "I warned you to clear this room," Sarah Pepys yelled. "You'll mend your ways or I'll take the skin off your backside with a flogging."

She flopped down on the bed. "Go and fetch a pasty

from Old Ginnie's stall. Tell her we don't want no horsemeat." She ran a pointed tongue around her lips.

Peg threw the child a couple of coins. "Buy three mutton pies. You look as if a square meal wouldn't hurt you."

Sarah Pepys lay fanning herself, panting for breath. "Lud, my heart ain't good. I took that young slut from a charity school but she's more trouble than she's worth. I'll make her dance to my tune, I warrant."

"Not while I'm paying the piper. It would be more to the point if you stirred yourself and fetched clean sheets and a warming pan. The place reeks of damp."

Sarah Pepys paused uncertainly at the door. "If you could let me have a trifle in advance. Times are hard since Mr Quinn went over to the other side."

"How much is the reckoning?" Everything had changed for the worse. The Sarah Pepys of the blowsy manner of dressing and the heedless optimism was much preferable to the querulous old woman time and hardship had made her. She hawked and spat on the floor. "Seeing as how we're old acquaintances, not to say friends; seeing as how I was mother to you when Violante deserted you; seeing as how I fed and clothed you..."

"For God's sake cut the cackle. What are you asking?"

"Half a sovereign including a home-cooked breakfast and a meat dinner prepared by myself," Sarah Pepys said sullenly.

"You who never cooked a meal in your life! I doubt me you know how to boil an egg." Peg tossed the landlady a crown. "That's all you'll get for the length I am likely to stay."

She had travelled sensibly in a drugget skirt and warm cloak, but put them aside next morning for something more fitting an actress in search of employment. Before leaving Dublin she had purchased the wardrobe of a grand lady in the second-hand shop in Francis Street she frequented. Shaking out silk petticoats, gowns, a moth-eaten fur which filled the room with the mingled odour of stale sweat and stale perfume, she promised herself that when she had established herself she would give the lot to Sarah Pepys and have a seamstress make her a wardrobe of new clothes. She decided to treat herself to breakfast in Buttons Inn where they served good coffee and hot rolls. She enquired about Billy off the serving maids and was rewarded with blank looks. It was as if the pot-boy, once the talk of the town, had never existed.

Covent Garden was heady with autumn smells, damp clay, fresh vegetables and the overpowering fragrance of flowers, smells she would forever associate with her early days in London, when she had run wild with Jennie Tatler. To cheer herself up she bought a unicorn's head as a lucky charm and a string of brightly coloured beads from a swarthy, dark-skinned pedlar. At a nearby stall, two men were bargaining for snuff boxes. Idly she noted that the younger of the two had the cut of the weavers who worked in the Tenter Fields in the Liberties of Dublin, stretching woollen cloth on hooks. Dark-haired, brown-eyed men, descendants of Huguenots who had fled France years before and settled in the Earl of Meath's Liberties. They spoke French and their children played a game that began "*Où Allez Vous?*" She turned away and didn't see the young man, who had been eyeing her, pluck feverishly at his companion. "Look over there where I'm pointing. At that girl with the red hair and green eyes. Did you ever in all your life see such a beauty?"

It was Sam Johnson's considered opinion that David

Garrick was moonstruck. Since reaching London he had spent his time chasing every girl with red hair that he saw. Several times he had been threatened by irate fathers and husbands. "The only female I see," Johnson said caustically, "is a wizened old woman haggling over a broken comb. Would you be in love with an Irish banshee by any chance?"

Garrick threw up his hands in despair. "She's gone. I've lost her. How can I describe her? Shall I compare her to a summer's day?"

"Don't for pity's sake! Leave that to Shakespeare," Johnson said grumpily, dragging his friend away. "I have a thirst that would sink a ship."

In Will's Coffee House where poets and writers met daily and where Johnson was fast establishing a reputation as a man of letters, Garrick soon forgot his morning vision but he was destined to meet her again before very long.

On the way back to Bull Alley that evening, Peg stopped at the local cookshop and bought spare ribs, peas and a cheesecake for her supper. Sarah Pepys's little slave was bent over a wash-tub in the kitchen. On an impulse, she invited the child to join her. She discovered that the child was sharp and streetwise, with a smattering of reading and writing, taught her by the mistress in the charity school where she had been brought up. The mistress had been sacked, she told Peg, for taking the children into her bed and making them do tricks. She didn't mind doing the tricks. Sometimes the mistress gave her a sweetmeat or cake.

"Did they give you a name in the orphanage?" Peg asked, remembering the foundling she had met on the Irish packet all those years before. The child hung her head. "Matron called me Chastity. The other girls laughed at me." Peg's heart went out to the orphan, the matron must have had a distorted sense of humour, either that or a peculiar belief in miracles. "It's a most unusual name," she said tactfully. "You can always shorten it to Chatty, just as my name which is Margaret is shortened to Peg."

Chastity smiled, her grimy face transformed, and confided that she was being shipped off to another country as an infant with her sister when she was rescued by Quakers. "Matron said we must always be grateful to God for our lucky escape." Her voice was wistful. "I wonder what would have happened to me if we hadn't been saved?"

Peg knew only too well. Unwanted children, not only of the poor but of the wealthy, were sold into slavery, taken down in baskets to the docks and offered to the highest bidders. It was known that a French princess of the blood had so disposed of six of her children born out of wedlock. "I shall train you and help you get a position as lady's maid in a great house," Peg promised, but Chastity would have none of it. One of these days she would join her sister in a bawdy house down by the docks. Her sister wore paint and powder and had fine clothes. Peg drew a gruesome picture of the dangers of such a life but Chastity's eyes glinted greedily when she spoke of the money she hoped to earn.

❦

She had been sure her Dublin success would open all doors but the London theatre was, if anything, more cliquish than that of Dublin. It was a handicap to be unknown, an even greater one to be Irish. She haunted Covent Garden Playhouse, Drury Lane, the lesser theatres, seldom getting past the stage-door. She tried small halls, little more than bawdy houses which were frequented by sailors and travellers who expected a girl to spend a night with them in a sleazy lodging house or lie with them under London Bridge. In desperation she struck up acquaintances with out-of-work actors who emptied her purse, ate her food, drank her wine; and promised introductions to important people that never materialised.

❦

She had been walking for hours. Leaning against a wall, she eased her aching feet out of high heels. A fishmonger hawking her wares examined her with beady eyes. "Business bad, dearie? It's the same all over. Only the redcoats left, recruitin' the old and lame now that all the young fellows 'ave took the shillin'. It's them Spaniards 'as has us distressed."

"If you must know, I'm an actress—as if it's any business of yours," she added under her breath.

"Actress, whore, one and the same ain't it?" the fishwife's face was knowing. "Ye don't look too 'appy. Wot you want ter do is meet Mr Rich."

"I'm not interested in any man, rich or poor."

The fishmonger shifted her basket. "'Aughty ain't we. Dontche know Mr Rich is the man wot owns the Covent Garden Play'ouse? 'E's iggorant same as me, carn't read, carn't write, all the same 'e invented that 'arlequin show, the pantomime, they calls it."

She brought out the word carefully and grinned with pleasure. "'Uts and 'ouses turned into castles, men and women into weelbarrers and toadstools and the likes. Magic it is. All done be means o' trap doors and mirrors and such. Ooh I'm fond of the play'ouse, I am."

"Where can I meet this Mr Rich?"

"Ye carn't. Yer'll not git past the stage-door. Won't see no female, 'e won't. Lives with animals, 'e does; frigs 'em he does, for all I knows."

"Tell me where does he live?"

"Wot is it worth ter ye, dearie?"

She rooted in her pocket and produced a shilling which the hawker bit. Satisfied, she put her mouth to Peg's ear, her breath stinking of stale gin and rotten teeth. "'E lives in Bloomsbury Square, red 'ouse, you carn't miss the sign. Arsk for 'is servant, little runt, mebbe a gold piece will do the trick. 'E 'as odd tastes like 'is marster."

When she reached the fashionable square, she put on a bold face and, ignoring the sign pointing to the servants' entrance, mounted the steps of the substantial redbrick house and resolutely pulled the bell. After a wait, the door was opened by a tiny man wearing his hair in a long grey pony-tail. He had two small button eyes in a sallow face. She was reminded of Rumplestiltskin, the malevolent dwarf in the story her mother used tell, who tricked the queen with his offer of help in spinning her yarn. "Today I brew, tomorrow I bake, the next day the queen's child I take." His payment for services rendered was the queen's infant daughter.

"No hawkers, prostitutes or pimps needed here." He had a surprisingly deep voice for one so small. Maybe money would soften him up. She held out a shilling. "Pray be so good as to inform your master that Mistress Woffington the celebrated Dublin actress wishes to see him."

It wasn't enough, she knew by his greedy eyes, and gave him a sovereign which vanished up his sleeve. "He don't like women," was all he said.

"At least give him my message. Tell him I'm here."

"Here thou art and here thou will remain," he grinned and slammed the door in her face.

In the weeks that followed she tried every trick she could think of to wear down the mendacious little man. Tears, temper, flattery—all to no avail. Chastity was her only confidante, sharing her evening meal, sympathising, swearing that the dwarf was a wizard like his master.

"Turns his enemies into cats. The place is crawling with them," she said ghoulishly. "I wouldn't go near that place if I was you."

Word had gone around the coffee houses and inns of her failure and she found herself shunned.

❦

There was the stale odour of mildew as she mounted the stairs. She caught her heel in a broken thread and twisted her ankle. Somehow it was the last straw. She was tired walking the streets, weary with disappointments, insults, rebuffs. Even Sarah Pepys had the temerity to give her a sly dig. Only that morning she had waylaid her in the hall to say her piece. "Lud, Peg, I hear tell Mr Rich is persecuted be some female who won't take no for an answer. His dwarf says she calls so often she has a hole worn on the steps of the house."

She would go back to Dublin. Surely by this time things would have improved, the theatre would have re-opened, Whaley would have forgotten she ever existed. People had short memories. She would count what money she had left, pack her bags and take the stage to Holyhead. Each morning she found a different hiding place for her purse, taking with her only what money she needed to see her through the day. It was a nuisance, but London was a hotbed of thieves and cut-purses and Sarah Pepys was not to be trusted with any money lying around. She prised a loose floor-board and rooted, then rooted again. She couldn't be mistaken. She had hidden the purse under the board less than six hours before. She searched feverishly, growing more frantic by the minute, emptying drawers, presses, looking under the bed, in the washbasin, even in the chamberpot that hadn't been emptied of the night's slops. She wondered hysterically what sentimental idiocy had brought her to Bull Alley in the first place. Would she call Sarah Pepys or Chastity, to help her search? No, they would cause such a commotion.

Was that a mouse or was Chastity spying outside? She put her eye to the keyhole, an eye stared back at her. She wrenched the door open and Sarah Pepys tumbled into the room.

"And what may I ask were you doing, behaving like a sneak thief?" She pulled the landlady to her feet. "Do you know anything about my purse?" Sarah Pepys tittered weakly. "Lud, Peg, but you are in a tizzy. As poor Mr Quinn used say, 'Who steals my purse steals trash.' Likely as not you squandered your few paltry pounds playing the lady around the town."

"What are you talking about, woman?"

"You can pack your bags and be off," Sarah Pepys shouted. "There are no thieves in this house."

"Don't lie, you slut!" She shook Sarah Pepys so hard that her wig tumbled off, revealing a head, bald as an egg. Her hairless state appeared to demoralise the landlady completely. Tears ran down her raddled cheeks. "Don't blame me, Peg. I didn't take your purse. That Chastity one I took in is responsible. She's run off, stolen every penny piece in the house, even took my buckled shoes. Me that was that good to her."

Silently Peg prayed for patience. "Put your wig back on, woman. You're like a plucked chicken."

"I'll set the constable on her," Sarah Pepys clapped her hands in a frenzy. "I'll have her in prison."

"Stop it for God's sake. You're as noisy as a beggar's clackdish. Chastity is gone, lost in the warrens of St Pancras or the sailor's whorehouse in Southwark."

Sarah Pepys rooted in her pocket, producing a dirty scrap of paper. "The little slut had the gall to leave you this."

With difficulty Peg deciphered the message written with immense labour and many blots. "Me sister send fer me and I tuk yer purse. I needs the money. I hope ye unerstan. I done a trick for the dwaref and he sez you ken see his mastor any time. I luve ye Peg. Ye was good ter me. Chastity."

"Well what did she say?" Sarah Pepys fixed her wig at an angle and, fully recovered, admired herself in the cracked mirror.

"She saw the dwarf. God only knows what he made the child do."

"Child my foot. That one was born bad."

"Oh, shut up. You're to blame. Working her like a slave. I intended to take her back to Dublin with me."

"To work in Margaret Leeson's brothel. Don't waste your sympathy. Maybe you should see the dwarf. Get something for all the money you've squandered," she said spitefully and made her escape just in time.

❧

Peg made her way to Bloomsbury Square on the following morning with the fishmonger's voice in her ears. "Lives with animals, 'e does; frigs 'em he does for all I knows." She remembered Chastity's whine: "I wouldn't go near that place if I was you. The dwarf is a wizard like his master."

Fornication, adultery, these were commonplace in the Playhouse, where girls sold themselves to managers, actors— even stage-hands in the hope of a part. They were equally ready to pleasure any old roué or painted fop to ensure a following. No one thought anything of it but bestiality was something else. "Oh, to Hades with it," she told herself despairingly. "If Máire Rua had the courage to face the Cromwellian despot, I'll not be put off by an ugly little monster and his master, whatever their vices." A house in a fashionable London square was not as daunting as the Hellfire Club in the Dublin Mountains.

Evidently the dwarf was expecting her. Putting a finger to the side of his nose, he beckoned her into a well furnished hall. She followed him up a flight of stairs and waited as he opened a door with a flourish announcing in sepulchral tones, "Mistress Woffington to see you, sir."

She had been holding her breath and now at the cosy domesticity of the scene facing her she let go and found herself laughing hysterically.

A small fat man was curled up in a chair with his pets. True they were numerous and different. Sleek Maltese and brindles, silky Siamese, long-haired Persians, cats bearing the scars of alley fights, toms with one eye or with chewed ears, felines licking their kittens, all looking remarkably well fed and well cared for.

She held on to the door-post for support, while the tears poured down her cheeks and she prayed for control.

Mr Rich was staring at her with puzzled baby blue eyes.

"I'm sorry," she choked. "It's just that I was expecting something else. I didn't realise you were only a cat lover."

His face dimpled. "No need to apologise. I like a good laugh meself, makes the world go round." He spoke in a mewing voice, was hairless as an infant newly born.

She managed to control herself and carefully closed the door behind her.

"Well, and what do you want?" he squeaked. "Why did you come?"

"I was leading lady in the Aungier Street Playhouse before it was forced to close because of the famine," she said, wiping her eyes.

He put his thumb in his mouth and considered. "Aye, I was expecting to hear from you. Alice Morgan is a connection of my own, lately married to that scoundrel Coffey. Off to Americay they've gone, following the footsteps of the Pilgrim Fathers. Wish they'd never been born if they meet up with the redskins. The stories I could tell you." He took his finger out of his mouth and examined it carefully. "How did you get in?"

"That servant of yours took a bribe of some sort from a young orphan I know. I shudder to think what he may have forced her to do."

He chuckled. "Chastity. You could buy her for a halfpenny but she must know a trick or two. The dwarf keeps them away with a pitchfork if necessary. So you want to be an actress, hey?"

She nodded. "I have a notice that appeared in *Faulkner's Journal*. Would you like to see it?"

He gave a prodigious yawn. "I'm no great scholar. Read it to me, Mistress."

She cleared her throat of dust and cat fur. "Young

Dublin actress makes stage history," she began. "Last night Peg Woffington titillated the town as Sir Harry Wildair capturing the very essence of that airy gentleman." A series of whistles and grunts filled the room. Looking up she saw that Mr Rich had fallen asleep, mouth open. She waited politely but the snoring continued. In a temper she screwed up the notice and flung it across the floor. Immediately a couple of frisky kittens pounced and began kicking the ball to each other. Mr Rich opened his eyes and beamed at his pets. "How clever, m'dear. When I play with my cat who knows whether I do not make her more sport than she makes me." Even before he had tugged at the rope bell, the door opened and the strange little man stood waiting.

A pudgy hand waved imperiously. "Show this person out."

Her heart sank. "Thank you for receiving me, sir. It was kind of you to spare the time."

He blinked. "No need to be formal, miss, it's not the last time I'll see you. Present yourself at the Playhouse tomorrow morning at the beat of the drum. No temper tantrums allowed. Actresses required to wear drawers on stage. Salary three guineas a week for the season."

She heard herself babbling like a youngster given her first walk-on part. "You won't regret it, sir. I'll work like a Trojan, keep your rules, be line perfect."

He raised himself to his full four foot ten. "Saying's one thing, doing's another." He took a few steps forward and the dwarf retreated hastily. "Show the lady out, little runt," he squealed, "and if the Duchess of Buckingham herself calls, say I am not receiving today."

Mr Rich had quite literally been born on the stage. His mother, a strolling player, had been seized by the pangs of childbirth during a performance in a makeshift theatre in a small town whose name she could never remember and had given birth to her son on the floor. She had christened him Rich because she said it would augur well for his future and in this she had been proved right. He liked Shakespeare's comedies, liked playing the clown, but his favourite part was Puck in *A Midsummer Night's Dream*. He could neither read nor write but had a phenomenal memory, that is until he sustained a fall on the head, after which he tended to have lapses. He worked as carpenter, scene-shifter, painting sets, even making costumes. His opportunity came when he conceived the novel idea of staging a fairy tale for a Christmas entertainment, complete with dwarfs, witches, warlocks, wizards, devil, angels, a fairy godmother, and a prince and princess. Out of this was born the pantomime and his name and fame were made. He ended up in that most enviable of all stage occupations, manager of his own theatre. Everyone agreed that he was a showman to his fingertips, with an unrivalled flair for publicity. And now for his latest production he had worked out a plan of campaign which was exceeding even his great expectations.

For weeks, London had been seething with rumours about an unknown actress whom Rich described as a "wild Irish rose." Posters outside the Playhouse announced the forthcoming production of an old favourite, *The Constant Couple*, in which a dazzling newcomer would make her debut in the part of Sir Harry Wildair. The first time an actress had ever played a breeches part on the English stage.

While Rich had leaked a few stories to the press, he had ordered Peg to speak to no one and to remain out of the public eye until after the first night. All this of course only added fuel to gossip. In coffee and chocolate houses, inns and clubs, stories were swopped about her life and loves. Young men who had never laid eyes on her boasted that they had bedded her. Journalists vied with each other digging up scandals and anyone with a story to tell found a ready market. Like most of such gossip there was a strand of truth woven into a web of fantasy. It was said she had started her stage career as a child, playing the part of Polly Peachum in *The Beggar's Opera* and had caused a riot in College Green in Dublin, as a result of which a well-known highwayman, a professor of mathematics and twenty students of Trinity College went to the gallows. A valet, known to be the current fancy of his aristocratic master, told his cronies that she had taken part in an orgy in a hunting-lodge in the Dublin Mountains, had danced with the devil, after which the lodge had gone up in flames and she had been forced to flee Dublin. The ruins of the burnt-out lodge, he said, were there for all to see. Then there was the Honourable Patrick Taafe. It was whispered in exalted circles that his marriage to the Lady Arabella Fitzsimons had been called off when Peg had ridden up to the church dressed as a man. She had invited Taafe up into the saddle and he had ridden away with her. And lastly, she was held to be responsible for the suicide of the Lady Jane and the drowning of the young heir to the title, Master Jeremy Sandford.

Stories of her family abounded. Her mother was said to be an Irish aristocrat. No one knew much about her father who, according to some, had been a stable-boy on the family estate, to others a God-fearing Puritan, brought to an early grave by his daughter's wanton ways. The whole of London knew that Máire Rua, or Red Mary the witch, had, if anything, been more scandalous than her great-granddaughter. Murdering no less than six husbands, seducing the Lord Cromwell himself, hanging herself by her own hair in a wood near her estate, haunting the County Clare. And lastly it was whispered that a curse, so terrible that it was never spoken of, followed her family.

Naturally all London determined to attend the first night to see the wild Irish girl for themselves. Fishmongers and porters from the great markets quarrelled and came to blows over gallery seats which they considered rightfully theirs by custom and tradition. Students of the King's Inns, craftsmen and shopkeepers, bribed the doorkeeper for seats in the pit or standing-room at the back of the stage. The Quality, as was their wont, sent footmen or blackamoors to reserve seats in the stalls, and if sufficiently influential, demanded boxes. Even the Prince of Wales had signalled his intention to honour the performance with his presence. He would attend with his entourage, numbering in all sixteen persons.

As the hour approached for the commencement of the play, a motley crew of beggars and cut-purses, bearded foreigners, whores and their bullies, poured off the warren of lanes that surrounded Covent Garden, to swell the crowd that watched gilded coaches and painted chairs set down their occupants. A space had been cleared by a guard for the passage of bewigged gentlemen carrying gold-headed canes and sporting embroidered coats, for the redcoated officers of the Footguards, for the ladies in silks and satins, for the swaggering dandies in broad-skirted coats, hands on dress swords, and last but not least, for the town's courtesans, painted, flaunting feathers and wearing the latest Parisian high powdered wigs. Young men about town, in periwigs and ruffles, threw halfpence to beggars and children, paid bawdy compliments to giggling maidservants and threatened to run the doorkeeper through with their swords if he refused them seats in the pit.

Inside all was noise, confusion and laughter, fiddlers scraping their bows, ladies calling out greetings to their friends, orange girls shouting their wares. A cheer went up as the Prince and Princess of Wales were escorted to the royal box under a canopy of scarlet silk decorated with gold tissues and tassels. Ladies-in-waiting settled themselves down in theatre boxes beside courtiers, while other boxes held titled gentlemen who had turned their backs on their clubs for the pleasure of finding themselves in the company of the prince. They would pass doubtful compliments if the play engaged their interest, gamble with dice and cards if they found themselves bored.

Backstage, a plump actress of uncertain years, who still bore the traces of former good looks, fiddled with Peg's costume, adjusted the cravat, added a beauty spot, settled the wig at a more rakish angle. Mrs Bellamy was a woman who lived on her wits and who had a shrewd eye for an up-and-coming actress. She stood back admiring her handiwork. "There now, sweetheart, you look as elegant as Beau Nash himself."

Somewhere around a stage-hand was whistling

"Greensleeves" off-key. Mrs Bellamy grimaced. "Do you hear that fool. Don't he know it's unlucky to whistle backstage anyway but to choose that of all songs...I'll send him about his business with a flea in his ear." She minced away but already the gangly youth was gone, only the plaintive notes of the reedy music came eerily back.

Peg wrapped her arms around herself as if for protection. Some people said that "Greensleeves" had been written for King Henry VIII's darling, Anne Boleyn. He had turned against her, ordered that she be beheaded and had played the song on his lute as she placed her head on the block. She had been very brave begging the executioner to dispatch her quickly, that she had a slender neck. Peg's mind ran on the last time she had heard the ballad, that night she had stood with Jennie Tatler outside Belle Tudor's house and Billy the pot-boy had poured out his heart in anguished enslavement.

Was she destined to be a failure? To be pelted off the stage as so many had forecast? She hated the role, hated the costume, had sworn after that night of torment in the Hellfire Club never again to don male attire. The experience was still with her, branded in her memory. Mad ride through the city, hard pull through Bohernabreena, doomed road ("ravens sating themselves with the blood of the murdered king.") She was icy cold as she had been on that journey when the wind tore across the mountain like a soul possessed and moonlight cast grotesque shadows on trees and rocks. And the lodge itself, sombre, sly, hugging its terrible secret to itself. Mr Rich had insisted on reviving the play and she knew miserably that her whole career depended on its success tonight.

One consolation, she told herself, was the costume she was wearing tonight, vastly different from that other—

richer material, better cut, fine lace at sleeves and neck. Dwell on the cut, the cloth and colour, the gold snuff box, the buckled shoes that pinched. Put everything else out of your mind.

These last few weeks had been a strain. She had been forced to disguise herself as she slunk in and out of rehearsals at the Playhouse, to avoid the men about town, the gossips. Of course it whetted their appetite for scandal. Everyone who knew anything about her had been approached. Sarah Pepys had enjoyed her brief notoriety as landlady of "the wild Irish girl." Peg thanked God that after tonight all the gossip would end. Even her fellow actors, their fears of the manager fuelled by jealousy, avoided her company, except for Mrs Bellamy, she who moved like a ship in full sail, conscious of past grandeur. Mrs Bellamy and that renegade Irishman, Owen M'Swiney, with his catamites, his flamboyant clothes, perfumes, wigs and his heart of gold. He had befriended her, praised her acting, called off the dogs. As she stood trembling in the wings he came up, debonair in well-cut breeches, painted face, to wish her luck, to examine her with a professional air.

The fiddlers played their last long-drawn-out note; one by one the candles in the house were snuffed and the heavy green curtain rose. A silence fell on the house, broken only by the fluttering of fans and the snapping of snuff-box lids, the slap of a groping hand, feminine laughter.

"Your cue," Owen M'Swiney whispering, kissing her cheek. "Good luck, my darling."

"I can't go on. I wish I were dead."

The parchment face creased in a smile. "Of course you do, so does every actor worth his salt on a first night. But who is out front to scare you? Harlots and their fancy men, fop-doodles and highborn sluts. Prince Fred in the royal box, afraid of his father, his mother. Why they say he goes in dread even of his wife."

Peg giggled nervously, but the silly words had broken the tension for her. Downstage an actor was reciting the prologue. The play was about to commence.

It was a repeat of her Dublin triumph, except now she was playing to the citizens of London, the most critical in the world; they could make or break any actor or actress. The theatre was part of their very lives. Their ancestors had known Will Shakespeare. For them he had written his plays. She was in another's skin, in another world, the past forgotten. Coffey, Taafe, the cottage in flames, the horror of the Hellfire Club—all the shadows might never have been. She was the essence of Sir Harry Wildair, airy, artificial, brainless, not a thought in his mind except wenching, gambling, duelling. She tripped around the stage, bowed, touched her feathered hat, shook out her lace, winked, paused for laughs, played to the gallery and they loved her, cheered, shouted, stamped. Someone in the royal box threw down a flower, at which the audience rising in their seats went wild, risking bringing down the house with vociferous applause. It was a night to remember. She curtseyed deeply to the prince and princess, saw through a blur the ladies smiling, gentlemen blowing kisses. Then Their Highnesses were leaving the theatre and she was backing into the wings, elated, exhausted, content to be led away by her triumphant keeper, Mrs Bellamy, who chattered like a parakeet in delight and relief.

❧

Sarah, Duchess of Buckingham, London's great hostess,

had scored another triumph. Her footmen had carried invitations to the aristocratic, the fashionable, the wealthy, bidding them attend a masked ball in honour of "the wild Irish rose," Mistress Peg Woffington, the night of her London debut. An invitation by the duchess had the effect of a royal command. For more than forty years Buck House had been the showplace of London. Designed on the lines of a ducal Palace the architect had admired in Venice, it consisted of a great main building flanked by side wings with open colonnades. A cistern which held no less than fifty tons of water driven by an engine from the Thames, supplied fountains, gardens, the house itself. All evening servants had toiled, pouring gallons of attar of roses into the waters so that scented sprays, glittering in the evening light, drenched the night. Rare shrubs and potted plants decorated terraces. Between groves of limes that lined the courtyard linkboys and footmen with flaming torches lit the way for the guests who alighted from the crested coaches. The great doors were flung back to reveal magnificent rooms, high vaulted painted ceilings thrown into relief by the light of wax candles in cut-glass chandeliers. Thick-piled carpets covered the floors, gold-flowered damask draped windows, spindle-legged sofas and love seats were heaped high with cushions; alcoves held busts of long-dead emperors, statues of nymphs, satyrs and pagan gods—booty brought back from many a grand tour of Europe. Portraits of ladies and gentlemen in Restoration court dress lined walls, the most striking of which was a painting of Charles II, surrounded by his spaniels, with his hand on the shoulders of his favourite mistress, Barbara Castlemaine, who bore a striking resemblance to the actress they had all come to meet. Another picture by the same artist showed two of Buckingham's children, a young boy with golden curls and blue eyes holding the hand of his baby sister. Eighteen years had changed the charming young aristocrat of the portrait with his wide-eyed innocence to an overweight dissolute, too corrupt for his years. His sister, the Lady Jane Buckingham, had died of the plague and now the earl stood to inherit not only the title and lands but his sister's considerable fortune. One day he would be the wealthiest man in the kingdom.

Musicians had been engaged to play the night away. A blind harper from Ireland who lived in poverty in the stews of London had been brought along, washed, deloused, dressed in a shag cloak, trews, buckled shoes, his forked beard combed and styled in the ancient manner. A supper providing every known delicacy would be served at midnight when the guests unmasked. Champagne, claret, brandy, whiskey, port would flow as freely as the scented waters of the fountains outside.

At the top of the great staircase stood the duke and duchess to receive their costumed guests. Harlequins, ladies of the harem, men dressed as birds of prey, as devils, as monks. Venus came up accompanied by Cupid, followed by a pirate and a slave girl. Most of them wore full-faced velvet masks attached to high wigs, or intricate head-dresses of pearls and feathers. Only Buckingham, old and frail, and the duchess, supremely elegant in cloth of gold, tiara crowning her upswept hair, and the slack-mouthed earl, were unvisored. Twin blackamoors in gold turbans and crimson silk sat cross-legged at their feet.

Peg had timed her entrance so as to be the last to arrive. As if in contrast to her role as Sir Harry Wildair and the extravagant rumours that had circulated the town, she had dressed with extreme simplicity. Her beautiful hair hung in rippling curls to her waist. Under her silver eyemask, her eyebrows and lashes had been skilfully darkened with kohl; her lips and cheeks were faintly touched with rouge. She wore no face patches. A sack gown of green silk fell in simple folds, her only ornament was the pendant in the shape of a dolphin, Conor O'Brien's last gift to his beloved Máire Rua. At her side padded an Irish wolfhound wearing a gold collar.

"Bewitching child..." drawled the duke, holding up his quizzing glass as she curtsied. The duchess passed no remark merely inclining her head with immense condescension. The earl painted, curled, foppishly dressed in sky-blue velvet, lace and high red shoes, offered her his arm and led her into the ballroom where two dozen violins were playing.

She seemed to have been dancing for hours, passed from partner to partner, in quadrilles, in slow stately minuets, in highland reels. Around her, masked figures whirled, bowed, made assignations behind fans, chattered. High-pitched voices, strident voices, drunken voices. A slave girl was telling her partner, "And would you believe supper was served on plates depicting such scenes." She giggled. "Men and men making love, women and women making love." Cupid was boasting to an overweight Columbine, "In Paris I attended a private ballet in the Duc du Montfort's chalet, all the dancers were naked but for their masks. After supper we had an orgy, what fun." A pretty young boy in velvet was stroking the earl's face as they locked in an embrace, and explaining, "Tonight I am wearing three face patches, the 'gallant', the 'rogue' and the 'kissing.'" The music was changing, partners were changing. A young man in brocade

and cheap buckled shoes slipped an arm around her waist.
Behind his mask she saw nervous brown eyes. "I have long
wanted to meet you," he whispered. "I was at the theatre
tonight and saw your enchanting performance."

"How kind," she gave him a practised smile, touched
him lightly with her fan.

"Your landlady told me of your early days in London
and how the great Mr Quinn was your mentor. I should
like to have known him," he squeezed her waist, the mask
giving him courage, "and you."

She had enough of this conversation, there had been
gossip and to spare without this brash young man adding
his meed. She had no wish to be reminded of the days
when she had run the streets with Jennie Tatler. "I spent
my childhood in Ireland," she said coldly, "and now if you
will excuse me." She stopped suddenly and scarlet-faced
he backed off.

"You have quite slain young Garrick," an amused voice
behind her remarked. She wheeled around. A man in black
velvet leaned negligently against a pillar. He wore no mask
and was eyeing her, she thought, insolently.

"And who is young Garrick?" Her voice was haughty.

"His brother is my wine merchant and also
Buckingham's. I understand the young man pleaded for
an invitation in the hope of meeting you. He is a personable
fellow. Even duchesses are not immune to charm."

"And to whom have I the honour of speaking now?"
There was something familiar about him. She was sure
they had met before.

"Oh the honour and pleasure are all mine and not for
the first time."

She caught her breath. It was all coming back. "I know
you."

He bowed. "'For ever, and for ever, farewell, Cassius.

If we do meet again, why, we shall smile!"

She said confusedly, "Forgive me, Lord Darnley, for the moment I—I had forgotten."

He took her arm. "We must drink to our reunion." Imperiously he called to a footman: "Bring wine to the Rose Arbour."

They went out of the room, on to the terrace, descended flights of steps to a lower terrace and into gardens, paced between avenues of shrubbery and with every step they took the sounds of revelry grew fainter. A footman walking behind set down a silver tray on a stone table and vanished as silently as he had come. Darnley gave her a glass. "To your very good health."

She stood looking out over the gardens. The scent was intoxicating. A million miles away stars glittered under the canopy of the heavens; only a fountain playing somewhere near and the song of a nightingale broke the silence of the night. London, the great mansion, the fashionable crowd might never have been. She sipped the wine. "I mustn't stay long."

He smiled. "Bide a little while. The night is young."

She stole a sideways glance at his face. In his late thirties, she judged, and quite stunningly handsome. What woman would not covet those sweeping lashes. Would not wonder how it felt to be kissed by those sensual lips?

As if he could read her thoughts, he put a hand under her chin and tilted her face upwards. She closed her eyes, her lips parted and her arms stole around his neck. She felt him brush her cheek and gently put her away. All evening she had been near to breaking point: first night nerves, then the excitement of the applause, the great house, the ball, the noise, people touching her, examining her, lewd hands, mocking eyes. And now this rebuff from a man whose company she had not sought. Something snapped and she slapped his face.

He caught her hand, twisting it back cruelly, his voice treacherously soft. "You did that once before, m'dear, and I forgave you, because you were but a frightened child. Do it again and you will live to regret it."

"I'm sorry," she muttered.

"I think it is time we returned to our hosts." He bowed and offered his arm.

She recognised his pride, knew with a blinding flash he might one day be broken on the wheel but he would never yield.

"Please," she begged huskily. "I have no excuse. I was overwrought with the night. I wanted your arms around me, to feel safe." She bit back the tears. "I too am proud and have paid for my folly."

His dark eyes bored into her. "You mean Patrick Taafe's death?"

She felt the ground move under her. "What do you mean?"

"Taafe was my cousin. I understood he died defending your honour."

She covered her face with her hands. "It was not like that at all. You know how he gambled...and there was the famine in Ireland."

Conor's dying face was before her, the cottage in flames, the night journey across the mountains, the old woman bending over her bed in that cottage. His arms were around her and words were gushing out, she was telling him things she had sworn never to divulge to a living soul. He gave her a handkerchief. The cool dry linen was comforting.

"There is no happiness for my family," she said

wretchedly. "Máire Rua hanging by her hair in the woods of Toonagh, my brother dead of the smallpox. He was too young. Until this moment I never told anyone what happened that night in the Hellfire Club. I think maybe my mother guessed. There were rumours...we never discussed it...it was not her way...she is close to my sister Polly. She gave me this pendant." She touched her throat. "All she had left of Lemineagh...it was Máire Rua's gift from the husband she loved. Maybe I could have been happy with Patrick Taafe, but it was too late when we met. I was in love with Charles Coffey. I shall never forgive myself for what happened."

He smoothed back her hair. "Hush, my dear. My cousin gambled away his life as he did your happiness and almost your life. We each have our devil who rides us." In the moonlight she looked young, vulnerable; he had an overpowering impulse to sweep her up in his arms, carry her off to a safe harbour. "You should go to your bed. You need rest." She shivered with exhaustion. "The duchess, the ball is in my honour. She will be displeased with my absence."

"I think not. You made the entrance she hoped, created the sensation she expected. Already she has forgotten you exist. The rest do not matter. They have other interests, appetites. Buckingham keeps the best table in London. They will eat to satiety, drink beyond their capacity, gamble at cards, fumble in corners."

He knew it all, had seen it too many times. High-born sluts, lecherous gallants licking between women's thighs, men pumping away mindlessly like dogs, while the object of their drunken lust lay in a drunken stupor. God how he despised them. On a night like this he longed for the cold clear air, the loneliness of his Scottish fastness.

"What will happen?" she asked distractedly. His lips curled in contempt. "An insult will be offered, a face slapped, a duel fought in Hyde Park at dawn. It is all part of a game they play."

She looked up at him, eyes shadowed with strain, her face that of a lost child. "You have been very kind, Lord Darnley."

"Believe me it was a pleasure meeting you again. Such functions as this bore me but I have certain matters to discuss with Buckingham. My coachman will see you safely home. Where do you lodge?"

"You asked me that question once before. Bull Alley behind Buttons Inn."

"Scarcely a suitable abode for a young woman who has, shall we say, acquired a certain notoriety."

She was suddenly angry. "Where I choose to live is my affair." She would not be patronised, by him least of all.

"Quite. Yet the district is not safe. The lanes and alleyways around Covent Garden are the haunt of cut-purses, footpads, criminals of every sort, as you must know."

Despite her fatigue, her taut nerves, she smiled. "Already I have lost my purse to a ten-year-old charity child employed by my landlady. She ran off to join her sister in a brothel down near the docks. To recompense me for what she took, she arranged that I be auditioned by Mr Rich. I shudder to think what price his dwarf extracted as payment.."

Darnley said drily, "Not money. He is wealthy, owns several houses of ill-repute. His appetites include, forgive me, buggery and penilingism."

She gave a small sigh. "Poor Chastity. That was the name given her in the charity school by some misguided Quaker woman."

"As a poet once said, 'No man's knowledge can go beyond his experience.' No doubt the same is true of the Quaker female." He bent and kissed her hand and she had a sudden wild urge to stroke his hair. Instead she said gaily, "Good-night, Lord Darnley. Pleasant dreams."

His eyes held hers for the length of a heartbeat. His voice was so low that she had to strain to catch his words. "'Those oft are stratagems which errors seem. Nor is it Homer nods, but we that dream.'"

He was gone and the flunky had materialised, was guiding her to the coach. As she watched a star fell through the heavens and with a pang she remembered another such sky, another such night. "Please God let me not fall into the same trap twice," she prayed. "Let me remember what happened, keep in mind that Lord Darnley is far above my station." Yet, given the chance, she knew her treacherous heart would betray her, as it had done on that night so long ago when she was young and knew no better.

1 4

"You are the talk of the town, my dearest," Mrs Bellamy breathed, breasts heaving with excitement. "I declare this to be elegant beyond belief." The buxom actress, painted, curled, wearing a scarlet velvet cloak trimmed with a ragged fur, had arrived uninvited at the apartment in New Bond Street to which Peg had but recently moved. Critically she inspected the bedroom with the fine four-poster, fingered the glass bowl on the dressing-table, tested the brocade chairs, then moved into the small study with its writing desk and bookcase and from that to the dining room with fine table and chairs and stools, tapestry cushions tied to the seats. Satisfied with her tour, she stood at the parlour window, sharp eyes approving the piano in one corner. "Kitty Clive is green with envy at your good fortune," she announced in satisfied tones.

Peg nodded carelessly. "Aye, Kitty Raftor that was. I knew her as a child in Dublin. I hear she recently married."

"A penniless beau·whom she keeps in the manner to which he was born," Mrs Bellamy said confidentially. "Kitty has herself beggared paying his gambling debts. Of course he was born into the aristocracy. But enough of the Clive." She leaned forward like a plump pigeon. "Has Lord Darnley made a settlement yet? A love-nest is a bower, but there's more to life than coupling. You should be worth five hundred a year to him and a carriage and pair. Strike when his passions are hot. I hear that Belle Tudor pleasures him in the French manner."

Peg feigned deafness. She would be damned if she would admit to the greatest gossip in London that she hadn't laid eyes on Darnley since their meeting that night in Buck House. A few days later he had sent word that he needed a tenant in an apartment he owned in New Bond Street, would she be prepared to pay a peppercorn rent of a shilling a year and consider herself in the nature of a caretaker? At first she was doubtful but Bull Alley had become something of a nightmare since her success in the Playhouse, besieged as she was on all sides by beggars who sought her help, slatternly neighbours who importuned her for loans, cut-purses who dogged her footsteps. She had written a brief note thanking him for his offer and a footman had delivered the keys. She wondered had he made the gesture because she was Irish. In that moment of madness in the gardens of the ducal mansion, she had confided her life story. She guessed he favoured the Stuarts; there were all sorts of rumours about his Jacobite sympathies. If he used the apartment as a meeting-place for fellow conspirators she would be one he could trust. Not that she cared. It was a matter of indifference to her who sat on the English throne.

Noisily Mrs Bellamy dragged back the green and gold hanging, to gape out the window at carriages and chairs setting down their fashionable loads. Most afternoons the *haut monde* liked to take the air, the shops in New Bond Street with their fashionable bow windows were positive repositories of all that was new in stuffs, hats, gloves, jewels. Rich young fops, known as the "New Bond Street loungers," preened themselves in their skin-tight coats and brimless hats and made assignations with young ladies scarcely out of the schoolroom as well as older matrons in search of diversion in the shape of a lusty admirer.

"Lud, but I am exhausted." Affectedly Mrs Bellamy sank into the *chaise-longue* and kicked off her shoes, admiring her well-turned ankles of which she was inordinately proud. "When I was Lady Tyrawley I had my own coach and four and a French maid to do my bidding. But then dear Tyrawley doted on me." Mrs Bellamy was fond of referring to herself as a titled lady, though such was not the case. Adopted as an infant by a lady of fashion, brought up in a licentious household, she had run away to Portugal with old Lord Tyrawley when she was only thirteen years of age and he a widower three times over. When she became *enceinte,* he had married her off to Captain Bellamy, an old mariner. Four months later she gave birth to a daughter, christened George by an inebriated clergyman who had got the infant's sex confused. To the relief of all, Lord Tyrawley had acknowledged his daughter and made her the ward of an elderly cousin. Later Mrs Bellamy drifted back to London, had a brief success as an actress and now spent her days hanging around the theatre, gossiping, playing cards, reliving her own past glories. An invitation to take breakfast with the Duchess of Buckingham stood on the escritoire. Peg hoped it had escaped the beady eye of her visitor.

"You must sample this brew," she said hastily, busying herself with the silver teapot. "I had these little iced cakes sent up from the cookshop next door. All the Quality shop there. The pastry maker is French and an Austrian girl has the lightest hand with the sponge. Her 'Queen of Hearts' is said to be favourite with the Princess of Wales."

Mrs Bellamy munched happily, greedily licking her fingers of cream and jam. "George Ann was honoured by the notice of the Prince of Wales. Lord Tyrawley recently settled an allowance of one hundred pounds a year on her, as pin-money." She mopped her cleavage with a scrap of lace. "When I was Lady Tyrawley, I had a professor of dancing call on me three times a week. I took singing lessons from Madame Corelli. His lordship used to liken my voice to a nightingale."

"'…I will roar you as gently as any sucking dove; I will roar you as 'twere any nightingale,'" Peg quoted in a bored voice.

Mrs Bellamy frowned and raised her quizzing glass.

"Shakespeare. *A Midsummer Night's Dream.*"

"Of course, the dear Bard of Avon," Mrs Bellamy cooed. "Lord Tyrawley was such a Shakespearean scholar."

ॐ

Peg sat stiffly upright in a hard-backed chair, marvelling at the activity all around her. It was the practice of Sarah, Duchess of Buckingham to conduct the day's business from her bed before rising at noon. Clad in an exquisite bedgown of silk and lace, she reclined on pillows and bolsters, dealing with the head housekeeper, the butler, dictating letters to her secretary, inspecting the rolls of silks and brocades, furs and jewels laid out for her pleasure. Seated around the room friends, relations, hangers-on, waited a sign that would summon them to the bedside where they would whisper the latest scandal into the ear of her grace. There was no intrigue, political or otherwise, to which she was not party. It was no idle boast that she was the most influential hostess in London.

She beckoned Peg nearer and clapped her hands, a signal that she wished the room cleared. Servants and tradespeople departed noiselessly, friends and intimates made their exits just as quickly but with more bustle, removing themselves to ante-rooms, where they would spend the morning drinking chocolate, playing cards, exchanging gossip until the duchess might have use of them again.

"You come of good stock on your mother's side, Mistress Woffington," the beautiful voice was languid.

"Yes, your grace. The MacMahons and O'Briens were powerful in the west of Ireland with castles in Bunratty, Clonroad and Clarecastle." Nervously Peg laced her fingers. "They were of the old Irish aristocracy, hereditary Lords of Clonderlaw, Earls of Ormond until their fall from grace after King Charles was beheaded."

The duchess raised well-marked eyebrows. She was within sight of her fortieth birthday, yet in the soft light of her chamber, she would have passed for a woman half her age. "Máire Rua intrigues me," she purred. "Tell me what you know of her."

Peg drew a deep breath. She had no idea why the duchess had summoned her nor what she wished to learn. "My great-grandmother married three times, the first time for family reasons, her second was a love-match, she contracted her third marriage to save her estates and the lives of her family and dependants."

"And to do so she seduced Cromwell's commander-in-chief in Ireland, General Ireton." Her grace allowed a faint smile touch her lips. "And sent the Cromwellian soldier to his death in her own good time. What matter, they don't breed such women in our age, more's the pity. I trust you have inherited something of her commonsense."

Thoughtfully she dipped a finger of toast in the chocolate on a silver tray at her bedside. Peg sat silent. Her grace had often been likened to a silken spider sitting at the centre of a web that bound London society but what possible interest could she have in an actress of no account?

"My son, the earl, declares he is smitten with you since the night of your stage debut in the part of a gentleman," the lazy voice sounded amused. "He wishes to set you up as his mistress. Now that I have examined you I think it no bad idea. It would be more satisfactory were you a matron. I had thought to marry you off to an elderly beau fallen on hard times, but my son will have none of it."

"I have no wish to wed anyone." Peg had an overpowering urge to leave this terrifying woman who had the confidence bestowed by centuries of power and privilege.

"Quite understandable given your unfortunate experience in Connolly's hunting club—what do they call it—the Hellfire Club? But enough of that." She wiped her mouth with a scrap of lace. "I shall make you a suitable allowance. Five hundred pounds a year with a small house on the outskirts of the city. You will of course give up the stage."

Peg made a strangled sound but the duchess continued blandly. "In time a suitable marriage must be arranged for the earl and the succession secured. My son has a weakness for pretty boys but if you are as intelligent and experienced as I am led to believe, you should be able to distract him from his particular vice. All cats are alike in the dark. If you play your part I shall see to it that a modest fortune is settled on you when the earl tires of your charms. Indeed with some skill you may hold his attention even when he marries. It has happened with the duke. So satisfactory."

She yawned, showing small pointed teeth and lay back on the pillows closing her eyes.

The sheer audacity of the suggestion kept Peg silent. She was only too well aware that Her Grace of Buckingham used people as pawns; chess was a game at which she was said to excel. Yet on reflection was the suggestion so outrageous? How many ladies of quality would be happy to accept the role of mistress to the earl, become protégée of a duchess ranking next to royalty? Sarah Buckingham would keep her word: Peg would never want, could secure her mother's future, take care of Polly. Women of good lineage had sold themselves for less. That she could never bear a child would, if anything, be an advantage. Her grace was not interested in bastards. She pictured the earl's hot eyes, loose mouth, recalled his stammering idiocies, his well documented salacious habits and knew that if her life depended on it, the price would be too high. Awkwardly she rose to go and the duchess raised heavy lids in surprise. "I have not dismissed you. There are other matters to settle."

Peg found her voice. "I must decline Your Grace's offer, but I am already satisfactorily housed and happy."

The duchess frowned. "Darnley has seen fit to adopt you as he would a stray kitten. He is known for such impulsive gestures."

"What Lord Darnley does is his own affair," Peg said heatedly. Damn this woman who rode roughshod over the feelings of others.

"Sit down and listen to what I have to say." The duchess patted the side of the bed and sulkily Peg obeyed. "The Scottish earl and I were childhood friends." The violet eyes clouded over.

She saw again Glamis Castle, her family home, grey

stone, battlements, turrets. Glamis whose thane Macbeth had perpetrated his dreadful deed at Inverness. A ghost, the "monster of Glamis," still haunted the castle. There were other ghosts too, an army of servants and retainers, great rooms filled with laughing crowds, the skirl of the pipes as an old highlander circled the terraces each morning. She was a Jacobite to the marrow of her bones, hated the Hanoverians, those uncouth foreigners who now wore the crown of Britain. She remembered idyllic days in the highlands with that dark handsome Scottish aristocrat, her equal in lineage, wealth, beauty. Mornings when they had gone riding. Ben Davoir tipped with gold and purple. She lied that her horse was lame and he had lifted her down, held her for a moment. They had laid side by side in the heather and he had fallen asleep. She had covered him with her cloak. She had loved him as she had loved no other man, had fooled herself that her love was returned. Even to think about it after all those years lacerated her pride.

She raised herself on her pillows. "Lord Darnley's favourite poet was Callimachus. I would hardly expect you, an ignorant Irish peasant, to have heard of a Greek who lived before Christ." She beat the silken covers with her fist. "I saw Lord Darnley weep his heart out, heard him recite the poet when his boyhood companion was killed." The words were branded on her brain. "'Still do I hear thy pleasing voice when nightingales awake...for death he taketh all away, but them he cannot take.'" The husky voice faltered.

"What are you trying to tell me?" Peg whispered.

"That the two were lovers. My brother issued a challenge because my honour was smirched. The young boy fought a duel and was killed. Darnley mourned his loss in the fastness of his highland castle for a year. He has a death wish."

Peg felt the room swim around. Any moment the canopy over the bed would collapse, smother her. "But—but there is Belle Tudor," she heard herself stammering.

"Bah. Men have risked their all for a night of Belle's lasciviousness. But what does it signify?" She pushed back her mane of blue-black hair. "Lord Darnley is descended from Henry II and Eleanor of Aquitaine. They were crowned in the abbey six hundred years ago. Henry was said to be the handsomest man in England. Darnley is like his noble ancestor." Her voice was bitter. "But what would one such as you know of chivalrous times and high deeds. Go away and practise what wiles you possess on the strumpets and rogues that fill the Playhouse. I shall make other arrangements for my son. A tour of Europe with his tutor, the professor of Classics at Oxford. It is no new dilemma. The ancient Greeks loved their own sex and married to perpetuate their line. In the excitement of foreign lands and new faces, my son will forget he had a fancy for an actress." She spat out the last word and Peg left the room, humiliated, depressed. "Sweet God," she thought bitterly. "Must I always make a fool of myself? Will I ever learn?"

During the cold of that winter and the soft days of spring that followed, with their burgeoning trees and green places, Peg buried herself in her work, reading plays, learning lines, battling for parts, doing her best to avoid the feuds and intrigues that threatened at times to tear the Playhouse apart.

Occasionally Darnley visited her, sometimes just pausing to drink a glass of wine and tell her some harmless gossip. His time was largely taken up at court and he frequently left London for short periods, never revealing his destination. She discovered that he disliked being questioned, was secretive by nature, yet he appeared to trust her and she basked in his attention when he was near. He was enormously generous, spoiling her with stuffs and jewels, treating her as though she were a well-loved younger sister. Despite her much vaunted will-power, she knew she could all too easily fall in love with him and was on her guard against this.

Night after night she would awake in the small hours to the dark thoughts that filled her mind. At such times she felt she was walking a tight-rope, that an unwitting jolt, a slip, would plunge her into an abyss. She knew that to Darnley she spelt a kind of distraction. He would welcome no ties, allow no liberties, was wedded to his secret dream, and nothing and no one would be allowed come between him and the cause he espoused.

Then on a night in April everything changed. He arrived unexpectedly, dishevelled, exhausted, throwing himself down on the sofa, telling her he had been on a journey to Rome where the exiled James Stuart held court.

She gave him wine which he drank thirstily and after a while he roused himself and began to thump on the piano, filling the room with ugly discordant sounds. Then he seemed to grow calmer and began to play more melodiously, breaking into an old Irish piece, the heart-breaking sound filling her with nostalgia for Ireland.

"You play that beautifully," she whispered leaning over his shoulder. "What is it called?"

"It has no name. No one knows who the composer was except that he was an Ulsterman. Torlach O'Carolan, last of the Irish bards, a blind old man travelling the roads with his servant, came to visit my uncle's estate in Limerick each summer. He taught me to play the harp and gave me a love of your country's music."

"Tell me more of your life." It was seldom he spoke of his early days. This was the first time he had confided in her like this.

"There's little to tell. My mother married my father when she was scarce sixteen years. His family had fought for the Stuarts and lost everything in the '15 rebellion. My mother was a great heiress. Her fortune restored the estates." He moved restlessly around the room, picking things up, putting them down. "And now the Hanoverians are in the saddle, with their thick guttural English, monstrous women, spites and jealousies."

She sought to distract him. "In Dublin they have a ballad about the king." She hummed it to herself, unsure of his reactions and he took up the words, singing gustily:

> *You may strut, dapper George, but 'twill all be in*
> *vain.*
> *You know 'tis Queen Caroline, not you that do*
> *reign;*
> *You govern no more than Don Philip of Spain.*
> *Then if you would have us fall down and adore*
> *you,*
> *Lock up your fat spouse, as your Da did afore*
> *you.*

She felt emboldened to ask him, "Is it true what they say? Did the old king imprison his queen in the Castle of Ahlden for thirty years because she had taken a lover?"

"Yes, very true. And brought over two mistresses with him from Hanover, the fat Duchess of Kendal, known as the Elephant, and the Countess Von Platen, nicknamed the Maypole."

"Does this king hate the Prince of Wales?"

"All the Georges hate their heirs. It's a family failing."

"Poor prince," she said sadly.

He laughed. "Oh, Frederick has his compensations. Good wine, rich food, fat women. His latest passion is Lady Middlesex; two stomachs, three chins and ten children."

"I can scarcely believe that."

He stretched and caught her hand. "Would I lie to you, sweetling? You're a good wench and a good listener and that is why I put up with your quirks and quiddities. Pour me a bumper of wine and I'll give you a toast."

She did as he bid and he raised his glass. "To the prince over the water."

"You mean...?"

"Charles Edward Stuart." He drank and smashed the glass against the fireplace. It was as if a black shadow from an alien world had crept into the room.

"Drink to the prince. Or will you betray me, my Irish rose?"

She swallowed the wine, coughed and said harshly, "Máire Rua's ghost haunts Toonagh Woods near her ancestral home. She would haunt me if I betrayed any Jacobite. Not that I care who sits on the throne of England." Her voice softened. "But I would never betray a friend."

He took her in his arms. His lips claiming hers. He was carrying her to the four-poster bed and, despite her misgivings, despite all the promises she had made to herself, it was what she wanted. She had not thought he would make love so tenderly, so gently. He who was so practised in the art of seduction, he who was Belle Tudor's paramour, he who had given his heart to another and maybe more than that if Her Grace of Buckingham were to be believed. It was the first time she had known a man since the night of her rape in the Hellfire Club and she found herself trembling, unable to match his ardour, but filled with gratitude for his compassion and understanding.

❦

On May Day he arrived early to take her to the fair of Brookfield, near Hyde Park. Elatedly she dressed in a dark-green silk gown with fichus of lace at the shoulders and neck and caught back her hair with a golden fillet. Milkmaids and milkmen, apprentices and serving maids were out on the streets celebrating the coming of summer. Children danced around maypoles set up on greens, women trundled carts covered with flowers and kettles and salvers festooned with silver. Chimney sweeps, faces whitened with metal, heads covered with periwigs, banged brushes and scrapers in time to the beat of itinerant musicians. From all over London people were converging on Tyburn Road where the highwayman Jimmy Maclean had taken his last ride in a cart bedecked with flowers. She saw once again the golden-haired giant treading his last measure with the hangman while the onlookers went wild with excitement. Her thoughts ran on to her return to Dublin and her meeting with Charles Coffey—that dark hair winged with silver, the cleft chin, the steady grey eyes. She shivered as she remembered and sternly reminded herself that she must concentrate on this day which a sixth sense told her would be different to anything that had gone before. She would put the past away, both his and her own, forget what the duchess had told her. He had been young, carried away by his boyhood friend. He was so handsome, so generous, so witty, so reckless. That quality she had always admired. A legacy from her great-grandmother who had not known the meaning of fear.

Swings and roundabouts had filled up with young men and their sweethearts, laughing, screeching as they spun and swooped. Hand in hand they explored what the fair had to offer, losing money to the three-card-trick men, tossing silver to jugglers, applauding the daring of the sword-swallowers, the grace of the rope-dancers. Darnley tested his skill at hoop-la and won a doll which he presented to her with a flourish. At a painted stall they bought pies and a string of freshly cooked sausages and cakes coated with sugar from the gingerbread man. A swarthy foreigner sold them wine and they wandered away from the laughing crowds to a quiet spot down the river. At the door of a woodman's hut they sat drinking the wine which was potent and filled her with languor. I shall remember this place forever, she thought; sunlight and rippling water, scent of wild flowers, even this midge on my nose and his shoulder my pillow.

"There's a stretch of river in my part where the salmon come up and almost beg to be taken." His voice had the edge of loneliness and she made her own purposely gay.

"I was once on a tour with the Aungier Street Players. We travelled to Cork and an actor I liked well, Dónal Bán from Eriskay, took me fishing. The boat overturned in the Lee and we all but drowned. I swear I never laughed so much in all my life."

He settled his arm around her shoulder and she shivered with pleasure.

"Divert me, Peg. Tell me stories of when you were young."

Snuggling close she recalled her childhood days running wild with Kathleen McEnroe and later Jennie Tatler. She described Mr Quinn painted and powdered, reciting Shakespeare, Margaret Leeson boasting of the bawdy house with ceilings of mirrors and licentious paintings she hoped to own one day, the quick wit of the fishwives in the Earl of Meath's Liberties. Best of all, a story of how all the beggars in Dublin had gathered in a house in Francis Street to wake an old gleeman in whiskey and poteen and how in the midst of their roistering the corpse had sat up demanding his share of the drink.

"Egad, you are as companionable as a fellow." Darnley wiped tears of laughter from his eyes. "You remind me of someone I once knew." He traced her jawline, caressing her face, stroking back the curls which had come loose. "The same hair, the same green eyes." He kissed her nose, "Even that bridge of freckles." He was whispering in her hair. "'Still do I hear thy pleasing voice when nightingales awake, for death he taketh all away...'"

"No," she said fiercely. "No, not that." She would not be bested by a ghost. She leaned over him, kissing him passionately, running her hand down his body, fondling his thighs, caressing him, loving him, sensing his pain, knowing he was lost in the past. Then arms locked, they were stumbling into the hut and she sank on a bed of green rushes as he undressed her and then himself. Naked they merged together and as his mouth took her breasts she felt the weight she had carried since that terrible night on the Dublin Mountains melt. She was conscious of the rising surge of his passion, glad that at last she could match fervour. Her heart was pounding, her hands clutching his hair as they strained together. She tasted his sweat, heard herself whispering, "Oh please, oh yes, darling, oh yes..." Held him deep inside her until the wave broke over, washed them and she was carried away to a distant shore.

Hours later they sat by the river, spent but happy, drinking the last of the magical wine. "I could remain here forever," she said, stroking an errant lock of his hair. He helped her up and with an arm around her waist walked her a little distance to a rustic bridge, pausing to lean over and watch small fish leap to the fly. "I have something to tell you, Peg. No matter what happens you will be taken care of." Someone was walking over her grave. His words had the ring of finality, as if they were at a crossroads, parting. He was telling her that he was going to marry someone else, and her head was filled with the sound of his words. "I am nearing forty," he was saying. "The path I have chosen is fraught with danger, intrigue. If I am lucky my end will come in a highland glen," his voice hardened, "but not before I have struck a blow for the rightful king."

"Rightful king." The words had no meaning for her. She beat his chest with her fists. "The duchess warned me. She said you had the death wish."

"Sarah meddles in every pool," he said tiredly. "I need a son to inherit, to carry on the family name."

"Damn your family," she raged silently. "Damn your pride and your fine lineage." He knew her shameful secret, that because of what had happened that night in the Hellfire Club she could never bear a child. Yet she also knew that if she were as fertile as Lady Middlesex he would not think her a fit mother for his children. She was tainted.

She was sick to the pit of her stomach. Was this to be the story of her life? Coffey's betrayal, Taafe's death, Darnley's mad dream in which she had no part. She choked back her tears. She was being unfair. He had never given her cause for hope. It was she who had seduced him, taken advantage of his lost dreams.

She tilted her chin. She would not beg, would cling to her pride. "When do you plan to wed?" Her voice was high, light.

He shrugged. "Sometime in the autumn. My grandmother will arrange matters. My intended bride is learning to be a great lady at the court of France." He turned her to him and she blinked angrily, tears stinging her lids. "Leave me alone."

"Don't, darling," he said softly and the kindness of his voice broke through her defences.

"You think I'm like Belle Tudor," she wept.

He laughed and gave her a handkerchief. "Dry your eyes and blow your nose. What a child you are. You would never make a great courtesan, your heart rules your head. Poor Belle."

She coughed. "Poor Belle indeed. I thought she was

great and successful and skilled in her profession. They say men have ruined themselves, died for a night of her love-making."

"True, and now she is dying. Already she lives on borrowed time. Arrangements have been made for her last journey to a convent in France where she lived as a child. There she will finish her days." His eyes were dark. "Belle was once the most beautiful woman in Europe, but to us all, death comes as an end."

Peg nodded mutely. There was nothing left to say.

"It is time for me to escort you home," he said formally and gave her his arm. Slowly they made their way back through the noise of the fair, grown shrill and menacing, two fashionably dressed people, she playing her part, prattling gaily, he flirting lightly. And she thought, does one ever know, and sighed for the past that could not be called back, for the day that had started out so brightly, so full of promise, and for the night that must fall.

16

I n the month of June Rich's dwarf was found in an alleyway with a knife in his back. He had terrorised the denizens of the sleazy streets and lanes around Covent Garden and amassed a fortune by bribery, blackmail and other means. Few mourned his departure. He left all he possessed to his cousin Priscilla Stevens, a minor actress in the Playhouse, mousy, with washed-out eyes, pale lashes, stringy hair and a complexion that even paint and powder failed to improve. She had spent much of her life in bondage to the dwarf and now that she had come into her own she set about donning a mantle of respectability, becoming a strict churchgoer, moving into the house in Bloomsbury Square and having the menagerie of cats put down.

"You have recently taken it upon yourself to engage Mrs Clive for the season's plays, promising her more than she was paid in Drury Lane. You will tell her that this cannot be," she told the bewildered Mr Rich who appeared to have lost the will to assert himself since the hunchback's untimely demise.

"For twenty years I have managed the Playhouse in my own way," he said, face mottled with anger.

Priscilla tightened her lips. "Allow me remind you that I now control the purse strings. Licentiousness and loose living in the Playhouse must cease. Peg Woffington is a kept woman. Her paramour Lord Darnley is said to have Jacobite sympathies."

"She is a fine actress and has a good following," Mr Rich protested but Priscilla swept on. "There is another matter which gives me pause," she fixed him with a beady eye. "It is not fitting that I, a Christian woman, should share a house with a man without benefit of clergy. I have decided to marry you and have fixed the date for our nuptials." Mr Rich's baby face crumpled. He had no wish to marry anyone, least of all this harridan who had taken over his home, murdered his cats and was now bent on destroying his theatre. He was a simple man who did not hold with learning but he remembered the late Mr Quinn, head thrown back, quoting from a playwright called Heywood, long since forgotten. How did the lines go? He dug deep in the recesses of his memory and triumphantly brought out the lines. "Oh God, that it were possible. To undo things done, to call back yesterday."

Priscilla gave him a look of mingled exasperation and scorn and swept out of the room. Left to himself the little man executed a dance of triumph. Unlettered he might be, but his brain was as good as the next. He would get the better of this woman yet. To cheer himself up he poured himself a large glass of port which he downed at one gulp, drinking to the downfall of the weaker sex.

Priscilla's maid, given to listening at keyholes, related as much as she could remember of the conversation to Mrs Bellamy who, in her role as custodian of the Playhouse, hastened to spread the news. Kitty Clive was enraged beyond measure. She had been wooed from Drury Lane by Rich with the promise of an increase in salary and two benefit performances a year. She needed the money. Her husband, Mr Eustace Clive, five years her junior, the younger son of an impoverished baron, spent his days gambling in clubs and coffee houses, toadying to the bucks of the town, ordering Kitty to open her purse as frequently as he ordered her open her legs. In a night of pillow talk with his wife he heard of the doings of the Playhouse, tittered over the dilemma of the reluctant bridegroom and agreed that mutiny was brewing amongst the actors. Next morning he sold the story to a newspaper hack and when it appeared in print there was uproar at rehearsal. Mr Rich in a fit of fury threatened Kitty and she smashed a vase on his bald pate. Peg, who had been sleeping badly, threw down the script she had been shredding to pieces and stormed out the door.

"Drat the Playhouse. I declare I am sick of Mr Rich and that woman Stevens, sick of Kitty Clive's tantrums," she grumbled to Mrs Bellamy who had insisted on accompanying her back to the apartment in New Bond Street. When Kitty had first made her appearance in the Covent Garden Playhouse, Mrs Bellamy had wavered in her allegiance to Peg but common sense had prevailed. Kitty was tough, hard, with a commanding presence and boundless self-confidence. She had no need of support.

Mrs Bellamy clucked in sympathy. "Mr Rich is losing his grip. Luring Kitty from Drury Lane, getting himself entangled with Priscilla Stevens all within a couple of days."

Peg held her aching head. "I cannot conceive of a more ill-assorted couple than that pair. I doubt me if the wedding will ever take place."

"Mr Rich has no choice. Priscilla holds the whip-hand. I can foresee nothing but trouble in Covent Garden." Mrs Bellamy eyed Peg speculatively. "You appear in low spirits.

Why don't you take a trip to Bath? All the aristocracy go to drink the waters."

Since the day at the May Fair she had been feeling out of sorts, no appetite, her dreams haunted by Darnley. It was time she forged a life of her own, free of any man. She would force Rich to give her better parts, more money, would be damned if she would stand idly by while Kitty Clive played leading lady in the theatre. Mrs Bellamy had scarcely departed before an irate Kitty arrived and without preamble launched into her grievances. "Mr Rich and that woman Stevens must be taught a lesson. Between us we fill the theatre." Peg could scarcely believe her ears. This from Kitty who never gave anyone credit for anything.

"It will go ill with you once they are wed," Kitty continued. "Like Caesar's wife I am above reproach but the world and his wife knows of your liaison with that Scottish rebel."

"Lord Darnley's politics are his own affair," Peg said coldly. Little did Kitty or anyone else realise that the affair had ended.

Kitty gave a sour smile. "The question is what are we going to do about Priscilla Stevens? Religious fanatics are dangerous. Why only last week she had the temerity to ask Mr Handel to put music to a hymn she has lately discovered called 'Sinners Obey.' Needless to say he refused. Like Rich, she's an upstart. They both started life as strolling players." She paused for breath.

"Let me remind you," Peg said, "that we both cut our stage teeth in Madame Violante's booth in Dublin."

Kitty looked down her long nose. "I quite forgot you came out of a run-down hovel in George's Lane and that my grandmother was forced to give your family credit."

"Your huckstering grandmother was paid every penny,

Mrs Clive. Is she still cheating the poor of Dublin?"

Kitty stood up. Her shadow threw a spider outline on the wall. Pulling her cloak around her in a parody of Hamlet, she recited in a deep-toned voice

She is dead and gone, lady.
She is dead and gone,
At her head a grass-green turf;
At her heels a stone.

Peg reddened with embarrassment. "I must apologise," but Kitty full of her own affairs was explaining. "My grandmother left me a considerable sum. It soon went to pay Mr Clive's debts. Like all aristocrats he has a mind above money."

Peg wondered, and not for the first time, why Kitty allowed the weedy creature she called husband to batten on her. "What do you suggest we do?"

"Deliver Mr John Rich an ultimatum."

"And if he sacks us?"

Complacently Kitty patted her wig. "Why Mr Fleetwood will be delighted to have me back." She gave Peg a sly look. "Only last week he was heard to praise your acting. If we hold firm Rich must yield. He cannot afford to lose his two leading ladies in one go."

❧

Rich, sprawled in his chair in the greenroom, listened unmoved to Kitty's diatribe. Peg said little. He would be glad to be rid of Mrs Clive with her temper and tantrums. She was a born troublemaker for all she was a fine actress. Priscilla might give him some peace if he sacked Peg

Woffington as well as Clive. If the rumours that Lord Darnley intended to wed with his cousin were true, Peg might find herself without a following. The bucks of London were notoriously fickle. Kitty scared him but Priscilla was worse. He had encouraged the dwarf's appetite for opium, would even fix his pipe. Perhaps his bride-to-be might be encouraged to develop a taste for gin. To his relief she had decreed that they would occupy separate bedrooms. Sex would play no part in their marriage. The thought of this gave him courage. Folding his pudgy hands on his paunch he delivered a broadside. "I filled the theatre before either of you shook the dust of Dublin from your feet. My advice to you Mrs Clive and to you Mistress Woffington is to take what little talents you possess elsewhere."

In a matter of hours Kitty was closeted in the manager's office in Drury Lane. But when Peg made her bid to join the company she was politely told that one temperamental Irish actress was enough in any theatre and shown the door.

❦

Peg opened her eyes. Darnley had come unannounced into her bedroom and now stood looking down at her with sombre eyes. He looked tired, travel-stained and with a week's growth of beard.

She pulled herself up, the effort was almost too much. "Where did you spring from? I thought you were in Scotland."

Briefly he bent and kissed her. "Further afield, my pet. I arrived back from France today and heard you had succumbed to the influenza. What's this I hear of trouble in the Playhouse?"

Mrs Bellamy launched into a saga of rows, sackings and the influenza that was sweeping the town. "I have nursed Peg as tenderly as if she were my own George Ann." She wiped away a virtuous tear. "I have quite worn myself out."

Darnley listened in silence then produced a sovereign. "A little fresh air will restore your spirits. A new hat, gloves, I believe such trifles are a panacea for all ills."

"What a fraud you are, Darnley, flattering her so wantonly," Peg scolded when the door closed behind the plump figure and gushing voice. "Now I shall be forced to listen to a litany of your virtues for weeks to come," she sighed. "I feel so downcast."

He settled her pillows. "The little girl I first met had more courage." Her eyes were puffy, her hair hanging in lank strands. Yet he thought she had never looked more desirable. "Maybe some wine will cheer you up; I fetched it all the way from the cellars of a dissolute French count."

❧

The bottle was empty. She touched his face. She had drunk too much, too quickly, and the room was rotating gently but it was a pleasant sensation. She held out her arms and they began to kiss, gently even calmly at first, then with mounting passion.

Evening shadows were creeping into the room. The little gold clock on the mantelpiece chimed the hour of nine. He rolled out of the bed and began to pull on his shirt. "I must go."

"I feel so much better." She smiled.

He turned and slapped her bottom. "Hippocrates once said 'For extreme illness, extreme treatment is most fitting!'"

"Advise me, darling. What should I do?"

"Join me in Bath."

"Are you serious, Darnley? Only today Mrs Bellamy gave me the same advice."

He chuckled. "A goodly woman. Her price is above rubies."

"That woman would sell her soul for a sovereign," she said sourly.

He leaned over and bit her shoulder. "Bring her with you to Bath. You'll need a chaperon."

Life in the house in the Crescent which Darnley had rented in the spa was pleasant. Each morning Peg and an overdressed Mrs Bellamy took the baths and drank the mineral waters. Afternoons they shopped, attended concerts in the Assembly Room or received callers. Tactfully Mrs Bellamy spent most of her evenings with new friends she had made while Peg read novels and waited for Darnley. He was in constant attendance on the prince at the gaming tables where a man might win a fortune in cornfields or lose a manor house on the throw of a dice, and it was often the small hours of the morning before he was free to join her. He was ardent, tender, passionate by turns and the thought that this might be their last time together only added poignancy to their love-making.

The month was drawing to a close. On the morrow the Prince of Wales would return to London and Darnley make the long journey to the Scottish highlands and whatever the future might bring. He had come to her early and she had ordered his favourite supper, oysters, chicken in wine, a sorbet and cheesecake. When the meal was eaten they sat on a love-stool beside a fire of bright seacoals. Later the pain of parting would tear her apart but now she felt warm, at peace. Gently he closed her lids. "I have a surprise for you."

She felt him move away. Then put something into her hand. Her fingers smoothed the velvet.

"Open your eyes, Peg."

She was holding a flat velvet box. He leaned forward and undid the clasp. "A last gift for my love."

A coal crackled, settled down, shooting flames lit up the room, the white diamonds glittered, emeralds threw off green sparks. Nestling in a bed of satin was a set of matching jewels, emerald and diamond necklace, bracelet and ear-rings. She drew in a breath. "They're beautiful."

"A memento of our time together. Do you love me, Peg?"

"So much that it hurts."

He was taking off her bedgown of ivory silk and lace, kissing her white skin, carrying her naked to the great four-poster bed.

Hours later, satiated, love spent, she stroked his face. "This is good-bye, Darnley?"

In the moonlight his face was carved ivory. "Tomorrow I leave for Scotland."

She felt a fierce stab of jealousy, longed with all her soul to be his wife, give him the son he wanted so much. Would the young Scottish girl learning to be a great lady in the courts of France make him happy? Would any woman satisfy the demon that possessed him? He was dedicated to the Jacobite cause and in her soul Peg knew that the cause was doomed. She had vowed that when the time came she would let him go gently and with good grace. She traced the lines of his face, high cheek-bones, dark hair in a widow's peak, eyelashes so long, so thick that a woman might sell her soul to possess them. He was the handsomest man she had ever known and the most generous.

"Promise me you will be happy, my darling," she whispered.

"Enough of this melancholy, Peg. Remember the first time we met when you enchanted me with Brutus's farewell?"

She pulled a face. "What a show-off I was!"

He chuckled. "When I was a boy an old astronomer called Walter Pope dedicated a poem to me. Let me see how it goes."

> *If I live to be old, for I find I go down,*
> *Let this be my fate: in a country town*
> *May I have a warm house, with a stone at the*
> > *gate*
> *And a cleanly young girl to rub my bald pate.*

"Don't Darnley," she begged. He saw her tears and his heart turned over. From the first moment he had set eyes on her she had the power to move him as no other woman ever could.

❦

It was customary for Frederick, Prince of Wales, to visit the pump-room on his last morning in Bath. Figures like painted puppets in satin and gold with monstrous wigs, faces covered with patches, formed lines and circles around the tables which held glasses of mineral waters. Small black pages carried pug dogs; ripe dowagers wearing too many jewels surreptitiously sipped cordials and pulled wry faces as if they were downing the foul-tasting mineral waters. Darnley, his hand on Peg's arm, led her to where the prince was holding court. He bowed. "Pray allow me present Mrs Woffington, Highness, the flower of the London stage. You will have seen her grace the Covent Garden Playhouse."

Peg curtseyed low and the royal blue eyes popped in surprise. Gad, Darnley had taste. She was a beauty and no mistake. He stroked his fine brocade coat, decorated with ribbons and honours. But for Lady Middlesex, he might honour this minx with his bed. He coughed. "I have enjoyed your playacting, ma'am. Pray let me know when next you appear on the stage." Her lips quivered. "Alas sire, I am without a situation. Mr Rich has dismissed me from the Covent Garden and Mr Fleetwood of Drury Lane has no place for me." She dabbed her eyes. "Pray forgive me, sire, I find myself in such low spirits."

Frederick was not noted for his sensibility but she was a deuced pretty woman, besides he wished to please Darnley who was a handsome loser at cards. All nonsense about his Jacobite sympathies. "Dry your eyes," he ordered avuncularly, "I shall be slow to patronise any theatre where my favourite actress is not welcome."

Peg kissed the bejewelled hand in gratitude and the prince moved off with Darnley gravely bringing up the rear.

"My dear, you will be much sought after." Mrs Bellamy's gushing voice filled the pump-room. "And to think you are his Highness's favourite actress. Rich and Fleetwood must be told of this. We must return to London at once."

Peg was in no hurry to leave Bath. Such news would travel fast. Let Rich and Fleetwood stew. The highest bidder would win. Mrs Bellamy would, of course, embroider the story, describe how the prince had invited Mrs Woffington to his bed, had begged her not to abandon the London stage. She should be able to dine out for a month at least on her story.

❦

Fleetwood received Peg with the utmost affability, kissing her hand, enquiring after her health. "One of my players has fallen ill," he said in the tone of a doctor telling a patient that after all he would live. "I find I have a place for you in the company."

She sank gracefully into a chair, shrugging back her sable-trimmed cloak, revealing the simple gown that set off her jewels, looking very much the *grande dame*, assured, knowing her worth. "Should I decide to join Drury Lane, I would of course guarantee to fill the theatre. Where the Prince of Wales goes, all London follows."

Fleetwood wrung his hands in an ecstasy of delight. "Royal patronage is all. I shall have the royal box renovated. It is my wont on such an occasion to stand at the entrance to the theatre, holding a silver candelabrum to escort royalty to their fitting place."

Peg shrugged lightly. "Should I join your company I would expect a salary of £250 per year."

Fleetwood's saturnine face grew longer. She had to repress a desire to giggle. "A sum way beyond my purse, I fear."

Studiously she swung a buckled shoe. "In addition I should expect a benefit performance each season, which, with my connections, should bring me £500 plus a costume allowance of £50."

Fleetwood loosened his cravat. "What you ask is impossible, ma'am."

She pulled on her gloves, fastening them carefully. "I do owe Mr Rich a certain loyalty. The Covent Garden Playhouse is where I first trod the boards."

Fleetwood knew when he was beaten. He despised Rich whom he considered a pantomime clown. It was not to be borne that the fat little man and his shrew of a wife should lord it over him. He must gain her services no matter how high the price. "You will ruin me, Madame. Were I wise I would not take the chance."

A dimple played on her chin. "Chance rules our life." Something made her add, "One day you will boast of my talents." She was twenty-two years of age but in her wildest dreams she could never imagine that she was destined to become in time the most famous actress on the London stage and all because of the genius of an unknown country boy who would, in turn, become a legend in his own lifetime.

The play's the thing
Wherein I'll catch the conscience, of the King.

(*Hamlet*, II,II)

17

O wen M'Swiney, making his way to Peg's apartment in New Bond Street, marvelled at the change that had taken place in London in so short a time. The very air of the city pulsated with life. Shrewd aristocrats, canny builders, men with their way to make were buying up derelict houses, farms, land around London, commissioning architects to design redbrick houses and mansions, arcades of shops, concert halls, offices. By now the boundaries of the city were extending beyond the green acres of Hyde Park, encroaching on Hampstead village, marching down Tyburn Road, swallowing up the village of Marylebone where the ghost of a former abbot kept his vigil in the ruins of the monastery, expiating the sins of his life. Old wives told tales that the abbot had melted down a gold monstrance to buy the life of his mistress charged with the murder of her husband. Afterwards she had married another and in despair he had hanged himself from a willow tree.

Shops were brightly lit, remained open until midnight and were better stocked and carried more elegant displays of goods than those in the fashionable Rue St Honoré, in Paris. Side by side with ostentatious displays of wealth were the casualties of a war that would drag on in Europe for another six years. Soldiers lacking a leg or an arm begged for alms to fill their bellies, to quench their thirst. Country girls once fresh-faced, rosy-lipped, now scarred and riddled with disease, plied their age-old profession down on the docks, in sleazy streets, under London's bridges, in brothels. Beggars, thieves, ragged children crowded the markets, stealing, fighting, scavenging, rotting their guts with the gin which they had drunk with their mother's milk. Spitalfields, once a thriving community of weavers, was now little more than a warren of overcrowded houses and dingy taverns.

M'Swiney had just returned from a year's sojourn in Rome where he had shared a palace with his lover, a young nobleman of impeccable lineage and dissolute habits. The dry Roman air had aged the actor, his once fresh Irish complexion was sallow and the wearing of the bright wig of a younger man only accentuated his years. Yet he was still the dandy, painted, powdered, with priceless lace at wrists and neck.

They had eaten well. Peg had ordered a ragout, chicken in wine, cheese, garlic bread, apricots in jelly. His favourite foods. Now replete, he sat back in an armchair, smoking his pipe, demanding to be given the theatre gossip. Peg twisted the stem of her glass, watching the bubbles dance. "The town is agog with the talents of a young man called David Garrick. We had a brief encounter the night the Duchess of Buckingham gave a ball. He was with an older man. If I remember rightly you were present and exchanged courtesies."

"Aye, I remember Samuel Johnson, a heavy and ponderously spoken man yet with some wit. But this Garrick made no impression. Is he a Londoner?"

"I believe he comes from Lichfield. I understand he enrolled at the Inns, but soon tired of the law and went into partnership with his brother, a wine merchant on the Strand. Lord Burlington has introduced him to the great houses of the city where he takes part in private theatricals."

M'Swiney took a sip of brandy. "I dislike the dilettante. Acting is a trade like any other and needs an apprenticeship."

"He is to appear professionally in a run-down theatre somewhere to the east of Aldgate next week. I should like to attend the first night." Peg gave him a charming smile.

The painted face creased in a smile of pleasure. "I will be honoured to escort you, m'dear. What news of Lord Darnley?"

"Darnley married his cousin last summer and has forsaken London to live on his Scottish estates." To be forced to speak his name was pain. Only at night in her lonely bed did she allow herself the luxury of tears. He had paid her a brief farewell visit and they had exchanged last gifts. His a small diamond brooch in the shape of a heart, hers a miniature of her head and shoulders, painted on ivory by a young French artist she had met in a shop near St Paul's Cathedral. His going was like a death. She wrenched her thoughts away from the past. Owen M'Swiney was talking about Scotland. "Jacobites everywhere plotting the return of the 'Young Pretender' as they call the Stuart. Your erstwhile admirer, Peg, owes loyalty to the House of Hanover."

Any criticism of Darnley hurt, but the words "erstwhile admirer" was like turning the knife. By what right, she thought passionately, did an Irish peasant sit in judgement on a man whose line went back to the Crusades and beyond?

She said angrily, "Surely you of all people, Mr M'Swiney,

should understand Lord Darnley's love of lost causes? Is his story so different from our own?" At that moment she hated him, only wished he were gone, that she could take herself to bed and weep herself to sleep.

He stuck out his lower lip. "You disappoint me, Peg. Are you by any chance a Papist?"

"I come of a long line of Catholics on my mother's side." She would be damned if she'd admit to this man that she hardly ever set foot inside a church.

"I hate all Papists." He spoke with a venom that shocked her and in a blinding flash she realised the truth. Without thinking she lashed out, "There speaks the apostate," and immediately could have bitten off her tongue at the look of blind misery on his face. He had been kind to her in the old days in Covent Garden, had called off the dogs, helped her with parts, even lent her money. But for him she might have given it all up, gone back to Dublin. Impulsively she leaned across and kissed his wrinkled cheek. She said softly:

> Bid me to live, and I will live
> Thy Protestant to be:
> Or bid me love, and I will give
> A loving heart to thee.

He smiled. "Graciously spoken, Peg, though I don't think the poet had religion in mind. Let's drink to it anyhow."

He left soon after and she thought no more of the incident, little suspecting that the few lines of Herrick tossed lightly across a supper table would be remembered by him as a pledge in the years to come.

❧

They were being carried across a bridge spanning the Thames, past houses with splendid façades which gradually gave way to mean streets of ramshackle buildings. Rain and wind had swept London for over twenty-four hours. Channels overflowed, refuse and dirt piled high, water-spouts poured their contents on the hats and wigs of people hurrying by, roof tiles splintered on cobblestones, signs swung crazily from shops and houses. With a lurch the hackney swung into the Weavers Quarter and the Tower of London loomed up, implacable, grey in the watery light. In a narrow street half-naked women hung out of windows or leaned in doorways, plying their trade. From every house hung a bunch of grapes, the sign of the brothel. Decay, urine, mildew, shit, mingled with the sweet rotten stenches that drifted up from the river, permeating everything.

Peg felt they had been travelling for ever, were on a Stygian journey of no return. "Where is he taking us? Has he lost his way?"

M'Swiney peered out the window. "We're riding through Goodman's Fields, what they call the stews."

Dear God. What a place to launch a career, thought Peg, and wondered if they should tell the driver to turn back but he was pulling up in a narrow street at a grey building with a playbill stuck to the wall and Owen M'Swiney was helping her out. While he paid the fare, she read by the flickering yellow street light

> *This evening at six o'clock, a concert of vocal and instrumental music will be presented in the Fleece Theatre, followed by a tragedy entitled*

> *The Life and Death of King Richard the Third*
> *by William Shakespeare. The part of Richard*
> *will be taken by a gentleman who has never*
> *before appeared on the stage. Places for boxes to*
> *be taken at the Fleece Tavern next door.*

After the damp cold and dank misery of the night outside, the tavern, low-ceilinged, spanned by oaken beams, exuded warmth; a fire burned in an open hearth and there were wooden benches ranged along smoky walls. A burly innkeeper was leaning across the counter, boasting to anyone who would listen of his nephew. "Mr Giffard's his name, sir," he told the newcomers. "Put himself out on a limb, he did, to help this new actor, Mr Garrick. Could mean the end of the Fleece, close the place. The nephew hasn't a licence to put on a play. He thinks he foxed them by charging for the concert, throwing the play in for free. How it will end no one knows for sure. Three shillings is the price of admission, and good value at that." He pushed two brass tokens across the counter, inscribed with the words "The Playhouse" and "The Fleece." "That'll be six shillings, if you please sir."

While M'Swiney paid the reckoning and engaged the innkeeper in further gossip about the production, Peg sat by the fire, sipping her port. A couple of sailors with their whores staggered in. Peg recognised Chastity at once though three years had elapsed since she had fled the house in Bull Alley for the brothel.

"Come here, Chastity!" she called. "I want to speak to you."

Reluctantly the painted and tawdrily dressed youngster sidled over. "I expects you're going to call the constable because I robbed your purse," she said sullenly.

Peg arranged her face in a suitably grave expression. "I wanted to thank you for arranging that interview with the dwarf. He kept his word and I got my chance."

Chastity grinned. She lifted her skirt, showing a grubby silk petticoat. "He was done in and small blame to the one responsible. He was a bad 'un, that little runt."

Peg thought the girl had aged beyond her years. "How is it with you, Chastity? Do you like the life?"

The painted blue eyes puckered. "It's not bad—better'n Sarah Pepys. I'm in the whorehouse around the corner and the pickings is good. Sailors on leave with money." Defiantly she settled her red-feathered hat. "I weren't going to be a slave all me life." For a moment her mask of bravado slipped and she looked the frightened youngster she was. "All the same I'd 'ave liked to see the world. Pity the charity folk rescued me from that ship."

For no reason at all Charles Coffey came into Peg's mind. He had taken ship with Alice Morgan for the New World like thousands more. It all seemed so long ago, as if she had known him in another life. "Why don't you go to America?" she heard herself saying. "I'm told there are great opportunities there."

Chastity's eyes lit up and Peg warmed to the idea she had thrown out so carelessly. "You're young, your life is before you. Women are scarce in the colonies. You could marry a decent man, live a normal life, have children of your own. You'll grow old before your time consorting with sailors, rotten with foreign diseases."

Chastity hunched her shoulders defensively. "Wot chance is there for me! A girl in the house is savin' ter git away, money hidden under the boards." She grinned. "I was tempted but I won't steal it on 'er. 'Er pimp gives her a time of it. Broke her nose he did."

"Would you go with her if you had the price of the passage?"

Chastity rubbed her eyes. "Ah what's the use of talkin'. Them old Quakers spoiled me chance."

Peg rooted in her bag but all she had was a couple of shillings. She unpinned the diamond brooch from her gown and put it in Chastity's hands, closing the nail-bitten fingers over the diamond-encrusted heart. "It's real, Chastity. A pawnbroker in a shop beside St Paul's Cathedral will give you a fair price, enough to pay your passage to New York. Tell him I sent you. Tell him I'll redeem it for whatever sum he gives you. He knows me. If you let me down I swear you won't have a moment's luck. Now hide it somewhere. Don't tell your companions."

"Take me for a fool. Fanks again." The brooch disappeared in a flash and, bending over, Chastity planted a moist kiss on Peg's cheek and was gone.

"Giving that slut your valuable brooch." Owen M'Swiney was standing beside her frowning.

"Don't lecture me," Peg said shortly. "I'll buy it back from the pawnbroker. I only hope he gives her a decent price."

"She'll drink the money or the whoremaster will beat it out of her."

Peg got to her feet and put a hand on his arm. "Chastity can contrive when it suits her. I know her of old. She's an odd little thing. I owe her a lot." She rubbed her head. Strange how often it ached these days. "She brought me luck before; maybe the same will happen again. She's my talisman."

M'Swiney grunted. What a strange girl was Peg, with her hair and eyes. In his own place she might be considered a witch like her ancestor, Máire Rua. Something told him she had the second sight.

Outside the inn someone was beating a drum, a sign that the concert was over and the play about to commence. Peg followed her companion into the dingy street. Chastity and her companions had vanished.

The interior of the Fleece was shabby, run-down, with damp walls. Already the broken seats were filling up with the poor of the place—garishly dressed women, men with grey lined faces in shabby clothes, though here and there a sober jacket lent weight to a respectable weaver and his bonneted wife or an embroidered waistcoat highlighted a precious dandy who with his fancy had come from afar to see the new actor. Orange wenches shouted their wares, their voices high and strident above the noise which continued unabated even when a young actor came downstage to recite the prologue.

Then it happened. From out the wings a hunched figure emerged, made a hesitant gesture. Pulling his plum-coloured robes about him he limped in front of a painted backdrop depicting a London street. Fixing his bright and piercing eyes upon the backless benches of the pit, he launched into Gloucester's opening speech:

Now is the winter of our discontent
Made glorious summer by this sun of York;
And all the clouds that lower'd upon our house
In the deep bosom of the ocean buried.

Gradually the noise died away and the house settled down, conscious that something new and strange was happening on stage. David Garrick, against all theatrical conventions, was acting naturally, his hunchback form casting the shadow of a grotesque crow on walls and the floor. His whispered words could be clearly heard in every corner of the house and Peg thought, for the first time I am seeing Richard Crookback as Shakespeare created him. Driven by ambition, twisted by deformity, subtle, treacherous, false, pitiful.

In that wonderful voice was the cry, the pain and bitterness of every cripple born:

Deform'd, unfinish'd, sent before my time
Into this breathing world scarce half made up...

Measured against Garrick's performance, the Lady Anne's reading was impossibly coy. She spat at Gloucester as a simpering milkmaid might and Peg bit her lips telling herself fiercely, "I'd sell my soul to be playing opposite him in that part."

The Lady Anne was gone, the corpse of the king carried away and the hunchback executed a little dance of triumph, his courtship of the queen concluded:

Was ever woman in this humour woo'd?
Was ever woman in this humour won?

He grinned evilly. "I'll have her; but I will not keep her long," made a ripple run through the theatre.

To the spellbound audience the play rolled to its inevitable conclusion and Richard, monstrous, terrible, half-crazed yet with a courage that had something of greatness, went to his death mouthing the words:

A horse! a horse! my kingdom for a horse!

Peg stumbled to her feet, scarcely conscious of her

companion helping her up. "I must go backstage to meet him."

He was in a ramshackle room, still costumed, face streaked with paint and sweat, surrounded by people, actors, friends, hangers-on. Sam Johnson was there with an ample middle-aged woman, over-rouged, patched, wearing hoops so monstrously wide she moved with difficulty.

He knew Peg was in the room, even before he saw her. Impatiently he pushed through the crowds and their eyes locked. He took her hand to his lips, then dropped it and laughed so lightly she wondered was it all part of an act. "You came all this way to see the play. Had I known you were in the audience I should have been quite unnerved."

"Nonsense. That was a splendid performance." They were like actors on stage, reciting lines they had learnt by rote. She wanted to tell him that something magic had happened in the shabby playhouse this night, that she had seen Shakespeare as if for the first time, but there were too many people, too much noise, too much confusion.

He was smiling at her and she thought he is slender, no taller than I and yet he gives the impression of height, strength. His voice, warm, captivating, was begging her to grant him a favour. Did he need money? An introduction to Fleetwood at Drury Lane? Of course she would do anything to further his career. "If I can be of any help..." the words sounded lame, grudging.

"If I could call on you. There is much you could teach me."

"You will be most welcome." She turned a brilliant smile on Sam Johnson. "Why don't you and your good wife join Mr Garrick when he visits me? Next Sunday afternoon would suit. The theatre is closed. Come at four of the clock."

Mrs Johnson said eagerly in her little girl voice, "Sammy likes nothing better than a dish of strong tea."

Johnson took her arm. "It is time we were on our way, Tetty."

Her red lips were set in a pout. "I had thought we were to join Davy for supper."

"He may have changed his mind," Johnson said stiffly and Peg took her cue. "You will excuse me. I have an early rehearsal tomorrow morning. I look forward to our next meeting. My apartment is in New Bond Street, two doors from the cook shop. You will have no trouble in finding your way."

They were laughing, talking; Garrick was kissing her hand gaily and Sam Johnson, who knew his friend better than anyone else, offered a silent prayer that the great Peg Woffington would be kind to this besotted young man who had no thought for his triumph but only for the girl with red hair.

❧

Each night the space between Temple Bar and Whitechurch was filled with coaches, hackneys, chairs, even crested carriages for the east end was the place to be seen and to see this new young actor play the part of the hunchback king. The Covent Garden and Drury Lane theatres were playing to half empty houses and there were rumblings backstage from managers, actors and the moneyed men who had fingers in every pie. Matters came to a head when the most influential critic in London visited the Fleece and wrote his assessment of the play.

Last night I witnessed The Tragedy of King Richard the Third *at the Fleece Theatre, Goodman's Fields, when the character of Gloucester was performed by an actor newly come to the stage. The reception given him was the most extraordinary ever known on such an occasion. This young man bears the hallmark of the truly talented. He has brought in a new natural acting style which I foretell will change the face of our London stage.*

Elrington and Rich combined to send a joint petition to the Lord Chamberlain to have the Fleece closed down. Their petition was granted and on the last day of April 1742, the final curtain fell on the little theatre that had made history in a few short weeks.

John Rich of Covent Garden moved first, offering Garrick three hundred guineas for the autumn/winter season, while all London waited for Fleetwood to make his bid. Garrick called to the apartment in New Bond Street on the afternoon of his meeting with the Drury Lane manager. A bright fire flickered, casting shadows on ceiling and walls, and the room smelt of attar of roses which Peg had sprinkled with a lavish hand, remembering the glory that was Buck House. She was wearing sprigged muslin, had bound her hair with a yellow ribbon and wore shoes with golden heels. Excitement and anxiety had lent colour to her face; her cheeks were flushed, her eyes bright. To the adoring eyes of Garrick, she was the girl of his dreams, whom he had first sighted in Covent Garden on a day in spring and with whom he was now hopelessly in love.

"Darling." He held out his arms. "Fleetwood has offered me six hundred pounds for the season with two clear benefits, together with an undertaking that I can choose my own plays. As part of the agreement he will employ Mr Giffard, who gave me my first chance in the Fleece. Giffard is to be the new assistant-manager of Drury Lane."

No other actor in the history of the stage had ever been offered such terms. Trembling with nerves, Peg filled two glasses with wine, splashing her gown. He was on his knees in a trice, mopping the stain, and she was thrilled and yet awed at her effortless conquest of this young man so gifted, the boyish figure who was already being talked about as the greatest actor on the London stage. "I am to make three guest appearances in Drury Lane before the season ends," he was telling her, "and you, my sweet Peg, are to play Ophelia to my Hamlet, Cordelia to my Lear and Lady Anne to my Richard." She was crying and laughing and they were hugging each other and he was prising open her lips with his tongue. Breathlessly she pushed him away. "Please, Mr Garrick. No."

He dropped his head. "Forgive me. I was carried away, but oh, please call me by my name."

Such a boy. She smiled. "It will be an honour to act with you, David." He was drunk with success, buoyed up with hope. "Someday you will look on me with more kindness. 'Your beauty that did haunt me in my sleep.'" She shivered. "Not Gloucester's courtship of the Lady Anne. Remember how you destroyed her in the end."

"Forgive me," he begged huskily and kissed her cheek. And after that they toasted each other, eyes promising success and perhaps something else.

❧

All London came to Drury Lane for Garrick's three guest

appearances and before the month had ended an offer arrived from Louis Duval, manager of the Smock Alley Theatre in Dublin. David Garrick and Peg Woffington were invited over for a summer season of plays. They could name their own terms. And so it was that on the first day of June they set out from Park Gate near Chester, *en route* to Dublin. After an absence of scarcely three years Peg was returning in triumph to her native city.

18

The early morning mist was breaking up over the Irish Sea as the ship made its way into Dublin bay. Overhead, gulls screamed and made swooping dives into the grey foam in its wake. Far out white horses were riding the waves. In her mind's eye she saw the fair-haired squire with the hot blue eyes, riding his horse in that sunlit valley, how many years ago? Strange how whenever she thought of him she saw the three weird figures on the heath and heard the words: "By the pricking of my thumbs, something wicked this way comes." Patrick Taafe had not been wicked but coming events had cast their long shadow.

She thrust the past away to greet the young man with the eager face who had come up on deck to catch his first glimpse of her city. From their first meeting she had marvelled at how vital he was, how bright his face, how alive his brown eyes, even his hair flecked with golden streaks seemed to radiate life, energy. His throat was bared and he wore a sober jacket, breeches and fine leather shoes. He was not an elegant dresser like Darnley. He might have been one of the weavers in the Earl of Meath's Liberties, quiet, hard-working men passing unnoticed in a crowd except on Sundays when they stood out in their colourful high-crowned wigs. Like them he was of Huguenot stock and had an abiding loyalty to the House of Hanover. Garrick was so very different to Darnley, that dark-haired Scottish aristocrat with his crazy dreams of another restoration, his willingness to sacrifice wealth, comfort, life itself, to put a Scottish king on the throne of England. She had never meant to fall in love with Darnley, had sworn after Charles Coffey's betrayal, after that night of hell in Connolly's hunting-lodge in the Featherbed Mountains, that she was finished with love; but in the end her heart had betrayed her. It would be the very last time it would happen.

David Garrick put an arm around her shoulder and she gave him a brilliant smile, practised, sweet, the kind I bestow on the bucks in the Playhouse, she told herself and was ashamed. Bells were pealing over the city, announcing the Sabbath. Christ Church shrill and impatient, St Patrick's sonorous and the sweet silvery bells of St Bride's. "I was born to the sound of the bells. Even when I am far away I remember them—and the street vendors." She threw back her head and sang out. "Cockles and mussels. Dublin bay herrings. Knives, combs or ink horns. Fresh river water. Fresh gingerbread."

He laughed. "What a good mimic you are."

"I'm a Dubliner, born and bred."

He held her close. "Oh, Peg, it's like reaching journey's end. We'll show Dublin what the theatre should be. It will be a challenge."

"How rash you are," she said lightly. "Dubliners can be very critical." She thought, particularly of one of themselves. What was it the Good Book said: "A prophet is not without honour, save in his own country." She had a foreboding that all might not go right. "Please God, let me be good," she prayed. "Let them like me and this young man beside me, though his confidence borders on arrogance."

She was first off the boat, was being hugged and kissed by her sister Polly, no longer the solemn-eyed schoolgirl she had left behind three years before but a fashionably dressed young lady, looking older than her sixteen years. Tendrils of light brown hair framed her oval face, her flawless skin, their mother's gift to her daughters. David Garrick would admire her. A match between them would be the perfect answer. Polly would make a charming hostess, enjoy furthering David Garrick's career, would delight in being patronised by Lord Burlington, know how to handle that old aristocrat. And Garrick, with his talent, his vaunting ambition would have a supportive mate. Like her mother, Polly had notions of grandeur. What was it that gypsy had promised him? (He had no secrets from her.) Riches, fame, a promise that he would mix with the greatest in the land and be buried with kings.

Chatting animatedly, Polly directed a porter to carry the heavy trunk to a waiting hackney. "Mother would have been here to welcome you but she had a chill and I persuaded her to remain indoors. Where's Mr Garrick? I thought he would have been with you."

Peg settled herself down loosening her cloak and the hackney took off at a clip. "I wanted to be first off the boat, Polly. Mr Garrick was anxious to pay his respects to Mr Duval of Smock Alley and some of the leading citizens waiting to greet him." She leaned over and touched Polly's cheek. "I have plans for a supper party, darling, to introduce you to all the actors. Mr Garrick is looking forward to meeting you."

Polly rooted in her reticule. "Here's a cutting from *Faulkner's Journal*. Just listen to what they say about you: 'The expected arrival from England of Mr David Garrick and Mrs Peg Woffington is welcome news. Mr Garrick has introduced a new method of acting which has taken London by storm. Peg is a native of our fair city. We look forward to seeing her once again in the part she made her own, that of Sir Harry Wildair in *The Constant Couple*.'" She leaned across and planted a kiss on Peg's cheek. "O darling, you're famous at last."

Peg deepened her voice. "Egad, m'dear! I make a handsome gentleman. Recruiting officers implore me to enlist and matrons hide their daughters when I appear. But to be serious, we are giving a season of Shakespeare and I promise you shall have seats for every play. In years to come you will be able to say you first saw the great Mr Garrick in Dublin."

Polly moved uneasily in her seat. "Promise you won't be cross at what I'm going to tell you."

"What have you done? Spent too much on gowns and fripperies?"

Polly chuckled. "Nothing so drastic. It's just that my friend Samantha Gunning has invited me to spend the summer at her home in the west of Ireland. We leave for County Mayo the day after tomorrow."

It was foolish to feel so disappointed. She had been looking forward to her time with Polly, shopping together, gossiping far into the night, exchanging confidences, planning the future. She bit her lips, lest she say something she would regret.

Polly was rattling on. "Samantha lives with her grandmother in a fine house on St Stephen's Green. You must meet the old lady; she is quite a character. When she was only fifteen years old, she eloped with her cousin. Two years and two sons later she ran off with an Italian count. She became in turn mistress of a Russian prince, an Italian artist and a Jewish goldsmith, went everywhere, knew everyone."

Despite herself Peg smiled. "And then what happened?"

"Would you believe, at the age of forty, when her days of joy were over, she returned to Dublin and the family home. Her long-suffering husband, Thaddeus Gunning, took a seizure on the spot and died leaving her the wealthiest widow in town."

They were leaving College Street, turning into George's Lane, a journey back in time...Putting on concerts with Kathleen McEnroe, dressing up in coloured rags, tinsel. Where was Kathleen now with her dark curls, her saucy ways, her high spirits? Wandering the roads of England, a strolling player, pleasuring some man in a brothel, or could it be that she had settled down? But no, Kathleen was too wild, too bent on having her own way to make a wife for any man. Half-way up the Lane, children, arms linked, were singing out in the sweet tremulous tones of the young, advancing, retreating, before one of their companions perched high on a stone. It had been her favourite game.

Stands a lady on the mountains,
Who she is I do not know;
All she wants is gold and silver
And a nice young man to love her...

She had a nice young man ready to lay his heart at her feet. David Garrick. It wasn't enough. She mustn't think of Darnley or the high-born lady he had married, groomed in the courts of France, fit *châtelaine* of the castle he had once described. "It's very old, Peg, grey stone walls overrun with ivy. There's a keep, stone floors, a great fireplace, that takes a ton of peat, a narrow window that widens; one can see miles of purple heather and the hills. It's the loneliest place in the world and the place I love most."

They had reached Aungier Street. Familiar signs hanging over shops and houses, Baker, Glover, Skinner, Shoemaker, Tallow-chandler, Clockmaker, Wax-Light Maker. An old lady wearing a silver wig was making her way down the street, with the aid of a silver-topped cane. Alice Ford had been a popular actress before falling on hard times. After that she went on the streets and was soon acknowledged to be Dublin's prettiest whore. Then when past her prime, she had the good luck to acquire a protector, a dissipated roué, old enough to be her grandfather. He had set her up in a hat shop and she had prospered. Alice had flair, a good business head; was soon patronised by the Quality, who enjoyed sitting on gilt chairs in her shop, drinking her chocolate, trying on her bonnets, ordering gowns and cloaks which she had her workrooms make up from the silks, brocades, velvets she imported from London. Everyone wanted an Alice Ford original. Now, reaching sixty, she was a pillar of society, charitable, attending service each Sunday in the fashionable Anglican church of St Bride's in the Liberties. The windows of her shop were wondrously dressed with silks and lace and the latest mannequin dolls wearing Parisian fashions. If I'm lucky, Peg thought, I could end up like Alice. It was a depressing thought.

The Aungier Street Playhouse had a shabby, deserted look. The company was on tour. For a brief moment she was again a carefree eighteen-year-old, travelling along in a creaking cart with Dónal Bán, the Scottish actor who had been her friend. What would have happened had he not been there to give her that draught! She had been desperate enough for suicide—her mind had indeed run on those lines—with no money, the famine all around and nothing left to pawn.

The driver had pulled up outside the tall narrow house and was carrying in the heavy trunk, grumbling that his back was broken. Her mother, looking well despite her pallor, was weeping, kissing her. Dottie Carey, thin-faced, shrewish, giving her the once over. Later the innkeeper's wife would give Mattie her verdict. "That Peg Woffington, painted and powdered as any whore," and the landlord would mop his leaking eyes, pat his crotch, say he must go to see his neighbour's child in the Playhouse and Dottie would sulk.

She looked around her. "Where's Mrs McEnroe? I thought she might welcome me home."

"The poor soul was buried a week ago in the Huguenot cemetery near your father and Conor," said her mother sadly.

In a homecoming there was always one absent face. She swallowed a lump in her throat. "She was the kindest person I ever knew, God rest her soul. Did Kathleen put in an appearance at the funeral?"

Dottie Carey sniffed. "Never a sign of her. But then what news would there be? I always knew she would end up in the gutter."

Polly had opened the trunk, was squealing with delight at the cascades of silks, brocades, muslins that spilled out, their colours a painter's palette, daffodil, cherry, sky blue, rose, moss green. "Are they for me?" She had planned on taking Polly to Alice Ford's workrooms, sketching out gowns, skirts, bodices, the latest from London. Wistfully she fingered a length of silk. "This was to make a gown for Mrs McEnroe. Purple was always her favourite colour."

Dottie Carey was draping one end of the stuff over bony shoulders. Purple was definitely not her colour with that badly dyed hair and the muddy complexion. "It suits me well," Dottie simpered.

"Why keep it, Mrs Carey." Slany Woffington was at her most expansive best. "My family were always known for their fine open-handed ways. Hospitality is a tradition in our family but then I come of good stock."

"A lady born," Dottie said insincerely and Peg hid a smile. Nothing has changed, she thought. I might never have left.

❧

Two days later she bade good-bye to the travellers at the Bleeding Horse, a coaching inn at the top of Aungier Street: Samantha Gunning, raw-boned with a horsy laugh and an atrocious taste in gowns, vowed she was sorry to miss the play-acting in Smock Alley, boasting about her cousins Maria and Elizabeth who lived in a castle and were reputed to be great beauties. ("When they are of an age they will go to London and create a stir.") Polly gazed in admiration at her friend, gushing, "I so long to visit the castle and meet the beauties."

A black-haired urchin, wearing red petticoats, had been sent up by Samantha's parents to escort his young mistress and her friend on the long and hazardous journey back to Mayo. He gave Peg such a merry smile that she tossed him a shilling and he danced a barefoot jig in the dust of the road, leaping up on the roof as the coach drove away.

She thought long after that she had passed the summer

in a daze. A heatwave had hit the city, water was scarce, drains stank, fever broke out. It was said that the cobblestones were hot enough to fry an egg. Soon after Polly's departure Slany Woffington took to her bed, talking in an exhausted voice of her old home, Lemineagh, remembering the great stone dairies, the gracious rooms, and recalling cool winds blowing in from the western sea. "This weather will kill me." Fretfully she rubbed her forehead, wet with sweat. Peg plaited back her mother's hair and worried about what would happen when the season started. With rehearsals and performances she would have so little time. "A month or two in that farmhouse in Rathfarnham would do you good," she suggested. "Remember that summer when Conor died, how kind the farmer's wife was. You came back quite restored to health." Her mother brightened up, remembering the long sunny days, the fresh air, the company. "Do you know I think it might do me good. I made a circle of friends. We used play cards, take walks, have reading sessions. I might take that novel of Daniel Defoe's with me. It's said to be good." Peg shook the pillows and settled the quilt. "There now you'll feel better. I must admit I enjoy Defoe."

"Tell me what's it about?"

"The days and nights of Moll Flanders. During her life Moll practised every known crime, suffered many misfortunes. She was five times a wife, twelve years a thief, sentenced to death, reprieved and transported to Virginia. But it has a happy ending. I won't spoil your enjoyment by divulging what happened."

Her mother looked doubtful. "I don't know if it's fit for me to read."

Peg chuckled. "I heard that the Princess of Wales quite

enjoyed it. Tomorrow I'll help you pack and then we can hire a comfortable hackney to carry you. I promise I'll go out to see you just as often as I can manage it."

"Maybe so. The Playhouse takes up all your life. I wish you were married. Don't forget to get me that novel. I might as well see what they've been reading in London."

Dublin had changed in the three years she had been away. Wealth and taste were reflected in the fine new bridges flung across the Liffey, in the handsome squares and houses where the gentry lived. Many Irish landlords had forsaken their country estates to take their seats in the House of Parliament, now completed after more than a decade of work, a noble building, with Ionic columns, spacious courtyards, arched colonnades. In the main they were serious men, intent on bettering life for their fellow men, Catholic, Protestant and Dissenter. But there were others, hard-riding, hard-drinking, who with their wives and mistresses engaged in a ceaseless round of pleasure. It was fashionable that hot summer to ride out on an early morning, or take a coach to an outlying village or hamlet, Ranelagh, Rathfarnham, Templeogue, for breakfast parties in one or other of the handsome villas. Afternoons saw the ladies drinking tea, playing cards, having their dressmakers call for fittings. In the evening everyone went to the theatre. The Lord Lieutenant of Ireland had set the tone for the town when he attended the opening night of the season and witnessed Garrick in the role he had made famous, that of the hunchback king in *Richard III*.

Before the week was out, Garrick was lionised by old and young, rich and poor. People boasted they had "Garrick fever" and the answer to the greeting "How are you?" was "Oh I'm as gay as Garrick."

❧

Until Peg's arrival, the principal actress in the Smock Alley company had been a golden-haired English girl. Susanna Cibber had fled London to escape the wrath of her cuckolded husband. She was the possessor of huge blue eyes and these, combined with her fragile air and beautiful contralto voice, made her much sought after. Underneath her air of innocence she had a ruthless streak and an ambition to become a great actress. Her honeyed flattery of Garrick was at times embarrassing but he appeared to love it. Peg did not even try to compete. She was not in love with Garrick; true he was important to her career but she would not pretend to an emotion she did not feel.

At the beginning of August, the principal actors in Smock Alley were invited to Sandford Mansion in Chapelizod one Sunday evening. Lord Sandford, an elderly don who had spent much of his life cloistered in Oxford before inheriting the title, was an avid theatre-goer. Susanna Cibber would sing an aria which Mr Handel had written specially for her in his new work *Messiah* which had recently been performed in the Music-Hall in Fishamble Street.

Peg was reluctant to accept the invitation, Chapelizod held too many bitter memories for her, but Garrick would brook no refusal. Sandford was a patron of the arts, a nobleman, wealthy, influential and on no account a man to be slighted. Riding up the great avenue of trees she caught her first glimpse of the mansion, stone façade glowing eerily red in the evening sun. Fit setting for the incestuous passions, the hatred, culminating in murder, that had been played out inside its walls. At that moment she longed for Darnley. Garrick, with his boyish looks, his brash confident ways, would never understand the dark passages in her life, the shifts she had been put to, the miseries, the jealousies. Compared to hers his lot had been carefree. A mother who had a good singing voice and a sanguine nature, a father who had wanted to act but instead had become a recruiting officer. Even when his father fell ill there was Mr Walmesley to help them, that kind man he spoke of with such affection. Success had come easily and early. Oh, like all good actors he could assume any mantle, interpret any mood, emotion, but when the curtain fell he shed the role as easily as the greasepaint, the stage costume he had earlier donned. She knew in her bones that the difference between them went deeper than race, tradition, class. Or she asked herself honestly was it that she was not in love with him and could never be. Why was she forever seeking flaws in him?

Supper was over, Susanna Cibber had entertained the company and now they sat, a captive audience in the dim over-furnished drawing room, that had hangings so thick that not a chink of light came through the window. Lord Sandford was holding forth on his pet subject, ghosts and hauntings, while his guests deadened their senses with brandy. It might be a scene from a drawing-room comedy, Peg thought. Sandford, wearing a blue velvet robe studded with stars and moons, like the high priest of some esoteric sect; his aunt, an ancient dowager waving her fan, eyes closed, swaying, recovering herself; an old actor surreptitiously picking his nose; an overdressed fop helping himself to stuffed dates, throwing languishing glances at Garrick who in turn was ravishing with amorous eyes Susanna Cibber arrayed in cloth of gold.

"This very house is haunted," Sandford's piping treble would have done justice to a three-year-old, not an Oxford don of mature years. "To escape her husband's brutality and unnatural passions, my unfortunate cousin, the Lady Jane Sandford, was forced to flee the house, taking her young son with her. Later they were found drowned in the lake. It is my belief that Coffey scuttled the boat. Since the night of the tragedy the ghost of the unhappy lady haunts the manor though I must admit I have not seen her yet."

Susanna Cibber dabbed her eyes with a scrap of lace. "Some men can be beasts as I know to my cost. Does anyone know what happened the man Coffey?"

Sandford replied with proper indignation and force. "Me cousin, Squire Whaley, saw to it that Coffey was run out of Dublin. Believe he went off to the New World. Hope the Indians scalped him."

A sudden gust of wind blew the curtains apart; candles flickered, went out and a scream rent the room. Susanna had fainted. There was pandemonium with servants running around with tapers, Sandford squealing imprecations on the Lady Jane's husband, the elderly dowager waving her smelling salts and the fop trying to comfort an irate Garrick. On an impulse Peg emptied a jug of water on Susanna who shot up giving her tormentor a baleful look. "What happened?" she moaned, rubbing water from her eyes.

"You screamed," Peg said flatly.

Susanna turned her great blue eyes on Sandford. "Your lordship's thrilling account of the drowning and hauntings so gripped my mind that for a moment I was on the verge of a higher experience."

Sandford danced with excitement. "What happened, m'dear? Did you see a manifestation of some kind?"

"I saw the Lady Jane looking in the window, water streaming from her hair, eyes anguished beyond belief."

"It is as I feared," Sandford said happily. "The Lady Jane is trapped between two worlds. It is given to few of us to see beyond the veil."

Susanna smiled bravely. "I feel unable to face the journey back to Dublin tonight," she whispered, closing her eyes.

Sandford helped her to her feet. "Of course you must stay the night, my dear. I shall give orders to the housekeeper to see to your needs." His lined face creased in a smile. "I am writing a monograph on hauntings and ghostly apparitions. This will be of immense interest to the London Society of Incorporeal Research."

Taking the hint the party soon broke up, chattering volubly of ghosts and murders. On the whole it had been a successful evening; it had resurrected a scandal long dead, brought a frisson of fear to the credulous, and was something on which to dine out for weeks to come.

Garrick had hardly uttered a word for the length of the journey back to Dublin. Peg was undecided whether he was sulking or nursing a passion for Mrs Cibber. When they reached the house in Aungier Street, he insisted on seeing her into the parlour. Moodily she poured him the whiskey he demanded and curled herself up on a sofa. "I am quite worn out with the evening's drama," she said sourly, "that and Susanna Cibber's histrionics."

"The child is intuitive," Garrick envied Sandford the nubile Susanna in his bed.

"Mrs Cibber is twenty years or more, hardly a child, though I grant you she can be an accomplished actress when it suits her book. She saw no ghost. She was sitting with her back to the window. Though I must admit what happened broke the tedium of an intolerable evening. I was never so bored."

Garrick swallowed his drink in one gulp and hiccoughed. "Lord Sandford is a gentleman and an excellent host," he brought out carefully.

"That's as may be. Sandford's version of the story is a libel on a decent man. I knew Mr Coffey. He was trapped into marrying Lady Jane. For years she had carried on an incestuous relationship with her brother, the earl. She drowned herself and killed her son for revenge."

"Was this much maligned Mr Coffey another of your conquests? I seem to have heard your names linked."

She had taken as much as she could stand. "The hackney is waiting to take you to your lodgings," she said coldly. "And now if you will excuse me I have the beginning of a megrim."

With immense dignity Garrick weaved his way to the door pausing on the threshold to deliver his exit line: "'Frailty, thy name is woman!'"

The driver caught him just before he tumbled down the steps.

1 9

She had left the Playhouse immediately after the curtain came down, scarcely giving herself time to change out of her costume, fighting her way through the hangers-on that nightly crowded the greenroom. After the day's heat, the air was cool and fresh. Perhaps she would sleep tonight. Matters were going badly between Garrick and herself. Since that night in the Sandford Mansion he had scarcely thrown her a word. He spent his time squiring Susanna Cibber around town, seemingly enjoying her inane prattling, her gushing insincerities. Not that she cared—or was she entirely honest with herself? I'm like a dog in the manger, she scolded herself. I don't want him, nor do I want anyone else to have him.

Around Fishamble Street the warren of lanes that went to make up the oldest quarters of the city were strangely deserted, though a bare half-hour earlier the place had filled with the well-breeched and aristocratic as they poured out of the Playhouse, calling loudly for chairs and hackneys to take them home, ordering their carriages to move further into Smock Alley while the common folk were squeezed against walls before escaping to Winetavern

Street and the many drinking taverns from which the street got its name.

The silence of the night was broken by the clatter of a horse's hooves on the cobbles. A solitary horseman came into view. "Want to be taken home, lady?" he called down.

It couldn't be, yet it was, that familiar much-loved voice. Her heart was pounding as he reined in his horse and leaning down swung her up on the saddle.

"Darnley. I don't believe it." His arms were around her waist, hands guiding the reins and the horse was cantering briskly down the street. "Where on earth did you spring from?"

"Sweetheart, when I heard you were gracing the boards of Smock Alley, I left the cousin's home in Limerick and quite wore myself out to reach you."

"Liar," she said fondly. "What are you doing in Dublin of all places? I had thought you were in Scotland."

"It's a long tale." His voice was chilly and he relapsed into silence. Christ Church was in shadows; Dame Street, bright with street lamps. A night-watchman went down College Green calling out in a monotonous voice, "Eleven o'clock, past eleven o'clock and a dark dry night." She would never hear that cry without remembering Conor's last hours. He felt her shudder and tightened his grip on her waist. They were riding through town's end lane out of the city. She wondered where he was taking her? And told herself that she did not care very much. Most of the harvest was in and the fields were thick with stubble and heaps of grain. They passed a farmhouse, a millhouse and a mansion half-built. On their left the Liffey flowed past. Beyond was Ringsend and beyond that again the hamlet of Irishtown, where the Dodder came down from the Featherbeds to enter the sea.

She remembered Charles Coffey telling her the story of how Irishtown got its name. Years before the native Irish had been driven from the city of the Pale by English decree but that was old history now. In the interim the inhabitants of Ringsend and Irishtown had fought, intermarried, fought again, come together again, bound by their mutual needs: fishing, smuggling and women. Darnley turned the horse's head down a dusty boreen and swung back around towards the harbour of Ringsend. A row of leaning cottages propped their backs against the jetty, staring out to sea. He lifted her down and she followed him through the open door into the end cottage where a fire blazed on the hearth, giving out welcome heat for all that the night was warm.

The table was set as if for company: a linen cloth, cutlery, dishes containing cold salmon, cheese, a salad, fresh bread, wild raspberries, clotted cream. For days she had been so unhappy that she hadn't bothered to eat but now she was suddenly ravenous. Wine cooled in a bucket. Through a door she saw a bedroom, light pouring through leaded diamond windows, a bed freshly dressed with a patchwork quilt like a coat of many colours.

The food had revived her, the comfort of the room enveloped her, happiness filled her being. She leaned across the table and touched his hand. "It's like a fairy tale. Everything ready, waiting. Who is the helpful dwarf?"

"No dwarf but my old nurse who married a man from Ringsend and lives next door. A simple arrangement." He raised his glass. "To you, my sweet. How long since we two met?"

She had counted the hours, the days. Fourteen months, ten days, six hours. She had longed for this moment; yet now that it had happened, that he was here, she found herself strangely dumb. The old intimacy had gone. There was something about him, watchful, like a lost child.

"I pray your wife is in good health?" Her voice was stilted, artificial.

He examined his glass. "She died in childbirth, as did my son. We were nine months married." His voice was chilling. "What was it Othello said, 'She that was ever fair and never proud.'"

She muttered some platitude, meaningless, commonplace. She felt unutterably depressed. Why had she come?

He filled his glass to the brim, held the golden bubbling wine up to the firelight. "Cold, yet it fills the veins with fire."

With a stab of pain she remembered the day at the May fair in Brookfield, the wine they had drunk by the river, the love they had made, how she had felt when he told her of his impending marriage, the girl learning to be a great lady in the courts of France. She swallowed. "What will you do now?"

"Follow the road I have chosen. I give you a toast, m'dear. *Deoch sláinte an Rí.* Health to the King."

She drank obediently, like a child. "Tell me about the prince."

"You would find him handsome. I think he is brave. Eight cardinals and a host of noble lords and ladies were at his birth. They say a bright star was seen in the heavens at the time of his birth. A sign of greatness, I am told."

"What will happen?"

"He will return to Scotland and I shall be there to support him. He must make the attempt soon." He held out his arms. "Come to bed."

"I love you," she said. "I have longed for you. 'In such a night/Stood Dido...upon the wild sea-banks, and waft her love...'"

His mouth dammed her words. He was carrying her to the bedroom with the diamond panes, undressing her, stroking her white skin, was on his knees, his mouth on the soft triangle of hair, his lips on those other lips and she was aflame with desire. She bent and caught his hair in her hands. "Take me, Darnley. I love you."

He undressed her, must have done so, undressed himself, she didn't remember, only knew they were naked together, arms, legs entwined. He will die for the Jacobite cause, she thought and held him fiercely, panting, straining, offered him everything, body, soul, all her being. He sank into her and she held him there, as if she was drowning and he alone could save her life. As if there was no tomorrow. "Nothing can take our love away," she whispered.

He eased himself out and she slept a little and then awoke to find herself stroking the soft flower between his legs, feeling it quiver, come to life. She was kissing the diamond of moisture at the pink tip and he was rolling over, taking her, whispering words of love. She was at peace at last. "I love you, Darnley," she said but he was asleep and the room was filled with broken lights.

She put out her hand and felt for him but he was not beside her, though his place was still warm. The room was in half-shadows. She could hear the soft murmur of voices, clink of china. Quietly she got out of bed and padded to the door which was slightly ajar. He was sitting at the table drinking from a mug. She got the aroma of coffee and marvelled that in such a place at such an hour he could command this luxury; then told herself that the rich had but to command and their every whim was obeyed. An elderly woman wearing a white cap was toasting bread at the fire, holding the long pronged fork in one hand, shielding her face with the other. He turned his head as if listening and a bearded man, shaking drops of moisture from his head, lifted the latch on the door and entered. He had the look of a seafaring man and with a sinking feeling Peg knew why he was there. In the darkness of the bedroom she dressed hurriedly, frantically flinging on petticoats, bodice, drawers, her gown, cursing the hooks, tying the waist with a cord, throwing a shawl around her shoulders.

When she went into the kitchen the old woman and the fisherman were gone and he was sitting beside the fire. He looked up and gave her a smile of such tenderness that she felt her bones turn to liquid. "You were leaving without saying good-bye."

"Darling Peg. I thought it better this way. You were sleeping like an angel."

"When do you sail?" She could hardly bring out the words.

"Very soon." He got to his feet and put an arm around her shoulder. "Walk with me down to the harbour."

Outside the mist was so thick that it caught her throat. Somewhere around the sea sighed away from them and they made footprints on the cleanly washed shore. The morning was lightening, the mist slowly melting before the sun's coming up out of the east. The tide had left hollows and there were tufts of gorse and salt puddles amongst the boulders. He took a sandy path away from the harbour. On the far side of the bay Howth was luminous, Hy Brazil, the promised land. To their right the mountains looked different, purple, shading into dark blue. He stopped on a sandy hillock and pulled her down beside him, holding her close.

Her green eyes filled with tears. "Don't cry, Peg," he begged. "Have pity."

"You can't leave me." She wound her arms around his neck. "I love you, love you. Stay with me, darling, we could have such a good life together. Oh Darnley, don't leave me."

"It's no use. I must go. I have work to do. You will never understand."

She clung to him. "No one means anything to you; there is nothing in your life but this mad dream. What drives you, Darnley? What do you want?"

"To see the Stuart on the throne."

"What difference will it make? What do they care in London, in Dublin? What better off will they be? The cities prosper, people grow rich."

His breathing was harsh. "Speculators, men who care nothing for the past, whose only God is money."

She sobbed. "I don't care."

"Darling." He turned her face up to his. "Look at me. Listen. Scotland is in bondage to England, the cotters starve, the chieftains exiled or gone to ground. They are clearing the highlands, turning them into pastures for sheep, the English grabbers, the Scottish lairds who betrayed their clans."

"What does Scotland mean to me?"

"Dear God, Peg, can't you see what's happening in your own land? Your people groan under the yoke of the penal laws, no stake in the land they till, forced to pay tithes to a religion not theirs, all professions barred to them." He laughed bitterly. "They cannot even own a horse worth more than five pounds."

She buried her face in his chest. "How much better off would we be under the Stuarts?"

He put his hand on her neck. She thought he would choke her, didn't care; instead he lifted her chin, kissed her mouth. "Darling, all over Europe men wait for the call, sons and grandsons of the Wild Geese who followed Sarsfield into exile, soldiers of fortune, mercenaries who have fought every battle but their own, who live out their lives waiting for a last chance to win back what was once theirs."

She pounded his chest. "What is it to you? Rich, aristocratic, a friend of the Prince of Wales. Do you know what you want, Darnley?"

"A return of the old days, of the days of chivalry, honour. My people and yours were civilised when the Saxons painted themselves with woad."

"You're mad," she said hopelessly. "Even you cannot turn back the clock."

He stroked back her hair. "God help me, I can try."

Tears were coursing down her cheeks, she didn't even bother to wipe them away. "Let me go with you, anywhere. I'll be your mistress, your whore, camp-follower. What shall I do without you?"

He got to his feet. She clung to his knees.

"Let go of me, Peg, for Christ's sake. I must go. You will forget me in time. Even the most deathless love wears out in the end."

"Will you come back, ever?"

"Don't count on it. For me the die is cast."

"Don't leave me."

Roughly he unclasped her arms. She fell on her face and lay there a long time sobbing her heart out. When she got to her feet the sea was empty, the only sound to be heard was the trickle of waves on pebbles, the soft plop of a fat-bellied crab in the thin channel of water that lay imprisoned amongst a cluster of rocks and the cry of the heron.

❦

Smock Alley was in turmoil. They were coming to the end of the summer season and Garrick was riding roughshod over everyone, driving the actors to the point of exhaustion. They had rehearsed *Romeo and Juliet* endlessly, and in the end it was Peg who broke, tearing her script to shreds, screaming in her frustration, "You are monstrous, David Garrick. My only regret is that I allowed you persuade me come to Smock Alley." Garrick ran his hand through his hair; he looked mad, yet his voice was cool, controlled. "And mine that I agreed to your coming. At the best of times you are an indifferent actress but in this, our final production, you are abysmally bad. Shakespeare is not for one such as you."

Trembling with anger she left the stage, hating him with all her heart, vowing vengeance for his daring to strip her of her pride before the cast, before Susanna Cibber with her simpering airs, her sly asides. Within the hour the whole town would know that she was a failure. What had become of her pride that she allowed the son of a recruiting officer treat her like dirt. She had lived before she met him, had made her name as an actress. By God she would show him. She would go on stage this very night and by the time the curtain had closed he would be crawling to her on his knees.

For the hours that remained she willed herself into the part, putting out of her mind the heartbreak of Darnley, the cold selfishness of Garrick, all that had gone before. And that night in the darkened theatre by some strange alchemy that she was never again to experience, she was possessed by the spirit of the poet's Juliet, high-born daughter of the noble house of Capulet. She was back in the sixteenth century, intoxicated with the scent of flowers in her father's garden, the savour of quince and honey in her mouth; she knew every stone in the streets and squares of Verona, was acquainted with its merchants and friars, the young men with their sly adoring looks, the musicians in her father's hall, who played to please her. She was filled with a wild delight when she met her love and when her old nurse gave her the bitter tidings, "His name is Romeo, and a Montague, the only son of your great enemy," her heart keeled over and she knew that her doom was sealed.

As if to match her interpretation of the love-stricken girl, Garrick appeared transformed, playing the role of the tempestuous lover with fire and passion. When the time came for him to take his last leave of Juliet in the tomb, and he spoke the most poignant farewell ever written:

O my love, my wife,
Death that hath suck'd the honey of thy breath
Hath had no power yet upon thy beauty

his anguished whisper reached every corner and moved the house to tears. Never before had Smock Alley produced such a performance. Never again on any stage would Romeo and Juliet act out their love story with such tenderness and such fidelity.

She took no curtain-calls, left the Playhouse still costumed, painted, ordered a chair to take her to her silent home. Wearily she prepared for bed, stepping out of Juliet's gown, now but a lifeless bundle of silk and lace, and like a zombie brushed her hair and creamed her face.

Garrick was in the room, admitted by the awe-stricken

little maid she employed, stock awry, shirt crumpled. He knelt before her, kissed her hand, whispering, "You were magnificent tonight. Try to forgive me." She was in his arms and he was kissing her gently then more urgently and she lay supine, too exhausted to struggle.

He sighed. "You are in love with Lord Darnley?"

She was too tired to explain. "I'll never see him again."

He kissed her mouth. "Marry me, Peg. I love you. I promise to make you the greatest actress on the London stage."

"I must have time." If only she knew the answer. "Go back to London, David," she begged. "There is my mother, my sister."

He wasn't listening. "Say yes! You must say yes." His eyes glittered. He would give her no peace.

She assented through fear, fatigue. Yet she knew she would postpone the day. Darnley was gone. There would be no life, no future for her on the London stage, alone, at the mercy of every drunken sot, every fop. Without a husband, a protector she would be fair game for any man. Garrick would be kind, would help her to become a great actress; it was the only thing left in her life. She would sleep with him, the price she must pay, even as Máire Rua had paid her debt to the Cromwellian general. She kissed him like an exhausted child. "I promise when I am ready I will come to you. There is no other man. Now go back to your lodgings and leave me in peace."

❧

He was alone in his room. He threw himself face down on the bed. Her face was before him, green eyes circled with fatigue, titian hair he wound around his throat. If she did not come to him...if he could not have her...

He had left and it was as if a great storm had subsided. She wandered the streets of Dublin, searching for something, anything to distract her mind. She found the answer in a house in the High Street, near where she was born, where her mother had lived as a young bride and beloved wife. The Woffingtons had come down in the world, but they were going up again; she would ensure that they did. She would buy the house for her mother, enlist the help of Alice Ford to furnish the rooms. And there would be a homecoming.

❧

"It's like an exile's wake," Slany Woffington said happily as neighbours and friends gathered in for the housewarming.

Polly, rested and happy from her stay in Mayo, twirled around on her toes. "In Westport they danced at the crossroads."

I am the exile, thought Peg sadly. There is a time to dance. On the morrow she would sail for London where her future lay. But Dublin would always be home, her refuge. Even far away, the sights, the smells, the sounds of her beloved Dublin would be with her: church bells pealing, weavers' looms clacking, children laughing and that ragged old gleeman at the corner of the High Street singing the ballad the street vendors loved to hear:

In Dublin's fair city, where the girls are so pretty,
I first set my eyes on sweet Molly Malone...

They still remembered Molly around Dublin, with her

bright hair, her bright eyes, who had laughed so merrily and who had died so young of a fever.

Would she end up one day like Molly Malone, dying as her father before her had of a fever? And after that would her ghost too haunt the streets of the town to which she gave such heartfelt love?

ACT IV

LONDON, 1743–1747

Shall I compare thee to a summer's day?
Thou art more lovely and more temperate.
Rough winds do shake the darling buds of May,
And summer's lease hath all too short a date.

Sonnet 18

20

I t was a bright October morning when Peg dismounted
from the lumbering coach at the "stop down" and
engaged one of the waiting hackneys to take her to Bow
Street where David Garrick had rented a house. The crossing
had been smooth but then had come the interminable
drive from Holyhead to London with seven overnight
stops at frowsy coaching inns, where she had been forced
to bribe landlords, maidservants even, to find her a place
where she could lay her head. Once she had spent a blissful
night on a bale of straw alone in a barn. It had been the
best night's sleep of the entire journey.

Darnley was gone. He had taken a road she would never
walk, lured on by the dream of Jacobite glory. Whatever
the dangers, hardships facing him, whatever the end,
success or failure, one thing was certain: it was a drama
in which she would play no part. For the future she would
trust no one, depend only on what wits and talent she
possessed, what meed of luck fate might dole out. She had
no illusions. The stage was hard, crowded with ambitious
men and women, rife with jealousies. Mr Quinn had been
thrown into the Thames and left to drown because of a

stupid challenge and the promise of a part that might last no longer than a week. The truth was that stage people were seen as the rogues and vagabonds the laws of England deemed them to be. What was it the fishwife had said that day on the London street, "Actress, whore, one and the same ain't it?" And the idea that most actresses were brash, self-confident—who had decided that? The only time her inadequacies, her fears were buried was when she donned the mask of another on stage. Probably this was as true for David Garrick as for the meanest neophyte treading the boards of Drury Lane.

David Garrick? Ah there was the rub! She was fond of him, enjoyed his company, was flattered by his attentions, touched by his wish to marry her but she knew something he had not yet realised. Their differences went very deep indeed. He had all the prejudices and conventions of his class. Some sixth sense warned her that he would shrink from the story of her rape in the Hellfire Club, be appalled at what had happened to Patrick Taafe, that she would be diminished in his eyes because she had lost her heart and more than that to Charles Coffey and because that broad-shouldered man with the grey eyes and the cleft chin had left her for another. Even still to resurrect that past tugged at her heart-strings.

She was not a fool. She needed Garrick's help if she was to make her name on the London stage. And this she was grimly determined to do. She promised herself she would not cheat, would repay Garrick with whatever resources she had. Would keep her side of whatever bargain they might make. She knew he was careful with money, a trait she disliked and strange in someone prepared to spend his emotions so lavishly on the theatre. "I was brought up to be thrifty," he once told her. "My father was forced to retire through ill health on half-pay and at times we went short."

And my family at times almost starved, she thought wryly, and yet money melts in my hands. Was her impulsive generosity, her inability to say "no" a weakness, a craving for love and acceptance, or was it her inheritance from that most reckless of women, the legendary Máire Rua?

Her feelings were mixed as she mounted the steps of the solid redbrick house: relief that she would soon be back on the stage at Drury Lane, misgivings about her reception. She would be judged hardly playing opposite Garrick, her work measured against his. Not for the first time did she fear for their future together. She, volatile, extravagant, with her tendency to act first and think later. He so different, meticulous, a perfectionist, so consumed by his work that, she often thought, nothing else really mattered to him. In his own way he was as great an enigma as Darnley. Both obsessed by their dreams, ambitions, one to put the Stuart back on the throne, the other to become the greatest Shakespearean actor of his time.

He opened the door, clad in a crimson silk dressing-gown, sleepy brown eyes, rumpled hair, rubbing her face with his. He was wearing a day's growth of beard. She grimaced. "You need a barber. What have you been celebrating?"

He stroked his chin. "Sam Johnson's good fortune. He has been commissioned to produce a dictionary of the English language and given a substantial advance. I didn't get to bed until the early hours."

"What of the great novel?"

"He needs the money. Tetty is threatening to return to Lichfield but he is determined to remain in London. But enough of his problems." He caught her up in his arms. "I have been counting the hours, sweetheart. Let me make love to you. Come to bed."

She pulled away. "For pity's sake, David, give me time.
I'm hungry, travel-stained. I haven't washed properly or
eaten a decent meal in almost three weeks."

A taciturn maid showed her to a room, heavy with
mahogany furniture, sombre with dark carpets, hangings,
and gracelessly brought a jug of hot water and a towel. She
washed, changed and joined Garrick in the breakfast room
where a table was laid with a cold repast: meat, a lump of
mouldy cheese, bread and a pot of lukewarm coffee. She
made up her mind that at the first opportunity she would
speak to the kitchen. If this was to be her home she would
see to it that some comfort was introduced, that at least
the food served would be warm and well-cooked, the table
linen clean.

A portrait of a gentleman in brocade and lace hung over
the fireplace. Obviously overcome by the grandeur of his
subject the artist had conceived an improbable setting. An
English castle formed the background, statuary urns and
vine leaves were strewn around. She felt an inane desire
to genuflect at the look on Garrick's face. "Lord Burlington,"
he announced proudly. "The portrait is his gift to me, that
and the Tompion clock in the hall. This house is his
choice." All London knew of Burlington, rich, powerful,
arrogant, a patron of the arts after the manner of the
Medicis. Like the great Florentine family he was said to
dominate those he helped, to order their lives. The house
was undoubtedly handsome, with a good address, a fitting
abode for an ambitious actor yet she had dreamt of their
finding a place together, a house on the strand, overlooking
the river, alive with painted ships, dark seafaring men. She
loved the sight and sound of water, maybe because she had
been born under the sign of the crab.

"We have much in common, Lord Burlington and I," Garrick was telling her. "A love of the theatre, a passion for Shakespeare. We both consider the Bard the greatest poet the world has ever known. One day I hope to own my own theatre, produce what plays I wish. His patronage will count for much."

Already the misgivings she had felt on the journey were becoming a grim reality. "Dear God," she prayed, "let us be happy; let me be wise in the ways of this man with whom I am fated to live."

❦

As soon as she settled in she engaged a new cook and maid, rearranged the furniture, covered the floors with Persian and Turkish carpets, ordered a new four-poster bed and purchased a collection of Chinese porcelain in her favourite pawnbroker's shop near St Paul's Cathedral. The bearded owner who wore a shabby skull cap lived over the shop with his granddaughter, a girl of about fourteen years whose dark pretty looks were marred by an ugly birthmark on the chin.

Whatever spare time she could spare from the theatre she liked to spend rummaging in the shop, a veritable Aladdin's cave of treasures. One day in a dim recess, she discovered a dusty statue of a boy poised on one leg, playing a flute. With sensitive fingers the old Jew stroked the marble, glowing golden in the shop's dim light, telling her a little of the statue's history. It had been discovered in the ruins of Pompeii, somehow miraculously preserved. In her mind's eye she saw the unknown sculptor modelling those shapely limbs, the head crowned with a wreath of flowers. Even before she asked she knew the old man would not part with his treasure. As if to compensate her he produced a magnificent pair of diamond shoe buckles, asking a price she could not refuse. She would buy them for Garrick. He would be pleased. It would prove she cared for him. She thought with a sigh how easy it would have been to cheat and marry him. Few, if any, in London would believe that it was she who held back, who refused to make a commitment she feared she might break if Darnley ever returned. She told herself she loved Garrick—his zest for life, his passion for the theatre, his knowledge of Shakespeare, his voice the most beautiful she had ever heard. He was such a good teacher, so kind. Oh yes, in certain moods, at certain times, she loved him but never with the wild stirring of the blood she had known with that dark handsome Scottish rebel.

Garrick was delighted with the buckles, trying them on, then spoiling the moment by announcing that he would wear them to the rout in Burlington House on the following night. She had no wish to be received by the earl or his friends, yet it irked that they behaved as if she did not exist and what infuriated her more was that Garrick appeared not to notice or, if he did, turned a blind eye. He was flattered to be asked to give readings in the mansion. He had told her that the earl liked to match quotation for quotation with him, liked to interpret Shakespeare, that his greatest pleasure was to show off his collection of manuscripts and memorabilia that had once belonged to the Bard of Avon.

"Wear the buckles whenever you wish," she said shortly. "Your friends should be impressed. They cost enough."

Unhappily Garrick shuffled through his drawer, eyeing a handful of bills, "I've been meaning to say this for some time, Peg. We are living far beyond our means. You should save your money, put it out to interest."

"For pity's sake don't keep harping about money." His eternal cheese-paring would drive her mad. "I pay my share of the household bills." Some devil in her made her add, "When we are parted you may keep the buckles as a memento of happier days."

His eyes darkened. "Don't ever say such a thing. I will never part with either the buckles or you."

"Which comes first? Oh David, we are behaving like children. Darling, it's a lovely day outside, maybe the last of the St Martin's summer. Don't let's spoil it squabbling about things that don't matter. Take me for a drive in the country."

He kissed her cheek. "'Why didst thou promise such a beauteous day/And make me travel forth without my cloak,'" he whispered. "'To let base clouds o'ertake me in my way...'"

She couldn't remember the next line of the sonnet and contented herself by saying lightly, "There will be no clouds I promise."

With a mock groan he stuffed the bills into a drawer in his desk. Peg in a coaxing mood was hard to resist. On days like this he missed Lichfield, longed for a sight of green countryside, the rich loamy smell of good earth.

As they left the city behind, he was filled with a sense of well-being. Peg, in a cloak of russet velvet over a yellow gown, had never looked more enchanting. Winding lanes had replaced noisy streets, green fields stinking alleyways. Chickens and geese were everywhere. A barefooted child waved and a daring fox retreated furiously at the approach of the small four-wheeled cab. Half-timbered cottages with thatched rooves and tiny dormer windows wreathed in honeysuckle and ivy, ran down to the river, hedges blazed with furze, bushes were heavy with great juicy blackberries, russet apples fell from trees with soft plops to the grass below. The fiacre pulled up in a village which boasted a cluster of houses, a blacksmith's forge, an apothecary's shop, shelves laden with coloured bottles, and an inn with a coloured sign showing the unicorn and the lion rampant. Inside the ceilings were criss-crossed with great black beams and though the evening was warm, a fire large enough to roast an ox burnt on an open hearth.

"It has never been allowed to go out since the house was first built in the days of Queen Elizabeth," the landlord said boastfully. "An ancestor of me own killed a traveller for his gold and buried his body under the hearth. Aye and laid a curse on whoever would let the fire be extinguished." He gave a great belly laugh and pushed tankards of ale and plates of oaten bread and goat's cheese across the counter. "Not that I hold with old wives' tales; still it's better to take no chances." Peg was tempted to tell him of the curse that followed her family but Garrick was holding centre stage and the locals, wary at first of strangers, were drawing near so as not to miss a word. He was telling them stories of freebooters and pirates the like of Drake who had destroyed the Spanish Armada and saved England for the red-haired Virgin Queen. Most of the stories were woven into the folklore of every hamlet and village the length and breadth of England but never before had the locals heard them so vividly described with an actor's change of voice and face.

In years to come Peg would remember her early days with Garrick as happy; her nights were no longer haunted by dreams of Charles Coffey or crazy Jane, or of wandering distraught through the ruins of the Hellfire Club. Tetty Johnson had finally shaken the dust of London from her feet and returned to her native Lichfield and Sam, lonely for company, became a frequent visitor to the house in Bow Street. Early on she discovered that he was an avowed Tory who blamed the Hanoverians for all the country's ills.

"I hadn't realised you were such a rebel, Mr Johnson," she said in a teasing voice on an evening when they lingered over the supper table. They had eaten well, a steak and oyster pie, a syllabub, cheese and coffee.

Garrick passed around the port. Sam Johnson filled his glass, saying reflectively, "We Tories never forget, ma'am, that since the overthrow of James at the Boyne, and the elevation of Dutch William to the throne, England has been dragged into one foreign war after another to satisfy the lust for power and fortune of military men."

She smiled provocatively. "I understand they are only waiting in Scotland for the return of Prince Charles to rise in rebellion."

Such rumours were common enough in tavern and club but that she gave voice to them enraged Garrick. "No doubt you favour the Jacobites like your one-time admirer Lord Darnley who plots treason behind the king's back," he taunted.

"By what right, David Garrick, do you assume that a man of whom you know nothing plots treason?" she demanded.

"I have it on the authority of Lord Burlington," he began and at the mention of the hated name she exploded. "I am sick and weary listening to the pronouncements of Lord Burlington, tired of hearing of the accomplishment of his adopted daughter. It sometimes seems to be that the man is the arbiter of our life."

Johnson helped himself to snuff. "For we that live to please, must please to live," he said judiciously and in the subsequent laughter the row was forgotten.

But later that night as they undressed in their room, Garrick playfully accused her of jealousy and she pretended to sulk to please him and they made up and fell into bed to make love, a niggling voice told her that this was the first real rift in their relationship. She feared it was a portent.

❦

Peg sealed a letter to which she had given much thought and announced in a satisfied tone, "I have made arrangements to send Polly to Paris to complete her education."

Garrick, immersed in a Shakespearean sonnet, read on. She threw down the quill. "You will have the goodness to answer me when I speak to you."

He closed the book and looked up. "And so Polly goes to the French capital to learn how to become a lady."

Damn him, she thought, how dare he be so superior. She thought of Máire Rua's people, aristocrats, ruling vast acres when the likes of Burlington were nothing but adventurers licking the heels of their masters.

"Allow me to remind you, David Garrick," she said icily, "that my sister is as entitled to as fitting an education as Burlington's ward or whatever he chooses to call her."

He smiled pityingly, "Violetta is a lady."

"Conceived on the wrong side of the blanket." Even as she heard herself say the words she was ashamed of her pettiness but was unable to hold her tongue. "Violetta is the daughter of a Viennese dancer," she said shrilly. "I wonder how her ladyship likes the idea of receiving the daughter of her husband's mistress?"

Garrick said patiently, "Lord Burlington has legally adopted her. They both dote on the girl."

Jealousy drove her on. "As she dotes on you."

"Indeed this is news to me." He looked so pleased that she itched to slap his face, instead she contented herself with spitting out, "The whole of London knows of her infatuation. Not that I care a fig, but be sure of one thing, David Garrick, his lordship, patron of the arts though he may be, will never allow an actor, even one of your stature, pay court to his daughter."

He held out his arms. "Enough of this foolishness, darling. You are the only woman I love." In the firelight, clad in a diaphanous gown that did little to hide her shapely limbs, she was indeed bewitching. He pulled her down on a heap of cushions before the fire, murmuring drowsily in her hair:

Shall I compare thee to a summer's day?
Thou art more lovely and more temperate.
Rough winds do shake the darling buds of May,
And summer's lease hath all too short a date.

This was the Garrick she loved with his beautiful voice, reciting her favourite sonnet. She snuggled into his arms. "Why do we quarrel, dear heart?"

"Because we are two of a kind; the theatre is our life's blood and we act out our loves and hates. The Bard said it for us: 'We are such stuff as dreams are made on; and our little life is rounded with a sleep.'"

That night she fell asleep with the taste of Garrick's kisses on her mouth, the feel of his hands on her body, yet it was of Darnley she dreamt. He was riding alone on a dark and lonely road. His horse stumbled and she saw that rider and mount were exhausted. "Take care," she cried but her voice was carried away in the night wind and she knew, the way dreamers do, that all his energies were concentrated on reaching his goal and that she was far from his thoughts. And in her sleep she wept.

21

Prince Charles Edward Louis John Sylvester Maria Casimir was closeted with the Scottish nobleman who had crossed the English channel and ridden hell for leather through Europe to reach the Palazzo Muti near the Castle of St Angelo in Rome where the exiled James held court.

On 20 December 1720, a salvo of guns had been fired in celebration of the birth of the heir but there were no celebrations on this the twenty-third birthday of the handsome prince with the reddish-gold hair and the well-marked features. Since childhood Charles had prepared himself for the day when he would win back the throne his grandfather James VII of Scotland and II of England had lost to William of Orange at those final and decisive battles of the Boyne and Aughrim in Ireland, more than half a century before.

The two men spoke in English. Darnley's nurse had been a native speaker from the Isle of Skye; later he had been fostered by a staunchly Scottish family who clung to the old traditions and spoke Gaelic as their everyday tongue. But to the prince, brought up in a polyglot court,

Gaelic was foreign. Perhaps the fault lay with his tutors. The Chevalier Ramsey, dispossessed of his highland castle and acres, exiled with a price on his head, buried himself in his books and gave little attention to his young charge. When Ramsey had died he had been replaced by a newcomer to Rome, a burly red-headed border man, whom the young prince had disliked at sight. No one knew much about James Murray's background. Once the prince had caught him rifling through secret documents and had threatened to kill him if it was found he was a spy. Next morning Murray vanished to reappear in London where he boasted of being in the employ of the Hanoverians. Later his body was fished out of the Thames. It was believed that he had been murdered by a highlander who knew of his treachery.

Thomas Sheridan, an Irish aristocrat, was the prince's last tutor. Sheridan knew no Gaelic, had little patience with pedantry and was choleric by nature. Though now an old man, he lived on at the palace in the hope that he would live to see the day the Stuart came into his own.

Darnley leaned his arms on the table and spoke earnestly to the prince. "Support for the Jacobite cause has never been stronger, sire. The French await your lead but time runs out. This war drags on. Soon there must be an end and when that day comes Louis of France will look elsewhere."

Not for the first time did the Scottish nobleman wonder if this tall elegant young man with his insouciant air would have the stamina, the courage to see the adventure through to the end. Though he was fair as his great-uncle King Charles II had been swarthy, yet the family likeness was strong: they both had the same careless air, both carried the burden of their heritage lightly.

"Louis is apprehensive." The prince made a steeple of

his fingers. "He believes that without English backing there can be no hope of success. He cautions me daily."

"With due deference, sire, you must be prepared to take the initiative." Darnley's voice was tinged with impatience.

Charles looked suddenly young, unsure. "It is what I most ardently wish. What do you suggest I do?"

"Leave for France as soon as possible, put your case before Louis himself. He will not refuse you." Hypnotic grey eyes held troubled blue eyes. "If you are agreeable, sire, I shall make arrangements." A narrow index finger traced a circuitous line on the map on the table before them. "That is the route I would advise."

The prince studied the map. "How soon would your plans be complete?"

Darnley made a rapid calculation. "Three weeks, a month at most."

The young prince's face lit up. In his smile was all the lazy charm of his namesake, the king who would go down in history as the Merry Monarch. He unfolded his long legs and got to his feet, he was taller even than Darnley. He crossed the room and took a bottle of ruby wine from a hidden alcove. "A rare vintage," he said, "kept for special occasions. He handed Darnley a glass. "I give you a toast. *Deoch sláinte an Rí.* Health to the king."

"And to the prince who is born to be king," Darnley replied, drank and smashed his glass against the fire in the traditional Scottish manner.

❧

Three weeks later, on a January morning, the prince rose before dawn. No one knew of his plans, not his father, not his younger brother Henry, not even the beautiful young

Spanish Contessa Marabella, with whom he might be in love. Darnley had thought it was better so. He was the puppet master who pulled the strings.

Servants sullenly polishing the chaise, in the dim light of the courtyard, were half asleep, courtiers astride their mounts blew on frozen hands, shivering in the wind that whipped sleet and snow around cobbles and castle. It was typical of the prince, they grumbled under their breaths, to decide on a day's sport, boar-hunting no less, on such a morning when all Christian souls still should be comfortably abed. He had too much energy, too much time to indulge in whatever pastime his fancy took. The sooner the rumoured invasion took place the better, they thought sourly, though they had no wish to exchange the comfort of the court for wild Scottish moorlands, no wish to leave Rome where spring came early, summers were hot, and dark-eyed matrons could be passionate. They exchanged meaningful glances as the prince changed his mind, ordering his ostler to bring out his favourite mare. Throwing his shivering aides an amused glance he swung himself into the saddle. "A brisk gallop will do me good, circulate the blood," he called down. "Follow after in three hours or four. No, I do not need anyone to accompany me. I prefer to ride alone."

They watched silently as he rode away leaving them free to make their way back into the comfort of the buttery. At least there would be time to thaw out, drink hot mulled wine, have a game of cards or dice beside a roaring fire. Four hours he had said. With luck the weather would have turned so foul long before that he would come scurrying back. A day's hunting indeed! Not even a boar would venture from his lair in such weather.

In a wood some seven miles west of Rome, a figure in

a monk's garb waited patiently. His sharp ears heard the mare's whinny even before the prince crashed through the undergrowth.

Darnley raised his hood. "You are alone?"

The prince dismounted, tossing the bridle over a bush. "I left them cursing me under their breath for dragging them from their beds on a morning like this. They will curse me even more in four hours' time when I am found to be gone."

Darnley took a brown robe from a saddle bag. "Bury your own clothes as best you can, the snow will cover our traces; with luck your coat and breeches will be found by a wandering beggar or leper who will carry them off for fear of losing what he has honestly come by."

A short while later two mendicant monks rode out of the woods in an easterly direction, then veered sharply north. In a woodman's hut a second change of clothes had already been hidden away by a supporter and the two pressed on in the guise of Neapolitan courtiers. Nearing the Tuscany border they bargained with a second-hand clothes dealer and set out on the last lap of the journey in Italy dressed as sober merchants.

They had been more than a week in the saddle. This was the last night they would spend together. Sitting by a great log fire in a remote country inn, drinking the rough wine of the district, they made their final plans. Darnley gave the prince a wallet of papers. "In there you will find money for the rest of your trip, papers, a passport, gift of the Grand Duke of Tuscany. It will see you safely through his kingdom. A boat will be waiting in Savona to take a Scottish merchant by the name of Graham to Antibes. Do not delay in Antibes but press on to Lyons. A trusty messenger will make himself known in the King's Inn in that city and will take you to a safe house where you can rest and be given conveyance to Paris."

At that moment Scotland seemed very near to the young Prince. All his life he had dreamed of a country of which he had heard much but never seen. He conjured up a picture of a fair land of brown bogs, black water, smoke rising from thatch, the mighty highlands tipped with drifting clouds, cleansing wind, soft rain and his own people waiting to welcome him home. He was filled with hope and yet daunted at the prospect before him. He gripped Darnley's hand. "You have been our most loyal friend. One day you will be rewarded."

Darnley's eyes were hooded. "The only reward I ask is to see the Stuart back on the throne,"—his voice was bitter—"and the hated Hanoverians sent packing."

Charles thought of the long hours he had spent in this man's company, sleeping rough, foraging for food, making plans, evading strangers and wondered about him. "What will you do now that you have set me on my path?" he asked curiously.

Darnley got to his feet and went over to the door, opening it, looking out into the black night. "What will I do?" he said softly. There were times like this, when bone-weary all he wanted was to return to London, snatch up Peg and take her with him to Scotland. Was it the physical exhaustion that made him think of a warm bath, a blazing fire, a soft bed and his darling in his arms. He wanted her, God how he wanted her! He fought back his desires, his lusts. She was softness and sweetness and pleasure but he had long ago chosen his stony road and there could be no going back.

He swung around with such force that the prince jumped and the door crashed. "What should I do but continue as I have begun. Raising funds, mustering support." Furiously he rang a handbell for the innkeeper. "You will ride out alone tomorrow morning, Your Highness. I shall be gone before you rise."

Grumbling the innkeeper shuffled into the room. Strangers, foreigners, keeping a hard-working man up half the night, smugglers most likely or possibly Tuscany's men engaged on some dangerous enterprise, he had met their like before. All the same the English m'lord had been generous with his gold. Still he would be glad to see the back of them. Sighing heavily he lighted them to their rooms.

On 29 January, three weeks to the day since he had set out from the Palazzo in Rome, Prince Charles reached the French court at Versailles. A fortnight later he set out in secret for the town of Gravelines, twelve miles west of Dunkirk, where preparations for a French invasion of England were under way. Seven thousand French and Irish troops under the command of the Marshal de Saxe prepared to embark on French transports and made ready to sail. The great adventure was about to begin.

"Pray God it will be more successful than the Spanish Armada," de Saxe said in his gravelly voice.

"God and St Andrew will guide us to victory," Charles said stoutly. He was filled with a young man's enthusiasm. He never doubted the expedition would succeed.

22

In the house in Bow Street, Garrick was entertaining his boon companion, Charles Macklin, to supper and celebrating the actor's triumph in *The Merchant of Venice*. Alexander Pope had written of Macklin's Shylock, "This is the Jew that Shakespeare drew."

Peg's smile was dangerous as she leaned across the table. She enjoyed baiting this giant of a man who had changed his name from McLaughlin on shaking the dust of Ireland from his feet and who hated to be reminded that he was Irish born. "You are such a mystery, Mr Macklin. What are your origins?"

Garrick looked daggers, but Macklin, swallowing a bumper of port in one gulp, gave her a conspiratorial wink. "Mixed. Like your own, my dear Peg. A mother who was a Papist, a father a Presbyterian. Twelve of my uncles took part in the Siege of Derry in 1689; six were William of Orange's men and six were Jacobites." He dabbed his chin with a napkin and leered over his glass. "I heard recently that your admirer Lord Darnley is still dabbling in Jacobite plots. He was sighted in Rome recently, conniving with the Stuarts."

"Much good it may do him," Garrick said bitterly. Peg wished that Macklin had not brought up Darnley's name but had to admit to herself that she had brought it on herself. It was like a red rag to a bull as far as Garrick was concerned, though she doubted that the two had ever exchanged more than a civil bow. They were so different, she thought wearily. Darnley was reckless, generous to a fault, Garrick weighed up every word, every course of action, never doubting himself, practising a thrift that was tantamount to meanness. No doubt it was his Huguenot heritage, so different to her own. She could understand Charles Coffey's betrayal; he had clawed his way up from his peasant background, feared disgrace, loss of face; she understood Taafe's gambling instincts, Darnley's passion for the Jacobite cause, could even understand Captain O'Kelly and James Maclean, the highwaymen, who had lived dangerously and gone to their deaths defiantly. But Garrick's behaviour baffled her. He had such breadth of vision in many ways yet in others could be so petty.

She turned her thoughts away from the past to concentrate on the conversation. Macklin was joking about the Jew-baiting that had broken out in the city. Since his interpretation of Shylock feelings had run high in certain quarters.

"It's about time Drury Lane changed the bill of fare," she said. "Take off the *Merchant*, replace it with a light comedy to make people laugh and forget their jealousies and prejudices."

Garrick stuck out his lip. Sometimes she thought he looked like a spoilt small boy. "The box office returns are good," he said ponderously. "We play to full houses as well you know."

"Must money always dictate our actions?" Her eyes

were flashing ominously. Macklin laughed loudly, delighted with the fires of dissent which he would help to fan. "Money talks," he said coarsely. "Who can blame the poor of London, bled white, driven desperate by avaricious Jewish moneylenders. Foreigners who should be run out of England."

With an effort she controlled her temper. "As I understand it, Mr Macklin, it is not the poor but wealthy ruffians who engage in Jew-baiting. So-called gentlemen. I call them scum. Gangs like the Bold Bucks, the Mohocks, never brought to justice because of privilege, connection. They should be strung up for their deeds."

"You are so pretty when you are passionate," Macklin mocked.

She stood up. "If you pass another such remark, Mr Macklin, I shall have you thrown out of this house, if not by your acquiescent friend here at the table, then by my servants. And now if you will excuse me."

She went out of the room, banging the door behind her, furious with Macklin, with Garrick and above all with herself, who had fermented the row. She should have known Macklin. He was vicious as a viper. As a young man he had put out the eye of a fellow actor in a greenroom brawl. Manager Fleetwood had paid the fine and Macklin had gone free but the incident had taught him control neither over his tongue nor over his temper. If ever the friendship between himself and Garrick foundered she feared what the outcome might be.

❦

"Dear God in heaven I just don't believe it." She stood in the doorway of the little shop in St Paul's Close, her eyes sweeping over the wreckage. Fine china smashed and ground underfoot, broken windows, shutters wrenched from their hinges, a broken marble flute beside a shapeless mass that had been the exquisite limbs of the marble boy. There was blood on the floor and when she bent down to pick up the broken head she saw it was streaked with blood and hairs. She felt tears of frustration and rage start to her eyes. The statue had been quite perfect, a work of art, mindlessly destroyed by barbarians. What had happened? Where was the owner? She called out, but there was no answer and with mounting fear she called again. "Zara, are you there? It's me, Mrs Woffington."

She heard a noise in a cupboard and flung open the door. A young girl, face streaked, hair hanging, gown in shreds, fell into her arms. She held the small sobbing figure. "What happened, Zara? Where is your grandfather?"

"They took him away. Before they left they broke everything in the shop."

"Did they harm you?"

"They tried to get me on the ground but grandfather saved me. He was dusting his marble—you know he loves it—and he threatened them, he who never raised his voice in his life. As they were dragging him away they were hitting him on the head. I hid."

"Do you know who they are?"

Zara wept into her hands. "They wore masks. They had knives. They were drunk or mad."

Peg remembered her own encounter with such a gang long ago on the London road. Only this time there had been no foundling to run for help, no Darnley to blast them to hell where they might burn. She must get the girl away to safety, the blood on the floor, the grey hairs of the old man that still clung to the marble were grim pointers to what had happened. "You must come home with me, Zara," she said gently. "It is what your grandfather would wish."

With the help of a constable she was lucky enough to meet, she searched the lanes and alleyways of the Jewish quarter of the city and spoke to the Rabbi, to elders of the sect, to anyone who could tell her anything. The gang had run riot, knifing men, raping women, setting houses on fire, molesting children. The following morning she learnt that the battered corpse of the old man had been found in the river. His body was given to his people for the rites. He was buried before sundown in the little Jewish cemetery. It was the custom. His malefactors were never brought to justice.

Garrick had been stunned by the death of the old man, by the destruction to home and property of a quiet and law-abiding community. He had lived with race memories of the persecution of his own people, was familiar since childhood of the story of the Revocation of the Edict of Nantes, when Louis the Sun King put an end to liberty of conscience for his Protestant subjects, offering them money, two sous for their conversion. The price of a sow for a soul, they said scornfully. Zara would be welcome to stay in his home for as long as she wished and she settled down quietly, attaching herself to Peg. She was skilful with her needle, had an unrivalled knowledge of herbs learnt from her mother, long dead. Her father had crossed the English Channel to the Low Countries with his pedlar's pack and never returned. Given time she would recover.

❧

London was swept by fears of a French invasion in the

spring days that followed. Inns and coffee houses were crowded with men in search of the latest news. At Charing Cross the Windsor House offered chocolate at twelve pence per quart with a free copy of each newsletter hot from the printing press.

On the beaches of Dunkirk there was utter confusion as the invasion force took off. Out in the channel the French squadrons soon discovered they were heavily outnumbered by the British fleet and, disobeying Admiral Roquefueille's orders, ran for cover. Back in port, more orders were given, countermanded, given again, countermanded again. This time the Irish Brigade under de Saxe would sail. Prince Charles, wildly excited, smashed a bottle of wine against the flagship and sank to his knees in a prayer of thanksgiving.

And then disaster struck in the shape of a mighty storm blowing down the coast. As the Irish moved into deep waters they were buffeted about, some of the ships dashed to pieces against rocks, men fighting the stormy seas for their lives. The few ships that survived limped back into harbour, their crew beaten, despairing. The prince had been saved but it was the death knell of the expedition. The French forces turned their attention elsewhere but a defiant Charles remained at Gravelines and refused to give up.

Word reached London that the French invasion fleet had been compelled to turn back in the teeth of a gale and bells rang out in the city in thanksgiving. It had happened before in the days of Elizabeth when the winds of God had risen up to destroy the Spanish Armada. Now once again God had been on their side and his mighty works had destroyed the French. The English believed, and not for the first time, that they were invincible. In St James's

Palace, the Hanoverians rejoiced.

Polly wrote from Paris of her own affairs, oblivious of the dangers of war, of the fact that change was in the air, that all around her history was in the making. She used thick cream parchment and her writing was upright, assured.

> *Darling Peg,*
> *I am enjoying Paris and the best society and speak French with a good accent, I am told. I had a letter recently from dear Samantha. She is to marry her cousin, an officer in the Guards, and they plan to make London their home. Last week I celebrated my eighteenth birthday. I took part in amateur theatricals in the home of a French noblewoman. We staged a play by Molière in which I had a small part. Madame Dumesnil, leading actress of the Comédie Française, honoured us with her presence. She has heard of Mr Garrick who is acknowledged to be a very great actor. She asked me were you his* amoureuse, *and I said you were betrothed and would marry soon. I should like to be your bridesmaid. It would be so exciting.*
> *Your devoted sister,*
>
> > *Polly*

She folded the letter in two and carefully locked it in a cedarwood box in which she kept her papers. Reading between the lines she knew what her sister wanted. To be married like her friend Samantha, live in London, move in society. Well why not? Polly was young, attractive, well bred, well educated. All she needed was a secure base from which to be launched. And only she, Peg, could help. She must marry David Garrick. True he had long since given up importuning her to make him an honest man. Indeed had been heard to boast to his friends of his bachelor status. Yet she was sure he would be relieved. Marriage would suit him. He had never been a philanderer. At heart he was still the conventional son of respectable God-fearing folk. Yet she feared he had changed in some ways; then consoled herself with the thought that he was a worried man, had been for some months. All was not well in Drury Lane, as she knew to her cost. Fleetwood was gambling heavily, dipping into the coffers to pay his debts. And they were all suffering as a result, salaries in arrears or not paid at all. Many of the actors and stage-hands complained that they were on the edge of starvation.

He had arrived home in the early hours as he frequently did of late, eyes bloodshot, stock awry. He had mislaid his wig. Always a bad sign. He sat down heavily on the side of the bed and she put aside the book she was reading.

"Charlie Macklin and I have decided on a plan of campaign," he announced in tones of doom. "We intend to apply to the Lord Chamberlain for a licence to open a new theatre."

She sat up in bed, pulling the covers around her shoulders. "You have decided what?"

"You heard me. We might rent the Opera House. Most of the players will secede with us."

She decided to take him easy. "What does your friend Lord Burlington say?"

He frowned. "I have not discussed the matter with him."

"It might be best if you did, David, better still talk it over with the management. Fleetwood won't like it. He will see it as betrayal. He saved Charlie Macklin from prison when that fracas occurred in the greenroom."

He moved uneasily. "If we show our hands, Fleetwood will find some way to circumvent our plan. All the principals are agreed. Kitty Clive and Susanna Cibber have already pledged me their support. We'll sign a joint petition and present it to the Duke of Grafton."

She could scarcely believe what he was telling her. He had actually discussed his plans with her rivals behind her back. She felt too angry to talk and lay back closing her eyes. "We'll discuss this in the morning. No doubt you intend sleeping in your dressing room. It will be nothing new." She couldn't keep the bitterness from her voice.

He caught her roughly by the arm, pulling her out of the bed. "Don't tell me where I may sleep. I want to talk to you, Madam."

She rubbed her arm. "It's a little late for talking."

He had the grace to look ashamed. "Don't make a fuss over nothing. It's just a matter of signing a piece of paper."

For the sake of peace she had given way time and time again, allowed him make all the decisions as to how much they would spend, what they would save, what table they'd keep, what friends they'd entertain. He had even measured out the amount of tea she put in the pot, complaining of the price, saying she spoiled Sam Johnson, making his tea too strong. She had endured his pettiness and his overriding belief in his own rightfulness because of her guilt that she could never love him as she had loved Darnley, but this time he had gone too far.

"Enjoy your night's sleep," she said icily. "I shall take myself elsewhere, but before I do let me assure you that I'll sign no paper tonight or at any other time. It's time you faced facts, David Garrick. Burlington may flatter you but when fortune no longer smiles you will get no support from Milord. As far as the Lord Chamberlain of England is concerned, actors are the vagabonds the law still deems them to be. "

He looked so stricken that she weakened. "Fleetwood has powerful friends at court."

"As you have the Earl of Darnley," he sneered.

She clutched at the rags of her self-control. "I'm only trying to help. You'll destroy yourself and the rest who follow where you lead."

"How dare you lecture me, you ignorant Irish trollop." His spittle sprayed her gown and at that her temper exploded. She slapped him across the mouth, her rings catching his lip. He tasted the blood and his face contorted with rage. He was shaking her like a rag doll and she heard herself screaming hysterically. "Blast and damn you, Garrick, and your cursed ambition. You want to be manager of your own theatre and to further that end you'll sacrifice everyone—but you'll not make a fool of me. I'm no puppet to dance to your strings."

"You'll do as I say or take the consequences." As they struggled together, her robe slipped from her shoulders revealing her nakedness. His eyes had a mad look as he forced her back on the bed, pounding her, feeling her. He had her on her back, was driving into her and she shuddered, aroused by his violence, passion driving all else from her mind.

❦

She gazed at the ceiling, a small smile playing around her mouth. Always in their love-making she had felt his diffidence. It was the first time he had taken her so masterfully, so careless of the consequence. She hadn't thought he had possessed such fire and she had quite enjoyed it. She kissed his ear, giggling like a silly young girl having made love for the first time.

"I have decided after due consideration to accept your proposal of marriage, sir." She snuggled closer. "We can't go on tearing each other apart like this, darling. As your wife I'll sign any paper you wish."

He turned his back on her. "Make whatever arrangements you please," he said sulkily and closed his eyes.

She got out of bed, pulled a robe around her naked body and padded across the room to the window seat. She opened the shutters and gazed out. The street was silent, empty; overhead was the blackness of night studded with stars. What was it Darnley used whisper as she lay in his arms:

The moon shines bright: In such a night as this...
Troilus, methinks, mounted the Trojan walls
And sighed his soul towards the Grecian tents,
Where Cressid lay that night.

She cradled her head with her arms. Oh damn your soul, she thought fiercely, where are you, Darnley, I need you. Why do I go on loving you? The spring of the great four-poster creaked, Garrick grunted, turned on his back and began to snore loudly. She shivered with cold. In all her life she had never felt so alone.

A hackney dislodged Madame Flaubert at the house in Bow Street on a crisp September morning. London's most fashionable modiste was accompanied by a very small black page staggering under the weight of a box of stuffs. Madame Flaubert was dumpy with flashing brown eyes, false curls and a black gown, heavily ornamented with pink roses and cut too low. She should have looked absurd yet contrived to look elegant as only a French woman can.

"I believe Peg Woffington is to marry Mr Garrick at last," a rosy-cheeked housewife who had stopped outside the redbrick house to watch the French woman's progress, remarked to her companion, a thin-faced woman with a large belly and an expression of deep discontent.

The companion sniffed. "It took her long enough to bring him to heel then. She's been living with him for nigh on three years. It's my guess she's expecting and that he fancies a son."

A neatly dressed young girl in cloak and bonnet came tripping along in time to hear the tail end of the conversation. "Mrs Woffington is not *enceinte*," she said severely. "Madame Flaubert promises the wedding will be *très chic*."

The thin woman gasped and the girl with a moue of displeasure disappeared down the basement steps.

"Is she French do you think?" the fat woman enquired of her companion.

"Jewish, more likely."

"They're not to be trusted," the thin woman said peering through the railings. "I wouldn't employ that one as a maid."

The fat woman said placatingly, "Still and all she's a good-looking girl, well turned out."

"Except for the terrible birthmark, God bless the mark." The thin woman patted her bulge. "I had a longing for strawberries all summer but my husband forbade me eat them."

"I had a taste for pork meself when I was carrying. For a full nine months I ate nothin' but pig's cheeks and bacon," the fat woman giggled.

"And the child was born with a pig's head?"

"Yerra go way outa that. He's the finest of the lot. Born with a lucky caul, he was. They say he'll never drown. A sea-faring captain offered him a sovereign for the caul but he wouldn't part."

"You Irish are full of superstitions." The thin woman tightened her lips. "That Peg Woffington is no better than a whore. An easy wench for any man."

The fat woman chuckled. "Faith then a man'd need money to bed her. The son I was telling you about works in Drury Lane, earns good money as a stage carpenter. Says she's the highest paid actress in London, earns eight hundred guineas a year and is very free with her money."

The thin woman hitched a cloak and prepared to move

off. "And with everything else, I doubt not. He must have a long spoon," she concluded ominously, "that must eat with the devil."

Madame Flaubert helped by the little blackamoor was opening boxes, spilling out stuffs. Tables and chairs were heaped with ribbons, chemises light as air, gold and white silk stockings, with matching ruched garters, stiff embroidered stomachers, elbow-length gloves. Shoes of brocade and velvet lurched drunkenly on one side or stood firm on high heels. There were gowns and petticoats of silk and muslin in a variety of colours, daffodil yellow, moss green, pale blue, lilac, red. Carefully she lifted out a gown of white silk interwoven with silver threads, trimmed with silver lace, with small panniers, sweetheart neckline and elbow-length sleeves. "Your bridal gown," she said through a mouthful of pins, "of an elegance beyond compare. With this you will wear a cap of Brussels lace."

As she fitted and tucked she chattered volubly, relaying the latest French scandal. "King Louis has taken a new mistress, called de Pompadour. Her coiffure is all the rage."

Peg strained to see her reflection in the long mirror but the French woman pulled irritably at the fabric she was draping. "Please not to move. I desire the gown to fall properly."

"You were speaking of Madame de Pompadour," Peg said soothingly.

"*Mais oui*. When the child was only nine years a gypsy foretold that she was fated to become the mistress *en titre*. From that day she was known as Reinette." She adjusted a pleat. "You will please to turn around slowly. Yes a tuck here and a small adjustment there."

"A gypsy once read Mr Garrick's future in his hand," Peg murmured. "She said he would fall in love with a red-haired girl with green eyes but would marry another."

The French woman sniffed. "She was a witch that one. She will be proved wrong." Beside her the small blackamoor moved uneasily. His grandmother had been a witch. Even the elders of the tribe had consulted her. She had warned him of the white man, said that one day he would be sold in the slave market. And so it had happened. He was taken to France in a ship and his mistress had bought him for gold in the market. If he was good and carried her parcels safely she was kind enough but sometimes he forgot to stand still and she beat him with a cane. He stood on one foot and she poked him sharply in the ribs. "Pay attention. If you displease me I shall sell you to the traders down by the river and they will make of you a galley-slave."

He blinked back the tears, his mistress hated him to cry but sometimes he couldn't help himself. He was only four years old. Surreptitiously he wiped his eyes with the hem of the wedding gown and in a temper she boxed his ears.

Peg patted his head of black curls. "Hush little one." She rooted in a box of comfits and found him an almond sweetmeat. "I should like to have a blackamoor of my own. My maid Zara is lonely for her family. You could help her."

He gazed speechless at the beautiful lady smiling down at him.

"What are you called?" she whispered in his ear.

"Mohamet," he whispered back.

"His price is only one hundred guineas, Madam." The French woman had a shrewd eye for a possible sale. She had paid the slave trader twenty guineas and was already regretting her buy. A girl would be more useful, she could teach her to sew and embroider. She was prepared to haggle over the blackamoor's price but to her delight Peg said grandly, "I can see he is worth his weight in diamonds."

Mohamet's face split in a huge grin.

Pleased with her morning's work, Madame Flaubert said brightly, "As I explained, yes, the young Reinette never forgot her destiny. When she became a woman she rented a cottage in the forest of Senart near Cloisy, the king's hunting-lodge. I was born in the district, you comprehend. Each day the Pompadour followed the king's hunt, driving a pink phaeton and wearing a blue gown or dressed in pink in a blue carriage. *Mon Dieu* what man could resist such a captivating sight."

Peg stifled a sigh. Some women plotted their destiny with skill. Things fell out as they wished. All her life she had been moved by impulses, emotion, had never given thought to possible outcomes, and now she was paying for her foolishness. She knew with a heart-sinking certainty that her life was collapsing around her. Garrick's days were taken up with the rehearsals, meetings with the management, from which she was excluded, discussions with his fellow actors in which she had no part. Of course they noticed his coolness towards her and acted accordingly. After the night's performance he usually adjourned to the Beefsteak Club with his intimates and it was the early hours before he returned home. Lately he had taken to sleeping in his dressing room so as not to disturb her rest he said. No definite date had been fixed for the wedding.

Zara was delighted with the small blackamoor. He slept in her bed and she taught him to wash carefully, eat properly and do as he was bid without sulking. He liked best to ride in "Mees" Woffington's coach, seated proudly beside the driver. Sometimes he was silent for long periods, Zara, ever watchful, would slip him a sweetmeat when a tear trickled down his ebony cheeks. But mostly his chatter could be heard all over the house. He frightened the maids telling them stories of the village where he was born, of the warriors who painted their faces and rode faster than the wind. Once as Zara sat at her embroidery frame, he told her a long rambling story of how the women of the tribe sought his grandmother's help when their man had taken another wife and the moon was full. "The mammas came with their bellies full." He puffed himself out like a balloon. "My grandma gave them a powder to drink with coconut milk and they went down like this." He drew in his breath and let out air.

"Hyssop, fleur-de-luc," Peg said from her seat by the fire. Herbs ground up and used to put an end to the unborn child. It was what the young Scottish actor had given her on that day long ago. The pain she had endured, the loss, had stiffened her resolve to make her way on the stage, become so rich that she would never be frightened again. Hyssop for sin, for despair, she thought bitterly.

"Hyssop, a purification for the coming year." Zara remembered the Jewish rites of her childhood at the time of Passover, her mother sprinkling water in the four corners of the room with twigs of hyssop. Holy water from the river Jordan, a gift from the Rabbi.

Mohamet, sitting at a hassock at Peg's feet, tugged at her skirt. "You promised you would read about the sailor. Zara and me is waiting." Peg patted his curls and he leaned his face on his chubby fists, just as Conor used to. Every evening before leaving for the theatre she would read Mohamet a chapter of *Robinson Crusoe*.

"You will remember how Crusoe was shipwrecked and how after many lonely days and nights a native of the island whom he called his Man Friday became his constant companion and friend," she reminded Mohamet. She opened the book which she had marked with a dried rose leaf and waited while Zara put away her frame and came nearer, the better to hear.

"'Enemies came and invaded and ruined their plantation,'" Peg read, "'but a storm came to their aid, destroying the canoes belonging to the invaders so that they were defeated. And after that they lived in peace upon the Island. During the ten years that followed they had some very surprising new adventures. Perhaps one day I shall give you an account of them.'"

"Did they live happily ever after?" Mohamet gave a great yawn.

"On a beautiful island where the palm trees grew and the sun always shone," Zara said softly, and lifting up the little bundle carried him to his bed. "Someday we two will go and live there in a hut like Crusoe," he whispered and closing his eyes drifted away to a sunny island where coconuts grew on trees. From the sea the great sailor called him to join them and he ran across the sand and into Man Friday's arms.

❧

That Christmas many of the actors and their families went hungry. Fleetwood was gambling, recklessly, in the vain hope of recouping his losses. Importuned on all sides by his fellow workers, Garrick decided that the only solution was to write to the Duke of Grafton requesting a licence for a new theatre. A week later he was summoned to meet the Lord Chamberlain.

He arrived back in the house in Bow Street on a cold January evening. Peg watching from the parlour window saw him get out of the hackney, press a hand to his forehead and stumble up the steps. Next he was in the room, shoulders hunched, face pinched and grey. He had managed to age ten years in the three hours he had been absent and not for the first time she marvelled at how he could will himself into acting a part.

Without a word she poured two whiskeys. She too was going to need a crutch.

He collapsed on to a sofa before the fire and gulped down his drink.

"What happened?" She was almost afraid to ask.

He held out his glass which she refilled.

"Grafton enquired how much I was paid as an actor. When I told him the truth, one thousand pounds a year, he threw the application in my face." His voice was a parody of the duke's arrogant drawl. "'One thousand pounds is an absurdly high sum for an actor. My sons earn less than half that amount in the service of king and country.'"

He tossed back his drink. "'Petition dismissed.'"

She knelt beside him, stroking his head. "Everything is not lost. Drury Lane cannot afford to lose their best actor."

"Ruin stares us in the face," he moaned. "'Machinations, hollowness, treachery and all ruinous disorders...'" King Lear to the life. Then she was ashamed of her smallness of mind and said coaxingly, "Fleetwood will come to his senses. Your only hope is to stand firm now that you have gone so far."

He looked at her sadly and with immense dignity got to his feet and went out of the room, murmuring, "'Put out the light, and then put out the light.'"

"Now he's Othello," she told herself and finished the whiskey in one gulp. She was in for a stormy night.

All London knew that Drury Lane was in deep trouble.

In the great houses of the town the aristocracy dismissed the actors as ne'er-do-wells, forever bemoaning their lot. In inns and clubs they were berated as feckless no-goods, squandering what they earned, sponging on others. Backstage, tempers grew brittle as the weeks passed and the actors and their families starved. It was during a performance of *Julius Caesar* that matters came to a head. Even Garrick felt the tensions, knew that many envied him because, of them all, he was sure of his salary. Lord Burlington saw to it that Fleetwood did not dare leave him short. But in their wildest imagining no one could have foreseen that a supporting actor of modest pretensions and a mild manner, driven to the edge of madness, had planned a terrible revenge.

Caesar, wearing the purple robes, the crown of laurels on his brow, bestrode the world like a god, undaunted by the soothsayer's warning or Calphurnia's tears. Around him the conspirators gathered, adulation in their faces, treachery in their hearts. The moment had come. The fates had spun their web. Casca lunged forward to stab Caesar in the neck, Marcus Brutus plunged in to deliver the *coup de grâce*...But something was terribly wrong. Garrick was on the ground and they were crowding around him, watching helplessly as blood pumped down his neck, staining his shoulders, his gown to a deeper purple. Someone screamed. Voices were raised. In the stalls people were craning to see what had happened. Peg in Calphurnia's robes was running downstage crying out, "Can anyone help? Mr Garrick has been stabbed."

❦

"Another fraction and the jugular vein would have been

severed," said the young surgeon as he skilfully bound up the wound and rubbed his hands. "You are a lucky man, Mr Garrick," he said. "How did it happen?"

"I was Marcus Brutus. I was supposed to stab him, when I looked there was blood on the dagger," Charlie Macklin said shakily. "I wasn't responsible though I will be blamed because I once put a man's eye out."

"It was an accident," Garrick said tiredly. He knew who the culprit was. A young actor playing Casca whose wife had left him and whose child had died only that morning, he had said of neglect.

Early the next morning Casca was found in his dingy lodgings hanging from the ceiling. When they got to him his body was cold. He had made a noose of the bloodstained toga he had worn on stage and kicked a broken chair from under his feet.

Fleetwood seized the opportunity to close the theatre and at this the actors lost their nerve and implored Garrick to make the peace. He swallowed his pride, met the management behind closed doors and at the end of the most acrimonious meeting in stage history, an agreement was reached. All the players would be reinstated with the exception of Macklin. Fleetwood had a private debt to pay the rumbustious Irishman whom he had once saved from the gallows.

❧

"Dear God, who is that?" The house was shaking to the reverberation of thunderous knockings. Pèg opened the bedroom shutters and looked down. In the shadowy light of the street lamp she could make out a wild figure. "It's Charlie Macklin," she whispered. "He's dancing around shaking his fists."

Garrick looked up from the papers he was sorting through, his face grey with fatigue. "I'll speak to him. Remain where you are."

Zara opened the door. Macklin pushed her aside and she fled for sanctuary to the basement. He was shouting for Garrick's blood.

"You reneged on me." He was very drunk. "Judas sold me for a handful of silver."

Peg came down the stairs to help. Macklin was beyond control, Garrick could not handle the madman on his own.

"Sit down, Charlie," she heard him say. "I'll try to explain what happened."

"Gimme a drink," Macklin screamed.

"Get him whiskey," Garrick ordered.

She ran into the study and was back almost at once. Macklin grabbed the glass, emptied the drink in one gulp and began to cough. His bloodshot eyes were darting around the hall, focusing on Garrick. "We can take the company to Dublin. Cock a snook at Fleetwood," he tittered. "Wha' say you, my friend?"

Garrick said patiently, "We got no offers from either Smock Alley or the Aungier Street Playhouse, though I tried the waters in both. If the theatre remains closed there will be more than one suicide. The actors are desperate. Fleetwood will take them back. I have his word for it."

"Except me." Macklin was hiccoughing while drunken sobs punctuated his words. He rubbed snot from his nose. "Fleetwood hates me. He is trying to make me the scapegoat. Asked me to support him but I threw in my lot with you." He shouted at Peg. "More whiskey."

"He's had enough," Garrick said wearily.

"I wanna drink," Macklin screamed. She handed him the bottle not caring if he collapsed on the floor. He put the bottle to his mouth, swallowed convulsively and said in a whining voice, "You hate me, Garrick. You and your whore. You've always been jealous of me."

Garrick held his head. "I did my best. Offered to take a cut in salary if Fleetwood would agree to reinstate you."

She thought, sweet God, he's crucifying Macklin's pride. There will be murder done this night.

Macklin lurched over then lifted Garrick up by the lapels of his coat. "I want no favours either from you or Mr Bloody Fleetwood. You shit, I saved your life when a decent actor tried to kill you." He threw back his head and laughed. "Me, Macklin, saving this sod. I should have struck the fatal blow myself. '*Et tu, Brute,*'" he mocked and threw Garrick on the floor. "'Then fall, Caesar.'"

They were rolling around struggling. Macklin had Garrick by the throat, trying to throttle him. Peg thrust her body between them. Macklin kicked out and she fell. But it had given Garrick time to draw his breath, gather his strength. He had Macklin by the hair, was beating his head off the wall, screaming at the top of his voice. "Get out of my sight, Macklin, before I finish you off. Never darken this door again."

Something of his demonic rage seemed to reach through to Macklin's drunkenness. He managed to free himself and lurched to the door. "'S all right," he mumbled. "We'll settle wi' swords. Have a—have a duel in Hyde Park. Arrange seconds." He tittered. "'Goo' night, sweet prince.'"

He was gone. Garrick locked himself in his study, refusing her pleas to let her in. Exhaustedly she dragged herself to her room and fell into bed. It was dawn before she slept.

How sweet the moonlight sleeps upon this bank!
Here will we sit, and let the sounds of music
Creep in our ears; soft stillness and the night
Become the touches of sweet harmony.

(The Merchant of Venice, V,i)

24

She could hear Zara opening the shutters, letting in the cold air. "Go away," she mumbled. "Let me sleep."

An aroma of fresh coffee, of hot toast, tantalised her senses and she opened her eyes, asking in an exhausted voice, "What time is it?"

Zara set down the breakfast tray on the bed. "Nearly midday, ma'am. The master left early." She settled the pillows and poured out a cup of coffee. "He asked me to tell you he's gone to Lichfield. He ate no breakfast."

"What did you say about Lichfield?" Peg pulled herself up so suddenly that the tray rocked and coffee slopped over the bed. "Now look what I've done," she said exasperatedly.

"Mrs Bellamy is below in the drawing room, impatient to see you." Zara put the tray on the bedside table and wiped the quilt.

"What in God's name does she want?" Impatiently Peg arranged a garment around her shoulders and poured herself fresh coffee. "Show her up and bring another cup, Zara. The fool of a woman is always hungry."

❧

Mrs Bellamy arranged herself comfortably in an armchair beside the breakfast tray and, helping herself to coffee, thoughtfully spread a slice of toast with butter and honey. "I met Mr Garrick this morning. He looked the worse for wear. He was taking the stagecoach. On a journey I'll be bound."

Peg put down her cup. "Possibly."

"He had no time to chat; gentlemen can be so taciturn. Dear Lord Tyrawley was a man of few words."

Peg swung herself out of bed and went over to the dressing table where she began to brush her hair vigorously, catching it up in a bunch of curls on top. "If you will excuse me," she said distantly, "I am late and have much to do."

Mrs Bellamy continued to talk through a mouthful of food. "So we are all to be reinstated, except Mr Macklin. He was uttering the most terrible threats last night." She belched, patted her false curls and, putting down her cup, got to her feet. "I have so many calls to make today," she said complacently, "but I thought I should spare you the time." She kissed Peg on both cheeks and went out, pausing at the door to say, "And Lord Darnley is back in town. I wonder why?" And she was gone, tripping down the stairs, calling to Zara in a loud voice to fetch her a chair to take her to Drury Lane.

"It's an ill wind," Peg thought sourly, knowing that Mrs Bellamy would have a field day acquainting Kitty Clive with her news, informing Fleetwood of Garrick's departure from London, sympathising with Macklin on how he had been treated by those ingrates in Bow Street. Everywhere she went she would exact payment of one kind or another, a meal, a drink, a pair of new gloves; she might even manage to borrow a crown if one of her cronies happened to be in funds.

So Darnley was back in London. It was three years since that last good-bye on the quayside in Ringsend, three years in which she had tried to forget him and failed. Of course there had been rumours. He had been sighted in Rome, in Paris, at the beaches of Dunkirk when the ships were beaten back. She doubted if anyone had the truth. What amazed her was that he had dared show his face in London, then realised that he was different: the wealthy, the well born were always different. They could afford to be, like the Buckinghams who made no secret of their hatred of the Hanoverian upstarts as they called them. Then too, Darnley had once enjoyed the friendship of the Prince of Wales and if rumour were true, the prince would allow no word of criticism of his former aide. Maybe it was because his father, the king, feared the Jacobites and Frederick hated his father.

She would seek Darnley out. Ask his help. Is that the reason? a mocking voice in her head demanded, and she reminded it fiercely of her determination to marry Garrick. Packed in her trunk were the wedding clothes, the exquisite gown, the cap of priceless lace. She had even planned the honeymoon in Italy. Maybe in some mouldering villa she would find another marble boy. She pulled the bell rope and by the time Zara came into the room she was pulling on her stays. "Lace me up," she said, holding onto the bedpost. "Tighter, Zara. I am going out on a visit. Lay out my prettiest gown and help me fix my hair and face. Just a little powder. No paint."

Darnley, wearing a robe of dark red velvet, was sharing titbits with his King Charles spaniel when she was admitted to the house in Berkeley Square. He looked older, his hair tinged with silver, his eyes tired; but his smile was friendly and his manners polished. He raised his eyebrows in surprise and then kissed her hand. "This is indeed a pleasure, Mrs Woffington. To what do I owe this honour?"

Her heart sank. This was how it would be. "My apologies for this unexpected visit, Lord Darnley," her voice was brittle. "I have come on a matter of some concern."

Idly he plucked a flower from a vase on the mantelpiece and began to discard the petals, reciting as he did so, "She loves me. She loves me not." She found herself smiling, giving him back the doggerel:

> *I do not love you, Dr Fell,*
> *The reason why I cannot tell;*
> *But this alone I know full well*
> *I do not love thee, Dr Fell.*

It was a foolish game they had played together in happier times, at least it broke the ice. Darnley scratched his bitch. "Do you suppose Mrs Woffington could be tempted to rendezvous with me this afternoon? We could visit the Chelsea Gardens and call in at a certain tavern in the town where they hold out the enticing offer:"

> *Here you may get drunk for a penny,*
> *dead drunk for two pence*
> *and straw for nothing."*

The bitch barked shrilly and Peg held out her hands in appeal.

"Darnley, I need your help."

His eyes softened. He put the spaniel aside. "'Being your slave, what should I do but tend upon the hours and times of your desire?'"

"I'm not playacting. This is serious."

He tilted back his chair and looked at the ceiling. "Pray continue, m'dear. I am all attention."

She tried to marshal her thoughts, to relate simply, methodically, all that had happened, as if he were an acquaintance, but he was not and it was difficult. She found herself telling her story in disjointed sentences. "Garrick is distraught...he took the morning stage to Lichfield. We are to be married...things are bad in Drury Lane. Fleetwood is gambling heavily, the actors are desperate. One tried to kill Garrick and then hanged himself. Charlie Macklin called to the house last night and Garrick and he fought. He is dangerous. He once blinded a man in the theatre. Garrick wants a licence. Could you help? Approach the Duke of Grafton?" She found herself weeping and was furious; she didn't want to beg for his sympathy, wanted to be collected, businesslike as if they were no more than old friends. She gave a hiccough and he tossed her a handkerchief. "Dry your eyes like a good girl. This seems to be my chief service to you."

She smiled mistily and his heart turned over. "Garrick may swing for all I care," he said gruffly, "but I cannot bear to see my favourite wench unhappy. I'll mention the matter to Grafton. That noble lord owes me a favour."

Impulsively she leaned across and kissed his cheek. "Thank you, Darnley. You do not know what a relief it would be."

He got to his feet. "If you will excuse me, sweetling. I have a pressing appointment with my tailor and a call to drink chocolate with some friends and catch up on the town's latest scandals. But if you will permit I shall call for you this afternoon and take you for a drive."

❦

Spring had come early that year. Darnley took her driving in Hyde Park, carpeted with daffodils and bluebells, to Cappers Farm in Tottenham where they drank tea under a willow and ate simnel-cake, delighting in the golden almond paste. They went to Hampton Court and heard an old man playing a lute while a choir of young boys sang madrigals. They wandered arm in arm through the palace where once a king had made love to a dark-eyed slip of a girl for whom he overturned his kingdom and church. Peg wondered sadly did love always grow stale in the end and what Anne Boleyn's last thoughts were when she laid her slender neck on the block.

Their idyll came to an end that evening when in balmy air they hired a barge to witness a water pageant on the Thames. Boats, gaily decorated with garlands of flowers, sailed down the river, skiffs raced each other from Westminster Hall to Waterman's Bridge, banners and pennants hung from riverside buildings and the evening sky was colourful with flaring torches and shooting rockets. As they rode back to the mansion in Berkeley Square, Darnley held her in his arms. "Remember Lorenzo in *The Merchant?*"

> *How sweet the moonlight sleeps upon this bank!*
> *Here will we sit, and let the sounds of music*
> *Creep in our ears; soft stillness and the night*
> *Become the touches of sweet harmony.*

She knew in that moment that she fooled herself, that he still held her heart, always would. Garrick forgotten, he carried her to his bed as he had done once before in that stone house by the sea with its diamond windows and the many-coloured quilt.

He wrapped his arms around her, looking down on the bridge of freckles across her nose which she hated and he loved, the huge green eyes, the sweet mouth. "Tomorrow I leave for France," he was telling her and it felt as if he were driving a stake through her heart. "What do you plan?" she whispered.

He put a finger to her lips. "No questions, Peg."

Her arms and legs were around him, silken living ropes that bound her to the body she worshipped, the beloved face close to hers: the fine aristocratic features, lines around the eyes, a deep ridge from nose to chin that hadn't been there before and the grey eyes that looked down on her with such love. There had never been anyone else for her. David Garrick was the dark side of the moon; Darnley was warmth, life-giving sun. He was kissing her passionately, touching her soft body, feeling her secret places, taking her and she was straining to give him all in an ecstasy of desire. They merged together, reached the climax of their love together, and she knew in her soul that this was the final act of their affair. After tonight the final curtain would fall.

❦

A few days later a buoyant Garrick returned to the house in Bow Street, borrowed a shilling to pay the hackney fare, took her in his arms and kissed her enthusiastically on the mouth.

She pulled away and he chucked her under the chin. "Hey now, don't look so woebegone. I had expected a warmer welcome."

She swallowed nervously. "And I a letter from Lichfield. I was sure you had quite forgotten me."

He grinned. "Quite honestly I hadn't time to write. Oh Peg, just listen what happened. Mr Walmesley turned up trumps. I have his promise to put up four thousand pounds to match my savings. I am to buy the interest on the Drury Lane Theatre. Fleetwood is resigning. The trustees are agreeable."

She felt an irrational jealousy. "You needn't have gone begging. My emeralds alone would have fetched as much."

His face darkened and she knew at once she had blundered, mentioning the jewels that Darnley had lavished on her.

"I prefer to manage my own affairs," he said briefly and turned away. "I need some air after a seven-hour coach ride. I must be first to break the good news to Charlie Macklin." At the front door he shouted back, "Don't wait up for me. I'll likely sup at the Beefsteak Club. I may stay the night."

She slept badly and when sleep did come her dreams were troubled. She was wandering through a mist, looking for Darnley. She was in the theatre and Othello was throttling her. As she struggled for breath, Garrick's face changed to the satanic monk's in the Hellfire Club.

Zara was shaking her awake, dragging her out of the nightmare. It was morning and there was a tray containing a silver pot of chocolate on the bedside table. Zara was opening the shutters. Mohamet, clad in a sheet, stuck his head around the door. "I am a ghost," he said in his piping treble. "I make you laugh."

"Take him away, Zara," she said nervously. She could hear Garrick's footsteps on the stairs, impatient, taking them two at a time. Zara caught up the blackamoor and fled as Garrick brushed past her.

She knew by the look on his face the storm was about to break and steeled herself for its onslaught. "It's about time you came home," she said boldly, though her hands shook so much she laced them together under the sheets.

He stood at the bedpost looking down at her. "There is one thing I have always admired about you, Peg, and that is your courage. Even when you are cornered." His voice was deceptively pleasant. He seated himself on the side of the bed. "And so, Milord Darnley assiduously squired you around London in my absence. No doubt you offered him the pleasures of your bed."

"Get out of my room," she said through clenched teeth. She would not let him see her fear.

He bent over and placed his two hands at either side of her head and pressed. Bands of iron were clamping her brain. She saw him through a red mist. "Let go of me you fool," she shouted.

"I would squeeze your head so,"—the bands were tightening—"if I thought it would destroy his image in your mind. Maybe this would serve better." He had her by the neck, choking her, muttering, "'Yet she must die, else she'll betray more men. Put out the light. Then put out the light.'" With a stupendous effort she twisted and bit his finger, she could feel the bone crunching and with an oath he let go. She fell out of the far side of the bed, tottered to the washbasin and scooping up a handful of water, swallowed. "If you can bear to abandon your role of Othello, I'll try to explain," she said painfully. "I called to Darnley to ask his help, to intercede with the Duke of Grafton on your behalf."

"You dared interfere in my affairs." The fury of his voice was like a physical blow and for the first time that morning she was truly afraid. "I acted for the best," she croaked. "Why do you think the trustees had a sudden change of heart? They had their instructions from the Lord Chancellor himself." She saw the hatred on his face and rage gave her voice. "What will you do now that you know the truth?" She wanted to stop this crazy tirade, but she could not control the flow of words that were pouring out. "Will you resign from Drury Lane? Refuse their offer? Explain to your well-placed friends in Lichfield that your mistress sold her favours to further your ends? But of course you won't. You would betray your every last principle to realise your ambitions."

He turned away, moved to the window so that she would not see his face. He had never dared let her know how much he loved her. She had quoted Pope's lines to him: "'No, make me mistress to the man I love. If there be another name more free.'" Oh she had been mistress alright, but another had held her heart. He thought of Burlington's gentle daughter. Violetta did not have Peg's radiance, her wild untrammelled beauty but she loved him. It would be good to be loved for one's own sake. She had exhausted herself, fallen silent. He turned back afraid he had injured her. She was crouched on the floor whimpering that she was sorry, that she had acted for the best. It was like a refrain in his head. His face was as expressionless as his voice. "You acted stupidly but no doubt you meant well. My appointment is a matter of expediency and not as a result of intervention in high places. Drury Lane has been losing money. Fleetwood is finished. The trustees need capital, need my services."

She licked her lips. "What can you do that Fleetwood could not?"

He passed his hand across his eyes. "Change the

theatre. Clear the gallants from the stage, ban those raucous orange girls." He thought for a moment. "I'll clear the boxes of titled fops who patronise the theatre merely to pass an idle hour, gamble, make eyes at every wench. Oh yes! I shall change attitudes, manners. Drama will be taken seriously. People will learn to appreciate what we are trying to do. If not they are welcome to remain away."

She felt sick in the pit of her stomach. He was obsessed but there was something she must know. "Did you intend to marry me?"

He shrugged, every line of his body expressing his boredom. "For a long time I haven't given it much thought."

She was screaming and the sound was lifting his head. "Then I'll decide for you. I'll leave this house today and except in the course of business I shall never speak to you again."

He said in an even tone, "It might be best. Shall I send Zara to help you pack? You will also take the blackamoor. I have little patience with young children."

She lost control and was hurling the contents of the breakfast tray at his head. He dodged and went out of the room. She remained gazing mesmerised at the chocolate, spreading out, staining the Chinese wallpaper she had picked with such loving care when she first moved in. Zara had come in and was holding her, reassuring her that everything would be all right. Mohamet was on his knees picking up the silver pot, the broken china, the sugar lumps. She saw the whites of his eyes and began to laugh, helplessly. Zara slapped her on the face and after that she wept and wept, until there were no more tears to shed.

❦

She took an apartment across the river and returned Garrick's gifts: the complete works of Shakespeare in one volume, an ivory fan, a peacock's feather, a ring with two hearts entwined which he had given her in Dublin in the first flush of love. It was worn by the fisherfolk of Galway as a token of love, a marriage band. She had never left it off until now. He sent back all the gifts she had given him, except for the diamond shoe buckles. They were very valuable and she wondered was this his real reason, remembered that autumn day when she had said, "In years to come... let them be a memento of our love" and he had sworn that he would never part with them, or her.

To console herself she dwelt on his everlasting economies, charged him with being a miser in everything, even in love. Yet in all honesty she knew she judged him wrongly. He was a consummate artist, had shaped her future, made of her meagre talents the actress she was. Maybe the truth lay elsewhere. Her mother often said, "You could live a lifetime with a man and still not know him." It was true of her years with Garrick. In some ways he was a greater stranger on the day they parted than on the day she had first laid eyes on him at the rout at Buck House.

25

It had been a dark and sullen day with occasional bursts of thunder and gusts of rain. As night fell a gale-force wind came driving in from the sea, screaming across the harbour, lifting nets, tossing refuse and small objects around, flinging its force against the town, battering houses and sending inhabitants scurrying for home. Mountainous waves crashed against the jetty, drenching fishermen as they ran for shelter before the storm.

"By the grace of God we made it," the tall figure wrapped in a black cloak climbed out of a fishing boat and paid the men who had battled the heavy seas to bring him to safety. Lurching awkwardly in the teeth of the gale he was soon lost in a maze of mean streets. In a smoky den he consulted with a couple of grizzled old men squabbling over a game of cards. Their rheumy eyes examined him indifferently. A stranger was no novelty in Dunkirk, where Irish and Scottish mercenaries spent their days gambling, wenching and drinking, waiting for Jacobite action and growing old and embittered as the years passed them by. He bought the ancients the rough red wine and rum they mixed in a draught of such potency as to fell an honest drinker and they directed him to an inn behind a cobbled courtyard.

Darnley and Captain Maurice O'Connor had been friends since childhood. The O'Connors had survived Norman invasion, Elizabethan plantations, Cromwellian wars, but had lost everything backing James at the Boyne. Their proud boast had been that they had continued down the centuries to hold fast to old customs and traditions, maintaining open house, sending their sons to be fostered by other great families as had been done from time immemorial.

Maurice, the last of the line, had been fostered by an uncle of Darnley's on the maternal side, at the Black Castle in County Limerick. As a boy, Darnley had spent summers from May to October in Ireland and so the scion of a once great Irish household and the young Scottish aristocrat had struck up a friendship. Together they had explored Ireland's golden vale, fished Lough Gur, the bottomless lake which claimed the heart of a human being every seven years, climbed Doon Hill where a golden eagle nested, explored Garret Island where almost four thousand years before men of the Bronze Age had built habitations of mud and wattles. Both their families were fiercely Jacobite. Maurice's father had perished beside the Boyne waters on that fatal day when James had lost his kingdom to William. On St John's Eve, with bonfires blazing on every hill for miles around, two boys on the threshold of manhood had taken a solemn oath to devote their lives to the Jacobite cause, gashing their fingers, mingling their blood. It was to be their last summer together. It was time for Maurice to return to his widowed mother, time for Darnley to take over the family estates in Scotland. But they would never forget that they were blood-brothers, never forget their boyhood dreams of a Jacobite resurrection.

Darnley tossed aside his sodden cloak and embraced his friend. "I am happy to find you well, Maurice. You know why I have come. I need an exact report of what France intends."

O'Connor was strikingly handsome, bearded, tanned with wind and sun. His smile was as sincere, his blue eyes as true as those of the young boy who had sworn to die for the "King over the Water," more than three decades before. Only the once raven hair now powdered with snow marked the years' relentless toll.

"Louis of France grows cunning," he said. "He has ordered that all the Irish in exile, from eighteen to fifty years, join the Irish Brigade or be hanged as vagabonds."

Darnley's lips tightened. "You sailed with Marshal de Saxe on the ill-fated expedition a year ago?"

"Yes and was glad to go. The marshal, Saxon bastard though he be, is the finest soldier in Europe. I'd follow his sword where the smile of the prince might not coax me."

A serving wench brought them ale, cheese, bread. Darnley ate hungrily. "Coming over we were forced to pump out in the storm, losing what provisions we had. I haven't tasted food or water for forty-eight hours." He wiped his mouth with the back of his hand. "Tell me what happened. The accounts I heard seemed intolerably garbled."

O'Connor frowned. "I sailed in the flagship with Prince Charles, our swords across our knees, our boastful talk of victory. It was the storm that defeated us. The winds of God." He filled a beaker with ale and studied it, his eyes bitter. "Six young fellows threw themselves into the raging sea. I battened the hatches and stood with drawn sword and pistol cocked while the men, half mad with fear, fought to get out, God help them. Some were sons of the Wild Geese born into the brigade and had never been to sea in their lives. We lost thirty-eight officers and men. Our ship crawled back here to Dunkirk. Had we reached London, de Saxe would have won a kingdom for the Jacobite. Now we who remain spend our days dreaming of campaigns lost and won and drinking old toasts." He raised his tankard. "A health to *Rí Séamus* and God save Ireland."

"Amen to that," Darnley said and drank.

O'Connor rapped the table for service and when the wench had replenished the jug of ale drew his stool nearer his friend. "Prince Charles has refused Louis's command to return to Paris."

Darnley said in a low voice, "Louis will not venture the best of his army again in a cause in which he no longer believes. How fares the prince? What of his company?"

"He surrounds himself with a small coterie of men, long past their prime. You will know most of them. William Murray from Scotland."

Darnley nodded. "Aye. He was attainted for his part in the Fifteen but to his clansmen is still the second Duke of Atoll."

"Then there's Colonel Francis Strickland."

"He's of an old Westmoreland Jacobite family."

"And Aeneas Macdonald the youngest of the bunch. He came over from Uist on his own business and fell under the spell of the prince. Add four Irish aristocrats and you have the company."

Darnley filled his beaker with ale. "Who are the Irishmen?"

"Sir Thomas Sheridan who saw service at the Boyne with my father over fifty years ago."

"Aye I met him in Rome. He tutored the prince."

"Sir John Macdonald, nigh on seventy and fond of the bottle. George Kelly who never saw service in his life. The only one worth a damn is Colonel William O'Sullivan, a seasoned veteran."

Darnley drank and turned his empty tankard mouth down on the table. "The prince is young and eager for a fight?"

O'Connor nodded. "He has courage, I'll grant him that. He offered to serve in Flanders but was turned down. He begged for men and arms to sail to Scotland, the Irish were wild to go. But Louis will not risk men and ships with scant hope of return. Meanwhile we rot in this hell-hole, and if we have a prayer it is that we be allowed strike a final blow before death overtakes us."

"If an expedition were to take place, Maurice, how many men could you raise?"

O'Connor pondered. "Seven hundred at least. We'd need ships. An advance carrying soldiers, powder, ball, flints, dirks, brandy, provisions. The cost would be high."

Darnley pushed back the bench. "It is time I had audience of the prince. Will you take me to him?"

"He frets his days out in a house near Gravelines about twelve miles from here. I ask no questions, but you will not raise our hopes needlessly?"

"I have sold my patrimony, Scottish and Irish estates, stables of horses, London property, what matter. It has taken time. London is a hotbed of spies, ready to sell their honour for gold or whatever it will buy. It was ever so with such men. At present the Hanoverians sleep peacefully. If money is all that stands between us and a last throw it shall be provided."

O'Connor grasped his friend's hand, smiling grimly. "It is time we were on our way."

Outside the storm had died down and the moon, cold, remote, glided over the rooftops. In the shadows an ostler waited with fresh horses. The conspirators swung themselves into the saddle and took the road west.

❧

George Ann Bellamy had left her father's house to join her mother in Drury Lane. She was a headstrong ambitious girl, determined to go on the stage and had lately become Polly's bosom friend. Thomas Sheridan, one-time school teacher, graduate of Trinity College, Dublin and lately actor, had taken to squiring the girls around London. He had left Dublin determined to make his way on the stage, so far with little success. He haunted Garrick, haunted Drury Lane, made overtures to Peg, paid court to Polly. At the end of June with money running short, he took himself off to Twickenham there to tutor young gentlemen for entrance to Oxford.

Garrick's appointment as manager had resulted in many changes in Drury Lane. Rehearsals were held on time, no excuse was accepted for unpunctuality. No member of the audience, however important, was admitted once the play had begun. Silence was enforced once the curtain went up; not even the orange girls were allowed sell their wares. Card-playing in boxes was forbidden and offenders were ceremoniously ushered out by attendants who could turn menacing if any resistance was shown. Garrick had assumed the mantle of authority with an assurance that belied his twenty-six years. True he still walked in Burlington's shadow and rumours ran rife that Violetta was pining away with love for him though whether anything would come of that was open to doubt. Lady

Burlington had been heard to declare that Garrick was an upstart who wished to marry above his station. A bastard Violetta might be but she was Burlington's daughter: Plantagenet blood flowed in her veins. The earl and his lady held fast to rank and privilege. But all this was merely gossip; no one knew what the truth of the matter really was, least of all Peg, who was being treated by Garrick with studied politeness in the theatre, ignored as if she did not exist if they chanced to meet elsewhere, slighted by her rivals, Susanna Cibber and Kitty Clive, and mocked by Charlie Macklin who had never forgiven her for being a witness to that night on which Garrick and he had come to blows. She fretted so with misery that she fell ill and was recommended a change of air by her physician.

❧

"Mr Sheridan and I are worried about you." Polly, polished and pretty in a yellow gown, dark curls tied back with a matching ribbon, looked down with concern at her sister as she rested on a *chaise-longue*.

Peg wondered what Sheridan was doing back in London.

As if he could read her mind he said smoothly, "I have come up from Twickenham on an errand for a friend of mine, a certain Colonel Caesar. He seeks a suitable tenant for his villa. He proposes to take up his quarters in the Tower during the present unrest."

Polly broke in excitedly, "Everyone is leaving London for fear of a French invasion. George Ann Bellamy and her mother have already set out to visit friends in Twickenham. Mr Sheridan assures me there is much polite society there and one can go boating on the river. Besides," she added persuasively, "a change of air would do you good. It would be such a relief to get away from the dangers of the Jacobites."

Peg said sharply, "What is this talk about an invasion?" Only the previous night she had dreamt of Darnley. He was at sea in the company of the prince. A British man-o'-war loomed up out of the mist and went into the attack and a cannonball hit the bridge. As she watched, horrified, Darnley seemed to clutch a rail that was no longer there and plunge into the sea. She had awoken from the nightmare to the thunder of guns and the screams of dying men.

Sheridan laced his thumbs in his coat. It was one of the habits she most disliked about him, that and the officious way he stuck out his chest. "The Young Pretender is poised to invade Scotland," he said with a smirk. "Rumour has it that the Earl of Darnley has beggared himself to provide men and ships. People say he has the death wish."

The Duchess of Buckingham had used the same expression. Was it true, she wondered? Some people called it the curse of Scotland. She had known since her early days that at times she had second sight. It ran in her mother's family. Was this to be how Darnley would die?

Polly gave her no peace: the villa was elegant; Colonel Caesar was charming; the Bellamys had been well received by the county; in Twickenham amateur theatricals were all the rage.

In the end she surrendered with as good a grace as she could muster and allowed Sheridan to carry her to Twickenham to meet Colonel Caesar, a middle-aged widower with a military bearing and a clipped manner of speech. He fell in love with Peg at first sight and she with Teddington Hall, a Palladian villa, set in acres of woodlands. She was enchanted by its classical lines, handsome portico, ceilings painted by the fashionable artist Verrio, the carved fireplaces the work of the master craftsman Grinling Gibbons whose name was on every lip. Within a matter of weeks she had taken possession of the house and sent Polly down to oversee the move. At the beginning of July she told Garrick she was taking a much-needed break and set out on the twenty-mile coach ride to her new home accompanied by Zara and the wildly excited Mohamet who insisted on riding with the coachman.

❧

On the morning of 16 July 1744, two ships moved slowly up the Loire estuary bound for the Hebrides of Scotland on the last great Jacobite adventure. Maurice O'Connor and Darnley sailed in the *Elizabeth*, a sixty-eight-gun frigate under the command of Captain Douaud. The ship carried a complement of seven hundred Irish and French mercenaries. The smaller ship, *Du Teillay*, carried the prince and his handful of advisers.

Four days later, skirting the west coast of Ireland for safety, they met a British warship. Immediately the *Elizabeth* went into the attack and the *British Lion* replied. Officers screamed orders, the cannon-loaders cursed, smoke belched, timbers splintered, men writhed in death agony as their guts spilled out. The brief encounter ended when a final shower of iron balls battered *Elizabeth*'s bridge, Captain Douaud's head was blown from his body and Maurice O'Connor was hit. Darnley stumbled across the main deck to where his friend had fallen, slipping on the bloody entrails spilling out of the dead body. A final explosion shattered the foremast and the mahogany rails he was clutching were no longer there. He was falling, hitting a solid sheet of water, going down into a green suffocating grave, lungs bursting. He surfaced, gasped for breath and managed to catch at a flat-bottomed boat that had come adrift. It took an eternity of time and herculean effort, but he managed to drag himself into the boat where he collapsed. He lay there under the brooding skies unaware that the encounter was over, the *Elizabeth* limping for port. He was not to know until a long time after that the *Du Teillay* like a toy ship had crowded all sail and slipped northwards. He lost consciousness and when he came to again he was alone. All around was the emptiness of sea and sky. After a long time a fishing boat came over the sea's edge, picking its way amongst floating debris, dead bodies, torn riggings, sails. He called for help but his faint voice was lost in the cries of the turbulence of sea, cries of scavenging gulls.

Three days later, the *Du Teillay*, with its tiny complement of men, reached Barra on the southern end of the Outer Hebrides. As she came in sight of the islands, the sun broke through the clouds for the first time since they had left France, a rainbow unfolded and a golden eagle hovered overhead. More wonderful still was the sound of the piping that filled the air. In the distance a kilted figure playing the bagpipes was moving across the strand. As he came nearer the watchers saw it was a bearded man with long flowing hair, wearing the MacNeil tartan. He was playing a lament that changed into a wild, triumphant march. The prince held his breath. It was a moment none of them would ever forget.

Aeneas Macdonald dropped on his knees before him crying out in a voice that shook with emotion, "Sire, the king of birds welcomes you home and MacNeil of Barra's piper has come to guide the ship to safe anchorage."

The dream had come true. At a spot on the little isle

of Eriskay, forever afterwards known as *Cladach a' Phrionsa* (the prince's shore), Charles first set foot on Scottish soil. No man had ever arrived to conquer a kingdom with so little, no gold, no arms, no followers except for the faithful seven, two Scottish lairds, an English nobleman and four Irish aristocrats. They would be remembered in Jacobite folklore as the "Seven Men of Moidart." Before night had fallen word was out that the prince had landed. Singly at first, then in ever-increasing numbers, the clansmen arrived to join the royal standard. Scotland was up. This time there would be no turning back.

❦

In the garden of Teddington Villa, Peg was entertaining the Bellamys. Zara had set out the tea-things under an oak tree: Irish linen and lace and fine bone china. The table was laid with plates of thinly sliced bread, small iced cakes, a bowl of fresh raspberries, another of cream, a plum cake and a silver tea-service. Mohamet came staggering across the lawn on his fat little legs carrying a dish of jelly. He stumbled and the quivering red mould disintegrated on the lawn. He broke into howls of rage and had to be comforted by Zara. Stuffing himself with marzipan he ran across to where the gardener's boy was working and they both settled down to examine a caterpillar slowly making its way across the grass.

George Ann, a handsome girl with the Tyrawley golden hair, accepted a cup of tea from Zara. "Polly tells me that private theatricals are all the rage at Versailles," she said to Peg. "Madame de Pompadour has set the fashion."

Mrs Bellamy helped herself to a wedge of cake, greedily licking her lips. "The Pompadour is adorable, skin like fine porcelain I'm told. Dear Tyrawley used praise my complexion."

"She is said to live on a diet of truffles, vanilla and celery in an attempt to satisfy the Bourbon appetite for love," Polly said airily. Mrs Bellamy belched. "Poor child, I can sympathise. Lord Tyrawley was a gentleman of such strong passions. He liked to spend every afternoon in bed."

"I should so like to visit Versailles," breathed George Ann.

Polly settled herself in her chair, gracefully spreading her skirts. She loved an audience. "I was invited to a masked ball there last year to celebrate the Dauphin's wedding. The whole of fashionable Paris was there—such a spectacle you cannot imagine: the palace illuminated inside and out, avenues ablaze with torches, brands, flares. All the apartments were thrown open and everyone was obliged to unmask when their majesties appeared. Prince Charles Edward was dressed as a Scottish harper. They say the eldest princess is quite enamoured of him but the king thinks no suitor good enough to claim the royal mesdames."

Peg sipped her tea in silence. The mention of Prince Charles had set her thoughts racing. Since the night she had dreamt of Darnley she had been on edge, as if waiting for news.

She was distracted by the sight of Tom Sheridan making his way across the lawn. She wondered irritably what was his errand and why had he chosen to deliver it on an afternoon when she had company. The more she saw of the Dublin school teacher the more she disliked him. Even before he reached them he was shouting out his news. "Word has just come through that Prince Charles has landed in Scotland and that the Scots are rallying in their thousands."

Mrs Bellamy shrieked, George Ann fluttered an ineffectual fan, Polly jumped up and Peg said stiffly, "You are causing a commotion, Mr Sheridan. All this has been rumoured before."

Unabashed Sheridan rooted in his pocket and produced a paper. "See for yourself. The *London Gazette* of 4 August. Read what it says."

Polly leaned over his shoulder and read aloud. "The government has offered a reward of thirty thousand pounds to anyone who can give information leading to the arrest of Prince Charles Stuart."

"Thirty thousand pounds!" Mrs Bellamy snatched the paper to see for herself. "Why it's a king's ransom," she squeaked.

Sheridan recovered the paper. "I have more news," he said smugly. "Captain Douaud was killed when the ship he commanded encountered a British man-o'-war near the west coast of Ireland. They are saying that Lord Darnley was drowned."

Peg closed her eyes. She saw the ship in distress, the noise, confusion, smoke. Darnley falling overboard into those deep treacherous seas. "If you will excuse me," she said faintly, "I think I shall take a stroll down by the river. No, Polly, I do not need company."

It was very peaceful. Water rippling over stones, the splash of a water-hen, a pair of swans floating downriver followed by their straggling family, a water rat gazing at her with bright curious eyes before disappearing into a clump of weeds. Some sixth sense told her that Darnley was alive. She would have been given a warning, would have heard the banshee's cry, had his end come. That fairy woman the harbinger of death combing her long black locks, followed his family even as it did hers. Scotland was up. A tear splashed her cheek. She told herself fiercely she would not grieve. One day she would walk on his arm in the Court of St James, be received by the bonny prince from over the water. They would meet again.

She wrote to Colonel Caesar, begging for information and he replied by return. King George had shipped the palace gold plate to Hanover, while at the mouth of the Thames, troops recalled from Flanders were disembarking under the command of the king's soldier son, the Duke of Cumberland. There was no word of Darnley.

❦

To distract her mind she gave Polly permission to stage a play at the villa. Sheridan had chosen Congreve's elegant comedy, *The Way of the World,* calculated to amuse the local gentry. Colonel Caesar, accompanied by his aide, a friendly tow-haired boy, the younger son of a penniless earl, arrived from London. The Honourable Robert Cholmondeley attached himself to Polly but the evening belonged to the stage-struck George Ann. She gave a scintillating performance as Mrs Marwood, upstaging Polly at every turn, made a pretty speech at the close of the play and disappeared with Tom Sheridan. They were not seen again until the party broke up at midnight.

Polly accepted Captain Cholmondeley's stammered proposal. "I do not have your passionate nature," she told Peg, "but I so long to marry and I know I shall grow to love my husband."

Peg thought of their mother in Dublin. "We should bring her to London, at least let her know."

Polly said nervously, "I cannot afford to wait that long. I must marry him when his passion is strong. I am afraid of Lady Cholmondeley. She refuses to meet me, says I am not good enough to marry into the family."

Peg kissed her sister. "Don't worry, pet. Colonel Caesar tells me that the earl is saddled with a rakish heir, mounting debts and two horsy daughters. On the day you marry your captain, I shall settle ten thousand pounds on you and furnish a house for you in the best part of London. Never fear you will get her Ladyship's blessing in the end."

Before the summer had ended, Miss Polly Woffington and the Hon Captain Cholmondeley were married in the fashionable church of St Mary-le-Strand by the Bishop of London. As the bride swept up the aisle on the arm of Colonel Caesar radiant in Madame Flaubert's creation of brocade and pearls and wearing a cap of priceless lace, Peg watched dry-eyed but Zara shed a tear for her mistress, for the gown she had never worn and the wedding that would never now take place.

MY BLACKBIRD MOST ROYAL HAS
FLOWN

*Upon a fair morning of soft recreation
I heard a fair lady making her moan.
With a sighing and with sobbing and lamentation,
Saying, "My blackbird most royal has flown"*

(Old Jacobite lament for Prince Charles Stuart)

26

For hours people had been gathering in the town of Edinburgh. Merchants and shopkeepers, craftsmen and their apprentices, housewives with their children, farmers and their labourers, with time to spare now that the harvest was in. They told each other that this would be a day to remember. They were good-natured, exchanging gossip, banter. Upstanding men, ruddy-cheeked women, boys and girls with vivid faces, dressed in tartans with blue ribbons and sashes. A great cheer went up as the first of the kilted highlanders, skean-dhus in the top of their stockings, swung in through the city gates to the skirls of the pipes. Old men wept and drank the Stuart's health in whiskey with the flavour of heather, passing flasks to each other. "*Deoch sláinte an Rí,*" they said. "Health to the king."

At the back of the crowd a buxom housewife was wedged between a tall handsome man with dark hair in a widow's peak and grey eyes fringed with dark lashes and her husband who had red hair and was small and squat. "I never thought to see the day," she said excitedly.

Her husband lifted their four-year-old holding him up. "Look well, *a mhic o.* When you are an old man you will tell your grandchildren you saw the prince himself at the head of the clans. Never forget the date: 17 September 1745."

All the child could see were heads. He set up a howl of disappointment and the stranger took the boy from his father, hoisting him high on his shoulder. He chuckled contentedly, his eyes caught by a tall young man, riding a horse, wearing a blue bonnet, a bright plaid and across his chest a blue ribbon and something that glinted in the sun.

He pointed. "Who is he? What's that?"

Darnley craned his head. "He's the prince and he's wearing the Star of the Order of St Andrew. He's on his way to the Market Square to have his father proclaimed king and himself his regent."

Only the word "prince" had any meaning for the child. His mother had told him he would see the prince but the noise and confusion were all too much and he rubbed his eyes in distress.

His mother held out her arms and he went to her. "With luck the prince will tarry awhile before marching on London," she remarked to the man who had been kind to her son.

Darnley nodded. "Has it been good for him since he landed in Scotland?"

The boy's father turned a face sharp with suspicion. "Who are you and why do you ask what everyone knows? Are you a spy from London? A renegade? Do you sniff the reward the usurpers in London have set on his head?"

"Let me just give one shout that you are a traitor and the crowd will tear you limb from limb," the woman threatened and sensing the change of mood, the little boy whimpered with fright. "Hush you now," his mother soothed him fiercely.

Darnley patted the child's head. "Do not worry. I am loyal to the prince," and at the sound of his voice the boy ceased his wailing. "I was with His Highness in France."

"What happened?" the woman demanded putting her face up. "Stories come easy to one such as you."

Her husband spat. "And mean nothing."

Darnley smiled.

Yet there was something likeable about the stranger, the man thought. Well spoken, the woman conceded, recognising a gentleman when she saw one despite the unlikely clothes he wore, shag cloak, saffron shirt, trews too short. "Tell us about it," the man demanded eagerly. They had been hungry for crumbs of news such as this.

"I sailed with the prince from Dunkirk," Darnley said. "Four days at sea and we were attacked by an English man-o'-war. I was swept overboard in the fight that followed. For hours I battled for life, praying that the prince would escape when I was not busy cursing the British guns that had consigned me to a watery end."

"Did you see pirates?" Jamie put in. His grandfather had told him how pirates had chests of gold and parrots that talked.

"Can you keep a secret?" Darnley whispered.

The child nodded.

"I sailed with them once in a ship flying skull and crossbones from the mast."

"Get on with your story," the father's voice was gruff yet he was listening with great attention.

"I was picked up by a fishing boat out of Ireland, and was nursed back to health by a handsome housewife like yourself." He winked at the woman and she preened herself. "As soon as I could stand upright I made my way here. I have heard so many different versions of what happened the prince that I scarce know what to believe. Is it true that he landed at Moidart?"

"Aye in Macdonald country," an elderly man, wearing a scholar's cloak, who had been listening intently, put in. "You know the glen where the river Finnan flows into the loch?"

"Glenfinnan is a place of great beauty."

"My nephew, the *file*, saw the chieftains, Lochiel and Keppoch, swinging down the mountains at the head of their clans, with well over a thousand highlanders." The faded eyes filled with tears. "*A dhia*, what a sight. Tearlach unfurled his standard while the pipers played and the *file* recited a poem of welcome:

> *O Thearlaich mhic Sheumais, mhic Sheumais, mhic*
> > *Thearlaich.*
> *Leat shiubhlainn go h'eutrom 'n am eighlich bhith*
> > *marsal.*"

"Charles, son of James, son of James, son of Charles,/ With you I'd walk lightly when the call sounds for marching," Darnley translated softly and around him people surreptitiously wiped their eyes.

"From Glenfinnan the prince and his followers made their way through mountains and glens, playing cat and mouse with Johnnie Cope and his men," the pedant continued. "By the end of August the road to Edinburgh was open to them and they pushing through Atholl country with crofters and their women and children, leaping over ditches and hedges to welcome the duke; they were wild with excitement. You know that Atholl was exiled by the cursed Saxons after the 1715 Rising."

"Two thousand and more of the clans have answered the call and still they are coming," the red-haired man interrupted, his Adam's apple moving convulsively.

"A far cry from the single piper who greeted the prince on the morning he arrived," the scholar declared and at the pride in that old voice, Darnley swallowed his own tears. It had all been worth while.

The crowd was moving, people calling out, "The chevalier has dismounted." Darnley put out an arm to protect Jamie and his mother. There was another heave and somehow he found himself in front, face to face with the young man for whom he had risked so much.

He bent a knee in homage. "Your Highness is welcome home."

At the sound of the well-known voice, the prince lifted him up, clasping him in his arms. "Darnley, my friend. I never thought to see you alive. You will have heard how fortune has favoured the brave, how the clans have rallied to my standard. Join me in Holyrood House and we will drink a toast to victory and exchange stories of all that befell us since we last met." His clansmen were closing in, he was swept away and Darnley was lost in the crowd. Beaming with pride the woman was telling her son, "Remember how the prince's friend stood you on his shoulders." And Jamie's father was laughing and kissing the boy, saying, "It is not a thing to forget, *a mhic o.*"

❦

In years to come, exiled Scots, sick for their homeland, would remember with pride how for the length of a week, Bonny Prince Charlie dined in public each day in Edinburgh and how they pledged their lives, their sons, all they possessed to his cause. Women would recall how as young girls they had danced the night away in Holyrood House, would hug the anniversary date, 20 September, to their hearts, still strangely young though withered with age and loss. For a few short hours they were the flower of Scotland, lairds and their ladies, in tartans, blue ribbons and white cockades, the prince in their midst. Treasured too was the memory of how the Jacobite army attacked and routed General Cope's regiments at Prestonpans. To their dying day, old people would nourish their hunger for glories, long past, with stories of how the Camerons entered Edinburgh, triumphantly bearing the colours captured from Cope and his men, while pipers played the old cavalier air, "The king shall enjoy his own." They had been so sure the Jacobite army was invincible.

And the child Jamie, now old and grizzled, would remember how he stood beside his mother in Edinburgh Square, watching the prince and his army set out. He knew they were marching on London and that his father was there, marching proudly with the rest. And riding beside the prince was the tall man in highland dress, who had lifted him high and who turned and waved to the child he had been.

❦

As the winter of 1745 closed in, the country continued to be rocked by rumours of rebellion. By now the whole of the North was up and the Jacobites, pressing steadily southwards, marched almost unscathed through five counties in swift succession.

A mellow autumn had given away to a winter of bitter snow and ice and still they pressed on. In London hastily erected defences were thrown up, the populace panicked, banks were stampeded, food ran short and in mean streets and alleyways, the poor, the homeless, the old, perished of hunger.

On a December afternoon of slanting sleet, Sam Johnson arrived at Peg's apartment on the Strand with a new lift to his heavy steps. He greeted her gruffly and she busied herself with the silver kettle and thought of how in the old days Garrick had scolded her for her extravagance, because tea was expensive and she lavish in its making. Strange how so trifling a matter should itch at her mind. She filled the round-bellied cups with the dark brown fragrant liquid her visitor had always relished, her heart warming to this ugly, heavily built man with the cumbersome wig. The men she loved had been attractive. Coffey all masculinity, dark hair winged with grey, cleft chin, fine intelligent eyes; Taafe, fair-haired, with reckless blue eyes; Garrick, brown-haired, brown-eyed, with his chameleon moods and voice that could coax tears from a stone, laughter from a dragon. And Darnley, black hair in a widow's peak, inscrutable grey eyes, shadowed with those incredible lashes and a smile of such charm. He was the handsomest man she had ever known, the most generous. Yet of them all she was most at ease with Mr Johnson, plain-spoken, blunt, kind. There had never been anything between them but friendship and she liked him all the more for that reason.

Impulsively she kissed his forehead. He reddened and cleared his throat. "I have news of your friend Lord Darnley."

She gripped the sides of her chair, knuckles white. "What news?" He patted her hand. "Good news. My neighbour in Gough Square interests himself in homing pigeons and has a brother in Edinburgh with similar tastes. They exchange scraps of information by means of their winged messengers. I checked afterwards and it seems the story I heard is true. Lord Darnley arrived in Edinburgh on the same day as the prince and entertained the crowd with a story of his near drowning and rescue by a fishing smack out of Connemara in your country."

Contentedly Peg sipped her tea, eyes on the dancing coals. "I think I should have known if he had died," she said softly. "And now he marches with the rebels?"

Johnson said glumly. "Their journey is hampered by snow and they seem not to have managed to march much beyond Derby on the London road, if the latest intelligences are true."

"What will happen?"

He shook his heavy head. "Public affairs neither vex me nor please me. But I have sympathy for the dreams of youth. The prince sets an example in courage and gallantry." He gulped his tea and held out the cup for more. "Fate spin her threads with a twisted wheel. A wise man once wrote, 'Might is right and justice there is none.'" He gave Peg one of his rare smiles. "Drinking tea with you on an afternoon like this, a dish of toast at my hand, a good fire at my feet— life holds few such pleasures."

Her eyes glinted with tears. She brushed them away. "I think I would rather be sitting here with you at this moment," she said, "than with almost anyone else."

He blinked. "And so the weavers of Spitalfields are arming themselves, preparing to fight for King George. What news of David?"

She gave a weary shrug. "Busy as ever. Drury Lane flourishes with entertainments and plays to boost the morale of the citizens. Each night I speak a rousing epilogue calling on all good men and loyal to pledge their allegiance to king and country. And all the time my heart is with Scotland."

He got to his feet, pulled his great cloak about him. "Good-bye my dear. Do not set too great a store on a Jacobite victory. When all this is over you should return to Dublin."

His words lowered her spirits, yet she knew he meant well and there was something she must know. "Does David mean to wed Burlington's ward, Mr Johnson?"

"Who can tell. He is very gifted and very ambitious." He kissed her briefly on the cheek and was gone.

❦

With the dawn of the new year the tide of war turned and bells of thanksgiving rang out in London at the news that the Jacobite army was in retreat.

On a bright April morning, Prince Charles Edward Stuart took his final stand on Culloden Moor against the Duke of Cumberland and suffered a defeat that spelled the end of Scotland's high hopes.

Horrific stories began to filter back. Cumberland's orders had been "Take no prisoners." It was said that his soldiers had bludgeoned or bayoneted to death every Jacobite flushed out of cottage and byre. Even the English were abashed at Cumberland's savagery and hard-pressed mothers and nursemaids scared children into obedience with the threat "'Butcher' Cumberland will get you if you don't behave."

Peg spent much of her time gazing out the window, brooding on recent events. She felt very lonely. All Polly's concerns were with her new husband and life. In Drury

Lane life was a treadmill of rehearsals, performances. It took all her will-power to ignore Kitty Clive's barbs, Susanna Cibber's whispered innuendoes, Mrs Bellamy's mindless strictures and boastful admonitions. Hardest of all to bear was Garrick's continuing coldness. But for Zara's kindness, the distraction of Mohamet's chatter, she would have been bereft. Yet she still had the hope that Darnley lived, that somehow one day they would be reunited.

Then on a night in May she awoke out of a dream to eerie wailing that seemed to echo and re-echo around her bed and she knew that the banshee, the faery woman who followed her family, had come to warn her of impending doom. She crossed herself and prayed as she hadn't prayed in years for the Jacobite army and Darnley. She waited for news. It came three weeks later.

Zara had taken Mohamet to fly his kite in the park and she was quite alone when Colonel Caesar arrived. He sat on the couch beside her, as she focused on his thinning hair, moustache, clipped speech. His hand held hers as he told her of what he had learnt. A young drummer in the prince's army had been captured. He was a commoner, a Roman Catholic, his death would be an example to others who might ever again think to engage in treason. Sewn into the young drummer's coat was a letter addressed to Mrs Woffington, which the colonel had managed to intercept. The paper was blood-stained, the writing erratic, as if done in pain and with much effort. She pressed her spine to the chair for support and unfolded the letter. Darnley's teasing voice was in the room as she read:

> Darling Peg,
> I am writing this in the fastness of a highland
> castle. My messenger, James Wilding, is but

*fifteen years of age and fought valiantly. I am
in hiding but it is only a matter of time before
Cumberland's men sniff me out. I have sworn
they will not take me alive. If young Wilding
manages to reach London, will you help him?*

*This is good-bye forever, darling, but
have no regrets for me. The adventure was well
worth while. I joined the prince in Edinburgh
and we set out on the long march south. We
should have pressed on to London but rations
were short and our men exhausted. We managed to retreat in good order and made our final
stand on Culloden Moor.*

She put the letter aside and closed her eyes, then forced
herself to read on.

*As the mist rolled back on that April
morning, the moor was an awesome sight.
Slowly the sun came up turning gorse to flame.
Far away to the south loomed the height of Dun
Davoir, the spires and towers of Inverness golden
spears in the sky. Big brawny highlanders wept
like children as they took their last leave of the
country they loved so well. Slowly Cumberland's
army advanced, grey and dim at first, then
gradually becoming clear in the morning light,
redcoated, black-gaitered, with fixed bayonets.
Closer and closer they drew near, until the air
shook with the beating of drums and the day
was bright with fluttering flags. At last the order
to charge was given and the highlanders, with
incredible courage, raced headlong into a with-*

*ering storm of grapeshot and musketry. They
were impossible odds. Before the day was out,
Culloden was littered with bodies. To the lone-
some strain of a piped lament, the flank swung
around and the retreat began. Gillie Macbane,
a giant of a man, made a last-ditch stand,
towering above the dead and dying, covered by
his round shield, his long hair streaming in the
wind. He stood like the ancient Cuchulainn
holding the pass of Ulster.*

Her hands were clammy as she turned the page.

> *And now my beloved, my hours are
> numbered. The sands are running out. "How
> sweet the moonlight sleeps upon this bank!...In
> such a night/Stood Dido with a willow in her
> hand/Upon the wild sea-banks and waft her
> love/to come again to Carthage."*
>
> *Remember our times together. I love you
> now and forever.*
>
> *Darnley.*

She was cold, cold as the grave in which Darnley lay.
"And his end?" she asked dully.

"Young Wilding, a medical student, had bound his
wounds. He was dead when they got to him."

"Thank God for that." In the street below someone was
whistling a Jacobite lament. She took up the words, singing
at first softly, then strongly, proudly, for Darnley, for what
was past:

Upon a fair morning of soft recreation
I heard a fair lady making her moan,
With a sighing and with sobbing and
                                                lamentation,
Saying, "My blackbird most royal has flown."
My thoughts they deceive me;
Reflections do grieve me
And I am over burthened with sad misery.
Yet death if it should bind me
My true love...

The colonel was holding her and she was weeping desolately, as she had not wept for years. Once she had sat by the river weeping because she was homesick. Now she wept because for the rest of her life she would never know love again.

"This will help." Colonel Caesar was pressing brandy on her and like a child, she swallowed, shuddering as the spirit took effect.

"Thank you." She composed herself. "Where are they holding the drummer boy?"

"Young Wilding is in the Tower."

"What will happen?"

Miserably the colonel tugged at his moustache. "Do you want to know?"

She said bitterly, "Soon the whole of London will."

He was telling her and her mind was shying away from his words. She looked out the window and saw a merchant ship moving upstream bound for some foreign port. What was it her father used read from the Bible:

Once in three years came the navy of Tharshish,
bringing gold and silver, ivory and apes and peacocks.

She longed to be on the deck of that ship, wind in her face, vast horizons before her.

She was dragged back to reality by his words. "He will be taken on a hurdle to Kennington Common, there to be hanged, cut down and quartered while still alive."

Her mouth was dry. She swallowed. "When?"

"Six weeks. The date has been fixed for 28 July."

"Can you help?"

"The charge is high treason."

"Oh merciful God." She stumbled across the room to the closet and vomited until all she could taste was bile.

Gently the colonel led her back to the chair, wiped her face, gave her water to drink. "At least you have the consolation of knowing that Lord Darnley loved you."

She started to laugh. "Love? What does it mean? Hold dear? Be amorous? Oh yes, they all said they loved me, but they loved something better still. Charles Coffey, a place in society. He was born a peasant but had ambitions to write. He was a man of letters. Pat Taafe was a gambler. It was his passion. Garrick cared for nothing but the stage; he got his wish to manage his own theatre. He worships Shakespeare. They say he would sell his soul to discover a play not yet produced."

She stopped.

"And what of Lord Darnley?"

"Oh Darnley. The duchess warned me, but I would not listen. He had a death wish, you know." She held out her glass. "Give me more brandy, please."

She swallowed, shuddered and then stood up, mistress of herself once more. "Let me tell you something, my friend, something you may now realise. Something no man will admit. Women love men. Men love money and power. They have their ambitions, their dreams of greatness, dreams that sometimes betray them. And Darnley,"—her voice broke—"Darnley had the maddest, most impossible dream of all."

N ow that all danger of invasion had passed, an air of gaiety, even recklessness, pervaded London. Summer had come at last and the parks were a-flutter with ladies in fly-away muslin caps and aprons, hooped gowns of coral and turquoise attended by wigged gentlemen, wearing tricornes, amber waistcoats, wine-coloured breeches and high-buckled shoes. But the mouth of the Thames was blocked by ships in which wounded clansmen awaiting exile lay naked. In their rat holes they could hear the hammering of the scaffold for the execution of three of the noblest of the Scottish rebels, the Earls of Balmerino, Kilmarnock and Cromartie. A new form of diversion was popular. Instead of bear and bull baiting, people now flocked to the Tower to see the condemned.

On a bright July morning, a week before James Wilding was due to die, Peg called at the house in Gough Square. She hadn't wanted to ask Sam Johnson for help. He was too close to Garrick but he was her last hope.

He welcomed her, kissing her hand with a gallantry that moved her strangely, and soon she was sitting in his study, drinking a glass of wine. She thought he looked grey and lined for a man in his thirty-seventh year. She told him of Darnley's letter and how he had asked her to take care of the drummer boy who had bound up his wounds, stayed with him until the end and then had been caught making his way to London carrying out Darnley's last wishes. "You will have heard of the sentence, Mr Johnson. I cannot bear to think of it happening. I have tried everyone of influence I know in the hope of a reprieve or at least that the boy should be granted a kinder death. Mr Rich, Mr Fleetwood, Mr Horace Walpole who is related to my sister by marriage. I even called on Will Hogarth, the artist in Chiswick. He was deeply concerned but like the others could do nothing."

Johnson scratched his wig with a quill and considered. "You must seek Garrick's help."

"He hates me."

"Hate and love are but opposite obverse and reverse of the same coin, my dear."

She said despairingly. "I am only an embarrassment. He is said to be courting Burlington's daughter."

"And the earl is one of the most powerful men in England."

"I would prefer to approach Wales himself."

"Young Wilding is charged with treason. The heir to the Hanoverian throne cannot help."

She knew what he said made sense but it was hard to beg of a man who had once loved her and who now treated her like an outcast. She yawned and whispered, "Forgive me, I have slept badly these past weeks. I will take your advice, Mr Johnson. Pray God I am successful for if Garrick fails me the boy is doomed."

She stood up to go and Johnson put an arm around her shoulder. She could feel his warmth, kindness seep into her pores. "Remind Davy of his youth in Lichfield," he said using the boyhood name. "He is not devoid of imagination. No great actor ever is."

She hesitated. "Should I offer him felicitations on his choice of a bride?"

"Our own felicity we make or find," he said austerely and returned to his books.

She sought Garrick out in the house in Bow Street where he still lived. Once she had mounted those steps sure of her welcome, of his love. They had made love in that narrow four-poster bed and they had laughed when he fell onto the floor. He had been so gentle, boyish and said that she had made him the happiest of men, that their love would endure. Now she came as a mendicant, wary, unwilling.

He received her civilly, ushered her into the drawing room as he would a chance acquaintance and sat opposite her, resting his hand on the chair, making no attempt at conversation. She handed him Darnley's letter which he read with an expressionless face. Then gave it back without a word. Her heart sank. This was worse than she had imagined. She would make one last plea. "For old times' sake will you help."

He got up abruptly and went to the window, gazing down at the street. His voice was bleak. "Lord Darnley was guilty of treason. Traitors deserve no mercy."

"How can you say such a thing!" she said passionately. "Darnley is dead, beyond either your mercy or pity. It is of young Wilding I speak. You know his sentence."

"He is but one of many."

She laughed bitterly. "Oh yes! I know how many examples to future traitors there will be made. Colonel Caesar told me. Three and a half thousand men, women and children captured. One thousand awaiting transportation in coffin ships to the colony. Few will reach their destination; for most the wide Atlantic will be their graveyard. One hundred and thirty have already been hanged. For the Scottish earls, the block." She swallowed. "At least theirs will be a merciful end not like the unfortunate drummer boy."

"All richly deserved."

"Young Wilding is only sixteen years." She had vowed to herself that she would remain in control but it was hard. Her head was throbbing. With an effort she controlled her voice. "The boy ran away from the university when he got into a scrape and joined the prince at Manchester, as any young blade might do. His father is a respectable Lancashire merchant loyal to the crown. His mother is dead."

"What has this to do with me?"

She got up so suddenly that the chair toppled back and was across the room, catching him by the arm, swinging him around. "Face me, David Garrick! Listen to what I am saying. That boy, a young medical student, will be taken on a common cart to Kennington Common, hanged, cut down while he still lives and then drawn and quartered. For God's sake are you made of stone? Cast your mind back to the time you were his age. You sat with Sam Johnson on the steps of Lichfield Cathedral planning your future. How often did you recall those days for me? Young Wilding has no future, only a nightmare of pain and..." her voice broke and she wept unashamedly. Garrick was stunned. In all the years he had known her he had never seen her so distraught. And as always in anger and sorrow, she was beautiful, green eyes great with tears, red hair dishevelled...Was this the face that launched a thousand ships?...Sweet Helen make me immortal with a kiss. She had always bewitched him. It was not safe to be in the room with her. She was pleading, begging. "Burlington's daughter will do as you ask. Bring her to the Tower, let her see for herself. She is a Catholic, as her mother, Burlington's mistress, was. So is the boy. It is the reason his death will be so horrible, an example to others. Do this for me, David, please and I shall never ask a favour of you again."

He stood with arms folded, only the twitch of his mouth showed strain. She thought wildly we are playing a scene. He is Julius Caesar, I am Calphurnia and he heeds me not.

He spoke and as happened on stage, his words filled the room yet seemed to come from a distant place. "Even an animal should have a more merciful death."

He opened the door and she stumbled past him out into the night air, too tired to reason whether she had succeeded or failed.

❦

On the day before James Wilding was to be dragged to Kennington Common Colonel Caesar took Peg to the Tower of London. She was unnerved at the prospect before her, scared to meet the boy whose end had haunted her but she owed him this much, owed Darnley this last service.

A press of people was waiting to gain admittance, amongst them David Garrick, sober in brown velvet, his hand on the arm of a lovely, graceful girl, moving with the grace of her mother, the Viennese dancer. For a brief moment Garrick's eyes locked with Peg's and an unspoken message passed between. He had done as she asked. Brought Lord Burlington's daughter. Then the earl with the cold arrogant face arrived, surrounded by lackeys, and the gates swung back.

There was fear in the narrow cell, palpable fear, she could smell the fear, feel, almost taste it. In one corner three men in the rags of their clan tartans, their bearing proud, despite their heavy chains that bound them to the wall. Because of their noble blood, the earls would die quickly, would place their heads on the block, the executioner would raise his axe, there would be a moment's pain and then oblivion. Unlike the bloody end of the fettered boy crouching low. Peg pushed her way forward and knelt beside him, touching his hand. "I am Mrs Woffington. You were with Lord Darnley. I was given the letter you carried."

He didn't raise his head, seemed to gather himself in so that his body diminished as if he were back in the womb, safe, secure.

Burlington's daughter had drawn close.

"He is only sixteen," Peg whispered distractedly. "Too young to die."

"What will happen?" She looked at Peg, scared violet eyes.

The boy raised his head, eyes dilated with fear. "I—they sentenced me to be...to be..." He choked on the words.

Violetta was holding him. Peg was kneeling beside them. They were praying together. "Hail Mary, full of grace, the Lord is with thee..." Soft voices, pitiful voices, strong voices of the earls, halting voice of an old highlander praying in Gaelic. The noisy chatter of the onlookers had died away; they stood as if made of stone. Burlington moved forward, the crowd giving way before him. As he reached Violetta she collapsed, a heap of velvet on the floor, violet velvet cloak she had picked to match the colour of her eyes. Garrick was lifting her up, carrying her out. There was commotion as the Governor of the Tower appeared, orders were being rapped out and in an instant the place had been cleared.

James Wilding was reprieved one hour before his execution. All London knew that Lord Burlington, moved by the anguish of his natural daughter, had obtained a stay of execution.

Peg had sought Colonel Caesar's help and advice. After that she did what she must: spending gold freely, bribing warders, turnkeys, soldiers on guard at the Tower to look the other way. Some said she had even bribed the Governor of the Tower but that was not necessary. He was a friend of Burlington's. No steps would be taken when the prisoner escaped.

In the early hours of the morning a week later, James Wilding was smuggled out of the prison while London slept to where Peg waited in a closed carriage by the Tower. She kissed his forehead. "You are safe, lad," she comforted him. "No harm can come to you now. Have patience and your passage to the New World will soon be arranged." He smiled up at her trustingly like a child and she breathed a prayer of relief. She had not failed Darnley, had done as he had asked.

❦

She sat alone at midnight at her escritoire, composing her thoughts, her fingers arranging parchment, quills. Two weeks had elapsed since the prisoner had been smuggled out. He had been ill at first, a fever, but Zara had nursed him to health and after that he had waited patiently while she sought out the captain of a sailing-ship bound for the American colonies, willing to take the risk for a purse of gold.

She had grown very fond of James Wilding, no longer a boy, but a man, standing tall and strong with bright eyes and a mop of fair curls. He was what her brother Conor might have been had he lived. "Only the young," she thought bleakly, "do not count the cost, are ready to gamble their lives for a dream." But it was true also for Darnley who had risked his all for the Jacobite cause. She brushed away a tear and taking up a quill wrote rapidly.

Dear Charles Coffey,

Mr Rich of the Covent Garden Playhouse, cousin to your wife, has given me your address. James Wilding, a young university student, fought valiantly with Prince Charles at Culloden, reports of which have no doubt reached the colony by this time. Young Wilding was later captured and taken to London where he was sentenced to be hanged, drawn and quartered for high treason. Due to the intervention of a noble lady his sentence was reprieved at the eleventh hour. He will tell you as much of his story as he can bear to relate when you meet, as indeed I hope you will before very long. When the ship on which he sails tomorrow soon after dawn reaches Philadelphia, the captain, on my instructions, will engage a guide to take him to Virginia. It is my earnest hope when he reaches your plantation, yourself and Alice will befriend the lad. I do not think you will regret any kindness you may show him. He is a fine young man, intelligent, kind. I shall be anxious to hear that all goes well with him.

She paused, chewed the end of her quill and then continued:

> *I do not think I shall remain much longer in*
> *London. My sister Polly has married and is*
> *living at present with her in-laws in Somerset*
> *and my mother is quite alone in Dublin. She*
> *lives in number thirteen the High Street. Her*
> *address will always find me.*
> > *I wish you both good health and content.*
> > > *Peg Woffington*
> > > *14 August 1746.*

She sprinkled the ink with fine sand and sealed the letter. She had done all she could.

❧

A cab rattled over the cobblestones, taking James Wilding on his last journey out of England. Small puffs of wind were blowing away the last of the night clouds, boat people were stirring, reading the sky, testing the wind with fingers, telling each other that the day would be fair. The hackney came to a stop on the quays and the young man wrapped in a warm cloak and the heavily veiled woman dismounted and waited while the driver lifted down the travelling box.

"You have the letter to Mr Coffey and the purse of gold hidden safely in the belt next to your skin," Peg said in a low voice. "Do not be tempted to game with cards or dice on the journey."

James Wilding smiled. "Zara warned me to heed your words. She was good to me. I shall miss her and the small blackamoor." His voice was wistful. "Perhaps some day when I am settled they will make the journey to see me."

So that is how it is, she thought. She had guessed that he had fallen in love with her dark-eyed maid. Zara was seventeen, a year older than James, but the Jacobite campaign, his time in the Tower and the misery he had suffered had made him a man. He had put away his boyhood, never again would he be totally carefree, never again heedless. She had guessed this, thought it as well. He would need all his wits for who knew what lay before him where he was bound. He would make good in the colonies, she did not doubt; he had courage, had acquired a certain shrewdness which would stand him in good stead for the men he would meet—gaolbirds, gamblers, even murderers, men who had fled their own land and kind— would kill for a crown or less. Zara would miss him. Her eyes had been suspiciously red this morning. Mohamet would be furious when he awoke and found his new friend gone.

All her life she had hated partings. And this parting was very hard indeed.

"I shall never forget that I owe my life to your kindness," he said gruffly.

She hugged him. "Take good care of yourself for me," she ordered. "When you are settled write so that Zara and I will be content in our minds."

A sailor had arrived to ferry him out to where a trading ship waited to sail with the tide. He gave her a last hug, turned at the jetty for his last sight of England, waved briefly and was gone. All his life he would remember her kindness, her last farewell, "God keep you safe," would keep the words in his heart.

❧

Since the Jacobite rising, Tom Sheridan had been uneasy. His namesake, Sir Thomas Sheridan, one of the "Seven Men of Moidart," had not lived to see the defeat. Somewhere in the Scottish highlands the old Irish aristocrat slept peacefully in an unmarked grave. The two had never met, were not related by blood, were of different beliefs, had different loyalties, yet because he bore the name of a rebel, the Dublin pedagogue was suspect. Matters came to a head when Garrick and he had a bitter quarrel about a matter so trivial that he knew there would be no future for him on the London stage.

He called on Peg, uninvited, to bid her farewell. Self-important as ever, he sat himself down, smoothing his well-filled breeches, and told her of an offer he had received from the Smock Alley Playhouse.

"Why not join forces with me?" His voice was jaunty, eyes calculating. "Between us we could set the very Liffey on fire. Your charm allied to my talents."

She was incensed at his insolence, yet knew it could be a straw in the wind. "I fear Smock Alley could not afford me, charming though I may be."

"They say the great man has tired of you." He smirked as a blush mounted her cheeks. She rose to her feet. "If you will excuse me, Mr Sheridan, I have no time for idle chatter." She pulled the bell for Zara to show him out and he bowed low, smiling sardonically. "Give my respects to your sister, Polly. If she comes to Dublin I shall be happy to receive her." He was gone, and she knew in her bones she had made an enemy. She prayed she would never have need of his help.

❦

Bells were ringing in the year 1747 as the lumbering figure with the pock-marked face and wig askew made his way along the Strand. Peg received him at the door of her apartment, kissing him warmly on both cheeks. "It is good to see you, Mr Johnson. Draw up to the fire." Johnson took off his cloak and with a sigh lowered his bulk into the best chair. "My apologies, ma'am, for this unexpected visit."

She said teasingly, "Something told me you would come. A dark-haired man crossing the threshold is said to bring luck on this night. See, I have all prepared." She indicated the kettle on the hob, the table set for tea with an array of good things: hot buttered toast, a meat pie, honey, cakes rich with cream and jam.

He watched while she spooned the tea into the silver teapot. "A spoonful for you, Mr Johnson, one for me, one for the pot, another because I am so happy to see you and one because it is New Year's Day." She poured on the boiling water and stirred. "And what have you been doing?"

He said sombrely, "I was at the Tower tonight, visiting Mistress Flora Macdonald."

"And now that the sound and fury has died away and they are all dead and gone," Peg said quietly, handing him the full-bellied cup he liked, "how fares the girl?"

Johnson sipped gratefully. "Strong tea is a tonic. I had need of that. Prince Charles was a fugitive with the net closing in when they met. Mistress Macdonald disguised him as her Irish maid, Betty Burke, and together they crossed the turbulent waters of the Minch to her home in Skye. They spent twelve days together and made their farewells at Portree."

Peg gazed into the heart of the fire. "Were they in love?"

Johnson moved his great shoulders. "The prince had

little time for the tender passion with a price on his head, hunted like a wild stag. Yet the maid painted a bonny picture of how it was. He kept his spirits high even when Cumberland's soldiers were sniffing around like half-bred curs. She told me that in the five months of his wandering he never spent more than one night under one roof."

In her mind's eye, Peg saw the handsome prince and the girl who looked on her companion with something that was akin to adoration. Had Darnley's Scottish bride been like Flora Macdonald? Brave, faithful, beautiful. He had spoken her epitaph, quoting *Othello:* "She that was ever fair and never proud."

She roused herself and refilled their cups. "And in the end the prince slipped the net?"

"Aye. On the morning of 20 September, the Young Chevalier boarded the *Lochiel* and sailed south west out of Loch na nUamh into the wide Atlantic leaving Scotland behind."

"And his people crushed."

Fiercely Johnson kicked a coal in the fire. It broke into a radiant blaze, before dying down into blackened ash. "His people loved him to the last. With a price of thirty thousand pounds on his head, not even the meanest beggar could be got to betray the last of the Stuarts."

Peg said sadly, "Was the rising worth the price?"

"Who can tell? The months the prince spent as a fugitive will be remembered as his finest hour."

Peg thought of the Scottish earls waiting in that narrow cell for their end; of Gillie Macbane, that giant of a man, shield held high on Culloden's field. What had Darnley said, "Like the ancient Cuchulainn holding the pass of Ulster." Of the thousands who had died, been exiled and most of all of the handsome man with the widow's peak and the grey eyes fringed with dark lashes who had husbanded his dying strength to write of his love in that highland fastness. They had sacrificed their all for a dream. And yet success had so nearly been theirs. What would her life have been had the Jacobites triumphed, she wondered. Would she have known the glamour of life at the Court of St James, been received by the Bonny Prince himself, danced the night away to the music of Scotland with Darnley? She stirred restlessly. "What will become of Flora Macdonald? Will she be executed?"

"I think not. There have been too many atrocities. There is talk of an Act of Indemnity. I believe she will be set free."

"Thank God for that."

Johnson took her hand in his. "And what of your future, my dear?"

She smiled wistfully. "Garrick plans on reviving *Romeo and Juliet*; it was our biggest triumph. Much will depend on the casting."

❦

She was in the greenroom at Drury Lane, her eyes taking in the list of names pinned to the board:

Romeo...Mr David Garrick
Juliet...Mrs Susanna Cibber
Lady Montague...Mrs Elizabeth Steele
Nurse to Juliet...Mrs Kitty Clive

Feverishly she read on.

Citizens of Verona
Men and Women, related to the Houses

Her name was amongst the extras: Mrs Peg Woffington.

"'Oh what a fall was there, my countrywoman,'" Kitty Clive's voice was at her ear. "But then you never could act, could you, my dear. You climbed to fame on the backs of your lovers, or should I say on their bellies?"

At the crudeness of the jibe, something snapped. Peg wheeled around, struck out at the mocking face. Kitty was pulling her hair and they were struggling, reeling around, fishwives in a drunken Saturday night brawl in the Liberties.

"That will be quite enough," Garrick's voice cut across the room and she let go. Kitty Clive sat on the ground whimpering. "She tried to kill me. She should be in Bedlam."

"I saw and heard the whole disgraceful episode," Garrick said coldly. "You are suspended until further notice, Mrs Clive."

Peg flung back her head. "What of me, Mr Garrick? Am I also suspended? Who will you find to replace me in the crowd scene, Mr Garrick?"

She was never to know how tempted he was at that moment to take her in his arms, kiss the flushed cheeks, smooth back the dishevelled curls. He had thought he hated her, but at that moment he wanted her, would have given all he possessed to take her to his bed. He put a hand on her arm and she flung him away. "Do not dare touch me. Lay a finger on me and I swear I will kill you."

He stiffened. "My advice to you is to gather up your belongings and quit the theatre, Mrs Woffington. I am exhausted by your jealousies, your histrionics, which are better off-stage than on. While I am manager of Drury Lane, you will not set foot again on this stage. Now get out of my sight, both of you."

❦

"You will drink this draught," Zara sat on the side of the bed holding a glass.

Peg said tiredly, "What is it, Zara?"

"Metheglin. Fresh honey with aromatic herbs, a tincture of whiskey and hot water. It will help you sleep."

Obediently Peg swallowed the drink which was pleasant and eased her aching throat. Gently Zara smoothed the quilt, drew the curtains around the bed and on tip-toes left the room.

Peg lay in a twilight land between sleeping and waking, her mind travelling down the years to meet the young girl who had run across the busy Strand below, to hide her hurt by the river. Broken-hearted because Jennie Tatler had let her down and she would never become a strolling player. She had in time become something much greater, the highest-paid, most famous actress on the London stage. But tonight her prayer was the same as the innocent thirteen-year-old she had once been.

"Please God let me go home. I swear I'll be good. Just let me go back to Dublin to my own, the people I know and trust."

She would take Zara and Mohamet with her, show them the places she had known as a child. Christ Church Cathedral, where the Norman Richard de Clare, known to history as Strongbow, had shrunk to dust after more than six hundred years. He had conquered Ireland at the behest of the cuckolding Dermot MacMurrough and the beautiful Dervorgilla, wife of Ó Ruairc of Breifne. Their story of shame, betrayal, passion still lived on in the folklore of their country. Strange how love could so change the course of a man or woman's life.

Her thoughts drifted beyond the city. She would take Mohamet to the cockle beds outside Ringsend where she had once made love to Darnley. She pictured him racing over miles of golden sand, shrieking with laughter, Zara racing after him, lest he be lost, be drowned in a few feet of water. Boiled cockles to eat, fresh buttermilk to drink, there is nothing to beat them, she thought sleepily. And remembered no more.

❦

In the end she went to Paris. Owen M'Swiney had persuaded her to accompany him to the French capital where he would spend some months before travelling on to Italy. Marie Dumesnil was the magnet that drew her. She had long wished to meet the greatest actress on the French stage and besides when the time came to return to Dublin her courage failed her. There would be no place for her in the Smock Alley Theatre; Tom Sheridan had never been her friend.

She left London in early April, without a word of farewell. There were none to wish her God speed. Sam Johnson was on a visit to Lichfield, Colonel Caesar was taking the waters at Bath. Mrs Bellamy was with George Ann in Dublin visiting Lord Tyrawley's sister, the Honourable Mrs O'Hara, while Polly had taken up residence in Somerset in Cholmondeley Hall. It was the end of a chapter. She would never see David Garrick again.

ACT V

LONDON,
1743–1747

Mock on, mock on, Voltaire, Rousseau:
Mock on, mock on: 'tis all in vain
You throw the sand against the wind,
And the wind blows it back again

(William Blake)

2 8

Paris was different from anything she had imagined. Noisier, dirtier than London or Dublin, at least in the old quarters of the town. She had often asked Polly to describe Paris but her sister dealt in practicalities, what she had eaten, the people she had met, the classes she had attended to perfect her French. She hadn't even managed to paint any sort of a picture of the faubourg where she had lived with an aristocratic family, fallen on hard times and forced to take in paying guests. Later when Peg visited the garden city built by the money of rich merchants she was quite taken with the fine houses of honey-coloured stone, the gardens leading down to the river where the boats and barges of their owners were moored. A contrast not only in wealth and taste but in period.

Of course Polly had told her all about the fairytale palace built on the marshlands of Versailles far from the noise and bustle of the city, had explained in her dry, clear voice how Louis the Sun King had held court there surrounded by hundreds of nobles, spending his days hunting, gambling, love-making and enjoying the festivals and fêtes that marked his reign. After his death in 1715, the palace had lain silent and deserted while the court moved to Paris and into the Tuileries, that great palace planned by Catherine de Medici, wife of Henry II, almost two hundred years before. When the boy king was twelve years old the court had returned to Versailles and that enchanting place came into its own once again.

In every capital of the world they knew the story of how three years earlier, the thirty-five-year-old monarch, Louis XV, had taken a pretty bourgeoisie of twenty-four, Madame d'Étoiles, forever afterwards known as Madame de Pompadour, as his mistress and shocked the court over which he ruled as absolute monarch.

Little wonder then, after seeing the glory that was Versailles, after living in the spacious mansion at the edge of the forest of Senart with her aristocratic hosts, that Polly had been so insistent that Peg rent the beautiful villa at Twickenham. She must have found it hard to return to a modest apartment on the Strand in London, unthinkable to return to the narrow cramped house in the High Street in Dublin where their mother still lived.

That first morning driving through Paris, Owen M'Swiney pointed out the sights, the grim fortress that was the Bastille, the Opera House where masked balls were held, the Tuileries, where he would lodge with an aristocratic admirer for the duration of his stay in Paris. "Except for the central pavilion," he said, "the rest of the palace is divided into apartments occupied by an assortment of officials, clergymen, members of the nobility fallen on hard times, sound bourgeoisie and writers, sculptors and painters who are making their mark on society." Yes, to have the Tuileries as an address was much to be desired.

From the Tuileries he switched to the Bastille where not only common criminals but anyone who upset the king or the even tenor of life at Versailles could be incarcerated for a year or a lifetime. Not but there was a difference in the treatment they received. A man without influence or wealth might rot away in the dungeons, while an aristocrat could command a comfortable room, furnished to his wishes, be waited on hand and foot by his own servants, eat and drink of the best that Paris could provide and receive a constant stream of visitors to while away the tedium of his days with cards, gossip and love-making.

"Armand, Duc de Richelieu, one of the most powerful men in France, has already been imprisoned three times in the Bastille," he said, glad to air his knowledge of the doings of the nobility. "You may have heard of him, Peg?"

Of course she had. Polly had met him at the salon of some Parisian hostess and had described him to Peg as feline. "Cats' eyes in a thin narrow face, an arrogant mouth and a soft, caressing voice that could lure anyone to his bed. If you closed your eyes you might think him the handsomest man in France." This from Polly, least sentimental of women.

"Why was Richelieu sent to the Bastille?" Peg wanted to know.

"Gad, the noise will deafen me." M'Swiney held his hands to his head. The cacophony of sound was rising to a climax in the narrow streets, which were clogged with coachmen, chairmen, drivers of carts and tumbrils, all screaming imprecations at pedestrians who spat and screamed back. Competing with the noise was the cries of street vendors selling brooms, fish, street ballads, lavender, oranges as well as the incessant pealing of church bells. Mohamet, hanging out the window of the coach, was beside himself with excitement. Zara, pale and wan from the journey, was doing her best to quieten him down.

The coachman manoeuvred his way into a courtyard, edging his way between horse boxes. M'Swiney cupped his ear. He was growing very deaf but would not admit to it. "What were you asking, m'dear?"

"Why was Richelieu sent to the Bastille?" Peg repeated enunciating each word.

"For refusing to sleep with his step-sister. They married when she was thirteen and he fifteen, an alliance of wealth, lineage, power. When he refused to consummate the union his father had him thrown into the Bastille."

"That was hard on a young boy."

M'Swiney laughed. "Richelieu was never young. He was bedding wenches before he was out of the schoolroom. He complained that his young bride had a foul breath which turned his stomach. Most people saw it for what it was, an excuse to thwart the father he hated. All that was asked of him was to beget an heir to perpetuate the line. After that they would both go their own way. It's the common French practice amongst the aristocracy. Marry for position, lust for pleasure. In Versailles husbands tell their wives, 'I'll allow you every latitude, Madame, except footmen and princes of the blood.'" He chuckled. "It should be beneath madame's dignity to couple with a servant and if she catches the eye of a prince of the blood, her husband is in danger of being banished to his estates."

On the invitation of Owen M'Swiney, Marie Dumesnil, leading actress of the *Comédie Française*, had rented a coach house for Peg for the duration of her stay in Paris. Once part of the stables of a mansion on the outskirts of the town, now fallen into disuse since the court had moved back to Versailles, the little wooden house was comfortable but over-furnished, containing three bedrooms, a parlour, kitchen, scullery and the usual offices and closets. But the use of the great gardens, fragrant with orange and oleander, more than made up for the proximity of the crumbling mansion. Peg promised herself early morning walks by the river that ran through the end of the gardens and was enchanted to discover a tiny pagoda covered with creeper where she planned to entertain Madame Dumesnil and the other friends she hoped to make, to afternoon tea in the English manner. It would be tranquil to live alone with only Zara and Mohamet for company and no man to pull at her heart-strings. She was weary of love and passion, sore with the ache of Darnley's death and bruised by the humiliations she had suffered in Drury Lane. Oddly enough she missed Garrick very much. The theatre had been a strong bond between them. She was pleased that Owen M'Swiney had moved into the Tuileries with his lover. At times she feared for Mohamet's innocence, the child was so young. The old Irish actor always acted the gentleman when he was with her but could one say as much for some of the young men he fancied. She had seen the way they had looked the small blackamoor over.

In the palace of Versailles, the Duc de Richelieu was in a fury, though no one could have guessed from his calm demeanour. In Versailles politeness was all. As First Gentleman of the Bedchamber he was responsible for the palace entertainments. Twice a week it was his custom to invite actors to perform for the king and court. On Tuesdays the members of the *Comédie Italienne* put on a tragic play or opera. On Thursdays it was the turn of the *Comédie Française*. Their choice was usually a light comedy which was well received by the king. Whenever a special celebration was needed, a royal wedding, birth, a victory, Richelieu would arrange a series of masked balls, ballets, fireworks and the like. There had never been any complaints. The fact of the matter was that the king cared for nothing except hunting and love-making. He had inherited his overpowering lusts from his Bourbon ancestors and complained that if he did not enjoy a woman at least twice a night and once during the day he suffered from headaches and biliousness. It was true that when bored he turned yellow. He had long since tired of the queen and in addition to stray fancies had a permanent mistress installed near his bedroom. The mistress *en titre,* as she was known, had always been of aristocratic blood, the Mailly sisters, duchesses all, had served in turn, protégées of Richelieu.

But now things had changed. Madame de Pompadour had taken the king's fancy. He had first laid eyes on her when he was hunting in the forest of Senart and she had crossed his path out driving her phaeton. He had sworn he had never seen a prettier sight, the young woman in blue, hair piled high and caught with a ribbon, seated in the four-wheeled open carriage painted a delicate shade of pink. Even the pair of horses had pink ribbons tied to their manes. They had met again and he had danced with her at the Ball of the Clipped Yew Tree, as it was known because he and his attendants had disguised themselves as yew trees. She had bewitched him and he had brought her to Versailles and raised her to the rank of Marquise.

Now she was setting the palace by the ears. Introducing her own circle of friends from Paris, led by the notorious Voltaire, taking it upon herself to arrange the king's entertainments. Even Richelieu, who hated her, was forced to admit she was graceful, with a ready wit, a fund of stories and a beautiful singing voice. In addition to these advantages she was an accomplished amateur actress. There was no doubt the king was besotted with her, indulging her latest whim which was to form a company of players drawn from the nobility of the palace. Everyone loved private theatricals and the marquise had drawn up plans for a small theatre, to hold an audience of no more than fourteen. The players rehearsed each morning while the king was out hunting and twice a week put on a play, concert or opera with the marquise taking the leading role. Only recently they had performed a romantic light opera in which she had played the part of Prince Charming and the king had been so intrigued that he had kissed her in public and said she was the most delicious woman in France. Really it was not to be borne. Richelieu had a taste for certain actresses and had enjoyed their favours when they paid their weekly visits to the palace. Now that had ceased. There was a perpetual double file of carriages being driven at full speed on the road between Paris and Versailles. French drivers were notorious for the risks they took and Richelieu had had one narrow escape. It would be too fatiguing to make such a journey simply for the fuck, but he liked to sharpen his wits against Voltaire's in some of the great Parisian salons.

In another wing of the palace, Richelieu's niece, the Duchesse di Condi, groaned and writhed in childbirth. Pride forbade her screaming so she bit on a small block of wood wrapped in a wad of cloth which her maid had placed between her teeth. She was nineteen with pear-shaped breasts and buttocks, a plain face and a heavy nose which she was in the habit of caressing. Even in her labour pains she managed to exude a strong mixture of perfume and animal sensuality. Her body arched convulsively as the head of her child emerged and she groaned with relief. Her maid changed the bloody sheets and gave her mistress a goblet of hot wine as the midwife wiped the child with oil and then held her up for the duchesse's inspection. "A fine bouncing girl, Your Grace, and strong as a young filly," she said ingratiatingly, though she knew what the answer would be. "Take her away," the duchesse muttered, "I don't want to see her again." The midwife, duty done, left the bedchamber with the child in a basket, casting a practised eye at the silver chandelier, the tables and chairs inlaid with mother of pearl, the built-in wardrobes, the four-poster over which the maid was throwing a quilt of priceless lace.

Quickly the woman went through the anteroom where the walls were covered with quilted satin and paused to arrange her cap and cloak at a Venetian mirror which hung over the marble fireplace and was decorated with flowers, beasts, and naked men and women. As she hurried down the marble staircase and went out of the palace she planned on how she would sell the infant to bawds at the quays of Paris. It wasn't the first time it had happened. The little girl would fetch a good price and the midwife knew how to keep her own counsel.

The duchesse told her maid petulantly that she had no choice but to get rid of the infant. Had the child's father been one of the nobility it wouldn't have mattered; she and her husband the Duc di Condi had long ago come to an agreement that each would go his or her own way. But she had been impregnated by a stable boy. If this was discovered the boy would be flogged to within an inch of his life—not that she cared—but she would be exiled from court to the family estates where she would be forced to spend her days in intolerable tedium. As everyone knew, to be banished from Versailles was a fate worse than death. Her trouble was that she was hot for every man she laid eyes on from gardeners to the dauphin himself who had repulsed her overtures. He was a prig like his mother, the queen. The duchesse had a fire in her belly and despite all her precautions constantly found herself *enceinte*. She had tried every known method of birth-control: drinking urine, riding around the forest in a rutted cart, sitting in a scalding hot bath drinking Hollands which was specially imported by a randy duchess from England, using tampons of seaweed, drinking noxious draughts of various kinds. She had even tried inserting a sponge soaked in lime juice into her vagina and pulling it out after intercourse by means of a thread. But nothing seemed to work. She was usually too drunk to insist on *coitus interruptus*, besides which it was such a bore. Her doctor had warned her that if she had any more abortions her health would be at risk. Next time she would visit a certain nurse in the stews of Paris who was said to be so good at her job that there were no ill effects. It would be worth the journey and the gold she would hand over in payment.

"And that Pompadour weeps because she constantly miscarries the king's seed," she said bitterly. "As if the king cared. Why you cannot throw a stone in Versailles without striking one of his bastards. That little bourgeoisie has all the luck."

❦

Marie Dumesnil was a frequent visitor to the little wooden house behind the Place Dauphine. Peg took an immediate fancy to her from their first meeting. The Frenchwoman was not only the most gifted actress on the French stage, but strong-minded and capable with marvellous dark eyes and hair which she wore in the pompadour, the high turned-back roll around the face made fashionable by the king's mistress. Madame Dumesnil spoke impeccable English but insisted that Peg speak to her in French. "It will be useful, *cherie*, when I take you to the *Comédie Française* to meet the cast. Who knows but we may even arrange a small part, if you will agree."

As a child Peg had attended a Huguenot school in the Weavers' Square in the heart of the Liberties and had made friends with the weavers' children whose first language was French. Violante liked to speak French and Peg was often called upon to translate her instructions for the benefit of the cast of *The Beggar's Opera* or anyone else who might be around. Later when Polly returned from Paris they had made it a practice to speak and read in French together each morning in the villa. Polly had a good accent and Peg a practised ear.

Marie Dumesnil had many admirers, but enjoyed most her long-standing relationship with the most famous intellectual of his day. Voltaire, now in his mid-fifties, was small, stooped with piercing dark eyes and a small amused mouth. He was the centre of a group known as the *philosophes*, whose avowed intention it was to produce a great encyclopedia of human knowledge, an ambition which got them into trouble with both church and court. Like his mistress, Madame Dumesnil, Voltaire lived in a blaze of publicity and Peg frequently met him in the salon of his niece, Madame Denise, where scholars and writers and artists gathered each week.

He was the sworn enemy of the Duc de Richelieu though politeness demanded that they behave as friends when they met. Voltaire admired the Pompadour and had befriended her years before when as a young married matron, she was striving to make her way in society. Her mother, Madame Poisson, was handsome, free with her favours and had several wealthy lovers. But her long-standing affair with Monsieur de Tourneham had set tongues wagging. It was he who had arranged the daughter's marriage with his nephew, given the newlyweds a fortune and provided them with an apartment in the mansion where he lived with Madame Poisson and her husband. Even by Parisian standards, it was a curious arrangement and there was much speculation as to who the Pompadour's father really was.

When Voltaire first met her, the young Madame d'Étoiles was frantically eager to be received in the best houses but everyone was suspicious of her, the ladies more particularly because of her charms and good looks, the way their husbands and lovers ogled her and her mother's reputation. Madame d'Étoiles always behaved with excellent good sense, deferring to her hostesses and their friends, treating her husband with love and respect. But how far could they trust her? When all was said and done there was no substitute for breeding. They even made sly jokes over the name she had borne before marriage—Reinette Poisson. How pretentious and how common. Madame Denise had laughingly filled Peg in on the Pompadour's background. "As a young married woman she begged be allowed attend my birthday celebrations and when I took pity on her came with her husband laden with gifts. By the time her own birthday came around she was surrounded by the nobility of Versailles."

"The marquise wields enormous power," Voltaire explained. "And yet," his eyes narrowed as he stroked Peg's red-gold hair and studied her skin and eyes, "she is not more beautiful than you, my little Irish rose. And you too are an actress of some ability, Madame Dumesnil tells me, and set London talking by your audacity in playing a breeches part. Did you hear that the marquise lately enraptured the king when she showed off her legs in the role of Prince Charming in the new theatre she has arranged beside the Ambassador's Staircase in Versailles? His majesty kissed her in public. Everyone was astonished. You should remain in Paris with us, *ma petite*, but it is necessary for you to find yourself a protector, a man of standing. Enjoy yourself while you are still young. Too soon will come the deluge and the old order will be swept away forever."

He kissed Peg's hand and Madame Denise took his arm. "Do not flirt with your Irish rose. She needs a lover to mend her broken heart and you, *mon petit* Voltaire, are the lover of your charming Marie Dumesnil." Peg had confided in the French actress her affair with Darnley and how he had died after Culloden. She wished that Marie had kept her secret but it seemed that nothing was sacred in French society and besides, everyone loved the Stuarts. Prince Charles Edward had sought refuge in Paris after the Scottish uprising but rumour had it that he would not be long with his friends. The Wars of the Austrian Succession were drawing to a close and it was said that the English were bitter and would not sign a treaty with France until he was sent packing to Rome where they said he belonged. So far the king had not agreed but it would happen.

❦

The Tuileries ballroom was crowded. As promised, Owen

M'Swiney had taken Peg to a masked ball but soon vanished in pursuit of a young scion of the nobility who wore rouge, high red heels and three patches, leaving her standing under a blaze of light from the glass chandeliers. She was feeling exhausted, hadn't wanted to come. For weeks she had been fêted with poetry readings in fine mansions in the faubourgs, had boated on the Seine, gone horse-riding in the forest of Senart and in an effort to forget the heartache and loss that had driven her to Paris in the first place, had engaged in a round of dancing and gambling. It was usually dawn before she got to bed.

Despite her fatigue she was looking very lovely. Zara had skilfully painted her face and helped her into a new gown of green silk, cut low at the waist and shoulders. She had draped a lace shawl, a gift from Voltaire, over her mistress's shoulders. Diamonds sprinkled in her hair like dust, dark green feathers lent sheen to the dark red curls which she wore down her back.

"Care to dance, carissima?" There was something about the slightly mocking voice, the dark unpowdered hair in a widow's peak, the black velvet suit, the mask, that brought back the past in an over-powering rush. She was remembering that night of her London debut, the ball in Buckingham House, the Duchess Sarah and her meeting with Darnley. She caught her breath; next the stranger was sweeping her on to the floor. She found that the room was rotating slowly and swayed. "I feel unsteady," she said faintly and without a word her partner helped her to an ante-room and gently laid her down on a couch. "Rest yourself and I shall get you something which will revive you." His English was perfect but accented.

He was back almost at once bearing a silver goblet of wine. He had unmasked and she studied his face as she drank.

"We have met before?" He was familiar but then she had met so many in the crowded salons and ballrooms during the months since coming to Paris. He bowed. "Signor Domenico Angelo Malevolti Tremamando, at your service, ma'am."

How could she have forgotten the most noted horseman and swordsman in Paris. Everywhere Signor Angel as he was known went he was fêted. Women swooned over him, men were careful not to cross swords with him. He was always the victor. Even the dauphin had taken fencing lessons from him. He was said to be well born, well educated, wealthy and reckless. "Forgive me," she said putting out her hand.

He covered her hand, her arm in kisses and she shivered. She could feel her command of herself slip away. Was the wine drugged? Reason struggled with fantasy. It was just that she was so tired and the wine was undoubtedly potent, she told herself. His mouth was on hers, his tongue prising open her lips. She wanted to push him away but his strength defeated her. Recklessness had always been like an aphrodisiac to her, besides which she badly wanted a man's arms around her, a man's mouth on hers, after so many months of abstinence, wanted love and to be loved.

Afterwards she wondered why she had yielded so easily and knew that it was more than loneliness; it was that the very air around her pulsated with a strange physical energy. People talked of love all the time, of the pursuit, the capture, the capitulation and the betrayal. The court at Versailles set the fashion for pleasure alone. But even the intellectuals amongst whom she moved and who constantly forecast doom, lived as though every day were their last. Eat, drink and make love was their motto, for tomorrow the deluge, when the old order will be swept away and the tumbrils roll. Even the very beggars on the streets seemed at times like dancers in some crazy ballet that would end in bloodshed and ruin.

After that first encounter it was accepted by the circle in which she was moving that she was having an *affaire* of the heart with Angelo. Afterwards she realised that during the time it lasted, a matter of weeks, she was possessed by a feverish gaiety that drove her on. He had none of the tenderness of Darnley or David Garrick or Charles Coffey but was skilled in the game of love and could match her climax with his. Yet she knew in her soul that it was no more than an infatuation on her part and that he would drop her as swiftly as he had laid siege to her, should it suit his books. Already the Duchesse di Condi was sniffing around. She offered him her insatiable lusts, her wealth and entrée to the court of Versailles, if he would become her lover. Meanwhile the Duc de Richelieu waited in the wings.

Richelieu would arrange, when the time came, that Signor Angelo be given a small room at the palace. It would be interesting to witness the meeting between the proud Marquise de Pompadour with her charm and power over the king and the swordsman from Leghorn with his reputation with women. Richelieu believed in propinquity where matters of the heart were concerned. Just let the marquise by a single look arouse the king's jealousy and she would be banished from Versailles and Angelo sent to the Bastille. The palace was too small to hold the Pompadour and himself. Only a few days before he had slighted her in some small way and as he helped the king pull on his riding boots the next morning, Louis had asked him carelessly, "How many times have you been to the Bastille, Richelieu?" It was warning enough.

❧

As that long hot summer drew to a close a masked ball was held in the palace of Versailles and as was the custom the state apartments were thrown open to the public. Anyone could go to the ball, all that was required was for guests to be properly dressed and for the gentlemen of the party to carry swords.

Of course the whole of fashionable Paris would attend. Who would miss such an opportunity to eat and drink in such surroundings at no cost to the purse, perhaps to catch a glimpse of the beautiful marquise, the handsome king. In all her months in France Peg had never seen Versailles and her first glimpse of the palace on that summer evening was to remain with her for as long as she lived. Hundreds of wax torches held aloft by uniformed servants turned night into day, lighting up flowers and foliage as brilliantly as the sun. Though autumn's traces were all around and the night held a hint of frost, tropical plants still bloomed as if the time was high summer. As they dismounted from their carriage they heard the sound of invisible musicians luring wanderers towards labyrinths and secret mazes. Around them playing fountains sent their perfumed waters high in the air, mingling their scents with late blooming roses and night stock. Perhaps it was the unreal air of the place, the feeling that she had stepped through the pages of some fairytale to a land of youth and beauty that made her behave as she subsequently did. She lost all restraint, all feeling of what was right and wrong and when the time came found herself flirting outrageously with the Duc di Condi and so setting in motion a train of events which very nearly ended in tragedy for all.

But all that would happen later. First there was the

palace itself to be enjoyed, the honour that Richelieu was conferring on them by joining their party to be savoured, the surge of vanity that Angelo couldn't keep his hands off her even though the Duchesse di Condi was throwing herself at his head.

Richelieu promised that later she would see the Pompadour and the king who were supping in their private apartments, perhaps he could even arrange that she meet the marquise. Meanwhile a ballet would be danced on the lawn and they would watch it and the canopy of fireworks that would follow, from the balcony of his apartment.

The night wore on and the revellers became more rowdy; excitement mounted as people danced to the many orchestras in different rooms, wandered daringly into the queen's apartments, searching for food, for the buffet tables groaning with salmon, roast boar, *foie gras*, duck, jellies, blancmanges, cheesecakes, crystallised fruits and decanters of wine.

There was a great surge forward as a door opened and the Pompadour and the king appeared and took the floor. Peg marvelled at this exquisite woman with her enamelled beauty, high coiffure, cloth of gold shimmering with jewels. Had to pinch herself that she was really here at this moment, not a stone's throw away from the most envied woman in France, dancing with the handsome king, powerful as a god. Then they were gone and, drunk with the night, the sights she had witnessed, she made no protest when a masked figure pushed himself between herself and Angelo and with exquisite courtesy invited her to dance. Behind her fan the Duchesse di Condi giggled and Richelieu's lips curled in a smile.

"You are enchanting," the stranger whispered and was pulling her into an alcove, covering her hands, her neck, with kisses, finding her mouth while she made no protest. Then Angelo breathing fire and brimstone was between them, pulling the young man away, throwing him to the ground so that his mask fell to the floor. The Duchesse di Condi pushed forward and put her hand to her mouth at the figure climbing to his feet. "You have struck my husband the duc," she squealed and giggled.

Angelo was challenging di Condi to a duel, shouting that Madame Woffington was his. She was trying to come between them, furiously angry, telling Angelo that they were not married. He had no claim to her. Marie Dumesnil was reasoning with Angelo, begging him to consider. He had caused enough trouble for one night. Duelling was strictly forbidden in Versailles. The penalty for any offender was instant death. Angelo was saying his honour was at stake. The young nobleman, face pale, was accepting the challenge. The duchesse was licking her lips.

❦

"But for Voltaire things would have gone badly." It was a week later and Marie Dumesnil was sitting in the parlour of the little wooden house with Peg while Zara packed their trunks. Owen M'Swiney had left for Italy with his friend when the scandal broke.

"What will happen?" She was almost afraid to ask.

"They are both detained in the Bastille. It was the only solution. Voltaire asked Richelieu to intervene and though they are enemies, he did. In a strange way they respect each other. Richelieu had arranged that di Condi seduce you; it was a question of a bet, I understand. He did not think that even Angelo would challenge anyone to a duel while in the palace."

"But what did he hope to gain by it all?" Peg said.

"Angelo would be disgusted with you and would turn to the duchesse. After that the dear god knows what he had planned. He is a strange man."

Peg sighed. "And yet the duel went ahead."

Marie Dumesnil patted her hand. "Cheer up, my pet. Angelo could have killed the duc as easily as he would swat a fly but he has sense that one. He pricked young di Condi in the arm and honour was vindicated."

"But they are both in the Bastille."

Marie Dumesnil shrugged her beautiful shoulders. "Richelieu has influence with the king. They will spend a year in prison. What harm. The duchesse will visit Angelo and they will make love. She has been hot for him these months past."

"And her husband, the duc?"

"He will not be lonely with his friends, his mistress. He will play cards, make love, gossip. He is to have his own cook. Later he will be pardoned and sent back to his estates with the duchesse. They will expire of boredom and spend their time importuning Richelieu to have them brought back to Versailles. Angelo will return to Italy and create a stir." She got to her feet and stretched. "It is how they live. I am glad I have other interests, the theatre, arts, Voltaire..." She smiled.

Peg said sadly, "I am glad I am going home to Dublin. I should never have come to Paris."

Marie Dumesnil kissed her. "You must give me a parting gift."

"Anything," Peg said fervently. "A ring, an emerald brooch, pearls?"

"Would you give me the small blackamoor? I have taken a fancy to him."

"Mohamet! Oh, Marie, anything but that. Zara would die. Her grandfather was killed. It was a tragedy at the time and she was bereft. I bought Mohamet to keep her company. I think she loves that little boy more than she will any child she will ever bear. I have promised that when he is older I shall give him his freedom. I could not, even for you my dear friend, break her heart."

"Do not distress yourself, Peg. I shall be happy to accept the lace shawl that Voltaire gave to you. I was jealous at the time. He promised me another such, but he forgets."

Peg smiled. "I had meant to give it to you. You will take it and this pendant to remember me by." She took a chain from around her neck and gave it to the French woman.

Marie Dumesnil arranged the lace over her high pompadour. "Will you take a word of advice from an older woman?"

"What is it?"

"When you return to Dublin, find yourself a protector. An older man, someone kind, undemanding. A woman, especially an actress, needs such a man."

Peg shivered. "I have been in love with three men. I do not include Angelo. He was a mistake, a short-lived infatuation if you will. I am nearing thirty years."

"And a very beautiful woman," Marie Dumesnil said briskly. "Consider the Marquise de Pompadour. She is near your age, has not half your talent as an actress and holds the king in thrall."

"If I can force Sheridan to give me work in Smock Alley, I shall consider myself lucky," Peg said wistfully.

"Nonsense, my dear. You will take over the Playhouse, make it famous, force this Monsieur Sheridan to pay you a great deal of money. It is settled."

They embraced for the last time and Peg watched the

French woman settle herself into her carriage, the coachman manoeuvre the horses around and with a last wave, the graceful motion of wrist and hand that only great actresses and princesses of the blood can achieve, coach and occupant had vanished from sight.

Rain was falling and the gardens once so invitingly beautiful were now dank and forbidding. She would not be sorry to leave Paris and yet she would never wholly forget it, the places she had visited, the Opera, the Garden City, the road to Versailles, her last sight of the palace brought to life by a thousand torches, riding in the forest of Senart with the sun setting behind the trees bathing the woodland in a glow of crimson light. She would remember her friends, Madame Denise, Voltaire, Marie Dumesnil, and now and again she would think with wry amusement of her hectic month with Signor Angelo. All in all, she would not be sorry to return home.

She was on fire. The crossing from France to Ireland had been the worst in living memory, lasting all of sixteen days. She had been deadly sick as had most of the passengers and crew. Only Mohamet and a couple of hardy seamen had weathered the storm. Mohamet had been beside himself with delight, climbing up riggings, free as a bird with Zara prostrate and too weak to protest. He had got completely out of hand for the crew had adopted him as mascot, said it was thanks to him that the ship safely reached harbour. Zara had recovered sufficiently to prevent him drinking a bottle of rum given him by some foolhardy sailor as a last gift.

During the journey, Peg had insisted on getting out of the bunk and staggering on deck but had been felled by flying timber. She didn't remember being carried off the ship or the journey by cab to the house in the High Street, didn't remember Zara's putting her to bed or her mother weeping torn between joy at her daughter's arrival and fear at her illness, had no recollection of the doctor bleeding her to bring down the fever.

She opened her eyes. Her head was aching, her body

on fire. Zara was telling her not to worry, that she was safely home and would soon be better. That was the last sensible thing she remembered. Through the mists of delirium she heard voices, but they could not hold her. She ran away. Charles Coffey was holding her hand, counting the stars...Darnley went by riding a white horse shouting that Scotland was up...she was a child once more picking cockles on Merrion Strand with her father. Waves splashed her legs and she shrieked with delight at their coolness. Nearby a heron stood on one leg balefully watching her, little sharp inquisitive eyes. She thought of Voltaire and giggled. She wanted to wade out to where land rose out of the sea. Was it Howth or *Tír na nÓg*? She couldn't rightly tell. Her father said no. It wasn't yet her time. She was on stage in the Drury Lane Theatre. Garrick was playing the part of Macbeth asking Lennox, "Saw you the weird sisters?" She opened her eyes. They were around her bed, heads nodding, tongues wagging, telling each other that she was finished, that Zara was a foreigner, that Mohamet had brought her bad luck.

"Double, double, toil and trouble," she said in a cracked voice. "Eye of newt and toe of frog. Wool of..." Three sheep's heads stared down at her and she whispered, "Baa, baa, black sheep."

Her mother was shaking holy water on the bedposts. Mrs Bellamy was talking about Macbeth being an unlucky play. Mrs Carey, the innkeeper's wife, was keening an Irish lament. She wanted to leave them but Zara was lifting her head from the pillow, begging her to take a little sip. She retched and Zara wiped her face and said gently, "Try to keep down a little. It's a good brew, marigold juice, purlane, garlic..." Her mind wandered. She couldn't take in the rest. Mohamet was reciting a spell he had learnt from his grandmother and the witches were running away.

She came out of the dream. "Are you better?" her mother asked.

"I'd like a cup of tea," she croaked. Her stomach refused the toast which Zara cut into dainty fingers, but she drank the tea thirstily, gratefully and almost at once closed her eyes and went down, down, down into a dreamless sleep.

It was morning and the sun poured in through the diamond-paned window and across the patchwork quilt. She sat up and yawned, and Zara who had been keeping vigil at the bedside said, "How do you feel?"

She smiled. "Much better. I'm suddenly ravenous."

Zara brought a tray of scrambled eggs on toast and a pot of tea and Peg balanced it on the bed, finishing up every last crumb and emptying the pot. "Where's mother?"

"She went to mass to pray for your soul," Zara giggled. "Mrs Bellamy and Mrs Carey were here yesterday. You thought they were witches. They'll never forgive you."

"It must have been the fever. What's Mrs Bellamy doing in Dublin for heaven's sake?"

Zara recovered the tray. "George Ann came over to Dublin months ago to act in Smock Alley. They're lodging with George Ann's aunt, the Honourable Mrs O'Hara in St Stephen's Green."

Peg nodded. "Lord Tyrawley's sister. I've heard of her."

Zara twitched back the curtains. "Your mother is coming down the street arm in arm with that Mrs Carey. Don't let her tire you out, whatever you do."

Peg said cheerfully, "At least they'll give me the news of the town." She looked at herself in a hand mirror and her eyes had a faraway look. "I feel I've been on a long journey—and I don't mean Paris—but oh, I'm glad to be back."

ॐ

"Dean Swift died a month short of his seventy-eighth birthday," her mother said, mopping her eyes. "They waked him all over the Liberties, with snuff and porter. They muffled the bells of St Patrick's and they tolled for three days."

"The crowds of the world came to the deanery, where he lay stretched," Dottie Carey put in. "I got close to the coffin and cut a piece of his hair for a keepsake—not that he had much. Next minute every fishwife in Patrick Street was doing the same. They had to close the doors before the poor man was scalped."

Peg burst out laughing. She was sorry to hear of the dean's passing but the vision Dottie Carey had conjured up was too much. "I can imagine his comments if he had come back to life," she said, wiping her eyes. "He never saw himself as a saint, otherwise you would have a first-class relic, Mrs Carey."

"Would there be a cure in it do you think?" Dottie rooted in her pocket and brought out a few wisps of grey hair tied up in a rag. She bethought herself of her position as wife to one of the best-known innkeepers of the town. "Not that I believe in such superstitions, being a loyal member of the established church, but half the city has aches and pains. It would be good for business. Mr Carey would be pleased."

"You'll die roaring for a priest, Mrs Carey, and you a cradle Catholic," Peg promised. "Mother, tell Zara I would like to wash."

She had lost weight during her illness. Zara pinned and tucked as she dressed. "You have a waist many would envy," she said comfortingly, "but your hair—lost its lustre." Vigorously she wielded two brushes, rolled and curled. "There now. A trace of rouge to camouflage your pallor but no beauty spots today."

Peg slipped a rabbit's foot in her pocket for luck and had Mohamet order a chair to take her to Fishamble Street.

In Smock Alley, a béggar woman, face half eaten away with leprosy, squatted outside the Playhouse, plucking at passers-by, calling plaintively, "Buy a lottery ticket for the love of God."

Something about the voice stopped Peg in her tracks. She wanted to blot out the past but an emotion stronger than fear tugged at her heart. She bent down, stomach heaving at the stench of vomit, shit, the mildew of poverty. "Kathleen, is it you?" she whispered.

The listless eyes gave no sign of recognition, grimed nails scratched a head crawling with lice.

She tried again. "You remember me, Peg, Peggy Woffington." Despite the rags, the sores, dark set eyes in the yellowing skin, she couldn't mistake her one-time friend, the companion of her lost youth.

"We used dress up in coloured paper, put on plays for the children in the lane. You wanted to be an actress. Remember the day we went to see Strongbow's tomb in Christ Church Cathedral?" Her voice was coaxing. "You used tell me stories of the long ago. How the Princess Dervorgilla ran away with the King of Leinster and brought back Strongbow and his Norman knights to Ireland." She bent down and whispered. "You ran away like Dervorgilla. What happened you, Kathleen?"

With a languid gesture, the woman put her hands to her ears as if to shut out the past and defeated, Peg gave her a sovereign which she examined with stupid eyes, turning the gold piece over. Muttering something incomprehensible, she scuttled off sideways, a crab on the run.

Peg was shocked at the wretch that had once been the prettiest girl in Dublin, with dark curling hair, cornflower eyes, a voice sweet as a singing bird and endearing saucy ways. Like her mother before her, she had been generous to a fault. "Kathleen is an imaginary girl," Mrs McEnroe used say half proudly, half in despair. "She has driven me mad with her talk of the Playhouse. Don't let her sway you, Peg. Be a good girl and do as your mother bids you."

"I could easily have ended up like her, diseased, in the gutter," Peg thought despairingly. Only ambition, the legacy of Máire Rua, had given her the courage to go on. She went in through the stage entrance of the Smock Alley Theatre, deaf to the greetings of the doorman who remembered her from her early days, blind to the admiring glances of the young actors who had heard stories of her beauty, her wealth and her lovers.

Tom Sheridan received her affably in his office. "Peg my dear, I read of your arrival in *Faulkner's Journal*. Naturally I had meant to call and pay my respects, but the demands of the theatre..." He threw out his hands. The great man burdened with the cares of office. He was acting a part. She distrusted the sleek body in the well-fitting redcoat, white trims, lace cravat, disapproved of the patronising way he bade her be seated. She drew off her gloves, smoothing each finger looking round the handsomely furnished room, noting the portrait in oils of the young David Garrick hanging behind his desk. John Lewis, one-time scene-shifter in Smock Alley, had painted Garrick during that season in Dublin—how many years before? He had invited her to sit for him. She had paid him twenty pounds. Garrick hadn't liked it much.

"And how are all in Drury Lane? Is the great Mr Garrick in good health?"

"We have parted company as no doubt you have heard, or has the London intelligence failed you?" Her voice was brittle as his was smooth. He smiled as if in sympathy for her reduced circumstances. "You heard I got me a wife? You must join me in a glass of Madeira?" His *bonhomie* rang false.

She had never trusted him, so decided she would waste no more time in idle pleasantries. "To come to the point, Mr Sheridan, you once invited me to join forces with you here in Smock Alley. Does the offer still hold?"

He filled two glasses, holding them up to the light. "A good wine needs no bush," he said pleasantly. "Mrs Bellamy will have told you that George Ann is the company's leading lady, a splendid actress. She is settled with her aunt, the Honourable Mrs O'Hara in St Stephen's Green. A patron of the theatre, I am happy to say."

Peg shrugged. "I doubt me not I could muster as much support and patronage as I did on the London stage."

Sheridan frowned, made rings on the table with his index finger. "What salary had you in mind?"

"Six hundred pounds for the season with two benefit performances."

She had startled him, made him sit up, take notice. "You can't be serious. Even Garrick did not command such a sum on his Dublin visit."

Peg put down her wine untasted. "I never jest about money. Naturally I guarantee to fill your theatre."

He leaned across the table, sincere, confidential, the helpful friend. "For old times' sake Peg I'll make you an offer. Seven pounds a week for supporting roles."

Play second fiddle to George Ann. She would sooner

sell oranges in the pit. She drew on her gloves. "Top billing and a commensurate salary. You have a week to consider my proposal. Good day to you, sir."

The shock of meeting the woman who had once been Kathleen McEnroe, anger at the reception she had received from Sheridan and pride carried her out of the theatre but as she left Smock Alley and went down by the river into the oldest quarters of the town, her confidence ebbed. Refusing a chair, she cut across into Winetavern Street where a drunken buck was singing a raucous ballad about the Young Chevalier. The words followed her into Castle Street. She wouldn't think of that eager young prince in the blue bonnet born to be king, now exiled forever, nor of Darnley's lonely death. "Damn Sheridan," she said so fiercely that a broadsheet seller stared at her and whistled. "Damn his insolence. Yesterday he was a nobody, a hanger-on in Drury Lane. Now he has the gall to patronise me."

She walked unheedingly, tears trickling down her cheeks and found herself in the Coombe where a couple of ragged urchins were paddling in the muddy waters of the Poddle that flowed down Patrick Street. She heard Mohamet's voice even before she caught sight of him tricked out in a green velvet jacket, a scarlet handkerchief tied around his head. He must have slipped out unknown to Zara; she would never let him out in such a get-up. His stories of the striped cat and other marvels he had seen at Southwark Fair brought him popularity with the other children. Bigger boys who had attempted to bully him left him severely alone when he boasted of his grandmother the witch and swore he knew spells that could turn them into toads. Peg could hear him explaining how he had once been shipwrecked and lived on a desert island. Robinson Crusoe's adventures which he knew by heart were proving a useful bible. He would come home later, bursting with health and vitality, hungry as a young lion and Zara would wash and feed him and listen to all he had done. Seeing him at play had distracted her, dissipated her anger. By the time she reached the house in High Street she was mistress of herself once more.

❦

Clothes were strewn everywhere, on chairs, on tables, on the floor. Zara was on her knees packing a trunk with bodices, skirts, gowns of brocade, petticoats, aprons, boots and shoes. Mrs Woffington, face flushed, hair undone, was in a tizzy, having to be restrained from taking her favourite ornaments, her pet cat, her favourite chair.

Ever since Polly had written inviting her mother to join her in England, the house had been in an uproar. One moment her mind was made up. She would not let Polly down. The next she had changed her mind, could not face the journey. She had heard tales of abductors. Peg forbore to remark that her mother's grey locks and thickening waist would no doubt keep her safe from what she considered was a fate worse than death. Zara prepared tisanes to calm her.

The matter was resolved when George Ann had a falling out with her aunt. "I do not mind you borrowing my clothes, my jewels, my furs," that put-upon lady lamented, "but when you borrow my wigs..." The Honourable Mrs O'Hara was famous in Dublin for the number and different colours of the wigs she changed four times a day. "A pox on your wigs," George Ann said pettishly, adding spitefully, "You are the talk of the town with your nonsense. Mutton dressing up as spring lamb."

Mrs O'Hara burst into wild lamentations and had to be led to her bed by Mrs Bellamy whom she despised while an unrepentant George Ann flounced out the door. She was bored with Dublin, bored with Tom Sheridan who was so bound up in his new wife that he had no time to flirt. She had been much taken by a captain of the guard at the castle but he had been suddenly transferred to Edinburgh. David Garrick was no doubt still lording it over them all at Drury Lane. She had heard that he could not make up his mind whether or not to wed with Burlington's daughter. He was finding it hard to get over his red-haired, green-eyed Irish rose. George Ann made up her mind. She would return to London, would seek out Mr Garrick. Beg for a role in his next production. She had youth, looks, breeding and even Mr Sheridan had been forced to admit that she was a damnably good actress. What Mr Garrick needed was a sympathetic ear and perhaps just a little encouragement.

Peg kissed her mother reassuringly. "You will be quite safe. If one can believe Mrs Bellamy she has travelled far afield. She once lived in Portugal. She will see you safely to Somerset where Polly is lying-in. I have promised to pay her expenses and George Ann is all agog to meet Lord and Lady Cholmondeley."

"Titles mean nothing to me," Mrs Woffington said loftily. "I shall remind Polly's in-laws that our family once owned castles in Bunratty, Clonroad, Clarecastle, and that my parents visited the Court of St James in King Charles's time."

Peg had no sooner seen the travellers off from George's Quay than Tom Sheridan arrived at the house in High Street, smug, self-important, stepping disdainfully over a puddle of water. Peg, watching from a window, thought balefully, he should have a Raleigh to lay down a cloak.

"I was compelled to fight the treasurer every inch of the way," he greeted her ponderously. "I managed to convince those of importance that you were worth the gamble."

She bit her lips to hide her amusement, longed to prick his self-esteem, said coolly, "This morning I took farewell of Mrs Bellamy and George Ann who accompany my mother to London. Too bad you have lost your leading lady. A difference of opinion with her honourable aunt over a question of wigs and gowns, I understand. A loss of patronage. Too sad."

He grunted. "'Tis of little consequence. George Ann needs experience on the London stage. She hopes to work with Mr Garrick."

Peg drew two chairs to the table. "You have the contract with the terms I specified?" Carefully she examined the small print, then satisfied, signed her name with a flourish. "'For this relief much thanks,'" she quoted lightly from Hamlet. "*Julius Caesar* is not my favourite play but I do make a rather excellent Calphurnia. We must drink a toast to our future, this time in the late Lord Darnley's favourite quaff." She poured out two glasses of sparkling wine. "To our partnership, Mr Sheridan."

"You perhaps overrate yourself," he began caustically. She frowned and he had second thoughts. "To your future, my dear, on the Dublin stage."

Now boast thee, death, in thy possession lies
A lass unparallel'd

(*Antony and Cleopatra*, V, ii)

30

L ionel, Duke of Dorset, stood at the window of his library looking down at the changing of the guards in the Upper Castle Yard. He did this every morning for he was a man of regular habits.

It was his second term as Lord Lieutenant of Ireland. Earlier he had spent ten years in office before being recalled to England. He had never forgotten his first sight of the city. Tall spires, churches, bells ringing a welcome, the town protected by mountains, the streets choked with carriages of the gentry, nobility in lace, velvet, plumed hats, privy councillors, judges in scarlet, officers of state, officers of the household in black and green and red. It had taken the procession four interminable hours to make a journey from the quays to Dublin Castle, a distance of just under two miles. He had given a state reception in St Patrick's Hall that same evening for some thousand guests. The poorer citizens, maddened with the free wine and ale distributed at every corner, lit bonfires in the Liberties, fought, made love, ate, vomited, drank some more and sang snatches of ballads both loyal and rebel. This time his arrival had been low-keyed at his request. He was too old for such hustle and bustle.

Now in his mid-fifties, the duke was developing a paunch, which he blamed on the boxes of papers that kept him at his desk and occupied most of his time. His hair too was thinning on top. His blue eyes, set a shade too close, were as sharp as ever and his mouth and chin were still firm. He was a fine-looking man with an upright bearing and had always hankered after the military life. He had served his time as colonel of his regiment and later had been adviser to King George. He had just returned from Aix-la-Chapelle in France where the peace treaty had been concluded. He yawned. It had been after midnight when he made his exhausted way to bed, worn out with the crossing, the speeches, the sycophancy of officials, the noisy complaints of the duchess and worse than that of her gorgon of a maid because they didn't like their quarters in the castle. He consoled himself with the thought that refurbishing and redecorating the apartments would keep Her Grace busy for some time to come.

Dorset told himself that he was a simple man at heart. He felt he had served king and country and now all he wished of life was to be allowed retire to his estate on the pleasant south coast of England and devote himself to overseeing the farms, to gardening, fishing and indulging in his favourite hobby, carpentry. It would be agreeable to ride out on a morning like this down the Dorset coast, the tang of the sea in his lungs. He got little opportunity to ride in Dublin and the stench of the Liffey at high tide was enough to poison a man.

He rang a bell and almost at once Winchester, his valet, came in with his morning chocolate and toast. He had developed a taste for French bread during the time he had spent abroad. His chef, elderly, cantankerous, had unsuccessfully followed a recipe from the kitchens in Versailles. Fortunately the duke's visit had been more productive. Certainly the whole of Europe was sick of the War of the Austrian Succession which had dragged on for years and which had just ended. The British were adamant that the Pretender had caused enough trouble and should not be allowed remain in sight of the English Channel lest he be tempted to renew his claim. Louis of France had a fondness for the Stuart and was so used to ordering his nobles around at Versailles that he found it hard to stomach the British, but in the end Marshal de Saxe had persuaded him that it was all for the best and the treaty had been sealed.

"You would be astounded at the pomp and ceremony that surrounds the king at Versailles," the duke remarked idly as his valet set down a tray containing a silver pot, a cup and saucer and plate of almond biscuits on a small table, and fastened a white linen napkin around his master's neck. Dorset took a sip of chocolate and nibbled a biscuit, pulling a face. "The chocolate is cold and the biscuits are stale. Louis would have his cook hanged, drawn and quartered for sending up the like." He held out his cup for replenishing. "Putting his majesty to bed is quite a performance," he chuckled. "Escorted to his chamber by a retinue of lackeys and gentlemen of the bedchamber. Whoever happens to be in favour has the honour of carrying the candlestick. No one of rank less than that of a duke may remove the royal breeches which are then wrapped in red taffeta, while it requires a Prince of the Blood to help his majesty into his nightshirt. His personal valet then approaches on his knees with a damp towel on a silver dish to wipe the royal hands, face and no doubt backside."

Winchester gave a dry cough but the duke was well into his stride. "Then the king hops out of bed to join the marquise for supper, followed by private sport. What a farce. Thank God we have nothing like that in Britain."

He put down his cup and fingered a small wooden horse which held pride of place on his desk. "Do you know, Winchester, had I been born into a different family with little or no responsibility, I should have been perfectly happy to work as an artist."

Winchester raised an eyebrow but the duke continued unheedingly. "I have it in me to be a sculptor. It would be satisfying to work with marble, but alas I must content myself with humble wood." Proudly he held up a carving of a horse he had laboured over for many weeks. Winchester who knew his master better than most preserved a diplomatic silence. The horse was no Pegasus, flying through the heavens. It looked to the valet's jaundiced eye more like an old farm horse on its last legs. He cast a practised eye over a stack of newspapers. The duke liked to peruse the news of the day while drinking his chocolate. They were all there, *Faulkner's Journal*, the *Dublin Mercury*, the *Dublin Intelligence*, the *Dublin Gazette*, *Pue's Occurrence* and the rest. It was a source of amazement to Winchester that a city the size of Dublin could support no fewer than ten newspapers to say nothing of the weekly journals and the English press though they invariably arrived late.

Pettishly the duke glanced through a few headlines. "Nothing but thundering editorials and comments about the peace and what it will mean to Europe. The Irish must be better informed about what goes on outside their own country than anyone else." He finished his coffee and got to his feet. "Did you know, Winchester, that there are thirteen bookshops in Dame Street alone and six in College

Green. I counted them once from my carriage window. I don't get enough exercise."

Winchester not only knew the bookshops of Dame Street and College Green but the fourteen to be found in Skinner's Row. He was as addicted to the printed word as any Dubliner. "It would appear," he said wickedly, "that every second person in Dublin is engaged in writing a book." The duke spoke interminably about the memoirs he would shortly engage on. He had even gone so far as to jot down a few dates which his valet had been called upon to provide. Not that the book would ever see the light of day.

"Do you tell me that, Winchester," the duke said in a cheerful imitation of an Irish accent. "Well at least it keeps them out of mischief."

Winchester took up the tray and departed while the duke opened the *Gazette*. A headline caught his eye. "Prince Charles Edward Stuart arrested." His eyes skimmed the closely printed paragraph. The Stuart had been apprehended outside the Paris Opera House and expelled from that city following a protest from London. Reports from Versailles said that the king was displeased and Voltaire had sent a letter of protest to King George of England.

The duke threw down the paper. Much good it would do Voltaire or even Louis himself. England had been seriously alarmed over the '45 rebellion, with the Hanoverians losing their heads, shipping gold and plate which they didn't own to Hanover. Thank God for once Ireland had been quiet. Years before he had told the Earl of Darnley what the outcome would be, but the man wouldn't listen. He liked Darnley, enjoyed his company, remembered an autumn week they had spent hunting and fishing in Scotland. Nights they had sat drinking and talking. Books, music, religion, philosophy and of course politics. Voltaire's name had come up, the uncrowned king of the *philosophes*. Voltaire, the French democrat, brilliant, scathing, armed with his matchless irony writing pamphlets, essays, plays, defining the Age of Reason, vitriolic about injustices and the Church—though he was Jesuit educated—making up lampoons, mocking the court at Versailles, which were circulated throughout all of Europe. How long could the French monarchy stand the onslaught of such men as Voltaire. What was the phrase the Pompadour was so fond of using? *"Après nous le déluge."* Indeed it might be so.

He had tried to argue with Darnley that while the Hanoverians did little good—George I a drunken dissolute, the present monarch with his petticoat rule and on his own now that Caroline was dead and Walpole in disgrace— at least they did no harm. What the British most disliked about the Stuarts was their belief in the divine right of kings, an outmoded concept. Darnley and he had agreed to differ and somehow the conversation had drifted to women and love. Darnley had mentioned a girl with green eyes and hair the colour of autumn leaves—russet red, he had explained.

"A lass unparallel'd," he had called her. How did the quotation go? "'Now boast thee, death, in thy possession lies/A lass unparallel'd.'"

Darnley was dead. Was his Cleopatra also dead or using her wiles on some other man? Was it Winchester who had told him that she was an Irish actress with red hair and green eyes. Odd they had never met, but then he wasn't fond of the playhouse.

His secretary, thin-faced, sidled into the room with a

pile of documents for His Grace's signature and seal. At times like this the duke envied Louis his mistress, the Marquise de Pompadour. Not as a bedfellow but as a companion. Women were easy come by—besides he was growing old—but it would be pleasant to have someone to confide in. He had met the marquise the time he had visited Versailles and found her a fine-looking woman, charming, witty, shrewd, with a good grasp of politics. And a damn good actress to boot. He had seen her on stage in Versailles. They were fond of amateur theatricals there. He could do with a woman such as the marquise in his life. The duchess was silly, vain and without a thought in her head except cards, gossip and fashion. But where in this benighted country could a woman such as the Pompadour be found?

P eg closed up her mother's home in the High Street
and rented a fine house in Capel Street, north of the
river but convenient to Smock Alley. Built of good red brick
it stood four storeys high, with long sash windows and fine
stucco work on walls and ceilings. She furnished the rooms
with plush and mahogany, hung gilt mirrors in all the
recesses and engaged a French chef, a kitchen-maid, parlour-
maid, upstairs-maid and a boot boy. Zara would continue
as her companion and personal maid. Mohamet was
enrolled in the Quaker School in the Earl of Meath's
Liberty, that Conor had once attended. She had a new and
fashionable wardrobe of clothes made by the town's best
dressmaker and engaged in the social whirl, attending
soirées, dinners, concerts in the Music-Hall in Crow Street
and in Fishamble Street where almost a decade earlier,
Handel had first performed his oratorio *Messiah* to a wildly
enthusiastic audience.

On New Year's Eve she was invited to a performance
by the Grand Scots Ballet company in the ballroom of the
Marchioness of Antrim's mansion in Merrion Square.
Watching the ballerinas in their white muslin tunics with

blue ribands, hearing once again the old Scottish airs, brought back other days and inevitably thoughts of Darnley and the glorious adventure that had ended in death for so many. He had promised to take her to the highlands some day. Now she would never see the Loch Ruighi, its silver shimmering under a heat haze, the purple peaks of the Cuillins and high over them the expanse of blue sky filled with the timeless northern lights. He had loved Scotland in every season. More than anything else she regretted that they would never take black winding roads, leading through the wine-red moors of Skye. Never see the island where the Bonny Prince had trysted on his last journey with his dark-haired Flora Macdonald. No, she would never see Scotland. To go there without Darnley would be to endure a second death.

❦

"What will become of Mohamet when he is grown to manhood?" Zara frowned over the fine hem she was sewing. Mohamet's future was never far from her mind. At the mention of his name the small blackamoor raised his head and said mournfully, "I was born to be a slave."

"To the master and your studies," Peg said briskly. "It is the fate of most children."

He tugged at a lock of his hair, letting it spring back in a curl. "I'd rather be the Lord Lieutenant's blackamoor. He doesn't bother with books. He isn't made to learn words, to add and subtract. All day he eats cakes and sweetmeats."

"And rots his teeth." Impatiently Zara jabbed a needle into the gown she was making. "No doubt he has tapeworms in his belly as long as the Liffey."

Mohamet sniffed and Peg gave him a handkerchief. He blew loudly and continued his saga. "Elias told me he is a slave. He said I was a slave also and that you could sell me whenever you liked. I punched his nose till it bled. I am getting tired of Dublin; I think I will get on a ship for America and join my friend James Wilding. He promised to write to Zara. Perhaps he forgot?"

Zara blushed and hid her face in the fabric. She had lost her heart to the young man she had helped nurse back to health. She pictured him in the New World to which he had gone and the pretty fair-haired girl he had probably married.

"Soon he will write and give us his news," Peg said confidently. Mohamet pondered and bit his thumb. "I think the savages scalped him." He smiled at Zara. "When I go to America I shall kill them and send you their heads." Zara burst into tears. Peg hid a smile.

❦

Autumn gave way to winter; snow fell, mantling town and country in white. Then came the great frost when the Liffey froze over. She remembered the day long ago when she had gone skating on the lake in Hyde Park with Violante. It had been so cold that when she puffed a breath it formed a little spiral of smoke. They had remained skating for hours until night fell in a black velvet sky, stars danced and all around them people jigged and sang and clapped in time to the music of a gypsy fiddler. It was an experience she could never recapture. She had been young and carefree. She would never know such happiness again.

❦

Polly wrote that she had given birth to a healthy baby boy.

> *To the delight of mother who prays that the family curse is at an end. I am fully recovered*

—her letter ran on—

> *but find Somerset somewhat irksome and expect to return to London shortly after Christmas where I plan to establish a literary salon. I have engaged a nurse but mother will take charge of my son. It is comforting to think that he will be in good hands.*

Hastily Peg skimmed over a long-winded account of nursemaids giving gin to their charges to make them sleep.

> *Captain Cholmondeley has decided to resign his commission and take Holy Orders.*

Polly continued:

> *I fancy myself as a bishop's wife which would suit me well. I intend to take a leading part in fashionable London charities.*

Impatiently Peg flicked through the next few paragraphs until she came to the news that would confirm the rumours sweeping Dublin:

> *David Garrick has married at last. Mademoiselle Violetta languished away and no one knew what ailed her. Even Dr Mead, the town's*

*most fashionable physician, was baffled. In the
end Violetta confessed that she was mad with
love for Mr Garrick. The earl sent for Garrick
and a contract was duly drawn up. Violetta was
given a dowry of ten thousand pounds from the
family estate and a gift of five thousand pounds
from Garrick who has also promised her seventy
pounds per annum, pin money. The happy
couple were married first in the Church of St
Mary-le-Strand and later in the Roman Catholic oratory in the Portuguese Embassy.*

So vast a sum to dower so suitable a bride, so generous
a settlement from Garrick who had been so cheeseparing
that he grudged the lavish way she entertained, counted
the spoons of tea she put in the pot for Sam Johnson's
favourite beverage. Yet memories crowded in, and she
remembered again his countless acts of generosity. Money
given to help starving actors, to buy them food, pay the
rent. He could never pass a beggar in the street. She recalled
how he paid the funeral expenses of the actor who had
hanged himself in despair. For months afterwards he had
been haunted by what happened that night, had sworn
never again to play the role of Julius Caesar. But in the end
he had capitulated, commanded by the "Butcher"
Cumberland who had carried out so many atrocities in
Scotland. Garrick would always bow the knee, except to
Darnley. He had always hated Darnley. Yet he had saved
James Wilding's life. True Violetta had been the instrument,
pleading with Burlington, but Garrick had set the board
and moved the pieces when the time came. His star was
in the ascent. The gypsy had traced a life line that was long
and happy. When death came he would be buried with

kings. It was the end of a chapter. The end of her days of loving. The years were passing. What was it Shakespeare had said: "All the world's a stage and all the men and women merely players." Seven ages: the mewling infant, the scholar, the lover... She had staked her all for the bubble reputation. With hindsight would she have acted differently or had it all been fated as the gypsy had foretold? She would try to forget the past...there was no going back.

❧

Upper Sackville Street, Capel Street, the Rotunda were now becoming fashionable quarters, as the city grew, spreading across the Liffey. Fine streets were ornamented with lamps, obelisks, shrubbery. Members of the Irish Lords and Commons, forsaking their rural retreats, had built handsome houses and were served by new assembly rooms, concert halls, shops. Nightly the theatre was crowded, money was plentiful, Dublin prospering. In Peg's first year as leading lady in Smock Alley, the company made a profit of four thousand pounds. She had a stormy interview with Tom Sheridan, forcing him to give her a share of the profits. She was now earning eight hundred pounds per annum. She was wealthy, secure, had a carriage, fine clothes, jewels. No risky schemes for her, like the South Sea Bubble that had ruined her father and left them paupers. Yet she could never pass a beggar, never refuse a plea for help. She had her unfortunates who depended on her: out-of-work actors, needy neighbours, orphaned children. She had many acquaintances, few she would call a friend. Most of the time she was lonely.

Polly continued to write frequently. She had given

birth to a second child, a daughter, Slany, named for their mother and for the child-aunt lying in the cold graveyard beside Lemineagh. The Princess of Wales was with child. Owen M'Swiney had died in Naples. George Ann Bellamy was contracted to marry a title.

So Owen M'Swiney lay buried in some foreign graveyard with none to mourn him. She offered a silent prayer for his soul, shed a tear for the kindness he had shown her as a young girl making her way on the London stage. Once she had written to him after her return from Paris, describing all that had happened after he left, the duel, the Duc de Richelieu's intervention, the prisoners in the Bastille. He had not replied. She wondered had he been shocked; he went in awe of Versailles and its denizens, impressed by their squandering of their days in aimless pursuits. Or would he have seen it for what it was, nothing more than a farce? Not that it mattered. Like Darnley and Patrick Taafe he had passed into the shadows and would be heard of no more. But in this she was mistaken. A short while later she learned that she had been named a beneficiary in his will. He had died a wealthy man and left her shares in Consols, sufficient to produce an income of five hundred pounds per annum. There was one condition. She must honour the promise she had made him many years before, become an apostate, turn Protestant. It was all coming back, an incident long forgotten. Supper in her apartment in New Bond Street. Bitter words because he had criticised Darnley's Jacobite loyalties. She had labelled him renegade. Then, because he was old and had once been her only friend in the Playhouse, had tried to make amends, tossing off a few lines of Herrick. How did they go?

Bid me live and I will live
Thy Protestant to be

What a strange man he was, hoarding her promise all these years. She was superstitious, her mother's daughter. Such a bequest would bring her no luck.

❧

She had been invited to supper to the Sheridan residence to celebrate the birth of a son and heir, christened Richard Brinsley Sheridan.

"He will be famous one day," said his father as he toasted the infant. "As famous as David Garrick." Peg nodded agreeably. Her christening gift of a silver mug had been well received. The claret was handsome, the port mellow. Her distrust of her host had dissolved in an agreeable cloud of fine wine, good food.

"What news from London? I believe your sister Polly keeps you informed?"

Mrs Sheridan, handsome, bewigged, laid a hand heavy with rings on Peg's arm. Her father had been a shopkeeper. She had married up. Peg sipped from her glass. "You will have known of Owen M'Swiney? He died recently."

"A scoundrelly renegade Papist," Sheridan's greedy fingers tested a ripe pear. There was something about the self-satisfied way he peeled the skin, testing the blade of the silver knife that made her shrink.

"Perhaps he was Peg's little friend?" Mrs Sheridan's words were barbed, or was it her fancy? "I liked him well," she said simply. "He was kind to the penniless girl I once was."

The disbelief on their faces urged her on. "He left me

a legacy." The moment the words were out she regretted them.

Mrs Sheridan's heavy eyebrows arched. "Indeed. I had heard his fancy lay—er, in another direction."

Tom Sheridan threw back his head and roared with laughter. "You heard right my dear, pretty boys. Your role as Sir Harry Wildair must have breached his defences, Peg."

"Our friendship was innocent," she said furiously. "His legacy was the result of an idle supper chat."

"How much?" Sheridan's eyes were wicked.

"Five hundred pounds per annum in Consols."

"On what condition?" Sheridan's eyes bored into hers. Stupidly she heard herself say, "That I become a convert to Protestantism."

"Which of course you will do." His voice was smooth as cream.

Peg thought of her great-grandmother Máire Rua, riding to Ireton, marrying a common soldier in the presence of a Puritan preacher. But her need had been desperate. "My family were cradle Catholics," she protested. "It is customary with old Irish aristocracy." The look on their faces goaded her on to add, "I shall die in the religion into which I was born."

"And which you never practise." Thoughtfully Tom Sheridan cracked a walnut. "And Polly turned Anglican. I hear her husband has been preferred in his ministry." He paused reflectively. "It would just be the matter of a signature."

On the table a candle spluttered, flamed for an instant before dying out. In that single bright gleam she had seen pictures, a coach riding to perdition across the Dublin Mountains, a white naked drugged body on an altar of hell, a rape, an old man in flames. Patrick Taafe twisting in pain, dying on the side of the mountain, buried no one knew where. That night she had learnt the bitter lesson that money mattered, had sworn an oath that neither she nor anyone belonging to her would ever be poor again. Yet stubborn pride made her say, though she had made up her mind otherwise, "I'll not refuse the legacy and I'll not renounce the faith into which I was born."

Tom Sheridan said slyly, "You always wanted it both ways, Peg."

She stood up angrily. "I want nothing from you, Tom Sheridan," but her hostess was calming her down, ordering her husband to apologise to their guest. Tom Sheridan was kissing her hand, laughing, telling her not to upset herself.

"Our country house Quilcagh is only fifty miles from Dublin," Mrs Sheridan was telling her, "and the vicar is most discreet."

"I could take you there in a matter of hours, sponsor you," her husband said temptingly.

Peg laughed nervously. "If Dublin gets wind of the word they will think we are eloping."

Mrs Sheridan gave a superior smile. "I hardly think that likely," and though it sounded reassuring there was malice in her voice.

Sheridan stretched out his long legs. "Dublin loves you, Peg, but once let them get a whisper that you turned your coat and they will rend you." He filled her glass with brandy. She had drunk wine, port and felt light-headed, carefree. With good friends who would care for her. She was very drunk.

"I trust you, Tom," she said thickly. She was to regret her trust. Bitterly.

Early on Easter morning while Dublin still slept the Sheridan coach set out for Quilcagh. That evening behind locked doors, Peg renounced Rome and became a member of the Church of Ireland.

She felt no emotion, but later when the housekeeper served a delicious supper she barely made it to the closet before she brought it all up again. Tom Sheridan was in high good humour toasting her in wine and whiskey until well into his cups he decided it was time for them to return to Dublin.

At midnight they set out and a few miles down the country road the thunderstorm that had rumbled and threatened all day decided to burst, sweeping the countryside in a deluge of rain. A tree struck by lightning blocked the road and with an oath the coachman dismounted from his perch and went for help to the nearest cottage.

Peg crouched back in her seat trembling with superstitious dread. Tom Sheridan laughing at her fears unscrewed his flask. "If you've damned yourself my dear, you might as well have a good run for your money. Drink up."

She giggled uneasily, slopping the brandy down her bodice.

Sheridan's voice was thick. "You owe me a lot, sweetheart. How about a little payment in advance." His hands were pawing her breasts, his breath was choking her, his words were searing her brain. He was forcing her back in the seat with one hand and with the other unbuttoned his breeches, pushing his penis into her mouth.

She would choke. This was worse than anything she could have conceived. As she struggled help came in the shape of running footsteps, voices shouting orders. The driver put his head through the window to tell them that everything was under control and they would soon be on their way. She felt sick with shame. Outside they were heaving, tying ropes to the horses while the coach rocked and swayed and the driver shouted, "Heave ho," to a small cheer from the crowd that had gathered from nowhere. Then they were on their way.

"That promised to be a pleasant little interlude," Sheridan's spittle sprayed her gown and she drew further back. "If you are kind to me, I will keep your secret and the town need never know."

At the cold hard look in her eyes his voice died away. He was not to know it but it was the same look that Máire Rua had given the Cromwellian soldier she had been forced to marry on the day she sent him to his death. "If you ever dare touch me again,"—Peg's words were low but the menace in her voice made him break out in a cold sweat—"I swear, Tom Sheridan, I will kill you with my own two hands."

Monsieur Jean had been born in the Liberties of Dublin, christened John Murphy, and had started life as a butcher's boy. After that fatal day in College Green when there had been a riot at the "Riding of the Franchise" he had been taken prisoner with the young weaver he had attempted to carve up but had made his escape. A friendly fishing boat had deposited him in Dunkirk and he had enlisted in the Irish Brigade, later finding employment in the kitchens of Versailles where he had married the sister of the Duc d'Orléans' chef, the finest cook in the palace. Antoinette, for such was her name, had nothing of her brother's temperament but much of his skill with food. She was also a good manager and with her new Irish husband opened an inn in the town of Versailles which at first prospered. When she fell ill and finally died, it failed and John Murphy, by now Monsieur Jean, packed his bags and returned to Dublin. There was nothing to keep him in France. He had no family and felt that there was little to connect him with the scared young apprentice who had fled his city more than twenty years before. In a fit of bravado he had accepted a job as cook to the Lord Lieutenant of Ireland, but then fate had intervened. Before taking up duty in the kitchens of Dublin Castle he had paid a visit to the Smock Alley Theatre, seen Peg on stage, fallen in love with her voice, her face and her figure in that order and hearing she was in need of a cook had hastened to the house in Capel Street and offered his services, much as Launcelot might have offered his sword to Guinevere in the Arthurian romance.

Peg had been only too happy to employ him even though he demanded double the wages she was prepared to offer and had warned that he was temperamental and did not like to be crossed. If she would leave the kitchens to him everything would be to her liking.

He was a law unto himself, and he was never happier than when Peg was entertaining guests to dinner or supper, serving strange and exotic dishes: dates, almonds, walnuts, cherries, oranges and plums in brandy replaced the traditional soups, as a first course, followed by lobsters, crabs, oysters, mussels and snails cooked in the French manner. The main course was usually game or duck served with juniper berries or beef cooked in a pastry, with side salads. In the winter months he produced an ice cream pudding frozen with snow brought down from the Dublin hills. Sherbets were served between courses to cleanse the palate and a good cheese board and a fine port finished the meal. He was a connoisseur of wines and when he thought the occasions—or the guests—were worth the effort he would create table decorations: butter modelled in the shape of a swan, a spider's web of fine sugar, and crystallised fruits cunningly shaped as flowers. He never deigned to visit the markets, delegating such chores to Zara who sallied forth each morning at an early hour with Mohamet in tow.

Her favourite haunt was the Castle markets at the corner of Dame Street which catered for the epicurean tastes of wealthy citizens; fresh pork, the swine raised on acorns, hams smoked in apple wood, succulent salmon, trout, oysters, imported truffles and fruits. She enjoyed the bustle of porters, traders, hawkers; made friends with the housewives and maidservants who liked to banter and haggle and exchange gossip. There were always children underfoot; pilfering from stalls, begging, quarrelling, laughing. In the way of the young. Mohamet was one of the noisiest of the bunch.

She was abroad early and as she filled her basket with fruit—the prunes and figs had been unloaded from the trading ship down at the port only the day before and were much in demand—she noticed out of the corner of her eye that Mohamet and a young coffee-coloured boy, splendidly dressed in scarlet and gold, were wrestling. An elaborate turban was lying in a pool of water near her feet. Angrily she put down her basket and hauled Mohamet away, clipping his ear; at the same time a soberly dressed man dragged off his charge.

"He is the Duchess of Dorset's blackamoor and impossibly spoiled," the man apologised. "Pick up your turban, Elias, and put it back where it belongs—on your head," he ordered severely. And to Zara, "I shall take a stick to his back when we return to the castle."

"We were only tricking," Mohamet said indignantly. "Elias is my friend."

Zara said in a resigned voice. "I have heard much of Elias. It appears they come to grips each time they meet."

The man composed his face in serious lines, though his eyes twinkled. "The boy your slave?"

Elias grinned wickedly at this and stuck out his tongue,

and once again they were rolling around. Without more ado the man banged their heads together. "You will learn to behave or I promise you will be sorry."

Mohamet yelled indignantly and Zara handed him the basket. "Home with you now. Do not delay or Monsieur Jean will have you boiled in oil."

"Wait for me, I'm coming with you," Elias shouted and they were lost in the crowds.

Zara sighed. "Mohamet needs a man's hand to keep him in order. My mistress, Mrs Woffington, is too kind."

"The actress of the Smock Alley Playhouse. I much admire her. Whenever my duties permit I attend the theatre. Are you fond of playgoing?"

"Yes, indeed," she said gravely.

To his surprise he heard himself say: "Could I persuade you to take some refreshments with me? The Castle Inn is respectable. They serve French toast and a good cheese."

Zara considered him. He inspired confidence, a man of mature years, well, if soberly dressed. Though his hair was scant, he wore no wig, which pleased her. It was his eyes she liked most. Clear grey, candid, looking on the world with intelligence, honesty. His voice was attractive, deep-timbred, warm.

"Perhaps a cup of chocolate?" she said uncertainly.

Masterfully he took her arm and led her across the road to the inn where they spent a pleasant hour drinking wine which loosened her tongue and brought colour to her cheeks.

She learnt that his name was Simon Winchester, valet to the Lord Lieutenant of Ireland, the Duke of Dorset. He had seen service with the duke, as his military servant, and had taken part in many campaigns.

"There is an inn near the place where I was born. It is

situated on Dorset land. The landlord grows old and the duke has promised me the tenancy whenever I have a mind to go back to England. I look forward to spending the autumn of my days amongst my own people."

She smiled shyly and he experienced the most curious sensation, as if something under his left rib had left his body and entered hers. He examined her as if he would imprint her face on his mind. So young, not more than nineteen years; violet eyes, hair black as ebony, olive skin. Oh God, he thought urgently, I don't want it to happen again. I don't want to lose my heart.

"My people came to England from Russia when I was very small," she was saying. "The Jewish quarters around St Paul's Cathedral in London is all I know."

"I should like to show you my native village some day," he said slowly, and he told her of the village green, the inn of good redbrick, sign creaking in the wind but inside all gleaming brass and pewter and sturdy oak benches. He was telling her about the life of the village, the mummers who visited each house on St Stephen's Day, the hobby-horse dance at the harvest festival, the maypole on May Day. "No fairies, alas. It is said they left England the time of Elizabeth the Queen."

Impulsively she put her hand on his. "You are all alone?"

"My wife died a long time ago in childbirth. She was fair, not like you."

She blushed and touched her face. "Damn," he swore under his breath. "I have offended her." It was the first time he had noticed the birthmark. It was of no importance at all.

She stood up abruptly. "It is time I returned to Capel Street. Mohamet will have spread a story that I have been abducted by a stranger. He has a vivid imagination."

He bowed stiffly. "I trust we shall meet again."

Of course he could not keep away. He struck up an acquaintance with the cook, got himself invited to the servants' quarters for supper, brought a gift of a good bottle of claret, entertained the staff with stories of his travels with the duke, spoke French to Monsieur Jean who considered Winchester a man of the world, like himself. It was clear to Peg that Zara was the magnet that drew him to the house in Capel Street but she kept her counsel, even when he asked her advice. "Zara is a girl with a mind of her own. I would like to see her happily married but the decision must be hers."

"I am prepared to wait," he said valiantly, and Peg was touched and gave him tokens for the Playhouse. "Zara is fond of the theatre," she said gravely. "She might be persuaded to accompany you to see a production of *A Midsummer Night's Dream* next week."

O n a dark November morning, a dilapidated cab rattled over the cobblestones of the quays coming from the direction of Sackville Street, turned right and finally shuddered to a halt outside the front door of the most imposing house in Capel Street. Bones creaking the ancient driver climbed down, his once black coat now green with age, fluttering in the wind. Looking like nothing so much as a scarecrow he abased himself, tugged his grey forelock, muttered "Your ladyship," held out a grimy hand to help the ladies down. With a moue of displeasure, the matron rooted in her reticule and disdainfully threw a few coppers on the ground. She examined the house, then satisfied, mounted the steps, followed by her two daughters.

Behind her the outraged cries of the cabby, cursing her seed, breed and generation, filled the street. "Beggars and whores is what youse are," he shouted. "Tuppence for a sixpenny drive, and not a halfpenny extra to wet me whistle. Sittin' thimsilves up as gentry, living on pratie skins," he told an audience of ragged children, a mangy dog and an old apple woman who had stopped by to watch.

A scullion with a dirty face whose duty it was to clean grates and light fires, and perform other menial tasks, but who preferred to idle her time gazing out on the street, recognised them at once. Indeed since their arrival the doings of the Gunnings had given the town food for gossip. They were described by some as beautiful beggars, dismissed by others as adventuresses. It was generally agreed that they had left a mountain of debts behind them in their native Mayo, and that Mrs Gunning was contriving to marry her dowerless daughters into the aristocracy.

Peg was rudely awakened by a slatternly voice in her ear: "Git up, mishtress, git up. 'Tis the Gunnings below, Peter the packer brung them in his oul' cab, and he cursin' them. Demandin' to see yourself, they are and won't take no for an answer."

"Pox take the Gunnings," she grumbled. "What brings them calling at such an ungodly hour. Send Zara to me at once. Hurry, don't stand there gawking like an idiot." Hastily she swallowed a cup of scalding coffee which Zara brought and descended to the morning room, pulling on a silk gown.

Certainly the girls were beautiful; translucent skin, wide-spaced eyes hyacinth blue, golden curls cascading onto shapely shoulders. Mrs Gunning still bore the traces of former good looks, though her face was marked with lines of discontent. She had been examining a portrait hanging over the fireplace and turned insolently as Peg entered the room. "It is a fair likeness," she conceded. "I have in mind to have Miss Maria and Miss Elizabeth's portraits painted. Who is the artist?"

"John Lewis. He started life as a scene-painter in the theatre. He has become fashionable, since the Duchess of Dorset patronised him. Her blackamoor sat for him. He charges one hundred guineas." She let the information fall provocatively, knowing that her visitors were living on credit, unable to pay even the meanest of their bills.

Mrs Gunning moved restlessly about the room. "You are doubtless at a loss as to why I should honour you with a visit."

Peg smothered a yawn. "Nine o'clock of a morning is uncommonly early. Or do you set a new fashion?"

"You may not be aware that my family is of some consequence," Mrs Gunning continued. "I am the daughter of the late Viscount Mayo. My husband has been dogged by ill luck. We are perpetually dunned by bum-bailiffs."

She was the most impossible woman Peg had ever met. A peasant in a mud cabin would have shown more breeding. "How then can I serve you, Madam?"

" We have been invited to the Castle. My daughters will be presented to the Lord Lieutenant."

"We have nothing to wear," Elizabeth said sullenly.

"We have tried all our acquaintances," Maria's voice was strangled.

Peg felt pity for the sisters, puppets dancing to their mother's strings. "You have a cousin, Samantha Gunning?"

"They are in trade. Naturally we do not meet." Mrs Gunning had more hauteur than the Marquise de Pompadour.

It was time to end the interview. "Miss Samantha is an intimate of my sister, the Honourable Mrs Robert Cholmondeley, but in the circumstances..."

Angrily she tugged at the rope bell and when Zara appeared said curtly, "Kindly show these callers out."

Elizabeth burst into tears. "Do not send us away empty-handed, Mrs Woffington. You are our last hope. All our friends have refused us."

"I remember Miss Polly," Maria said faintly. "She came to Castle Mayo once with our cousin. She sent me a doll from Paris, dressed in the height of fashion. It was my most treasured possession."

That hot summer's day was vivid in Peg's mind's eye. An excited Polly, cheeks flushed, eyes shining with excitement. Her horsy friend Samantha loudly commenting on the passengers entering the stagecoach, the young servant boy who had danced in the dust for a silver coin.

"Fair daffodils, we weep to see you haste away so soon."

Youth went so fast. She drew in a deep breath. "I shall indulge myself by playing fairy godmother one more time. It always was my favourite role."

Mesmerised the girls stared at her and she took them by the arm. "Come with me. You shall have the pick of my wardrobe. Gowns, petticoats, baubles, shoes. What is your need?"

❦

His Grace of Dorset, Lord Lieutenant was dressing for one of the interminable receptions he was forced to hold, and commenting freely to his valet on what had happened the previous night. "What a dragon is that Gunning female, and her husband's a parasite. Never saw service in his life. Who fathered her litter of beauties, eh Winchester?"

His valet fixed a flower in the brocade buttonhole. "The young ladies created quite a sensation I believe, in the borrowed finery."

"Borrowed finery, eh! Who was the donor? Her ladyship and most of the guests were curious to know. The duchess is not on speaking terms with me because I danced twice each with Mistress Maria and her sister Elizabeth. What I do elsewhere she cares not." He shrugged, "But one must observe the rules: *Noblesse oblige*. Should I bring her some gossip she will unbend."

Winchester handed his master a jewelled snuff box. "I understand the Gunnings called on Mrs Woffington at her residence in Capel Street, sir. They had been refused help by all their acquaintances. Mrs Woffington moved by their plight fitted out the young ladies with jewels and whatever was needed. She is a person of wide charity as well as great charm," his voice shook.

"Smitten, eh?"

"No, sir." Winchester was shocked.

"There is someone in the household."

"Mrs Woffington's maid, Zara," the valet said stiffly. "I fear she is too young for me, barely nineteen years of age."

Dorset guffawed. "Nonsense, man. They are at their best at that age. Older and they are overripe." He fingered his moustache, "Peg Woffington, the actress in Smock Alley, eh. I have a mind to make the lady's acquaintance. I often wondered who she was. Lord Darnley in his cups described her as 'a lass unparallel'd.' Cumberland hunted him out, you know, but he was dead when they got him, I'm glad to say. Then there was young Taafe who was in love with her, I believe, and that actor fellow Garrick who wed with Burlington's wench. And of course Sarah Buckingham's son. She would have none of him. It was the first time in my life I have known Sarah put down. Yes, I must meet the lady. You will arrange that she is presented to me at the next levee." He sighed. "Life grows stale. I need some diversion in this benighted land."

❧

"It would be an honour, to have your grace sup with me."
Peg gave the Lord Lieutenant of Ireland a smile of great
charm. She was gowned in gold brocade, wearing Darnley's
emeralds. Her hair was piled high, her rouge skilfully
applied. Dorset was delighted with her. They had discussed
books, poetry, music, politics. She knew Voltaire. He
quoted Shakespeare. She had capped his quotations. She
was determined to further their acquaintance. "I am
fortunate in possessing the best cook in Dublin." Her voice
was deceptively meek. Dorset chuckled. "Should my cook
hear of it, he would throw himself into the Liffey." He
kissed her hand. "And now, I must attend to my social
obligations. Be assured I shall give myself the pleasure of
attending the Playhouse tomorrow evening and shall call
on you at a later hour."

Dorset was still a handsome man though lines of
boredom and dissipation were deeply etched on his face.
He was reputed to have had more concubines than the
ancient Persian king, Darius the Great, who had lived five
hundred years before Christ and enjoyed a harem of ten
thousand beautiful girls. Peg wondered what would be
expected of her; then told herself she did not much care.
His visit would create a stir, impress Sheridan who had the
whip-hand since she in a moment of drunken weakness
had signed that wretched paper renouncing Rome.

Peg's praise of her cook was no idle boast. He had never
wavered in his devotion to his mistress and felt it a tribute
to his talents as cook that she should entertain the greatest
in the land.

Dorset's visits to the house in Capel Street quickly
became the focus for the kind of scandal the town loved.
On his first visit Peg steeled herself to lie with him. She
was in no position to refuse the most powerful man in the

kingdom. The coupling was brief and unsatisfactory. Courteously he explained that this was a reflection neither on her looks which he found enchanting, nor her passion which she had simulated well, but that he was hard to arouse. His voice was composed and she looked suitably grave. When the need arose he preferred to visit Margaret Leeson's house. The Dublin whoremistress had imported various aids from abroad to excite and titillate her clientele; in addition to which she procured pretty virgins. "The daughters of fishwives divert me most," Dorset said simply. "A taste I share with the only Stuart I ever admired."

"The Merry Monarch," Peg said and laughed. "I have been hearing stories of Restoration England since childhood. Perhaps as Scheherazade did with the sultan I can entertain you with stories."

He fell into the habit of calling a couple of times a week after the Playhouse had ended and enjoyed her stories of the beggars, hawkers, raggle-taggle of the town who followed her whenever she went driving in the carriage and for whom she carried a purse of silver. Madame de Pompadour had never tried to impress Louis and Peg, taking a leaf from her book, regaled the duke with stories of her early days spent running the streets of Dublin with Kathleen McEnroe or of London with Jennie Tatler. Billy the pot-boy's story interested him greatly. He believed in reincarnation, told her once that she was her great-grandmother, Máire Rua, reborn. But the story he loved best and had her repeat again was of how all the beggars in Dublin gathered in the house in Francis Street to wake an old gleeman in porter and whiskey. And how the corpse had popped up in the middle of the roistering, demanding his share.

Mr Quinn had taught her every trick in the gambler's repertoire: palming, slurring, knapping, and now when she played cards with the duke she was usually the winner. She repaid her debts by a kiss, he by a purse of sovereigns, a gold bracelet, earrings. In some ways it was like the old days with Darnley, except there was no love, no passion, nothing but friendship. He often asked her advice and she knew he trusted her as he did few.

❧

On New Year's Day, 1750 Zara accepted Mr Winchester's proposal of marriage. They would settle in Dorset and run the Inn, as the duke had promised, and Mohamet would make his home with them.

Peg was delighted that the girl she had grown to love had at last found happiness, but the little blackamoor was distraught. "We were to go to America," he wept. "I liked James Wilding better than anyone else, even my friend Elias. I will not go with you to England, an old country where there are no Indians and no golden rivers." Elias had been filling his head with stories of gold found in Indian creeks and he had set his heart on voyaging to the New World.

Zara had never forgotten the grey-eyed boy who had touched her heart but four long years with never a letter had passed since he had bidden her farewell. She would never know love's wild passion with Mr Winchester, but he was kind, he loved her and she needed the security he could give.

Then a week before the wedding, a letter arrived from America. Even before Peg slit open the sheet she knew who the writer was, and called Zara and Mohamet to hear the news. They seated themselves on hassocks at her feet, faces alive with delight.

"*Dear Mrs Woffington*," she read.

> *You will be surprised to hear from me after such*
> *a long interval, my excuse being that so much*
> *has happened in the intervening years. I reached*
> *Indiana after many adventures, and was well*
> *received by Mr Coffey and his good lady. For a*
> *time I helped oversee the estate but Mrs Coffey*
> *is frail and is not long for this world. After*
> *lengthy deliberation they sold the plantation*
> *and accompanied me to the city of Philadel-*
> *phia, where I resumed my medical studies,*
> *which are now finally completed. I am very*
> *content. And now for the matter that is nearest*
> *my heart. I have never forgotten Zara; it would*
> *make me the happiest of men if she could be*
> *induced to join me here. Mohamet would be*
> *very welcome. I realise the decision will be a*
> *difficult one. Spring or early summer is the best*
> *time to make the journey. I have dreamt so long*
> *of our meeting that my life will be quite de-*
> *stroyed if we do not come together.*

Peg smiled in pity for the extravagances of youth. What was it Rosalind had said in the forest of Arden: "Men have died from time to time, and worms have eaten them, but not for love." Once she too had been young and believed that love endured. Now she accepted Shakespeare's ironical truth.

She continued:

I promise you that I will love and cherish Zara as my wife, while there is breath in my body. Mr Coffey has encouraged my hopes here and I depend on you to do all in your power to help me realise my dearest wish. I have rented a fine house adjacent to the Medical School in the centre of the city but meanwhile I shall send a scout to meet each ship that arrives from the London port. In gratitude,

James Wilding.

❦

"You have everything you need for the journey?" Peg examined the trunk. "Gowns, and petticoats, hose and gloves."

"And the book of Robinson Crusoe that you promised to give us," Mohamet said, eyes shining with excitement.

"You have sewn your purse into the hem of your gown and concealed your papers. I have arranged with Le Touche's Bank to transfer monies to Philadelphia. You will receive £500 per annum." She had made over Owen M'Swiney's legacy to Zara and Mohamet. It had not been an impulsive decision. The legacy had been too dearly bought, she would never touch a penny of it. But anything might happen Zara or Mohamet in the New World and she was determined that they would be independent.

"You are too good, ma'am," Zara wept. "I am foolish leaving you—and disappointing Mr Winchester—and taking Mohamet on a long and dangerous journey."

"It will take all of six weeks," he beamed with satisfaction. "If we are lucky we might even be shipwrecked." His listeners burst out laughing, then sobered up.

"I shall miss you sorely," Peg hugged Zara, stroking back the black hair. "You have been closer than a sister to me."

Zara wiped her eyes. "If only you would come with us."

"Perhaps some day." She caught the blackamoor up in a hug and though he wriggled free and blinked his eyes, he managed to kiss her back. "You promised me *Robinson Crusoe*," he said.

She held up a parcel. "Here it is all tied up, and a magnifying glass which will catch the sun's rays and help you light a fire if ever you find yourself on a desert island. And you must also bring a net to catch fish."

"Elias showed me how to fish in the river," Mohamet boasted, "and there will be berries and coconuts and other things."

Anxiously Zara touched her face. "What if James Wilding has forgotten how I am marked?"

"How vain you are," Peg scolded. "Already two men have fallen in love with you. I swear neither is aware that you bear a small blemish." She kissed them both. "Be good, Mohamet. Do as Zara bids you and all will be well. Take care of her for me."

"If she is captured by pirates I promise to rescue her," Mohamet said fiercely. Then his face split in a wide grin. "I do not think it will happen. I will find much gold and we will be very rich. Elias will be furious."

❦

At the quayside Zara took her farewell of Simon Winchester. Peg had remained at home. She hated partings, beside he was entitled to Zara's last moments in Ireland.

"You will never forgive me for what I am doing." Zara

was in tears. She held up her face and he kissed her, feeling her heart flutter against his breast. "Once I was young as you are, and wanted to see the world," he whispered. "If this James Wilding is not good to you he will have me to contend with. If you are unhappy in your new life, my dear, remember I am always at your service."

She touched his cheek. "And what of your plans to return to Dorset and set up as innkeeper?"

He blew his nose and dabbed his eyes. "The wind makes them water," he muttered. "His Grace the Duke thinks I am too old to make a new life. He has need of me. It is one of the best things in life to be needed."

Zara nodded, her thoughts speeding across the broad Atlantic to where a grey-eyed young man waited impatiently for her coming.

Brawny sailors were heaving trunks and boxes on board, lowering the rope ladder.

"It is time for you to go. Fare well on your journey," Mr Winchester said with mock cheerfulness. He did not tell her that it felt as if she was taking part of him with her.

A gust of wind blew down the river and the creaking canvasses were tied securely, as the ship lurched, righted itself and the great sails billowed out. Slowly the ship began to move along the quays.

"Good-bye, Mr Winchester," Zara called from the deck.

"Good-bye, Elias," Mohamet shouted to the slim brown figure in the bright turban who was running along the quays.

"Wait for me. I am coming with you," Elias called out - but his words were lost in the screech of the gulls and the swell of the sea.

Mohamet cupped his mouth with his hands. "I am Robinson Crusoe bound for a great adventure."

George Faulkner sat in his office composing his thoughts. He had been invited by Thomas Sheridan to the opening night of a new production of *Antony and Cleopatra* at the Playhouse, and later to be entertained to supper at Daly's Club in Castle Street. Faulkner was an elderly man with twinkling eyes which belied his gruff manner. Everything about him was sober; grey thinning hair—he seldom wore a wig—a pock-marked face, with the long nose and high forehead of his Puritan forebears. He invariably dressed in grey: coat and breeches, shirt, hose. His only concession to fashion was a trace of lace at cuffs and a gold snuff box. He had once been a frequent guest at Alice Morgan's musical evenings in the house in Smock Alley, and had disapproved when Charles Coffey fell in love with a red-haired girl, young enough to be his daughter. When the Sandford scandal broke he had counselled Coffey to marry Alice Morgan without delay. He was not a man given to introspection but what happened later caused him sleepless nights.

To the owner and editor of the influential *Faulkner's Journal*, little that happened in Dublin was secret. He knew of Peg's rape in the Hellfire Club, and Taafe's murder on the Featherbed Mountains, but a word from certain quarters had ensured his paper's silence. All that appeared in print was a brief account of the fire at Montpelier Lodge and a briefer notice of Taafe's death. The harm had been done and no useful purpose would be served by revealing facts or apportioning blame. Peg's life was in sufficient jeopardy without further scandal. He had discussed her future with the physician who had attended her in that remote cottage in the Dublin hills and they had agreed that it was better she take the money and leave Dublin and all that had happened behind her. Her future they predicted lay on the London stage. A wise decision as it turned out. She had achieved the success she deserved.

He smoothed a sheet of parchment and commenced his review of the play he had seen the night before, writing in the clear script demanded by his printers:

> Antony and Cleopatra *in the Smock Alley Theatre is one of the most stylishly conceived and stylishly acted productions ever seen in Dublin. Lavishly costumed and with beautiful sets it created a fitting setting for the Queen of the Nile in the days of her greatness. No expense was spared in mounting this production. A live camel carrying Cleopatra—played by our own enchantress Mrs Woffington—lent verisimilitude to the scene. She is indeed "a lass unparallel'd." This is a play not to be missed and ends a most successful season of Shakespeare.*

He helped himself to a pinch of snuff and sneezed

heartily, he would be glad when this task was finished. He liked to devote himself to more weighty topics but Sheridan expected a favourable notice. He dipped his quill in ink and on a separate sheet wrote:

> *Dublin is to follow London's lead in establishing a Beefsteak Club, and as in the case of the London club founded by Mr David Garrick, the Irish club will have a membership of twenty. Certain members of the acting fraternity as well as artists, men of letters and noble lords have been invited to become members. Mr Sheridan, manager of the Smock Alley Theatre, will host a dinner in his home once a month. The Lord Lieutenant of Ireland has indicated that he will honour the Club with his patronage, and Mrs Peg Woffington has graciously agreed to be the Club's first President. A unique departure, since London confines its club members to the sterner sex. The ladies of the town will rejoice. Liberal Dublin has again pointed the way forward.*

Faulkner allowed himself a sardonic smile. It would not be politic to add that it was Dorset's express wish that Peg be invited. The club had been Sheridan's idea and he had spared no expense in refurbishing his home for the meetings but the Smock Alley manager was no David Garrick, nor could the members expect the wit of a Samuel Johnson at their dinners. In Faulkner's experience gentlemen, denied the company of the fairer sex, were prone to wine and dine not wisely but too well and generally finished up under the table. Dorset, sophisticate that he was, wished to guard himself against such tedium. The presence of the bewitching

Peg would be a civilising influence. There would be much heartburning amongst the ladies of the Georgian mansions in the squares when the story was bruited abroad.

❦

Peg seated alone in her boudoir mused on the first gathering of the club which had taken place the night before. His Grace of Dorset had been obsequiously received by Tom Sheridan, and she had taken the place of honour at the head of the table with the Lord Lieutenant sitting on her right and Sheridan on her left. From then on the evening had run its predictable course. The beefsteaks had been good, the wines of an excellent vintage; that wily fox, George Faulkner, had related some excellent titbits of gossip which could never appear in print. He was an amusing raconteur. A Trinity College don brought up the topic of the identity of Shakespeare's Dark Lady of the sonnets, and there had been wild speculation as to who she was. How Garrick would have relished that particular discussion. She dismissed the thought. Nostalgia was a luxury she could no longer afford.

After dinner they had played charades; then Sheridan had rendered an aria from a little-known opera and when the duke yawned openly, she signalled young Lord Fermoy, a talented musician, to accompany her on the piano. She had sung Dorset's favourites "Greensleeves" and selections from *The Beggar's Opera*. Mellow with port, the members had contributed to the night's gaiety with ballads, stories, and one young officer contributed a particularly daring recitation. Sheridan had been gratified at the success of the evening, had congratulated her on her contribution. Not by the merest flicker did he reveal his thoughts. He was too skilled an actor for that. But she knew he resented her presence at this table. He had always been jealous of her success on the Dublin stage, even though he reaped material benefits. But for Dorset's friendship he would have found some way to dismiss her from the Playhouse long since. Owen M'Swiney's legacy was never mentioned, nor the mockery of her "conversion to Protestantism" which had taken place in the house Quilcagh. Never mentioned, but never forgotten.

Pensively she fingered a Sèvres bowl on her dressing table. Many were envious of her style of living; her elegant home, fine furniture, jewels, wardrobe, acquaintances. She entertained whomever she pleased and was received by the quality of the town. She had dozens of acquaintances but no real friend, no confidante. It was more than three years since Zara and Mohamet had set sail for America. She missed the young Jewish girl who had been maid, companion, friend, more than she had thought possible; was lonely for the child who had been her blackamoor. Of course Zara had spoiled him. So had she. She told herself defiantly she wasn't sorry she had accepted the legacy. Had she refused the allowance it would have gone to Owen M'Swiney's dissolute prince who had more money than he could ever spend. She had signed it over to Zara when she set sail for the New World. Money might not ward off hardship, but at least it would soften the blow. It would also in time give Mohamet his independence and allow him make his way in the world. Her heart contracted with pain when she remembered the childish chatter, the quick patter of footsteps on stairs, in rooms. Strange how children never walked, always ran, as if eager to meet each new experience. Mohamet would have enjoyed riding with her in the fine carriage, would have waved to the people passing, shouted back to the orange girls, fishmongers, beggars, apprentices, who greeted her whenever she rode out. They delighted in her success. She was one of their own, generous, with an open purse and a sympathetic ear for their troubles, but once let them get a whiff of her apostasy and she could never again set foot on the Dublin stage. Above all else they hated a "turncoat" as Tom Sheridan knew. It was the Damoclean sword he held over her head.

Zara wrote frequently. She was happy. Mohamet was thriving. Her husband James Wilding was making a success of his profession. She was *enceinte*. If the infant was a girl they would call her Peg, if a boy Charles after Mr Coffey who had recently suffered the loss of his wife. It was seldom Peg thought of her first lover; it all seemed so long ago. He would be quite elderly by now, in sight of his sixtieth year.

Critically she examined her face in the mirror, noting new lines of fatigue at eyes and mouth. She used henna to brighten her hair. It had been Zara's idea. She was moving into middle age; yet she still had her quota of admirers: army officers, lawyers, surgeons, wealthy merchants, titled bucks. Gracefully she accepted their tributes of flowers and trinkets, would allow no liberties. Dorset would not have approved any liaison, and in truth she was not tempted, contented to be her own mistress.

Yet sometimes in the early hours, in her lonely bed, other voices and faces came sweeping back, unbidden, to haunt her hard-won peace.

Charles Coffey, as she remembered him. Wings of grey

in his raven hair, cleft chin, strong hands guiding his favourite chestnut mare through the Phoenix Park, down the quays, glad to shake the dust of the house in Chapelizod from his feet, eager to return to Dublin, to her. "My salad days when I was green in judgement," she thought—the days when she had been possessed of a fever, a madness she was never again to feel about any man.

Tow-haired Patrick Taafe with his hot blue eyes who had loved her after his fashion and had perished so needlessly on the Featherbed Mountains. Gambling had been his passion, his downfall, she had been the innocent instrument of his violent end. She would carry a sense of guilt to her grave.

Garrick in his early days when he had swept her along on the tide of his passion. "Sweetheart, the whole world is ours for the taking," he had promised in his beautiful voice. "Love is not love which alters when it alteration finds" he had quoted, and she had believed him.

And Darnley, the Scottish aristocrat, dark, proud as Lucifer, reckless, possessed by his dreams of a Jacobite rising. He had spoiled her, given her the carefree youth she had never known, had encouraged her in all she did. They had laughed together, had fun. He was everything she admired in a man: handsome, generous to a fault, a law unto himself. Darnley who had husbanded his dying strength to write a last letter:

> *Remember our times together. I love you now and forever.*
>
> "In such a night
> *Stood Dido with a willow in her hand*
> *Upon the wild sea-banks, and waft her love*
> *To come again to Carthage."*

Only now he would never come. A long time since his mortal remains had crumbled away in that dark Scottish glen where he had died. Did his spirit haunt the lochs and hills he had so often described? When he had died he had taken her youth and joy of living with him. She shivered and thought how true were the words of the French writer, Montaigne:

If you pressed me to say why I loved him, I can say no more than because he was he and I was I.

From the morning the Gunnings had visited the house in Capel Street she had received no word, no acknowledgement of her help. Even before they had left Capel Street she had ceased to exist for them. Not that it mattered. She had been more than repaid, by her meeting with Dorset. Once she dreamt of them, and wrote and asked Polly for news, and a couple of months later her sister replied.

Dear Peg,
You were interested in the doings of the Gunning sisters, and so I must keep you up to date. When they first arrived in London they created such a stir in the town that people stood to watch as they rode by in their carriages, and an enterprising shoemaker made his name known, by displaying their slippers in his shop. Elizabeth's most ardent suitor was the Duke of Hamilton. He called to the house when mamma and Maria were conveniently absent, and became so hot and impatient that he married the

> girl at half past midnight in a chapel in Curzon
> Street, using a bed curtain ring as a wedding
> ring. The pair are so proud that they eat only
> from gold plate and converse only with each
> other when out in company.

Peg was amused, yet she had sensed tragedy in the younger
girl's haunting beauty and wondered what her future
would be.

A year later in one of Polly's rambling letters she heard
the final chapter in the story.

> You were interested in the doings of the Gun-
> ning sisters as I recall. Maria realised her ambi-
> tion, married the Earl of Coventry and became
> the toast of London. Her every gesture was
> copied, her gowns and furs admired in the most
> extravagant manner. Bucks likened her to the
> legendary Helen of Troy. She had adopted the
> fashion of plastering her face with a powder
> which is the rage at the court of Versailles. But
> the powder contained a deadly ingredient, white
> lead, which has destroyed the little countess.
> She lies alone in a darkened room which she has
> forbidden to all, even her husband and mother.
> Her maid alone attends her. Her once beautiful
> face is ravaged and scarred with festering sores.
> They say death will be a happy release for the
> most unhappy of women.

Polly had paid a visit to the French capital, and gave
a glowing account of that city and meetings with old
friends; yet she ended her letter on a sombre note:

Sadly Paris is in ferment. Madame de Pompadour has spent more than six million francs on her château at Bellevue, and the French, groaning under the weight of taxes, are outraged at her extravagances. In cafés and clubs the intelligentsia talk treason, and on the streets there are bread riots every day.

Dark clouds were gathering in France, portents of the deluge to come which would sweep away forever the older order of power and privilege.

In Dublin too there was unease. A bill had recently been introduced to the Irish parliament to have a portion of the English national debt paid out of Irish revenue. The country was slowly recovering from centuries of misrule and for the first time, Catholic, Protestant and Dissenter alike were united in opposing this measure. "Why should the Irish be expected to pay for England's wars?" an editorial in *Faulkner's Journal* thundered. "Why should Ireland pay for the prodigal squandering of England's peers, for the mismanagement of her government?"

In the early spring of 1754 the Irish parliament by an overwhelming majority rejected the bill. Toasts to Ireland's liberty were drunk in elegant Georgian mansions and victory bonfires blazed in the Liberties, where reckless men got drunk on poteen, the lethal native brew, and plotted dark and awful deeds. Dublin Castle, the seat of English power in Ireland, was the object of their hatred, the Lord Lieutenant reviled.

On an evening in spring, as the Beefsteak Club met for their monthly dinner, a ragged crowd gathered outside Sheridan's house in Upper Sackville Street, and urged on to a frenzy by a ragged cabman who had been evicted from his slum only that morning, commenced to throw mud at the Lord Lieutenant's coach. When Sheridan heard of this he sent out his servants with iron bars to beat them away. In the ensuing panic the horses attempted to bolt, the carriage was overturned and a man crushed under the wheels. At least half a dozen of the scattered crowd nursed broken heads and limbs.

❦

She was torn out of her sleep by a thunderous knocking. By the time she had pulled her robe around her and descended to the hall servants were passing among them a broadsheet attempting to decipher the words. She sent them back to the kitchen, ordering them to bring her up a pot of coffee and slowly climbed the stairs to her room, reading the ominous message which an unknown printer had run off somewhere in the town. "Death to Dorset. Death to the Beefsteak Club. Freedom and liberty for all." Scrawled in ink were the words: "You are warned only because of your charity to Dublin's poor."

The posters were all over town, pasted on walls, pinned to stable doors, being scattered like dust by little gusts of wind along the streets. Sheridan was in his office in Smock Alley reading a manuscript when she arrived. She held out the broadsheet and he wrinkled his nose in distaste: "And so you are to be spared because of your goodness to the poor. Little they know."

It was there, the veiled threat.

With an effort she controlled herself. "We are all under attack. You went too far last night. Don't you think it's about time that you wound up the Beefsteak Club."

Sheridan bridled. "That, madam, is a matter for me to decide." He tossed the manuscript across the table. "Your sister had the goodness to send me a new play by Voltaire called *Mahomet the Imposter* which has taken Paris by storm and which she has taken the trouble to translate. Take it home with you and occupy your time studying it and leave matters of importance to me." He turned his back. "And now I beg you excuse me I have work to do."

❦

A bookcase lined one wall of the room, a terrestrial globe in a wooden frame stood on one end of the marble fireplace over which hung her portrait painted in oils. A long case clock in mahogany and marquetry ticked away the hours. She had spent weeks searching for a carpet to match the blue-seated straight-backed chairs. She got to her feet, rearranged a bowl of flowers on a table and moved a handscreen which she used to save her cheeks from scorching at the fire. She was proud of the room, her favourite retreat. David Garrick would have enjoyed working here. Darnley preferred to see her by soft candlelight in her boudoir, fragrant, hair loosened, gowned in lace and silk. She knew she was wasting time, moving bits and pieces, knights, castles, men. It wasn't a game of chess she was playing. She was attempting to distract her mind, distance herself from the play she had read. Voltaire had spared nothing in either dialogue or plot, depicting a starving peasantry, angry citizens, intrigue, chicanery in high places and corrupt politicians. He must have been bitterly angry when he wrote it. She could see his face, the cynical curl to his mouth, the black darting eyes, the small hunched shoulders.

Why, in God's name, had Polly not consulted her! But then her sister was self-willed, did as she pleased, liked to dabble in politics and had no interest whatever in anything Irish. "You dramatise everything," she frequently lectured Peg in her letters. "You are your own worst enemy. You think Tom Sheridan should walk in Garrick's shadow. You should have married, secured yourself a place in society."

If Polly but knew. She had kept silent about that night in the Hellfire Club saving her mother pain, guarding her sister's innocence. Instead she should have told the world what she had been forced to endure and it came to her in a moment of blinding truth that Darnley had saved her sanity by listening to her story that night in the gardens of Buck House.

❧

Sheridan came stumbling into the room where she had been put to wait. He wore a crumpled dressing gown and his eyes were puffed.

"Why this early call?" For once he was petulant, querulous, as Mohamet might have been if suddenly roused from his sleep. "It is not yet nine of the clock, madam."

Peg sank into a chair uninvited, sweeping back her hair with a hand that trembled with fatigue. "I have been awake most of the night studying this." She tossed the play across the table. "Do you seriously intend to stage such an explosive work in view of all that has happened? Have you taken leave of your senses, or what?"

His face reddened. "I am manager of Smock Alley and you will obey my orders. Otherwise..." The threat hung in the air between them, palpable, sinister. He would destroy her if he could, but in so doing he would destroy the Playhouse and all he had striven, worked for.

She sighed wearily. She knew when she was defeated. "So be it then. You asked for my opinion. I have given it. The decision is yours and the outcome is your responsibility."

❧

On the opening night the place resembled a powder keg. Every seat in the house was filled, but no light badinage was heard, no reassuring hum of voices sounded; even the strident orange wenches were hushed for once. Copies of the play had been circulating the town, and actors, stage-hands, carpenters, everyone in the audience, the very dogs in the street knew that before the night was over there would be trouble.

To a grim-faced audience the curtain swept back and the actors made their entrances and exits. There was an ominous silence. Then came the moment they all had been anticipating. Alcanor, a citizen of Mecca, came downstage to recite a freedom speech to his fellow citizens:

And bring them to account, crush those vipers
Who, singled out by their community
To guard their rights
Shall for a paltry sum sell them to the foe.

From the gallery came a slow hand clap, and the house shouted, "Encore." Four times the unhappy actor was forced to repeat the lines. He escaped to a chant from all sides: "Sheridan! We want Sheridan!"

Swiftly Peg made her way to his office, not waiting to

knock. He was at his desk, gathering his belongings, muttering to himself. "They have no right to call me. I'll not obey them." His wig was awry. She wondered was he drunk or drugged. She caught his arm: "For the love of God will you go out on stage." In the distance they could be heard chanting. "Listen. They are almost out of control." Baulked of their prey, they were roaring now. Lions in the arena—ready to spring, to devour anyone who got in their way.

He didn't answer and she put her face up to his. "Apologise. Tell them it was a mistake. Offer to refund their money. Anything to quieten them down."

He pushed her roughly aside. "Slut, go on stage yourself. Face them, tell all." His face twitched and tears started to his eyes. "It's all your fault. Dorset's whore."

She could scarcely believe her ears, but in this nightmare anything was possible. "Are you mad, Tom Sheridan?" she said and even to herself her voice sounded weak, tinny.

He tittered insanely and for a moment the demon of lust looked out from his eyes before vanishing. With a sickening jolt she realised the truth.

"They know now of your scheming ways," he was whining, spit was dribbling and he made ineffectual movements with his lace. "Jesus, I laugh when I think how you fooled them for so long."

She swallowed back bile. "Do as I beg," but he knocked her aside in his haste to leave and went out the door, the black box with the night's takings under his arm.

She felt old, defeated as she stumbled back to the wings, to where frightened actors were cowering. An old stage-hand took her hand: "Go out front, Mrs Woffington," he pleaded. "You are the only one they'll heed."

She shook all over. Sheridan's words belled in her ears;

he had betrayed her secret.

"Please go out and quieten them," the actors were begging, and she pulled herself together. Máire Rua had journeyed from Lemineagh to Ennis town to meet with Ireton, not knowing what she faced, but unafraid. Her great-granddaughter would show no less courage. With head high she stepped out of the wings, downstage, while the noise continued unabated. She threw out her arms in appeal and a man shouted, "Silence, let her speak."

At this the uproar died down. It was even more menacing than the tumult that had gone before. Her mouth was dry. She swallowed, found her voice, called out, "Good people of Dublin. Friends."

"Romans, countrymen, lend me your ears," a student in the pit called up. "I come to bury Dorset, not to fuck him," a wag in the gallery shouted back to a gale of laughter. Peg joined in, hoping to swing their mood. An orange came winging its way across the proscenium to smash against her breast, and for a moment she was stunned. She rallied, smiled, said in a carrying voice: "Thank you for your tribute. I see you remember my origins."

"God's truth she has courage!" a man said admiringly. "Where in hell is Sheridan?"

"He sent me as a peace-offering," she said, and there was another wave of laughter. Thank God the worst is over, she thought, but already it was too late. A harridan climbed on to a bench in the pit and was screaming: "Tell Dorset's strumpet to get off the stage. She turned her coat, changed her religion, sold her Maker for thirty pieces of silver. A man his face convulsed with fury ranted, "My son was killed under Dorset's coach." He spat at Peg. "Apostate. You caroused, drank, whored, while our children starved."

She was being pelted with rotten fruit, eggs, stones. Worse than the physical abuse was the hatred, the naked fury that debased her, rent her asunder as had happened that night in the Hellfire Club.

A young man in a box stood up and shouted with mock servility. "God bless His Majesty, King George, with three hurrahs."

As the cheers died away the audience fell to work in an orgy of destruction, ripping the canvas wings, pulling out candle sconces. Men were hacking seats to pieces, piling the wood in a pyramid to make a bonfire of the building.

Outside the Playhouse the mob were waving torches, screaming for Sheridan's blood, but he had long since gone to ground. No one bothered to stem the riot. Even the Lord Mayor refused to come out, pleading illness, and neither City Sheriff nor magistrates could be found. It was safer to let the mob have its way. And so for the third time in its chequered history, the Smock Alley Playhouse was razed to the ground.

EPILOGUE

She sat by a window looking out on the garden, an oasis of peace in the turbulent town. She had not ventured outside since the night the Smock Alley Playhouse had been destroyed, a week before. But the morning air was bright with promise. Crocuses, primroses, raised their faces to the sun, clumps of daffodils, that appeared as if by magic each year, encircled the trees.

Fair daffodils, we weep to see you haste away so soon.

That deep-timbred voice, that starry night when it had all begun.

An inquisitive blackbird hopped across the grass, head cocked to one side listening, yellow beak busy rooting. Once she had spent another such day at a May fair with Darnley and a young bird had landed beside them, inspecting with bright inquisitive eyes the gingerbread she had crumbled on the grass. They had made love on a bed of green rushes. It all seemed so long ago.

She rose stiffly from the window seat, went out into the garden, scattering breadcrumbs. Tentatively a sparrow alighted at the foot of the tree and began to feed. He was joined by a robin, a couple of blackbirds, and their young. New beginnings, a new life. Her career on the Dublin stage was finished; all she had known of the theatre she had loved in ruins.

She was thirty-six years of age. Máire Rua had been thirty-six when she made the wild dash to Limerick to General Ireton. Three husbands for Máire Rua, three lovers for her great-granddaughter.

Would she haunt the streets of Dublin, even as the great

lady of Lemineagh haunted Toonagh Woods?

Impatiently she swung around and the startled birds rose as if to a secret command, circling the tree-tops. The blackbird lazily ruffled his feathers; a bird whistled, another answered, and the air was filled with their song. Overhead a line of sea-birds flew by, split, formed a Vee, following their leader by plan, instinct. Who knew? She watched until they were lost in a blue haze, felt the sun warm her face, experienced once again the wild exhilaration she had known in her youth. Spring had always been her favourite season.

She would make a new life. Travel maybe; join Zara in America; visit the growing city of New York; follow the Indian trail in Virginia where the Princess Pocahontas was married and brought to England, laden with Indian gold. She, Peg, had gold and to spare. Mohamet would die with excitement.

But first she would return to London to warm herself at the fire of her mother's love, make a guest appearance on the London stage for Polly's favourite charity. It would make her sister happy. Was that her weakness, or was it her strength? All her life she had sought to please others, act a part, play fairy godmother, seek love…

She was playing a street game in George's Lane with Kathleen McEnroe. It was a game she had loved. She could feel the excitement, as the line of children advanced, retreated, holding hands, singing out:

Stands a lady on the mountains, who she is I do not know.

All she wants is gold and silver and a nice young man to love her.

She was the lady on the mountains. All she had ever truly wanted was a nice young man to love her and keep her safe.

By midsummer she had disposed of the house in Capel Street and taken farewell of Dorset and Simon Winchester, whose eyes were sad to see her go. In her purse she carried crested letters. One was for the attention of Mr Rich, Manager of the Covent Garden Theatre commending to him the outstanding actress Mrs Peg Woffington. The second was addressed to the Governor of Pennsylvania commending to him the friend and confidante of the Duke of Dorset. They were by way of royal commands.

Carefully she mounted the ladder of the boat at the North Wall, due to sail with the morning tide. As she reached the safety of the deck she looked for the last time at the grey misted hills, gazing down on a town of graceful squares, narrow lanes, squalor and wealth. Dublin her city, its people a hybrid race of Norse, Norman, English, Huguenot, Irish. In time to come when she thought of Dublin she would remember church bells ringing, cries of street vendors in the Liberties, screaming of gulls in the bay.

Once long ago she had wept over some small loss and her father had comforted the child she had been with biblical words. How did they go?

To everything there is a season, and a time for every purpose under the heaven...A time to weep, and a time to laugh; a time to mourn, and a time to dance...A time to love...

Was it too late? Tears pricked her eyes. She straightened up, stood tall. She would have no regrets. There was always a time to love.